*I'd always thought all I wanted was to g[...]
have money and success, but I'd come to [...]
wanted was love. Without that, what do [...]
things that can be sold and a whole lot of nothing in our hearts.*

THE SUITE LIFE

**Suzanne Corso's companion novel
to her stunning literary debut**

BROOKLYN STORY

Chosen as one of *USA TODAY*'s "New Voices of 2011"

"*Brooklyn Story* rings true. . . . A universal story of longing, loyalty, and growing up. . . . Corso gets the Brooklyn dialect pitch-perfect and keeps the pace brisk."

—*Publishers Weekly*

"Corso puts her straight-talking personality into her well-written debut novel."

—New York *Daily News*

"A familiar story . . . [that] escapes the formula with a true female voice."

—*The New York Times*

"A wonderful and moving nostalgia trip. Corso is a gifted and sensitive writer, and her debut novel is straight from the heart."

—Nelson DeMille, *New York Times* bestselling author

"Wonderful. . . . You're hooked from the first sentence."

—Olympia Dukakis, Academy Award–winning actress

"Tragic yet triumphal . . . a must-read."

—Lorraine Bracco, Academy Award–nominated actress

"This story explores the mind and heart of a young girl struggling for her identity in a soulless world. Heartbreaking and sensitively written. A very unusual coming-of-age story."

—Armand Assante, Emmy Award–winning actor

ALSO BY SUZANNE CORSO

Brooklyn Story

THE
SUITE
LIFE

Suzanne Corso

GALLERY BOOKS

New York   London   Toronto   Sydney   New Delhi

G

Gallery Books
A Division of Simon & Schuster, Inc.
1230 Avenue of the Americas
New York, NY 10020

Copyright © 2013 by Suzanne Corso

First Gallery Books trade paperback edition September 2013

GALLERY BOOKS and colophon are registered trademarks of Simon & Schuster, Inc.

For information about special discounts for bulk purchases, please contact Simon & Schuster Special Sales at 1-866-506-1949 or business@simonandschuster.com.

The Simon & Schuster Speakers Bureau can bring authors to your live event. For more information or to book an event contact the Simon & Schuster Speakers Bureau at 1-866-248-3049 or visit our website at www.simonspeakers.com.

Designed by Esther Paradelo

Manufactured in the United States of America

1   3   5   7   9   10   8   6   4   2

Library of Congress Cataloging-in-Publication Data

Corso, Suzanne.
The suite life : a novel by / Suzanne Corso, Author of Brooklyn Story.—First Gallery Books trade paperback edition.
    pages   cm
1. Finance—New York (State)—New York—Fiction. 2. Wall Street (New York, N.Y.)—Fiction. 3. Corruption—Fiction. I. Title.
PS3603.O7785S85   2013
813'.6—dc23   2013005656

ISBN 978-1-4516-9818-3
ISBN 978-1-4516-9819-0 (ebook)

For Samantha,
the greatest gift a girl like me could have

God bless the child that's got his own.

—*Billie Holiday*

PROLOGUE

Brooklyn, 1982

"... twenty-five years to life ..."

Those were the words uttered by the judge as he passed sentence on Tony Kroon, my longtime abusive boyfriend and soon-to-be ex. A loyal mafia henchman who had managed to kill someone in the course of a botched bank robbery and get caught, Tony was being sent down—and I was finally free of him. As he was being led away in handcuffs our eyes met briefly. Tony's were as stony cold as ever and mine were already fixed on the future—at nineteen, I finally had a future to look forward to.

The Brooklyn Bridge and all in between that separates Bensonhurst, the world in which I grew up, from the fascinating and fulfilling life that I was certain was awaiting me in Manhattan. And I finally had my passport in hand—an appointment that very afternoon with an editor at an important New York publishing house who had read my manuscript and wanted to meet me. For as long as I could remember, I'd been writing, keeping journals, and dreaming of being a published author. Somehow I'd always believed that my writing would someday provide my ticket out of Brooklyn. Now it seemed that day had finally come.

Nothing was going to stand in my way and everything was going to be different from that day on. The destitute life my frail, divorced mother lived would never be mine. There would be none of the alcohol and drugs that were her crutches, none of the sickness in body and mind that had consumed her. None of that for me.

"Samantha Bonti?" a smiling young woman asked as she approached me in the publisher's waiting room, hand outstretched in greeting. "I'm Kim, Lucy Hastings's assistant. Sorry to keep you waiting. I'll take you in now. I know Lucy's been looking forward to this meeting."

And with that, no more than two hours after seeing Tony being led off to prison and out of my life, I was sitting across the desk from the woman I absolutely *knew* would be my future editor. Her comfortable but cluttered office was piled high with manuscripts, and, as I looked around, I was flattered that, of all the submissions she clearly received every day, she had thought enough of mine to schedule this meeting.

Lucy was probably in her mid-forties, casually but professionally dressed in what I would soon learn was the quintessential New York professional's black sweater and tailored slacks. As I started to tell her about the many truths behind the fiction I had written—including growing up with an alcoholic and drug-addicted mother, living on welfare and food stamps, and being trapped in an abusive relationship with Tony, all the while receiving constant support from both my Jewish grandmother and my church—it seemed as though she was as taken with my stories in person as she had been with my novel. As we finally said our good-byes Lucy assured me that I'd be hearing from her soon, and I left feeling pretty good about myself, confident that they'd be making an offer. I was already envisioning my book stacked up in front of the store at Barnes & Noble.

After pretending to have a doctor's appointment to take the meeting that would launch my career as a writer, I went back to my office temp job at a financial firm on Wall Street and then home to my five-story walk-up studio in Bay Ridge—and I waited. And waited. But as the weeks dragged on and I had yet to hear the words that would change my life forever, I couldn't stand it any longer. I needed to know what was happening.

The first time I called Lucy's office to follow up, Kim of the warm smile and outstretched hand told me that Lucy was "away from her desk." The next time she was "on another call." As my calls become more frantic and the excuses less believable, I spent my days at work jumping whenever my phone rang, afraid even to go to the ladies' room for fear that I'd miss that all-important call. At night I curled up in bed with my arms wrapped around a pillow and my fingers wrapped around my rosary beads, endlessly repeating my Hail Marys.

When Lucy finally did return my calls, she was apologetic but brutally honest. Unfortunately, she said, they wouldn't be able to publish my book after all. My stomach bottomed out before she could even finish the sentence. I was crushed. I gathered my wits and thanked her for her time before asking her reasons for passing. She paused, momentarily at a loss for words, and then sighed and admitted: "Because my publisher can't take the heat . . . I'm so sorry, Sam. I wish . . ." *Things were different? Yeah, me too.* "I wish you the best of luck with your book."

That's all I needed to hear. I had visions of Tony's underlings making thinly disguised threats from a series of smelly Brooklyn phone booths. There was no point even trying to argue with her. It was clear to me that I'd never be able to change her mind, not with Tony continuing to meddle in my life from behind bars. *Shit!*

ONE

New York City, 1996

In retrospect, I can't imagine why I had never considered that Tony could reach all the way from his prison cell across the bridge and into that publisher's office to continue controlling my life. I should have known better, but I was, after all, only nineteen and still naïve, despite everything I'd been through with him and with my mother.

Now, just over ten years later, I'm a bit wiser if not yet much better off. Whenever I think about all my big plans, I remember the old saying, "If you want to make God laugh, tell Him your plan." If that's true He must be doubled over and splitting a side at the cosmic joke that has been played on me.

I'd had to set aside my dreams of going to New York University and graduating with a degree in literature, and instead got a job straight out of high school to support myself. But whenever I began to doubt my path in life or feel sorry for myself, I thought of the foundation of love and encouragement I'd been given by my grandma Ruth and my faith in the Blessed Mother.

With the constant presence in my life of these two women who were always "there" for me, I knew that I'd be able to do whatever it took to achieve my goal of being a strong, independent woman and, ultimately, a published author.

I'd already come quite a way from the time when my mother died and I had to borrow money from friends just to pay for her funeral. I had steady temp work at a new brokerage house and had recently been put in charge of payroll, so let's just say I added a few hours here and there. I had to eat, right? With the bump in hours and pay that came with that mini-promotion I was already eating a little better and had a bit less stress when the rent came due. And the best part—I no longer owed anyone a dime.

Once Tony was transferred to a federal penitentiary in Kansas about five years ago, I'd stopped looking over my shoulder and jumping every time the phone rang. Although the manuscript for *The Blessed Bridge,* the novel I had written based on the years I spent with Tony Kroon, had been gathering dust on a shelf in my closet for years, I was submitting short stories and features to minor outlets, and I was deep into another novel that I was sure was destined for a better fate—as was I.

All things considered, my life wasn't all that bad, and I was still on track, albeit not in the express lane. I told myself that I was simply living my own version of *Girl, Interrupted,* and it could have been a lot worse. They say that when one door closes on you, God opens another. I still had my whole life in front of me, plenty of time to find that door, and I reminded myself to focus more on the positive, as Priti, my best friend at work, was always counseling me to do. Priti Sarma was a pretty woman with finely chiseled features who had emigrated from India with her family. Things hadn't been easy for her family either before or after they landed in America, and yet Priti was full of life and optimistic to a fault. Although I tended to guard my privacy and not get too friendly with the people in the offices where I'd worked over the years, Priti's exuberance and the hope that she exuded were infectious. I'd become accustomed to keeping friends and coworkers at arm's length—my suspicious nature a by-product of my entanglements with the mob. But after a decade of cautiously looking over my shoulder, I began to let my guard down and was grateful for my friendship with Priti. She taught me about India and her family's customs, which intrigued me, and she introduced me to the Buddha and the Hindu faith, which fed my curiosity about all things related to God. Her beliefs didn't threaten my own, as I'd already decided long before that every path of pure worship had the same end.

And she was equally open to learning about Jesus Christ and the Blessed Mother. Now and again she would join me for the short noon Masses at Our Lady of Victory, located just up the block from our office, every Monday, and would ask about my rosary-collecting hobby, which had started when I picked up a string of white plastic beads I had almost stepped on in the street when I was walking to my mother's funeral. Priti seemed to be fascinated by that glimpse into my past, as she was by everything I had to tell her about the rites and rituals of Catholicism.

One day, on impulse, I grabbed her hand and dragged her along with me to Mass. On hot summer days when you could actually see the heat rising in waves from the tar-covered streets and it was too hot to sit outside on a bench, we'd often sit in a cool, dark pew and talk quietly about the mysteries of faith, or pray silently in our own ways. In the peace and quiet of Our Lady of Victory, I am always reminded that I still find comfort in church—and that is no small thing.

That said, however, it was often harder to keep the faith in other areas. Yes, I was still writing, but also still waiting for the break that would allow me to actually live in Manhattan instead of just working there. When my mood got too bleak, Priti inevitably sensed when I was feeling low and was always there to cheer me up.

"What's with the long face?" she'd ask, her lively dark eyes peeking over the partition between us.

"Nothing," I'd answer, automatically fingering the rosary that found its way into my hand whenever I was anxious. "Just thinking about things."

"You girls working?" our ever-vigilant boss would invariably roar through the open door of his glass-enclosed office across the aisle.

"Yeah," I lied every time he asked the same question. I figured if he hadn't already fired me for my less-than-stellar typing skills, he wouldn't send me packing just for having a little over-the-partition chat with my friend.

"Who's zoomin' who, Ms. Bonti?" he asked, quoting the Aretha Franklin song. "Get back to that projection I've been waiting for too long already."

"Keep the faith, Sam," Priti would whisper as she sank back into her cubicle.

Okay, okay, I said to myself, turning back to my keyboard. *I guess everyone is waiting for something.* Despite a rush hour commute that would depress a saint, Priti's encouraging words generally kept me in a positive frame of mind until I got home, where I was greeted by the painting of the Blessed Mother that hung above my bed. *There are a lot worse roommates,* I told myself every time I saw it.

Some days, however, as I was preparing my go-to, cheap-but-healthy brown rice and broccoli dinner, the dreariness of my surroundings and the bleakness of my prospects really got to me—and on those days neither Priti nor the Blessed Mother could raise me out of my funk. I was in just such a mood one morning when I heard a familiar voice behind me at the bus stop.

"My, oh my. I'm not sure the Big Apple is ready for you today." It was John, my old friend from Brooklyn, who worked near my office downtown.

I smiled and gave him a peck on the cheek, self-consciously

smoothing the skirt of my blue-and-white-striped suit. Mom had bought it for me at a thrift store—it was so old that it had become retro and it was still in good shape all these years later because I had long since learned how to take care of the limited wardrobe I had. The skirt was pencil straight and clung to the curves on my petite frame in the right places but demanded to be worn with heels, which was okay with me. I'd always hated the way women look rushing for the train or the bus in their business suits and clunky sneakers; talk about not knowing how to feminize a suit.

"Nice suit, Bonti. I don't know how anyone in your office gets any work done with you walking around in that getup," he said, draping an arm across my shoulders and nudging me closer.

"Easy, John—it's just a suit," I retorted, elbowing him playfully and secretly loving the compliment. I'd been in a funk for so long, wondering how I'd become one of the dreary corporate drones commuting to Manhattan every day, that I'd forgotten how nice it was to get a little male attention.

"What can I say—you wear it well!"

I loved John for how sweet, honest, and supportive he was. He was a few years ahead of me in high school, and knew Tony, so he knew where I had truly come from, which scared most guys. But not John. He was always a gentleman, always ready with a compliment or kind word—and we both knew he'd always wanted to be more than friends, but the spark just wasn't there on my end. We rolled into lower Manhattan and stopped at a cart for coffee before parting ways with our customary two kisses and a hug.

I looked at my watch and picked up my pace—I was late already. I'd walked those two blocks from the bus to the office so many times that my feet took me there without my even paying attention to where I was going. I was still deep in thought when, steps from the glass and steel monolith that was my home away from home, I squeezed the white plastic rosary in my pocket and, without looking up, took a sharp left toward the door. As I did that, something caught my shoulder and spun me around. I lurched awkwardly to prevent myself from falling and spilling my coffee. "What the . . ." The words were almost out of my mouth when I looked up—and up—into the deep, laughing blue eyes of the giant who had almost bowled me over. The guy was huge . . . and gorgeous. At least six foot two and about two hundred thirty pounds, he had a full head of wavy black hair and an impish smile that compelled me to smile back. His perfect teeth were whiter than white against his tanned skin, and as I glanced down at the arm still on my shoulder, I could feel myself beginning to blush. That wasn't like me at all. But there was something about this man that took my breath away—and it wasn't the force of his blow to my shoulder.

"I'm sorry," he said, even though he didn't sound very apologetic. "I hope I didn't hurt you, but I think you're beautiful and I couldn't think of any other way to get your attention. My name is Alec, by the way."

"Well, thank you, I guess. You certainly do have a forceful way of introducing yourself, Alec," I shot back, having finally regained at least some of my composure. "I'm Samantha."

"Pleased to meet you, Samantha. And I'm truly sorry if I scared you. If you don't have a boyfriend or a husband, I would love to take you to brunch or dinner." He glanced at my left hand—the surreptitious ring check—and I realized I was still clutching my rosary. He turned on his thousand-watt smile: "You're not a nun, are you?"

Now it was my turn to smile. "Don't worry," I said, "I'm not married, and I'm definitely not a nun" (although my social life had been about as active as a nun's even now that I was free of Tony). "But I am very late right now." The guy had a nerve, but he was so charming that it would have been impossible to stay angry with him.

"So am I," he said, grin widening.

"Look, Alec, it's been great and all that, but I really have to go now," I said with as much conviction as I could muster.

"Yeah, I missed the opening bell, too," he confessed. Then he reached into his pocket, pulled out a card case, and leaned in close to my ear. "Call me, Samantha," he whispered, slipping a business card into my hand and allowing his fingers to brush mine for the briefest of instants, "next time you have an open Saturday or Sunday." And with that he turned and disappeared into the crowd.

I took a deep breath and steadied myself. *Holy shit, what just happened there?* I thought, shaking my head in disbelief as I pulled open the door to my building. *By the way, what is brunch?*

TWO

Fingering Alec's stiff business card, I tried to slip unobtrusively into my cubicle and look as if I were busy at my desk. I propped the distinctive slate-gray card with white lettering against my monitor and stared at it as I considered the brash but beautiful man who had given it to me: Alec DeMarco, Managing Director, Transglobal Equities. There was something tasteful yet assertive about the font, I thought. Just like Alec.

"I'm dying to know the reason for that ridiculous grin on your face," Priti teased as she poked her head around the partition.

"Very funny, P," I said, shuffling some paper.

She glanced toward the boss's office. "Okay, I'll let you catch up now, but I expect to hear everything at lunch. Twelve-thirty sharp at the bench," she hissed, retreating into her cubicle.

I shook my head to get rid of the overwhelming flood of emotions produced by my sidewalk encounter with Alec and tried to concentrate on the pile of paper in front of me.

"You gonna give me more than 'Just some guy I met,' or do I have to beat it out of you?" Priti complained as we settled on our favorite bench with our sandwiches. "Give it up, Sam. You're killing me."

"It all happened so fast, I can hardly remember. It's all a blur, really. This big guy grabs my shoulder right outside the building and spins me around. He asks for a *brunch* date, of all things. I mean, what's brunch anyway? We exchange a couple of pleasantries, he whispers in my ear to call him, and then he disappears."

"Is he hot?"

"I'd say that's putting it mildly."

"Really? That's saying quite a bit, considering it was *all a blur*."

"I know," I said, "but he just made a huge impression. He's rough and smooth at the same time, and his magnetism is really . . . powerful."

Priti grabbed my elbow gently. "Whoa, girl. Slow down. I know it's been a long time, but we can't have you rushing off to do him in his office."

Priti's name meant "delight, joy," and I couldn't help laughing about how much of both she got from my obvious discomfort.

"I know, P," I said softly. "But I've never met anyone who had such an effect on me so instantly."

Priti nodded. "I can see that," she said. "I'm just worried that you're going to be suckered in too quickly and end up hurt by some slick operator."

In an instant my relationship with Tony flashed through my mind. "Don't worry, Priti," I assured her. "That isn't going to happen to me—not again."

"So are you gonna call him?" she asked, obviously still concerned.

"In a day or two . . . or three."

"Good." She nodded. "Just so long as you keep your pretty little head screwed on straight."

✧ ✧ ✧

At home that evening, and for the two evenings after that, I jotted a few notes in my journal. Alec was never completely out of my mind. *What if John and I hadn't stopped for coffee that day? What if Alec and I hadn't both been late? If there'd been a speeding fire truck or an ambulance, or some other distraction that slowed either of us down for just a moment?* I decided that the whole thing must have been, in one of my Jewish grandma Ruth's favorite Yiddish words, *beshert,* meaning "destiny" or "fate."

Late on the third day after meeting him, the phone on my desk was beckoning me, but I was also a bit worried about dating someone whose world was completely foreign to me. Truth to tell, I wasn't even sure what "brunch" was. I knew it was some kind of combination of breakfast and lunch that people "went out for" on Sundays. But I'd certainly never had a brunch date in my life. What exactly did people eat for brunch? Where I came from, we didn't eat brunch. When we ate in a restaurant, which wasn't often, it was a local Chinese or Italian place, or sometimes a family-owned diner. A fancy meal was whatever the neighborhood nightclub was serving so all the young men (and the underage girls they supplied with fake IDs) would keep on dancing and buying drinks.

My courtship résumé consisted of a convicted felon who had cheated on me constantly and abused me in every other way, and a few nice guys trying to climb the ladder in the Financial District who didn't do it for me. I could already tell that Alec DeMarco wasn't like anyone else I'd ever known, much less gone out with.

So far it had always been the guys who didn't measure up to my standards, but what if this time it were different? Alec was far more sophisticated than I was or anyone else I knew for that matter. His entire demeanor exuded money and privilege. *What if this time I'm the one who doesn't measure up?*

Nonsense, I told myself. *Samantha Bonti is special, and if this guy is as special as you think, he'll know that.* So I pulled Alec's business card out of my purse and picked up the receiver.

The phone only rang once. "Hello."

"Alec DeMarco?" I asked.

"That's me."

"Samantha Bonti."

"So that's your last name." Alec chuckled. "The best day I ever had on the Street just got a whole lot better."

"Congratulations."

"It seems I haven't lost my touch after all, Samantha Bonti." The way he said my name sounded like a caress. "I'm telling you, I couldn't stop thinking about you, and then you call, and to top it off, it turns out you're Italian."

"Half."

"Let me guess: the other half is Native American."

"Jewish," I replied.

"Had to be one or the other." Alec laughed.

His easy manner made me comfortable. "You can laugh, but I promise, everything else about me won't be that easy to guess. You don't want to know how crazy my life was growing up."

"*Au contraire,* Samantha Bonti. I want to know everything about you, and I can't wait to get started."

Just listening to his voice sent a tingle down my spine. "Brunch this weekend would be nice," I managed, hoping that I didn't sound too anxious.

"Hang on a sec," Alec said, and I could hear paper rustling on his end, probably checking his calendar. "I've already got a date for Saturday. Let's do Sunday at eleven."

He's either crazy or brutally honest. "That's fine," I said. "Just tell me where to meet you."

"Not a chance," Alec said. "Give me your address and I'll pick you up."

"Well, actually, I live in Brooklyn," I confessed, sure that he'd change his mind.

"No problem," he replied without hesitation. "It's not every day a guy meets a girl worth driving to." He took down my address and added, "See you Sunday, Samantha Bonti."

"I'm looking forward to it, Alec," I said, which was the understatement of the century.

My apartment buzzer rang promptly at eleven on Sunday. *No way he's seeing this place right now.* "I'll be right down, Alec!" I called out of my second-floor window, then checked myself in the mirror. The simple vintage white cotton sundress I'd chosen (not like there was a lot to choose from) was cool, crisp, and, I knew, flattered my figure. I grabbed a small teal leather purse off the counter and dashed out the door in the heels I'd dyed to match.

"Unbelievable," Alec said, and smiled as he placed his hands on my shoulders and stepped back to get a better look, which also allowed me to get a good look at him. His blazer was no off-the-rack purchase. Looked to me like expensive Italian threads, and his tie had those tiny horses on it that I knew from the ads in fancy magazines meant it was Hermès. I vowed not to let his beautiful white teeth and wavy dark hair distract me too much. "You look great, Samantha."

"Thanks, Alec. It's just a sundress."

"That's exactly what it is about you. Anyone else would have got themselves all dressed up to impress me." I blushed. "You're nothing like any other woman I've known. I saw that from a block away."

"A girl could get hooked on that kind of flattery," I said as he led me to a black Range Rover parked at the curb.

"Full disclosure, Samantha: I plan to hook you, period," he said, smiling as he handed me into the passenger seat. *That's quite a statement considering we have barely begun our first date,* I thought. The butternut-leather bucket seat swallowed me up, but Alec's bucket seat contained him perfectly. He was massive but perfectly proportioned, and he exuded a sense of power and confidence that made me feel secure in his presence—the first time I'd ever felt that way with a man. Tony's power had always felt menacing rather than comforting, and I was beginning to understand the difference.

"Nice ride," I said with a dollop of syrup in my voice.

"Just one of my toys," Alec said as he pulled away. "Mostly for when I go fishing and for Sunday visits with the family at our beach house."

Please don't tell me you're springing your family on me today!

"I blew them off this morning," Alec continued as we headed for the Brooklyn Bridge. "Just like I would have blown off my fishing trip with the guys yesterday if that were the only day this weekend I could see you."

So that was the "date" he'd mentioned . . . "You go fishing often?" I asked, certain that this conversation would eventually get around to his real dates.

"Whenever I get the chance. Work is keeping me pretty busy right now."

"Is that a good thing?"

Alec flashed a jumbo grin. "You bet it is."

"It's nice to see someone who enjoys what he does."

"I freakin' *love* my work, Samantha, but it doesn't mean anything unless you have someone to share the ride," he said as we rolled onto the bridge.

Alec didn't find it necessary to keep talking, and I appreciated the few quiet moments as my mind raced with thoughts about what it would mean to share his ride. I'd vowed to myself that I would never let a man derail my future again. Not after what I'd gone through with Tony. So there was part of me that was afraid to let my guard down with Alec. I didn't want to lose sight of my dreams of becoming a writer. I had laid my life bare in *The Blessed Bridge* because I hoped that sharing what I had gone through would help at least one other girl like me. Getting it on paper had been an emotional and sometimes excruciating experience, and the effort to get the book out there had so far been disheartening. Now, sitting next to Alec, I renewed my vow to let nothing stop me from trying.

"You seem far away," Alec said.

"Just thinking about where I've been and where I'm going."

"Where you've been is history I'm dying to know all about. And as far as 'going' is concerned, you're going with me."

I felt my face flush. Grandma flashed into my mind. I'd been a love-struck teenager standing next to her and stirring the potato and onion mixture for her famous latkes, and now her words were as clear as if she were saying them from the backseat: *It's gonna be all right, bubelah. You'll see, the right man will come along and all will be great in the world.* I missed a lot of things about Grandma, but none more than our Saturday afternoons talking and cooking together.

"Where are you taking me?" I asked.

"Just a nice little café in my neighborhood."

"And what neighborhood would that be?"

"Tribeca."

I knew the area—the Triangle Below Canal Street—but only from reading the society pages. The old low-rise buildings that had long housed sweatshops and starving artists' studios were now filled with trendy boutiques, art galleries, fine restaurants, and expensive condos with floor-to-ceiling windows.

"Sounds great," I said, as Alec pulled into a garage. As soon as he'd put the car in park, he bolted around to my door before I could get it half open.

For a big guy he moves pretty well.

"The place isn't far," Alec said as he grabbed my hand and led me up the ramp to the street. "And anyway, it's a gorgeous day for walking a couple of blocks."

I was surprised to discover how at home I felt in a part of the city I'd never been before, and how natural it felt to be holding Alec's hand. I may have been different from any woman he'd ever known, but he was also nothing like any guy I'd ever dated, either. I'd held large hands before, but none that was callus-free and with buffed nails. His pride in walking with me was as palpable as his power had been earlier, and I felt as if I were floating a foot or two off the sidewalk.

Alec was true to his word and just a couple of blocks later he stopped before the heavy, wood-framed glass door to a café, pulled it open, and waved me inside. There were butterflies in my stomach that I attributed both to his attentiveness and to my anticipation of the meal we were about to share. I planned to take my time studying the menu and wondered how much of it would be Greek to me.

Everyone in the restaurant seemed to know Alec and they nodded or waved as a hostess right out of *Elle* magazine escorted us to a large corner booth in the rear. Most of my friends liked to sit right up front and next to a window so they could enjoy the comings and goings outside. Personally, I'd never enjoyed eating in a fishbowl, and certainly not now, when I didn't want anything to distract my attention from the food and, most of all, from the man I was with.

No sooner had we been seated than a waiter showed up at the table with a bottle of champagne in an ice bucket on a pewter stand. As he filled two crystal flutes I could see that the label read Taittinger, a name even I knew meant the best. Alec thanked him by name and raised his glass, saying, "To the most beautiful woman I've ever met." I held my breath as he took a healthy swig. "I never thought I would be smitten with a Brooklyn girl again," he said, grinning.

I didn't know if I should take that as a compliment or a criticism, and I guessed it was a bit of both, but then there it was.

As if reading my mind, Alec clarified: "I come from Brooklyn, too, you know, born and raised, so I'm allowed to say that."

I grinned at him. After all, I hadn't spent much time thinking about what it would be like to be with another Brooklyn guy, either. Yet somehow Alec was fundamentally different from all the other guys I'd known from the neighborhood. "Life is full of surprises," I managed to say.

Alec took another swig as I let a small taste cross my lips, and he must have signaled our waiter in some way because he reappeared as if by magic.

"We'll start with some cheese bread, rigatoni pesto, and the risotto, Jason," Alec said, grabbing a roll from the basket on the table between us.

So much for studying the menu.

"Certainly, Mr. DeMarco," Jason said. "Do you want me to put in the other dishes now, or later?"

Other dishes? Pasta, risotto, and a loaf of bread sounds like a lot of food to me, but Alec is a big man; what do I know anyway? Maybe that's what everyone around here eats for brunch.

Alec leaned toward me as Jason refilled his glass. "You pressed for time?" he asked.

I shook my head no, and he grinned. "Great. I have all day! That will be all for now, Jason. We'll order the rest later."

As the waiter withdrew, Alec leaned toward me again. "Try a brioche, Sam," he said, reaching for his butter knife. *So that's what they call a roll in this place.* "They're to die for."

The fact that he'd just called me Sam gave me chills. "Funny," I said, "that's what my family and close friends always call me."

Alec shrugged his shoulders. "Just seemed natural," he said. *Like the handholding felt.* "And feeling close to you, even though I hardly know you, feels natural, too," he added, slathering his brioche with butter from a little pot.

I took a sip of champagne and watched him from above the gold rim of my flute. There was something so refreshing about the way he wore his heart on his sleeve even though he seemed like a really tough guy—I found his confidence intoxicating.

"Getting to know you . . ." I sang softly as he took a healthy bite and swallowed it, seemingly at the same time.

"You a fan of Broadway, Sam?" he asked, and I must have looked puzzled because he added, "That song, it's from *The King and I.*"

"Oh, yes, I remember. I just heard the gang on *Cheers* sing it."

"I love that show." Alec beamed.

Loves his job, loves Cheers. *Two down, and countless more to go. Everything about this guy is probably over-the-top.*

"I usually end up at the theater a couple of times a month," Alec said. "I'll get us seats for any show you want. You free after work next week sometime?" he asked before draining his glass.

"You move fast."

Alec laughed. "You should have seen me in my football days."

"Really?"

"The Jets had their scouts on me before I busted up a knee. Took three surgeries before I could walk straight."

"That's too bad."

"Probably worked out for the best. Got me started sooner on my career."

"Trading stocks?"

"Slaying dragons, Sam," Alec quipped just as the first dishes arrived. "Slaying dragons." He looked up at our waiter. "I'll serve, Jason. And tell Carl he can fire up the angry lobster now."

"Yes, sir," Jason said, topping off my flute and refilling Alec's before he slipped away.

"Angry?" I asked.

Alec laughed and said, "Wouldn't you be if you were swimming in a four-by-four-foot tank all day long and knew you were about to be thrown into boiling water and seasoned, only to be eaten by a guy like me?"

Alec palmed the serving spoon, which looked like a teaspoon in his hand, scooped up a hefty portion of rigatoni, and picked up my plate.

"Just a taste, please," I said. "I have to save some room."

It looked and smelled delicious.

"This pasta is fabulous, Alec," I gushed after a couple of bites.

"Wait until you taste the cheese bread," he said, polishing off his rigatoni. "And the risotto is sublime."

I nibbled a corner of the warm bread and picked up a forkful of risotto, just as plates of eggs Benedict and French toast dripping with maple syrup appeared.

"So how did you end up on Wall Street?" I asked.

"That was natural, too, because my dad, who owned his own brokerage firm, had already made something of a name for himself there. I'm part of the next generation taking over."

Just like the Young Turks, Tony Kroon, and the Boys who were in line to take over for the mafia dons in Brooklyn. "Is your dad retired?"

"Semi. He still has his hand in a few things. I want you to meet him. I know you'll love him."

There's the family again. "What about the rest of the DeMarcos?" I asked, suddenly curious to know more about where this guy came from.

"My older brother, Franco, is a hotshot plastic surgeon on Park Avenue. Married with two kids. Only the inner circle calls him Franco; it's Frank or Dr. DeMarco for everyone else. My sister, Gianna, is about your age," he went on, spearing three rigatonis at once and popping them in his mouth. "Looks a little like you, too." He leaned toward me then and touched my hand gently. "Not as beautiful, though, I might add."

I blushed yet again.

Alec palmed another brioche, broke off a chunk, and wiped his plate clean with the bread. "Hmmm," he sighed contentedly, "I never get tired of Carl's sauces . . . Just like I know I'll never get tired of being with you," he went on, as if reading my mind.

"What about your mother?" I asked.

"Employed full-time as the mistress of two homes and the family event planner. She fills in any gaps with shopping and decorating. But what about your family, Sam? Tell me about them."

Before I could answer his question, Jason showed up with two portions of the so-called angry lobster, so I got a bit of a reprieve before having to answer his question. "Would you like some butter, miss?" he asked.

"Yes, please," I said, my mouth already watering in anticipation. *I could feed myself for a few days with what will be left over in this bowl.*

As Jason dashed my serving and then covered Alec's with the herbal buttery blend, I considered just how much to tell Alec about my mother. I would have preferred to avoid the topic of my family altogether. But clearly family was important to him—and I liked that about him.

"I think Samantha here has got me off my game, Jason," Alec said. "Can you get us a bottle of that New Zealand Sauvignon Blanc? I should have remembered to ask for it sooner."

"Right away, Mr. DeMarco," Jason said, dashing off.

Jason set two glasses of white wine before us and made fast work of popping the cork.

"Before I forget again, Jason," Alec said, as the waiter filled the glasses, "you can pop the cork on an '82 Barbera, too. We'll be having the osso buco."

"Here's to you again, Sam."

"Likewise, Alec," I said, clinking his glass.

"It's still your turn, Samantha Bonti," Alec said, massive palms on the edge of the table.

He didn't need his size to command a scene, as his voice alone could get the job done. I squeezed my purse on the banquette and felt the rosary beads inside, giving me the courage to speak. "My mother died almost ten years ago, just a couple of months after my grandma passed on."

For the first time since we sat down, Alec stopped eating and drinking, and it was the first time I saw him without any trace of a smile on his face or a gleam in his eye. "I'm sorry to hear that, Sam," he said quietly.

"Probably for the better," I replied without thinking. *In for a penny, in for a pound.* "They loved each other and God knows they both worshipped me, each in her own way, but there was always some kind of *tumult* in our lives—or, as my grandma would say, *tsuris.*"

Alec filled the pregnant pause. "I'm familiar with the term."

"If it wasn't my Jewish grandmother versus my Catholic convert mother, it was my mother versus my choices in everything from hairstyle to boyfriends. Grandma always backed me up and encouraged me to write more, while Mom would never read a word. She would pump me up by telling me I was pretty and then make sure to follow it up with 'too bad you're not taller,' just to deflate me. I think in her heart she knew I would manage to find a way out, which she never did, and I think that pissed her off. Her only escape added to drugs was men."

"Sounds like your life should have come with a scorecard." Alec chuckled, lightening the mood. "But then again, Italian family gatherings are never exactly prayer meetings, and I speak from experience on that!" Then he leaned forward and resumed his assault on his food.

I seized the opportunity for another nibble, and Alec refilled his glass, giving mine a splash that wasn't necessary. "So what about those boyfriends?" he asked.

"Nothing special except for one Brooklyn boy I met when I was sixteen."

"There's plenty of them around."

"Maybe, but they're not all mobbed up like mine was."

That must really have gotten his attention because he put down his fork and his glass.

"Still doing time somewhere," I continued.

"I'm sorry to hear that, too, Sam."

"I'm not," I said, taking a slug of my wine that could have rivaled one of Alec's. "I'm glad to be rid of him."

"I can only imagine what you went through."

"It was all downhill after the first couple of months. You wouldn't believe the crap that happened to me—I can still barely get a grip on it. But I survived and it happened for a reason." I reached for my wine again.

"We can change the subject if you want, Sam."

"There really isn't much more to say, Alec, other than I had to break up with him three times before I was finally free of him."

"The persistent type."

"You don't know the half of it. Tony had me followed while he was in prison, and any boyfriend I had got a visit from one of his associates. He had me looking over my shoulder all the time, day and night."

"I don't care who he was 'with,' I would have had someone take care of him."

I knew he meant well and was also flexing his muscles to impress me, but, truthfully, Alec was sounding a bit too much like Tony at that point to make me entirely comfortable. And furthermore, I wasn't really looking for someone to "take care of" anything for me. For better or worse, I'd already been taking care of myself for a very long time. But all I said was "Thanks, Alec, but I'm at peace with all of it now. Past is prologue and all that."

"And speaking of the present, my lovely date," Alec said as he tipped his glass in my direction, "you won't be able to forgive yourself if you don't have some of that osso buco right now."

"Is the rest of your family as big on food as you are, Alec?" I asked as I obediently separated a sliver of veal from the bone with a touch of my fork.

"They give me a run for my money. Food is an important part of our lives. It brings us together."

I couldn't help thinking of Mom and Grandma, and how food—or not having enough of it—always tore us apart. I longed to be a part of the kind of family that enjoyed spending time together—cooking, eating, talking, laughing. And there was something about Alec that promised the whole package. "You'll meet them soon," Alec said between forkfuls.

"You *do* move fast, don't you?" I said.

"Sam," he said, "I only play one way—all in."

He wasn't smiling, but his face wasn't entirely blank, either. *I suppose that's the look he uses on competitors sitting across his desk.* I took a bite of my osso buco and rolled my eyes in delight—it was delicious. "You were right, Alec. I wouldn't have forgiven *you* if you let me get out of here without tasting the veal. It practically melted in my mouth."

Alec placed a hand on mine, gazed into my eyes, and said with all sincerity, "That's not the only melting going on here, Sam." He paused then, as if he needed to get a business matter out of the way, and continued, "Listen. I want to be straight with you. About my past. A guy would have to be stone cold dead not to succumb to the temptations put in front of him in my line of work. I've been with models, aspiring actresses, daughters and sisters of movers and shakers. You name it." He paused again, hands resting on the edge of the table, and my antenna went up. "I've even been around, how shall I say . . . professional women." *Now there's a bulletin—hookers on Wall Street! I'm not the only one here who's had an abnormal normal life.* "A lot," he added. "From strippers to ten-thousand-dollar-a-night escorts, porn stars, and world-class madams who work out of thousand-year-old castles."

I swallowed.

He paused, taking in my expression.

"It's Business 101 in the financial world, Sam," Alec continued. "But truthfully, there have been times when those pursuits had nothing to do with any deal . . ." Alec looked down at his hands, clearly wrestling with just how much more to say. "And while I'm in confession mode . . . I've even been married once. Katie was my high school girlfriend and everyone just assumed we'd get married, so we did. However, she was more a Maserati without the engine, if you know what I mean. It was stupid and we both knew it was a mistake almost from the beginning. It didn't last long—not even two years—and luckily we didn't have kids. She was the only woman who ever told me I would never amount to anything and never make more than forty grand a year . . . Boy, how things work out when you feel the need to put someone else down and not realize what they're capable of. I knew right then and there this was never going to work. By now it's ancient history and sometimes I almost forget it ever happened."

Honesty is such a lonely word, I thought to myself. And, as Billy Joel had written when I was in my previous life, honesty was also what I needed most from a guy. "I appreciate your candor, Alec." *Let the chips fall where they may.*

"Trust me, I could write a book about what goes on among the power brokers, just about all of whom are married."

I thought of my own manuscript languishing on that closet shelf. "But you aren't married," I said, proud of my powers of recovery. "You're still young, and there's still plenty of time to sow your wild oats."

Alec leaned forward and placed a hand on mine as he had earlier, catching me off guard as I was beginning to realize was his specialty. "The thing is, I'm almost thirty-six years old—or young as you say—but I haven't been in a serious relationship for years."

There was nothing I could think of saying to fill the pregnant pause that followed.

"I'm old enough to know what I'm missing, Sam," Alec continued. "Every fiber in my body tells me it's going to be a whole lot different with you."

My face flushed and my stomach fluttered. "I'm touched, Alec."

"I mean it," Alec said with a smile. He polished off a last bite of osso buco, leaned back, and motioned to Jason, who appeared almost immediately.

"You can clear our plates," Alec said, "and wheel the dessert cart over whenever you want."

I stared at the heaps of food left on our plates. *I guess it'll be a huge faux pas if I ask for a doggie bag.*

"Yes, sir," Jason said and he waved to a busboy. "Will you be having coffee, cappuccino, espresso, or tea, miss?"

"Yes, two espressos," Alec answered for me.

"Sure thing, Mr. DeMarco," Jason said as he departed.

"We'll be having our own little Viennese table too, Sam," Alec said.

As we sampled Neapolitan and Venetian pastries and sipped espresso, the conversation flowed easily. Something felt really good about being with this total stranger, but I could not define what that was. I hoped it was because Alec was being honest with me, and that was what felt so refreshing.

We talked and talked for almost an hour, and, as corny as it sounds, we never wavered from holding each other's gaze. When our conversation died down, I declined the grappa Alec had ordered for a "nightcap," and which, he explained, came from the last press of wine grapes, and opted instead for some Mandarin orange tea.

"You're through and through Italian, aren't you?" I asked as he savored the last mouthful of his wine.

"Sicilian." Alec grinned. "One hundred percent."

"Not the same thing," I said, and gave him a smile. "I know all about that. In fact, I even wrote a book about it."

"No kidding?"

"Nope. A novel called *The Blessed Bridge*."

"I knew there was more to you than met the eye, but I never figured you for a writer."

"My ex Tony didn't, either, and he wanted no part of seeing it in print. He reached out from prison and derailed my writing career before it even got started. I shouldn't have been surprised; he had connections everywhere—most mafia men do. But for some reason I'd fooled myself into believing that publishing was too far outside of his sphere of influence to infiltrate. I was wrong. Turns out it was easy for him to get to my publishers and stop the deal from happening. That's what life with Tony was like: when he was with me he tried to destroy me and when we were apart he still tried."

Alec let out a low whistle. "Well, Wall Street guys have connections too . . . I'd like to look this creep up."

Please, no.

I didn't wonder what Alec was capable of. As far as I could see, he did pretty much whatever he wanted, and I didn't need him resurrecting Tony Kroon. But I did appreciate the fact that he seemed so ready to defend my honor. "Last I heard he's in the witness protection program," I said.

"So he's both a lowlife *and* a rat," Alec said, draining his pretty cordial glass. "How did you survive that relationship?"

"My faith sustains me."

Alec smiled. "I didn't figure the rosary you were clutching when I ran into you was some kind of new costume jewelry statement."

Jason appeared and disappeared, refilling Alec's glass in the process.

"All kidding aside, Alec—*are* you an observer?"

Alec did justice to the healthy pour and looked me in the eyes. *There's that ear-to-ear smile!* "I could be."

"What does that mean?"

"My dad is a devout Catholic, and Mom is right behind him, but it didn't exactly rub off on me. I guess I was more consumed by Dad's financial teachings. Still, they're both always after me to practice my faith more."

"I don't belong to any congregation or go to church every Sunday, but I do find peace every time I go to Mass and every time I pray. Maybe your father knows what's good for you."

Alec squeezed my hand. "As I said, I *could* be an observer." My smile nearly matched his, as he drained his glass and leaned toward me. "You ready to leave?"

So that was brunch. "I enjoyed it immensely, Alec. Thank you."

"Maybe this is the beginning of a beautiful friendship," Alec said, quoting that famous last line from *Casablanca* as he slid from the booth and took my hand, ushering me toward the exit.

Jason said good-bye to us and slipped a small shiny pink box with a sheer white lace bow into my free hand as we left. "Some chocolates for you, miss," he said.

"Thanks." I beamed, still tethered to Alec.

"What about a check?" I whispered, but he didn't slow down.

Oops. Faux pas?

"My AmEx card is on file," Alec said as he we emerged into the late-afternoon sun.

I floated more than walked back to the parking garage, where an attendant stood beside the passenger door of Alec's Range Rover, already idling on the ramp.

How did Alec arrange that?

"Thanks, José," he said as he slipped a folded bill into the attendant's hand.

The Sunday traffic was light and so was the conversation. Alec wanted to know what I'd liked most about our brunch, and he seemed pleased when I told him that getting to know each other better was the highlight for me.

We rolled onto the Brooklyn Bridge and I couldn't help thinking for the umpteenth time about living in Manhattan. The energy was different on this side of the river and I desperately wanted to be a part of it all the time. *When is that going to happen for me?*

"Let me walk you to the door," Alec said as he double-parked in front of my apartment house.

This time, enjoying the attention, I waited for him to come around and open my door. When he took my hand once more and escorted me to the front stoop, the tingly feeling I'd felt on the phone with him came back in force.

At the door, he placed his hands on my shoulders as he had done before, and he saw everything in my eyes. "I'm going to see you again, Samantha Bonti," he breathed, giving me the gentlest kiss possible. His eyes lingered on mine for a moment as he released my hand. He smiled as he turned toward the curb.

I stood there for a long time after his Range Rover disappeared around the corner.

THREE

As soon as I got home, I curled up in bed with my little box of chocolates. Recollections of the food and the conversation I'd had with Alec played through my mind as I popped a hazelnut truffle into my mouth and let it melt on my tongue.

Not the only melting going on, that's for sure.

My humble surroundings seemed different somehow. The setting sun streaming through the double windows in the living area seemed to fill the empty vase on the kitchenette counter, and the colors of my shabby furniture seemed more vibrant than usual. *Maybe the present changes when the future does.*

I was dying to share my day with someone who gave a damn about me, but there was no one to call. It would have been cruel to babble on about Alec with John, and Priti lived with her parents, who, I knew, wouldn't have appreciated her talking on the phone for as long as it would take for me to tell all. That conversation would just have to wait until lunch the next day.

I wish I could talk to Grandma about Alec.

I switched the TV on and thumbed the *TV Guide* I'd palmed from my dentist's office. I knew Grandma would love hearing how attentive he'd been, but she'd also give me grief because he wasn't a "nice Jewish boy."

As for Mom, I could never win with her no matter who the guy was, even if he were Richard Gere, who had just popped onto the cracked TV screen with Julia Roberts in *Pretty Woman*. I sank deeper into my pillows as Julia sank up to her neck in a luxurious bubble bath. The phone rang before I had a chance to give myself a pity party.

"Hi, Samantha Bonti," Alec said, and I could see his grin.

I switched the TV off. "You *can't* be home yet, even if it is Sunday," I said.

"Nah, I just couldn't wait to talk to you," Alec said.

Having a guy call a day, or even two, after a date is exciting, a rather big deal. The significance of a call on the same day didn't escape me.

"Hell, I couldn't even wait till I got to the bridge."

This is a HUGE deal, Samantha. "You pulled over somewhere?"

"I'm in the Range Rover."

I'd heard about car phones, but didn't know anyone who had one. "I didn't see a phone when I was in the car."

"Tucked away in the console. Sure comes in handy sometimes."

"I'll bet." *The rich have a lot of handy things, like savings accounts and vacation homes.*

"You a gambler, Sam?"

"Not really," I said, without adding that I didn't have any discretionary income to spend on such frivolities.

"Well, just say the word and we'll be off to Vegas to find out for sure."

"That's not high on my list of places to visit."

"Where would . . . whoa!"

"What happened?" I screeched. "You all right?"

"The sunset . . . I just wish you were here with me on the bridge to see it."

I wish I were, too. "Funny . . . I noticed the light just a minute ago."

"Just one of the many things we're going to share, Sam."

"That's so sweet, Alec."

"A mere bag of shells, as Ralph Kramden says."

"I'm just a tad worried about you talking and driving, Alec."

He chuckled. "Now look who's being sweet."

"I mean it, Alec. I don't want to be responsible for a crash."

"I'm in good hands with Allstate."

"Why don't you just call me back when you get home?"

"I'm five minutes away. Don't go anywhere."

As if. "Take your time," I said.

A full day had just gotten overstuffed, and there was more to come. *This calls for a celebration.* I popped another truffle into my mouth. *Julia's got nothing on me right now.*

Pulling the set of rosary beads from under the pillow where I kept them handy, I called my blessings, past and present, to mind, and rattled off a Hail Mary and an Our Father, finishing just as the phone rang again. *Maybe Alec will "observe" with me someday.*

"Miss me?" He chuckled.

"Counted the seconds."

"Then count on being with me Tuesday after work, Sam. We'll see a show and have a late supper after."

This guy certainly moves fast. He could teach the Flash a thing or two about speed.

"I won't take no for an answer."

"What if I told you I already had a date?"

"I'd tell you to break it."

"You're pretty sure of yourself, aren't you, Mr. DeMarco?"

"Let me put it this way, Sam: if there's a guy out there you'd rather be with, then I want to meet him."

"Is that so?"

"Yup."

"To work him over, I suppose."

"Nope," Alec deadpanned. "I'd just want to tip my hat to him."

I laughed. "You're a regular riot, Alec, to paraphrase your friend Ralph Kramden."

"I'm crazy about you, Alice," he parried, and we both laughed. "I've got plans for your Monday, too."

"Oh? And what might those be?" I asked. I had to admit, his confidence was a big turn-on.

"Pop up to Saks right after work," Alec directed. "Go to the eighth floor and ask for Evelyn. She'll help you pick out something nice."

I paused, stunned. A smile spread across my face.

"That's also very sweet, Alec," I managed, "but . . . but very unnecessary." Unnecessary or not, it would certainly be a rare treat to be able to choose a new dress that came from a famous Fifth Avenue department store instead of a thrift shop. And I was too flattered, and too smitten, to think about the implications of allowing a guy I hardly knew to buy me such an expensive gift.

"I know it's not necessary," he said, "but please indulge me."

How could a girl refuse? Now I really *feel like Julia Roberts in* Pretty Woman. "I'm speechless right now, Alec."

He laughed. "That's how I like my women all the time."

"Been nice knowing you, then," I cracked.

We talked for two hours that seemed like two minutes, sometimes joking and sometimes speaking seriously. I was more than content to let him do most of the talking, and, stallion that Alec was, he was pleased to show off a little.

He told me that he had done extremely well as a specialist on the floor of the New York Stock Exchange, matching buyers with sellers as a market-maker to keep trades flowing smoothly.

He said that he seemed to have a great talent for handling tricky decisions on a daily basis and incredibly stressful initial public offerings (IPOs) every week or so. He had made a steady climb up the Wall Street ladder. Delivering lunches and coffees was a thing of the past. It was a fierce game of great wealth that only very few knew how to play well enough to survive, much less thrive. Alec knew when he would deliver his last lunch in much the same way that a mafia guy knows that after his first murder he will be "made."

He had just become a managing director at Transglobal, an independent specialist firm, and was well on his way to becoming a partner. I knew he'd gotten his start as a result of his father's connections, as had many others on the Street, but by his own admission he was bound and determined to become a titan in his own right, and, based on fierce determination alone, I knew he'd accomplish whatever he set his mind to do. From where I sat, he was already wildly successful, and his presence, which I'd experienced up close and personal, seemed natural, too. I couldn't remember the last time I'd let my guard down with another person, much less with a man.

"So Sam, *The Blessed Bridge*—I can tell by the way you talk about writing just how passionate you are about getting your book published. I'm not that familiar with publishing," he said, "so I'll be calling around this week to anyone who owes me a favor. We'll see if something shakes loose."

"Nothing you could do for me would be sweeter, Alec," I gushed. *Is this guy for real? Or did I make him up?*

I floated to work the next morning, and the thought of choosing a new outfit for my wardrobe was but one of the winds of possibility that had carried me along. Priti was in my cubicle before I even had a chance to sit down, a reception committee of one. "A heavy date has done wonders for your punctuality," she said. "It's still forty minutes before the bell."

"I swear, P, I've never looked forward to a Monday the way I did last night. But don't give me any medals—I'm leaving early."

"Another date already?"

"Tomorrow. *Phantom* and a late supper."

"He's a slick operator, all right."

"He is just so real, so alive. I have never been out with a man before who knows exactly what he wants and says it, out loud. If he wasn't so brutally honest and transparent about his intentions, I'd be inclined to agree with you. The brunch was indescribable, P."

"That's saying a lot for a writer."

"I'm not just talking about the food, which was pretty amazing in itself," I said as I slid into my chair. "I wanted to take three or four doggie bags home with me."

Priti laughed. "That you didn't says a lot for a former food-stamper."

"I kid you not—I'd never heard of half the stuff he ordered for us, let alone tasted it. But the conversation was even better, and his attentiveness, the way he put me at ease, was best of all."

"I'm going to the nearest kite store on my break." Priti chuckled. "If I don't get a tether to hold you down to earth, I'm afraid you'll disappear into the stratosphere. Did he hit on you?" Priti asked, getting down to brass tacks as usual.

"All we did was hold hands as we walked, but that felt as natural as if we'd been doing it for years."

"No kiss good-bye?"

"A peck on the lips is all. It was so fast it was as if it didn't happen."

"You sure he's not just setting you up?"

"If he is, he must have written the book on how to do it. We talked for hours last night."

"He called?" Priti shrieked. "Get out!"

"I'm telling you, P, Alec's not like any guy I've known, or even heard about for that matter. Maybe I read about one someplace, but I'm not even sure of that."

"Maybe you should write about him, then."

"Way ahead of you, P. I filled half a steno book last night and fell asleep with the pen still in my hand."

"Sweet dreams, I bet," she said and we shared a laugh. "So, what's with leaving early?"

"You better sit down."

Priti reached around the partition, wheeled her chair over, and slumped into it, ready for a long visit.

"Alec referred me to a wardrobe consultant at Saks," I began, and Priti's eyes got bigger. "I'm going there after work to pick out a dress for tomorrow night."

Priti exhaled. "This is serious, kiddo," she said as a flower delivery boy materialized at my cubicle.

"Ms. Bonti?" he asked.

"That's me," I said with my best imitation of Alec's big smile.

"These are for you." The boy smiled back as he set a huge bouquet of virgin-white lilies on my desk. *I don't think the teal ribbon around the vase is a coincidence.* "Have a nice day."

I reached for the teal envelope tucked into the ribbon and read the note, written in a man's hand.

"You gonna keep me in suspense?" Priti pleaded.

"'These will keep you company until I do,'" I read.

"This guy is some smooth operator." Priti sighed. "If you don't let me go with you to Saks tonight I'll never speak to you again."

Tuesday morning, I floated into work and hung a sleek black garment bag on the partition that separated Priti's and my cubicles. "That suit is a winner, Sam," she said, smiling, clearly delighted that I'd picked her favorite. I was counting the hours until I could change into the fabulous royal blue suit I'd bought the night before. With a fitted jacket and slim skirt, it was just tight enough to show my curves without being too clingy. I knew I looked great in it and couldn't wait to show it off to Alec.

"You should have taken the heels Evelyn suggested, too," Priti gushed. She said the consultant's name as if they were old friends.

"I've got a decent black bag and heels to match, P," I said as I sat at my desk and eyed the blinking red light on my extension. "I'm not a gold digger, you know."

"With this guy you could be."

I smiled. "I'll have to be on guard about that." It flashed through my mind that even accepting the dress was too much, but I quickly dismissed that thought. *Alec just wants me to do him proud when we go out tonight.*

"You'll have to be on guard, period." Priti chuckled. "I shudder to think what kind of bill he's going to present you with for the swag."

"I told you, P, Alec's not that kind of guy."

"And you're not some sucker, right?"

"Right," I said as my extension rang, causing my stomach to flutter again.

"I'll leave the two of you alone," Priti teased as she disappeared into her cubicle.

"You a psychic now, Priti?" I laughed, reaching for the phone. "Ms. Bonti—how may I help you?"

"Let me count the ways," Alec boomed. I blushed. "Where've you been?" he asked, semi-serious.

"It isn't even nine yet, Alec."

"I've been dialing your number every five minutes since eight-thirty. I stopped leaving messages a call or two ago."

I glanced at the flashing red light again. "I'll have to be more prompt about clearing my phone messages from now on."

"You all set for tonight?"

"Thanks to you. And thanks for the flowers—they're gorgeous!"

"As you are, Sam." *There's that flattery again.* "Even Evelyn noticed you were a keeper."

"I'm sure she was just being nice."

"*Au contraire,* buttercup. She said it's been years since she's seen a young woman who didn't need makeup."

"She's very sweet, Alec."

"That's because she knows I'm sweet on you. But I think what really got her was the fact that you didn't beat up my American Express card."

"I would never take advantage, Alec."

"I'm begging you to, Sam. I mean it."

"Well"—I laughed—"if you insist."

"Hurt me, baby," Alec said, laughing.

I glanced at my boss, who by now had arrived at his desk. "I have to go, Alec, or I won't be able to get out of here on time this evening."

"Okay, okay, but I'm telling you the day is coming when I won't let you go no matter what."

"I'm duly warned."

"My car will be waiting for you outside your building from five on. Can't wait to see you."

"Me too," I whispered before hanging up.

The boss picked up his phone shortly before five, which came in handy as cover for my early escape. I slid my chair back, stood halfway, grabbed the garment bag, and headed for the ladies' room.

Not bad, I said to myself as I modeled my new dress in the mirror and fluffed up my hair. *Not bad at all.*

"Wow," Priti said as soon as she came through the door. "Looks even better than it did last night."

"Thanks, P," I said, handing her the garment bag. "And thanks for taking care of this."

"Knock him dead, kiddo." She gave me a thumbs-up as I reached for the door handle.

It seemed that more men than usual were eyeing me as I rode down in the elevator, and I was feeling pretty great until I pushed through the revolving door and froze in my tracks.

How am I supposed to know the car?

With all the black sedans double-parked from one corner to the next, there was no way to tell one from another. But, as I should have known, I needn't have worried.

"Ms. Bonti?" A voice came from behind me.

I turned around and saw an elderly man in a dark suit and chauffeur's cap. "Yes, that's me."

"Right this way, miss," the man said, waving his hand toward the stretch limo parked directly in front of the entrance.

The chauffeur opened the rear door and ushered me inside. "Help yourself to the bar and the snacks in the fridge," he said as I sank into the cushy leather seat. He closed the door and reappeared a moment later in the driver's seat. "We'll head on over to Mr. DeMarco's office," he said over his shoulder, "and I'll have you at the Majestic Theater in no time." As he eased away from the curb a smoked glass panel rose from his seatback, sealing him off from the rear.

Alone again . . . but not for long.

The intercom crackled a couple of minutes later. "We're outside Mr. DeMarco's building, Ms. Bonti. If you need anything while we wait, just press that blue button above your head."

I was in a fairy tale and the only thing I wanted was for my prince to appear. I stared out of the tinted window for ten minutes that seemed like an hour until Alec emerged from the stock exchange. He strode toward the limo and I slid over as the chauffeur got out and opened the door for him.

"Sorry to keep you waiting, Sam," he huffed, pulling me close and giving me a peck on the cheek as the door closed behind him.

"This isn't such a bad place to wait," I said, gesturing to the bar and the luxurious upholstery.

"Just another toy, Sam," he said, eyeing the bar. "But I see you didn't crack a bottle."

"I'm fine."

"Well, I'm not," Alec said with a chuckle as the driver eased into traffic and headed for the West Side Highway. "But I will be soon."

Ignoring the tongs set on top of the ice bucket, he reached in and filled his glass with a single scoop of his giant hand. Then he opened the small refrigerator under the bar, removed a jar of olives, pried one loose with a pinkie, and dumped it into his glass. He repeated that twice more, grabbed one of the crystal decanters from the bar, and poured a liberal amount of the clear liquid it contained over the ice, topping it off with a few drops of dry vermouth.

"Nothing like a Reyka martini after work, especially when there's something to celebrate," Alec said and my eyes opened wide.

"I didn't think this evening could get more exciting, Alec," I said sincerely.

"Well, hold on to your hat," he warned, slipping an arm across my shoulders and bringing the drink to my lips. "You first, Sam," he said, tilting the glass. I obliged with the tiniest of sips but recoiled from the taste. Then, after putting a huge dent in the martini, he said, "It's not every day that your bosses connect you to Grigor Malchek."

"That's wonderful news, Alec," I said. I didn't follow the ins and outs of the Financial District closely, but everyone knew that Malchek had quit college and joined the stock exchange in the early seventies as an eighty-dollar-a-week listings clerk, and that he had rocketed through the ranks to become an icon of capitalism by using his extraordinary interpersonal skills. To him, the trading specialists who made the markets were always more important than new products and new trading technologies.

"Yeah, I'm gonna be working with him on some deals," Alec said. He took another swig, which just about drained his glass, and leaned back in his seat. "The first one is huge, and as soon as it's put to bed I won't be delivering coffee and lunches anymore."

"*You* have to go out for food?"

"Well, in a manner of speaking, Sam. What I mean is, I'm going to stop serving other people's interests and start serving my own. I'm going to be making my own trades instead of helping others with theirs. Bottom line? I've paid my dues and I'm done kissing ass."

"Good for you, Alec."

He looked at me and rested his free hand on my knee. "Good for *us*, Sam," he said softly. *There he goes, talking about* our *future again.*

He slipped a Stephen Bishop CD into the player, sat back, and polished off his martini as the prophetic words of "It Might Be You" poured from the speakers:

> *Something's telling me it might be you*
> *It's telling me it might be you*

As the chauffeur turned off of the West Side Highway and headed east toward the theater district, Alec refilled his glass. He had downed a second martini by the time we pulled up to the curb in front of the entrance. Alec slipped out the door opened by the driver and took my hand. I felt like a movie star as the crowd on the sidewalk watched me exit the limo.

They must be tourists.

Alec leaned in to me as we approached the door. "You're the star in my life now," he whispered, and I broke out in a jumbo smile that remained plastered to my face all the way to our box and throughout the musical. You could count on one hand the number of times I'd been to a Broadway play or Radio City Music Hall, and this evening was truly magical for me. After the curtain came down the adrenaline was still flowing as we climbed back into the limo, which was waiting at the curb.

"Unbelievable, Alec," I gushed.

"Trust me—supper at Le Cirque will not be an anticlimax."

All I can say is that Alec was right again. The elegance of the room, the deferential treatment we received, and the superb food and wines that he once again ordered for both of us were light-years beyond anything I'd ever experienced before.

Back in the limo, Alec hit the PLAY button and pulled me close. I rested my head on his massive shoulder, closed my eyes, and felt his whole body relax as we once again listened to Stephen Bishop:

All of my life
It's you, it's you I've been waiting for all of my life

"You're the best, Sam," he said, breathing heavily as he kissed my hair.

FOUR

A whirlwind week was followed by a whirlwind July and early August. It was as if Alec were some kind of fairy-tale prince who had ridden into my life on a white stallion, pulled me up beside him with his big, strong arms, and snatched me from the mundane daily grind that had been my life for so many years. I certainly hadn't been seeking or expecting rescue, but I can't say that I wasn't relishing every minute of it. We were together until the wee hours almost every night, and all day on weekends. He took me not only to the finest restaurants but also to art gallery openings, jazz performances, and baseball games, which we viewed from a private box. He even managed to extract me from my office cubicle for a couple of lunches each week. What I cherished most of all, however, were our long walks in Central Park after we'd visited the Guggenheim or the Metropolitan Museum of Art, and his phone calls every day when I was at work and every night when I was at home, even if he had just dropped me off.

I had to practically drag myself out of bed to get to work after one of those endless evenings, but Alec never seemed to be affected by the pace we were keeping. On the contrary, he seemed to thrive on acting as my teacher and guide. More than once I wondered what my mother, who didn't know a brioche from a bagel, would have thought about the life of pure indulgence I was leading, thanks to my white knight.

He was introducing me to many of his super-rich, high-flying friends, and I couldn't help but worry that I had neither the clothes nor the background to be traveling in such rarefied circles. Alec solved the first problem a couple of weeks into our relationship by sending me on a no-holds-barred shopping spree. But more important, I continued to remind myself that it was *me* he had chosen when he could surely have had any girl he wanted. No matter what happened, I fully intended to remain true to myself. I was still the edgy girl from Brooklyn who had raised her fists in defiance of the short haircut with curls that her drug-addled mother had forced upon her at twelve years of age. I wanted Alec's friends to like me, but they needed to like *me,* not some phony façade I put up in order to fit in.

After a while my friend John began to complain, albeit politely, that I hardly ever rode to work with him anymore and that we hardly talked on the phone the way we used to. But whenever we did talk he also was anxious to know all about what I'd been doing. I could also tell that Priti, who was certainly vicariously enjoying every minute of my new life, was also a bit annoyed that we almost never went to noon Mass together or ate lunch on our favorite bench anymore. I certainly didn't want to hurt either one of them, but, truthfully, I was so swept up by the whirlwind of Alec's courtship that I couldn't really think about much else.

In the office, I could barely keep my mind on my work. The distractions that came with my new dashing, powerful, and considerate boyfriend would have made a member of the Queen's Guard at Buckingham Palace desert his post. My mind was filled with recollections of past dates and wonderings about what was to come, and I automatically checked the light on my extension first thing each morning and whenever I returned to my desk, regardless of how long I had been away. Each time I settled into my desk chair, I vowed to fight the loathing that had set in and the guilt that visited me when I deserted my own post with flights of fancy.

I'd never pretended to love my job as an executive assistant, but I'd always managed to deliver an above-average performance. After I met Alec, however, it would be a stretch to say I was earning a satisfactory rating. My boss, bless his soul, never said a word to me about my slacking off, but I still felt guilty about all the time I spent being absent in body and mind.

"So where is he taking you tonight?" Priti asked over the partition as I slipped into my cubicle.

"Don't have a clue, P."

"I'm sure you will soon," she said.

My phone rang and Priti did her level best to stifle a laugh as I picked up the receiver. "Ms. Bonti here."

"I wish you were *here*, Sam," Alec drawled.

"Me too."

"Ready for some more fun later?"

Alec was always up for fun. He'd been positively childlike in his delight when he took me on a late-night helicopter ride mere hours before, and I must admit that just the memory made me feel like a kid on Christmas morning all over again. However, the boss's eyes burning into my back cut short the joy of that particular recollection. "I can't take a long lunch again today," I whispered.

"Me neither. The merger I'm working on with Malchek is heating up," he said, the excitement obvious in his voice. "But I plan to celebrate over dinner at Ariel's with some friends who've been dying to meet you."

"I'm thrilled things are going forward, Alec, but I really can't talk now."

"That's two *can't*s in less than a minute," he said, sounding miffed. "In any case, I won't be able to pick you up until seven, so you can give that boss of yours a couple of extra hours."

In our relationship so far, Alec had been the one in charge, but this was the first time I'd experienced for myself what it might be like for those who weren't willing to follow his lead, or had the audacity to contradict or cross him. His displeasure gave me a flash of discomfort, which dissipated as quickly as it came.

"An hour is all I could stand, Alec," I said as sweetly as I could. "Pick me up outside Our Lady of Victory."

"Say a prayer for me, will ya?"

Ariel's was a trendy Bay Ridge restaurant I'd been to a couple of times with Tony and the Brooklyn Boys, so at least I'd be on familiar ground for a change. It was a fine dining establishment that was both a destination for the upwardly mobile and a neighborhood hangout for local families.

Alec parked his Range Rover just past the front door. "Keep an eye on my ride, Dino," he said, tossing his keys to the valet.

"Sure thing, Mr. DeMarco. Would you like us to give it a quick wash?"

"Knock yourself out," Alec said. "I'll catch up with you later."

The Brooklyn Boys had catered to Tony because they feared his power, but Alec's hold on others was different. They deferred to him out of respect and admiration. I'd experienced the glow of his approval for myself and knew what it felt like to fall under his spell.

As we entered the restaurant, the maître d' came forward to greet us. "Your guests are waiting for you, Mr. DeMarco," he said, appreciatively eyeing me in my new linen sundress. "Right this way."

"Thanks, Carlo," Alec said as he took my hand. We made our way through the main dining room and out to a small patio in the back, where three couples were already seated at a large round table. The three men, all dressed in expensive suits with dress shirts open at the neck, as was Alec, stopped chattering and rose from their iron chairs as we approached.

"Hey, guys," Alec boomed, holding me close. "This is the gal I've been telling you about."

"Ad nauseam," the guy closest to us said, with a smile and nod toward the others, who laughed. He appeared to be a couple of years younger than Alec, with dirty-blond hair framing his handsome, tanned face. "No offense, Samantha," he said as he shook my hand, "but Alec here never stops singing your praises. It's getting so bad there's not much work going on these days."

"Sam, I'd like you to meet Victor Falco," Alec said, cutting Victor short. "He's prone to exaggeration and if he doesn't behave himself I'll get his ass fired." All the guys laughed then, their easy camaraderie making me feel right at home. "To Victor's right is his hot wife, Sofia," Alec continued. Her perfectly coiffed, shoulder-length, jet-black hair was set off by a figure-hugging white blouse. Flawless makeup, perfectly manicured nails, and obviously expensive jewelry completed the picture of a pampered trophy wife.

"Nice to meet you, Samantha," Sofia said, smiling thinly.

"Likewise, Sofia," I said.

"Going around the table," Alec said, "that's Jack and Patricia Bronson—no relation to Charles—Roger Haberstein, and Ellen Marbury."

"Pleased to meet all of you," I said.

"The pleasure is all ours," Patricia said.

"We've got some catching up to do, Sam," Alec said as he pulled out a chair for me and reached for the champagne bucket that was already on the table. He filled all our glasses, emptying the bottle, and motioned for the waiter to bring another. "And be warned," he went on, "this crowd isn't shy about eating off your plate or draining your glass if you give them the opportunity."

"Not so," Patricia said. "Pay no attention to him."

"I'm used to him by now, Patricia," I replied.

"Call me Pat."

I liked her right away. More understated and a bit older than the others, she wore her auburn hair in a Streisand bob. Her makeup was subtle, and the navy blazer with gold crest that she wore over a white boatneck T-shirt was smashing. Jack's eyes matched his wife's ice-blue ones, and I could picture him at the helm of a sailboat on Long Island Sound. The couple's self-assurance was immediately apparent, and I figured it had more to do with breeding than with age.

"You can't be used to Alec's appetite yet," Ellen said as the new bottle of champagne arrived at our table. "We go back years," she continued, smiling with her eyes fixed on him, "and I still can't keep up."

"Who could?" Roger added.

"Certainly not you." Victor chimed in to a chorus of laughter. "Try as you might."

Alec rested a hand on mine, and I doubted I'd ever tire of that gesture. "I don't keep Roger close because of his prodigious appetite, Sam. It's his prodigious ability with numbers that makes him indispensable. Jack, on the other hand, can give me a run for my money when it comes to wine. I'm trying to get him to will his cellar to me.

Jack chuckled. "Not a chance, pal."

I looked toward Ellen. "Have you and Roger been dating long?" I asked, and the men again erupted in laughter.

"Heavens, no," she said with a dismissive wave of her hand.

"They're not together, Sam." Alec smiled toward the two. "Just very good friends of mine."

Well, they certainly look like a couple. "Sorry," I said, reaching for my champagne.

"No apology necessary," Roger said.

Alec leaned in and whispered into my ear. "Ellen is a lesbian. Heaven forbid the NYSE finds out about that. We're a boys' club, Sam. But she runs a huge firm and makes so much money, no one will out her."

"That's kinda sad that she can't say who she really is."

"Yeah . . . when you're making millions, you tend to shut up." *You mean you tend to live a fake life,* I thought to myself.

Alec waved the waiter over again. "I don't know about anyone else here, but I'm starved."

"What a surprise! I'm shocked that it took you this long to order," Victor said teasingly.

"Must be because he's on his best behavior this evening," Roger said.

"Ol' Roger here is a closet comedian, Sam," Alec said. "We're all getting bored with his old jokes, so he's always looking for a new audience."

"Stick a fork in it, Alec," Roger shot back, "like you stick a fork into everything else."

Everyone laughed then.

"See?" Roger said, puffing out his chest. "I haven't lost my touch after all."

"You're touched, period." Alec guffawed.

The waiter stood beside Alec and rested an arm across his shoulders. "What's your pleasure tonight, Mr. DeMarco?"

Alec squeezed my thigh gently under the table and addressed the gathering. "Shall I order for everyone?" *Will anyone say no?*

"Would you have it any other way?" Victor asked, waving an arm for him to proceed.

"Let's start off with the mussels in white wine sauce, Paolo, some garlic bread, and my usual Sauvignon Blanc."

"Will you be having the black truffle risotto?" Paolo asked.

"Do I ever come here and not order that?" Alec asked, as if he'd been insulted.

What's a ninety-dollar dish between friends?

"Just wanted to be sure, so we can get it started."

"No one's in a rush here," Alec said. "I'll let you know about the second course in a bit."

"Very good, sir," Paolo said, then silently retreated.

The evening proceeded much as it began, with Alec doing all of the ordering as well as most of the eating. It became clear as they bantered back and forth that, despite their constant teasing, they all respected Alec for his fierce competitiveness as well as his willingness to take calculated risks that, more often than not, paid off.

When they momentarily took a break to concentrate on their food, the women had a chance to get a word in edgewise. During one of these moments, as yet another course arrived at the table, Patricia spoke up. "Enough, you guys," she said. "We've heard it all before. What about you, Samantha? You don't strike me as a Wall Street type."

"She's a writer." Alec beamed. "Just working there until she gets her big break."

"Hush, Alec," Pat said. "Let Sam speak for herself."

"It's just something I've done for as long as I can remember," I said softly.

"Good for you!" Pat said with a wink. "You won't be getting your hands soiled with all that filthy lucre."

Alec leaned toward Pat and smiled. "I don't see you giving any of yours back," he taunted.

"Of course not," Pat said, not the least bit intimidated, as she looked toward her husband. "Our families have earned every dime, and we aren't slouches, either. It's just that stocks and mergers and acquisitions aren't for everyone."

They're not my cup of tea, that's for sure. "Being happy no matter what you do is what counts," I said.

"I'm happy digging into these mussels," Alec said, and everyone dove in with him.

I was starting to understand what made this Wall Street crowd tick. The boisterous way these guys carried on reminded me of the Brooklyn Boys, but what Alec and his contemporaries shared seemed to have much more substance behind it than the macho posturing of the wannabes in Bensonhurst. The Boys thought muscle cars and muscling "marks" were where it was at, and that Ariel's was the pinnacle of the dating scene. Alec and his friends, on the other hand, knew what a "score" was all about in the real world of Manhattan and how to entertain a lady. I was happy that he had such loyal friends, and happy to be among them. I must have met with their approval because, just a few days later, he informed me that we'd be having dinner with his sister, Gianna, and her fiancé. Was this some kind of test, or was he just eager to show me off? Although I was fairly certain it was the latter, I couldn't help being a bit nervous.

As usual, the limo was waiting outside my office, and before I could remind myself not to become too attached to the luxuries that had become more or less routine over the last several weeks, Alec jumped out sporting one of his biggest smiles.

The driver took off, heading for the FDR Drive, and, with Alanis Morissette singing in the background:

You treat me like I'm a princess
I'm not used to liking that

We had a couple of glasses of champagne and finished off a few crackers slathered with goat cheese.

"You're gonna love Mr. Chow," Alec assured me.

"I'd love any place you took me, Alec," I bubbled.

He leaned over and gave me a peck on my cheek. "You're gonna love my sister, too, Sam."

"I'm sure I will," I said, even though I was secretly intimidated by the very thought of meeting any member of Alec's family—his sister in particular . . . the sister he had described as being so perfect, who had the college education I'd dreamed of having and a childhood straight out of the secondhand Disney books I'd read to myself as a child. "I hope she likes me," I added, bringing the glass of champagne to my lips. "From what you've told me, she's got it all."

"Including a fiancé."

"You get along with him?"

"Gary's from Brooklyn, although he isn't Italian. He still lives in the Heights. Seems like a nice, sincere guy. I helped get him his job, so we'll find out soon enough what he's made of."

He fell silent then, and I was content to watch the yachts, some with helicopters on the aft deck, that were moored in the East River.

I'd found out a lot about Alec, and myself, over the previous month. I did love every minute of every experience we'd shared, loved the way he courted me and the fact that he was driven to make a name for himself.

As the limo deposited us, hand in hand, on the sidewalk in front of Mr. Chow, I smiled up at Alec, realizing that I would have been just as happy if he were a schoolteacher who took me to a deli for Hebrew National hot dogs and kosher pickles—I just wanted to spend as much time with him as possible, no matter where we went or what we did.

The Asian décor of the restaurant and fresh-cut flowers on every table were inviting, but the dining room was more spare and open than other restaurants we'd been to. The stunning Chinese hostess, with long, straight, jet-black hair, pearly skin, and a champagne-colored satin gown that was open to the waist in back, led us to a table in the middle of the room.

"Xudong will be with you shortly," she said as we took our seats. The simple, darkwood-stained, low-backed chairs seemed almost too delicate for Alec's massive frame, and I wondered if his would give out before we'd finished the first course.

"Thank you, Lijuan," Alec said. "To save him a trip, please tell him to have a bottle of Perrier-Jouët Rosé in hand."

"Yes, Mr. DeMarco," Lijuan replied. "Enjoy your dinner."

"No need to stand on ceremony," Alec said as Lijuan moved away; he kept one eye on her swaying hair. *Can't say as I blame him.* "We'll order something to tide us over until Gianna and Gary show up."

The staff here, as everywhere we'd been, knew Alec well. Crispy seaweed-wrapped squab and pork satay were delivered with a flourish soon after the champagne was poured. Halfway through this "nosh," as Alec referred to it, he smiled ear to ear when he spied a young couple following Lijuan to our table.

Gianna was tall and quite zaftig, with shoulder-length dark hair, large brown eyes like her brother's, and a loose-fitting flowery sundress. Gary was barely as tall as she, but good-looking despite a receding hairline.

Alec wiped his mouth with his napkin and stood to greet them. "Sis, Gary, this is Samantha." He beamed.

Gary offered his hand as Gianna bent over to give me a peck on the cheek. "It's about time we met the girl who's stolen my brother's heart," she said as they took their seats.

I breathed a sigh of relief that my jitters about this meeting had apparently been unwarranted.

Alec filled their flutes and topped ours off. "Lose the tie, honey," she said to her fiancé. Gary obediently unknotted it and tucked it away in a jacket pocket, as Gianna reached over and opened two buttons of his shirt.

Alec raised his glass. "A toast," he said, and the rest of us raised ours. "To the happy couple." *I assume he means Gianna and Gary.* We took a sip and started to put our flutes down. "Hold on a second," Alec continued as he tipped his glass my way. "We also have to toast the newest member of our family."

I swallowed. *What is that supposed to mean?*

"You making an announcement, Alec?" Gianna squealed.

"No"—he grinned—"but I'm working on it." He clinked my glass, Gary and Gianna tilted theirs toward me, and we all sipped again.

"How's work going?" Alec asked Gary.

"Not as well as yours," he replied.

Gianna beamed at her brother and leaned toward me. "Not many can keep up with Alec," she said. "He's quite a catch, Samantha."

I rested a hand on Alec's arm and looked into his eyes. "I'm blessed."

"I'll drink to that," Gianna said, sampling the champagne again.

Alec pointed with his chin to the appetizers. "Why don't you guys finish those? Meanwhile, I'll order some Peking duck and a sea bass."

"Get me a lychee martini, too," Gianna said. "You want to order a drink, honey?" she asked, turning toward Gary.

"That's okay. I'm good with the champagne," he said.

"When are you two tying the knot?" I asked, looking at Gary.

"Late next year," Gianna responded, as she toyed with the four-carat round stone on her finger. *Does Gary from the neighborhood have that kind of money?* "Haven't made my mind up where yet."

"You have any ideas, Gary?" I asked as Xudong arrived at Alec's side.

"Whatever Gianna wants is fine by me." He smiled.

As Alec orchestrated another epicurean spread, everyone engaged in some light conversation about work, our backgrounds, and the DeMarco family, and I managed to go on a bit longer than usual about my writing when it appeared they were genuinely interested. Gary did more smiling than talking, but I was happy to learn that he and his German family were originally from Bensonhurst.

When the main course was just about finished, Gianna pushed her chair back and announced she had to go to the ladies' room. "You want to join me, Samantha?"

"No need," I replied, hoping to take the opportunity to chat with Gary about our old stomping grounds. Alec, who was happy enough to be alone with his food and drink, didn't seem to mind the couple of minutes Gary and I spent exchanging stories about old times. We reminisced about Coney Island, the neighborhood pizzerias and restaurants, Sugar's shoe store, and Cue Ball, the billiard parlor and bar that my friend Janice's father had owned, a favorite hangout of the Brooklyn Boys and the mobsters they sucked up to. Gary had even been to the Feast of Santa Rosalia, and we wondered if we had actually met before without knowing it. I looked forward to getting to know him better.

"Let's see what they have for dessert," Alec said after Gianna returned to the table. He waved Xudong over, and soon enough the Chinese version of the wedding dessert buffet was set before us. I was blown away by the green tea ice cream and vowed to try skipping the main course next time so I could do the fancy desserts more justice. Alec and Gianna were happy to dig in with gusto, and I was happy that Gary was more of a hunter and pecker, as I was.

"Wait until you meet the rest of the family," Gianna said to me between mouthfuls.

"I'm looking forward to it." *I think.*

"I'm sure Alec told you about our older brother."

"A plastic surgeon of some renown in the city," I said.

"Franco was a real catch, too." Gianna beamed again. "Monica sure hit the big time with him." She turned to Alec. "Why don't you bring Samantha to the beach house to meet everyone?"

Alec faced me. "You have plans for Labor Day weekend?"

As if. I shook my head.

"Then that's the perfect time to do it." He turned toward his sister. "Don't blab to Mom and Dad."

"I wouldn't think of it, Alec."

"Then how did they know about Samantha before I told them?" Alec growled.

Gianna blushed and Gary grinned from ear to ear. "I was just so ecstatic when you told me. I knew they'd be, too."

I smiled, flattered that I was a topic of conversation within their family. "I'm sure she meant well, Alec," I said.

Gianna grabbed my hand and smiled softly at Alec, a playful glint in her eyes. "It'd be nice if I had a sister, instead of just a big oaf of a brother."

"You're lucky I'm in a good mood, Gianna, or I'd wring your neck," Alec said, his signature grin back in place.

Gianna nudged Gary with an elbow. "Let me pick up the check, Alec," he said.

"It's taken care of," Alec replied, rising from his chair, which had managed to survive his weight. "Maybe next time."

I stood and put an arm halfway around Alec's waist. "It was nice meeting you two," I said.

"Likewise, Samantha," Gary said.

"See you at the beach house," Gianna said, smiling softly.

Alec took my hand and headed for the exit. "Sisters," he muttered. "Can't live with them; can't live without them."

Alec called me at work the next morning to invite me to his apartment for dinner that evening. I was excited because this was the first time I'd get to see the place where he lived. But I was a bit nervous, too. Would this be the moment he finally put the major move on me?

"You've been a dynamo around here today," Priti said from her side of the partition late in the afternoon. "You turned down lunch on our bench and you've waved me away every time I tried to talk."

"Sorry, P," I said as I reached for the phone. "I just wanted to clear my desk so I could get out of here on time." *And without any guilt for a change.*

"I would have covered for you."

"You've done that plenty already. Can't let the boss think he could do without me completely," I said as I dialed Alec's number. "At least not yet."

"Haberstein here," said the voice on the other end.

"Hi, Roger. It's Samantha. Is Alec available?"

"'Fraid not. He bolted out of here a couple of minutes ago. I'm covering for him."

"Thanks, Roger. I'll catch him at home then."

I dialed Alec's home number and he picked it up on the fourth ring. "Hello," he huffed.

"Hi, Alec, it's me."

"Got my hands full," he said, his voice slightly muffled as he cradled the phone on his shoulder, the faucet running in the background. "Wish it were with you."

"I won't keep you. I just wanted to let you know that I can pick up dessert."

"Already made plans for that," Alec said, chuckling. *Uh-oh.* "See you at six."

I caught a cab outside Our Lady of Victory after I'd lit a candle and said a quick prayer. I said another one as the cab pulled up to the curb in front of the imposing Tribeca high-rise where Alec lived.

The young, European-looking concierge picked up his phone as soon as I breezed into the marble lobby.

"Ms. Bonti is here, Mr. DeMarco," he said with a French accent. It no longer surprised me when someone I'd never met knew me. "Yes, sir," he said and hung up the phone. "Take the elevator to the right, Ms. Bonti. Penthouse D."

"Thank you," I said, and I crossed the expansive lobby to the elevator bank, feeling his eyes on me every step of the way.

Alec's door was open, but I pressed the bell anyway.

"Come right in, Sam," he called from somewhere inside.

I was greeted by "A Girl Like Me," a Smithereens hit, on the sound system, as well as the Manhattan skyline, which filled the wall of glass on the other side of the sunken living room, and by a warm smile as Alec emerged from the kitchen and swept me up off my feet.

"Couldn't wait for you to get here," he said before locking his lips on mine.

"It will be all downhill after that." I smiled as we unclenched.

"You may change your mind once you know what I have in store for you," he said. *Dessert?* "Curl up on the couch," he said, waving toward a cream-colored leather sofa. "I'll be right back." And, true to his word, he returned minutes later with a platter of hors d'oeuvres and two champagne flutes.

"I like what you've done here," I said, surveying what seemed to be the ultimate, over-the-top bachelor's pad. The dominant accessories were a pair of whimsical but explicitly rendered naked female figurines that looked as if you could take them apart like a puzzle.

"Thanks. But it was all the decorator. I honestly had nothing to do with it," he said as he set the tray and glasses on the beveled glass cocktail table and sank onto the couch next to me.

"Not my taste, really, except for the wooden wine rack and the sexy figurines."

"They go nicely with the wide plank floors."

"I prefer marble. The place I'm checking out now will be all my doing."

I took in the skyline again. "Why would you leave *this* place? Is the rent too high?" I wanted to take back my naïve question, as soon as it left my lips.

"It's only thirty-seven hundred," Alec said as he reached for the champagne bottle nestled in a bucket on the table. *Only? That's more than a month's salary for me.* "This building was voted the number-one rental in the city, but it's pedestrian to me, Sam. One bedroom, too far from the river, small gym, and no swimming pool," he said, filling the flutes. "Too many mirrors, too," he added.

A girl can't have too many of those.

"You work out regularly, do you?" I cracked.

"Plan to," he said. "Gotta get in shape for the sprint that's coming."

"The merger?"

"That's just the start, Sam." He handed me a flute, raised his, and made yet another toast to our future.

I was warmed by the wine and his words, and by the lyrics playing in the background:

London, Washington, anywhere you are I'll run
Together we'll be

I took a healthy swig and eyed the bruschetta and stuffed mushrooms on the table. "Dig in," he said, enveloping a slice of toasted Italian bread topped with diced tomatoes in his over-sized paw.

"I will," I said, reaching for a piece.

Alec and I finished the appetizers, the lion's share consumed by my Wall Street lion, and moved to adjoining seats at a round glass table in the small dining area two steps up. The umber upholstered armchairs were as plush as the soft leather couch. Alec reached for an open bottle of red wine and filled two large goblets halfway.

"Hmmm," he said after the next toast. "Can't beat Chianti, if it's the right one."

"I wouldn't know," I said with a smile.

"But you will, and sooner than you think. I want you to know everything, Sam."

I tipped my goblet toward him. "Bring it on."

"I will," he said, sliding back from the table. "Starting with the next course."

The homemade manicotti, accompanied by fennel sausage, were as good as any I'd ever had, and the sauce was as out of this world as the apartment. "Superb, Alec," I said after I finished my last bite. "Really, you are some cook; you should own a restaurant one day."

If he's fattening me for the kill, this isn't a bad way to go.

"Family recipe," he said, beaming with pride. "I'll always keep my traditions, Sam, but I'm ready to change a lot of other things," he added, refilling his glass. He was moving the bottle toward mine, but I covered it with a hand and shook my head gently.

I looked around the apartment again, ran a finger around the edge of my goblet, and looked him in the eyes. "You hardly have to do that on my account, Alec."

"Well, let me be clear, anyway, so there's no doubt about where things stand—at least on my end." Alec emptied his goblet. "I've had four women hanging on to me for the past month, and I've been shedding one a week since we started dating. Being with meaningless women is not what I'm into anymore."

I looked down as I processed his words. It stung knowing that he was keeping up appearances with all of these other women even though he was pursuing me so persistently. I knew it was silly to expect otherwise; we weren't even sleeping together. And Alec had remained a perfect gentleman with me the whole time. He just had a way of making me feel like I was the only woman in the room. *What if he's just a really good actor?* I fretted. I dismissed the thought as quickly as it came. The fact that he did the honorable thing and waited to clear himself of all entanglements before putting the moves on me made me feel a surge of love for this man. I reached for his hand and looked him in the eyes again. "You're not the only one here who's growing up."

Alec squeezed my hand and kept his eyes on mine. "Team is everything to me, Sam."

He raised my hand a few inches, and I marveled at how light his touch could be. "A man and a woman make the team that matters most to me." He lowered his face to my hand, and the gentle touch of his lips on my outstretched fingers was heavy enough to rock my entire world.

FIVE

Alec didn't put the major moves on me that night. He didn't so much as hint at sex or even show me his bedroom, but he did leave me with another soulful, prolonged, and probing kiss at the elevator outside his apartment. That one lasted for days after the limo took me home, as did my ponderings about when—or if—I'd ever be sleeping with him.

Since he left on an extended business trip to Miami the day after our dinner, I had more time than I wanted in which to consider where we stood. I was both flattered and miffed that he hadn't swept me up into his arms, carried me to his bed, and taken me as he no doubt had dozens of other women. I was really trying to understand what made this guy tick. You could count on one hand, with a couple of fingers left over, the number of men I had gone all the way with, and maybe I gave off signals indicating that I was untouchable. I wanted to believe that Alec was simply being chivalrous and wanted to keep me on a pedestal but maybe I was just kidding myself.

Meanwhile, I took advantage of his absence to throw myself into my work and make up for lost time. I missed hearing his voice during the day when he was busy in meetings, but my boss was no doubt pleased to have a full-time assistant for a change.

I also took the opportunity to attend a noontime Mass at Our Lady of Victory, and even managed a trip to Our Lady of Guadalupe in Bensonhurst, where I ran into Father Rinaldi, my old priest, whom I hadn't seen in years. He greeted me warmly and seemed genuinely pleased to see me, even remembering to ask how my writing was going. When I confessed that I hadn't really made much progress in that area, he reminded me that God has a plan, on His own schedule, for every one of His children. And when I told him about Alec, he remarked that true love is pure. *Does he somehow know that we haven't consummated the relationship yet?* As we said our good-byes, he told me that he had always kept me in his prayers and would continue to do so. I was in a hurry to get home in case Alec called, but I stopped long enough to put some money in the collection box. Even though my attendance hadn't always been as regular as it should have been, the church had always been my rock when everything else in my life seemed so unstable. Throughout my childhood, throughout all the abuse I received from both Tony and my mother, it was my place of refuge mentally and emotionally, and my faith remained constant, whether or not I attended a Mass.

I hurried home, not wanting to miss a call from Alec from Miami, but he didn't call that evening. I worried that something was wrong, and prayed myself to sleep, Mom's rosary beads clutched in hand, in hope that he'd phone the next day.

And he did—as upbeat and excited as ever about his work and our future. He told me he was cutting his trip short by a day, not only because he had wrapped things up sooner than expected, but also because he missed me terribly. I momentarily considered that he was not being entirely truthful about the latter, but when he quickly added that he had turned down a deep-sea fishing expedition with his buddies to get back home and pleaded with me to be in the limo when he was picked up late the next day, I knew he was sincere. And I realized how much

I'd missed him, too, how much I'd come to rely on his massive presence to fill up my life.

I practically jumped out of the limo at LaGuardia Airport as soon as he emerged from the arrivals terminal, and threw my arms around his neck before he even had time to drop his bags. "Maybe I should go away more often," he said kiddingly. I took his hand and started to lead him into the backseat, but he pulled me back, twirling me around as he had done on the day we met, and planted a kiss on my lips. "I wanted to do that the first time I laid on eyes on you, Sam."

"If you had, maybe I would have called you sooner."

"Or maybe you would have run away screaming," he said with a chuckle.

We slid into the rear seat to the sounds of his favorite Alanis Morissette album, and Alec draped an arm across my shoulders as I presented him with his favorite martini, which had been chilling for ten minutes. "Hope this meets with your approval," I said, beaming at him.

"It does, and I don't even have to try it." Alec smiled, then took his usual gulp while drinking me in with his eyes. "Perfect," he moaned, and I wasn't sure whether he meant me or the cocktail. Both, I hoped.

"I'm glad you like it so much."

"I was referring to you," Alec said, pressing the privacy partition button. He took another swallow and pulled me close. "You won't mind if I just drop you off?" he asked after another soulful kiss. "I'm pretty burned out."

I stretched my arm across his broad chest and pressed my cheek into his shoulder. "Not at all," I whispered. "I'm just glad to have my conquering hero back."

"I've got more worlds to conquer, Sam," he said, lowering his head until his lips found mine.

✧ ✧ ✧

Luckily my boss left early on Friday to start the long Labor Day weekend, so he wasn't there to see that I too was deserting my post at two o'clock. I fussed with my hair in the ladies' room just as I had fussed with packing that morning, and with my thoughts all day. I knew that my wardrobe would be sorely tested over the holiday, and I worried about what Alec's family would think of me. But those weren't my only concerns. Our heavy petting was driving me crazy, too, and I knew it wouldn't be long before we finally slept together—provided, that is, no alarms about Alec or his assembled family went off in my brain.

Alec was waiting in the Range Rover, which now had two shiny new bicycles, one yellow, the other strawberry red, strapped to a rack on the back. As soon as he saw me, he reached across to open my door. I was moving as fast as I could with a large pocketbook and the only suitcase I owned, a relic from my youth that had seen better days.

"Here, let me take that," Alec said, grabbing the suitcase and tossing it onto the rear seat as if it were no heavier than an accent pillow. He gave me a peck on my cheek as I buckled up and put the Rover in gear.

"You look great, Sam," he said as we pulled away from the curb.

"It's just jeans and a simple cotton shirt," I sighed, "but thanks anyway."

"They hug you like I'd like to do right now," he said with a grin. "You'd make painter's overalls look hot."

"Double thanks," I said, but fretted still. "Are you sure the way I look will be okay with your parents?"

"They aren't judgmental, Sam," Alec said, turning north onto Water Street.

"Aren't we taking the Drive?"

"If it's all right with you, I gotta make a couple of stops first."

"Sure," I said. *I can use all the time I have to get my head on right.* "So tell me," I ventured, "what's with the bicycles?"

"The strawberry one is a birthday present for Gianna," he said, "and the yellow one is yours. It's a family tradition to take a bike ride on Labor Day weekend and we couldn't have you running along behind us, now, could we?"

"Thanks, Alec; that was really thoughtful of you, and it sounds like fun," I said, remembering how to ride a bike.

Five minutes later we were in the heart of Little Italy, where Alec stocked up on a variety of Italian cold cuts and pastries. *Just in case his parents don't have enough for us to eat?*

I was nervous and looking forward to the weekend, desperate to make Alec proud and eager to be around a normal family for once in my life. I was glad I'd already met Gianna and Gary, so that I wouldn't feel like a total stranger, and I had to admit that not having to worry about food or money was starting to feel pretty good.

We headed north again and took the Queens-Midtown Tunnel to the Long Island Expressway. As we passed the rolling hills of Calvary Cemetery spread out to the right and left of the highway, I thought of Mom and Grandma buried in another cemetery not far from where we were.

Traffic opened up as we crossed from Queens into Nassau County, and Alec pressed his size-thirteen foot on the accelerator. The sixty miles or so to the end of the expressway flew by as Alec filled me in on the history of the beach house. His father, he said, had grown up the son of immigrants and worked his way through college as a waiter. Twenty years ago, right after he brokered his first major deal, he had bought the house, and Alec, true to form, swore he'd more than match both the deal and the real estate purchase someday soon. I have to admit that just knowing his background made me feel a kinship with Giovanni even before I'd met him.

We headed toward the North Fork of the island, and traffic slowed to thirty miles an hour as the highway went from three lanes to two. A few miles farther along it narrowed again to one lane and we slowed to a crawl, causing fast-moving Alec to grit his teeth and curse quietly under his breath. "Fucking tourists," he spat out as he lowered the side windows and opened the sunroof.

"Maybe they own houses, too, you know," I offered, hoping that thought, along with the fresh, salty air, would cool him off.

"Whatever," he muttered. "A helicopter will solve the problem."

What problem?

"It's so magical out here," I said. "Why don't you just enjoy watching all the vineyards and farms rolling by?"

Alec yanked the wheel to the right and pulled up to a farm stand. "Thanks for reminding me," he said, jumping out of the car with the motor still running. "Almost forgot the strawberries."

I was happy to see a grin return to his face as he reappeared a moment later with a flat of fresh-picked berries he deposited in the rear seat.

"They'll probably be gone by Sunday, considering the vultures waiting for us," he cracked as he nudged the Rover back into the line of traffic.

A couple of miles later we turned onto a narrow dirt road leading to Great Peconic Bay. We passed a few driveways, and although most of the houses were hidden behind tall trees and bushes, I caught a few glimpses of wood-shingled roofs and gray siding along the way.

Finally, Alec steered through a gentle curve and my breath caught in my throat as I saw the postcard-gorgeous white clapboard house, with a pair of double columns framing the entrance and the bay stretching for miles behind it. Alec drove between the low stone columns abutting the entrance to a white seashell driveway, rolled past two Mercedes-Benzes and a BMW parked in front of a detached garage, and pulled up to the wide portico. He turned off the ignition, tapped the horn a couple of times in quick succession, and grabbed my hand.

"We're home, honey," he said, smiling broadly.

From your mouth to God's ears.

A couple in their sixties, who I assumed were Alec's mom and dad, came through the door as if on cue. Dressed in a light blue golf shirt and pleated white shorts, Giovanni was over six feet tall with a wiry build and a full head of silvery hair. I could see immediately that Alec got not only his height but also his broad smile from his father. Filomena was large-boned but slim and trim, with light blond hair that fell just below her chin. Dressed in a cotton blouse and slacks in soft earth tones, she was the picture of relaxed elegance.

As Filomena smiled softly, her arms crossed over her chest, Giovanni ran down the two steps to give Alec a big bear hug and a kiss on the cheek. "So this is Samantha," he said, turning to me, and grabbing my hand with both of his. "Pleasure to finally meet you."

Giovanni led me by the hand to the porch. "Thanks so much for having me, Mr. and Mrs. DeMarco," I said.

"We're delighted you're here, Samantha," Filomena said. "There's plenty of room." *Room . . . I never asked Alec about the sleeping arrangements.* "And if you don't call us Gianni and Fil, we'll be getting off very much on the wrong foot."

"Yes, ma'am," I said softly.

"Gianna!" Alec bellowed, reaching for the strawberry-red bicycle on the roof of the Rover.

She bounded through the front door and said a fast hello as she brushed by me. "For me?" she exclaimed excitedly, seeing the bike. "Thanks, big brother, I totally love it!"

Alec unpacked the Rover as his parents escorted me into the house, which was as breathtaking on the inside as it was outside. The wide-planked wood floor and contemporary furniture were set off by a plush hand-woven area rug with a geometrical design in browns and beiges, and the walls were hung with colorful contemporary paintings. The ceiling was honeycombed with white wood beams and elaborate moldings. A sunroom filled with white wicker furniture was off to the right, and the bay was visible through French doors at the rear of the living room.

"The others are waiting out on the deck," Filomena said, leading the way.

Monica was nursing her drink on a lounge chair as Franco marshaled their two young daughters on the lush green lawn below the deck. He was half Alec's size, but just as handsome, and she was much plainer than I'd expected the wife of a plastic surgeon to be.

Gary stood up as we came through the doors. "Nice to see you again, Samantha." He smiled.

"That's right, you two have already met," Filomena said, introducing me to Monica as Franco arrived on the deck with children in tow. "And this is Franco and their six-year-old twins."

"Well, well," Franco said, eyeing me up and down. "So this is the girl who's got the Wall Street lion's mind off business."

I shook his hand politely and bent over to the young girls. "And what are your names?"

"I'm Melanie," said the one who was clearly the spokesperson, as she pulled her sister close. "And this is Elizabeth."

"How precious they are," I said, giving Monica a hug.

"More than a handful." She exhaled. "Feel free to take them anytime."

Franco laughed. "We're working on a boy," he said. *All Italian men have to have at least one.* "The more the merrier."

"Easy for you to say," Monica shot back. "You're never home."

Giovanni came up behind me and rested a hand on my shoulder. "Can I get you some champagne, Samantha?"

"Yes, do that," Filomena said. "And some pâté, too."

"Thank you, Mr. De . . . Gianni," I said.

"That's the spirit, Samantha," Filomena said, smiling encouragingly. "Excuse me while I tend to dinner." Champagne, caviar, and pâté . . . I certainly wasn't in Bensonhurst anymore.

I sat next to Gary on the love seat facing the bay, and everyone did their best to include me in the conversation and make me feel at home. Still, I was counting the seconds until Alec showed up, and consequently I finished my first glass of wine much faster than usual.

"Here, let me refill that for you," Gary said, reaching for my flute.

"Alec tells me you're fond of Our Lady of Victory," Giovanni ventured.

"Yes. It's my oasis in the city," I replied.

"Did you know I lead the prayer group there every Monday evening?" he asked.

"No, I had no idea. Alec didn't tell me," I said, "and I'm never there after seven."

"Well, I'd love it if you joined us sometime." Giovanni smiled warmly as Alec and Gianna emerged from the house side-by-side.

"I will," I assured him.

"Will what?" Alec boomed.

"That's for me to know and you to find out," I said with a chuckle.

"A feisty one, isn't she," Franco said, smiling. "Looks like pillow talk tonight will include some interrogation, little brother."

"She'll give it up long before that," Alec said, grabbing the bottle of champagne as Filomena returned. "What are we having for dinner, Mom?" he asked her.

"Swordfish kabobs, Italian tomato salad, and corn on the cob," Filomena said, taking a seat.

"I'll fire up the grill," Giovanni offered, and got up.

Alec plopped next to me. "Comfy?"

"Totally," I said. *Other than wondering about the sleeping arrangements.*

"Make sure she stays that way," Filomena said. "Such a nice girl. You better hang on to her."

"Not like your usual floozies, Alec," Franco cracked.

"Behave yourself, big bro, or I'll plant you in the yard next to the raspberry bush."

"Boys, boys," Filomena chided. "I won't have you scaring Samantha off before the weekend even gets started."

"Aw, we're just playing, Mom . . . please relax," Alec said.

"Speaking of playing," Gary piped up, "who are the Yanks playing tonight?"

"C'mon, Gary," Gianna scoffed. "It's Boston."

"Oh, right. How could I forget?"

"I won't have you ignoring Samantha all night," Filomena said to Alec, "holed up in the den glued to the TV."

"I don't mind," I said quietly.

"Well, I do," Filomena said. "We've got enough sports widows around here."

"What's that about widows?" Giovanni asked his wife as he rejoined the group.

"The ones those damn Yankees create."

"Now, now, Fil," Giovanni said, planting a kiss on his wife's head. "Don't talk like that about the team that was home to Joe DiMaggio."

"Yeah, Mom," Alec chimed in. "Or you'll have Joltin' Joe turning over in his grave."

"The way you all carry on about that team will put me in an

early one," Filomena cracked. "And I swear, one of you will probably bring a portable TV to my funeral."

Franco tousled the twins' hair. "Careful, Mom. If you carry on like that you'll scare off the next generation of Yankee fans."

"I'd burn those season tickets if I could." She sighed.

Filomena squeezed her husband's hand. "Be a good host, dear, and refill their glasses."

Giovanni winked at me. "Yes, dear."

The easy banter and obvious affection all these people had for one another brought home to me again how much I yearned to be part of a warm and loving family.

After the next round of drinks, we all moved to the large round table at the end of the deck. The warm salt air fueled everyone's appetite, and the dinner Filomena had prepared was as delicious as any of the fancy meals Alec and I had enjoyed in the city. The wine flowed freely, and the conversation remained spirited as I got to know everyone, including Alec, much better. I loved seeing how he interacted with his family and how genuine their connection really was. I was seated next to Monica, who complained about raging hormones, even though she was only in her mid-thirties, and about the medical conferences that took Franco away from the family several times a year. She warned me about her husband, whispering that he was something of a flirt and that women seemed to melt in the presence of doctors, especially plastic surgeons.

I began to wonder if all of the calls he *had* to make during dinner were related to medical issues, but found myself liking him because he seemed to be totally lacking in the macho controlling gene that most Italian men had.

Giovanni didn't have the gene, either, and I was being more and more drawn to him as the kind father I'd never had.

I was actually relaxing and enjoying myself when Monica

leaned toward me as Filomena and Gianna cleared the dinner plates, and asked, "What's your favorite dessert?"

"I just love strawberries and fresh whipped cream," I said, thinking of the flat Alec had bought on our way out.

"I'll be sure to have them when you come for dinner, then," she said.

Filomena and Gianna returned with a pot of coffee, a platter of the pastries provided by Alec, a huge bowl of strawberries, and two large ramekins filled with powdered and brown sugar.

"I'll get the prosecco," Giovanni announced.

"Have you ever had them like this?" Monica asked me as Giovanni filled a wine goblet halfway with the sparkling wine.

"No, I haven't."

"Follow my lead, then," she said, spearing a ripe berry with her fork, dunking it into the sparkling wine, which caused a flurry of bubbles, and dipping it into the powdered sugar. "I can never make up my mind which sugar I prefer," she said before taking a small bite of the strawberry.

I copied her routine and was blown away by how such a simple dessert could be so rich.

"Amazing, isn't it?" Alec asked as he speared his catch.

"I was searching for the right word," I said after swallowing a berry that had burst in my mouth. "That one will do."

As Alec had predicted, the berries were gone within minutes. He clearly wasn't the only DeMarco who relished fine food, and I too was undecided about which sugar I favored on my strawberries.

"It must be the sixth inning by now," Alec said, pushing away from the table.

"Go, go, all of you." Filomena sighed. "You can take your coffee and pastries with you. You'd just be underfoot in the kitchen, anyway."

The men left en masse and the women stayed to chat over

coffee and pastries. Afterward, Monica took the twins upstairs and I followed Filomena and Gianna into the kitchen.

They made me feel right at home in that woman's sanctuary, and I could tell that their excitement about my being with Alec was genuine as we scraped plates and stacked them in the dishwasher.

"I've been telling Alec for years to forget those model types," Filomena said.

"And the stiff business broads, too," Gianna added.

"Exactly," Filomena said. "I've asked him time and time again why he can't just find himself a regular Brooklyn girl." She and Gianna both laughed. "Like you, Samantha."

I may be from Brooklyn, but there's nothing "regular" about me.

We made quick work of the cleanup and joined the men, who were sitting on the edge of their seats, glued to the TV. Monica had already rejoined Franco on the love seat.

"What's the score?" Gianna asked.

"Up a run with two outs to go," Alec said. "C'mere, Sam," he said, extending an arm without taking his eyes off the screen.

I rested my butt on the stuffed arm of his chair and he leaned in and gave me a peck on the cheek, also without taking his eyes off the screen.

Filomena slid gracefully onto the couch next to her husband, and Gianna squeezed in next to Gary on the other armchair.

"That's teamwork, huh, Gar?" Alec said when the game ended.

"They define the word," he replied.

"No postgame show tonight," Filomena said, and the men groaned. "I'm checking the weather and shutting it off."

The forecast for Saturday was picture-perfect, which made everyone happy. Giovanni served cordials from the bar, and I broke my normal routine by not only draining a glass of

Amaretto but also accepting a refill. Filomena announced the next day's plans, which would start with breakfast in the sunroom at nine, followed by a bike ride along the beach.

"I don't know about you young folk," Giovanni said, rising and taking his wife's hand, "but it's bedtime for us."

"Good night, all," Filomena said with a wave, as they headed out of the den to the master suite on the other side of the house.

"Good night, and thanks again," I called after them.

Monica stood and pulled Franco up from the love seat. "Bedtime for us, too," she said. "The girls will be up before anyone."

"Nice meeting you two," I said as they followed in the hosts' footsteps.

"Same here," she said over her shoulder.

"Just give a shout, Samantha, if you need someone to rescue you," Franco cracked in the distance.

Gianna gave Gary a wet kiss on the lips. "Now's as good a time as any, right, honey?"

"Whatever you say," Gary said agreeably. He and Gianna inched out of their chair and continued the procession.

Alec labored to extricate himself from the thick, soft cushions. "We're right behind you," he said, and took my hand as we followed Gary and Gianna up the stairs. They stopped at a door on the right and giggled as they opened it. "Good night, you two," she said as they slipped inside. "Don't make me have to drag you out of bed tomorrow, big brother," she added, closing the door.

Three doors left. Why didn't I think to ask about the sleeping arrangements this morning? Why didn't Alec think to let me know in advance?

I was both annoyed and embarrassed, but at the same time I was drawn in by the power of his control. Perhaps it should have occurred to me that choosing his parents' home as the place to consummate our relationship was less than thoughtful of him, but it didn't.

Alec still had my hand as we passed two doors and reached the one at the end of the hall. "Here we are," he announced, letting go of my hand and reaching for the doorknob.

He had taken three steps by the time the door closed behind me. In an instant my eyes took in the large, dimly lit corner room with dramatic photos of Yankee celebrations hanging from every wall, memorabilia covering the top of a massive maple dresser, and two seats that must have been from the original Yankee Stadium, bolted into the wood floor in a small alcove lined with trophy-filled shelves. A king-sized bed dominated the room . . . and my thoughts.

Alec turned around as he unbuttoned his shirt, releasing a spray of dark, curly hair on his massive chest. "You just gonna stand there all night?"

His huge grin did little to calm my nerves. "I . . . I . . . I'm not sure I'm ready for this," I stuttered.

I'd been waiting for this moment, and now that it had arrived, I was suddenly unsure. Alec, however, moved toward me and backed me up against the door, placing a palm flat on either side of my head as he leaned toward me.

"I am," he said with a low breath, his lips moving gently to my mouth and his groin pressing on my thigh. He was plenty ready, and my stomach fluttered as his lips sucked gently from one side of my mouth to the other. "No time like the present," he whispered, and his soft kisses became more insistent.

"Your parents are okay with this?" I asked when he came up for air.

"Franco did the heavy lifting for me and Gianna." He chuckled. "Took several dates to his bedroom before I got around to it."

I grabbed his waist with my hands and extended my arms a fraction of an inch. "Let me freshen up a bit," I said.

"Bathroom's right next door," Alec said, sliding his palms

over my breasts. "Don't keep me waiting too long," he whispered, straightening up, "or I'll be passed out when you get back."

Not a chance. I've seen you drink a lot more than you did tonight without showing even a hint of being drunk. "Just let me get some things," I said, moving to my sad-looking suitcase, which someone had deposited on the chocolate-brown leather bench at the foot of the bed.

I squeezed my pocketbook for a long moment, and grabbed my vinyl toiletry case and sheer black sleeping jacket with matching panties as Alec removed his shirt and unbuckled his slacks. I knew his eyes had never left my back as I slipped out of the room.

I fussed as long as I could in the bathroom and said my prayers, including one that I wouldn't meet anyone in the hall on the way back to Alec's bedroom, and then took a deep breath.

I couldn't look at the bed when I entered. Candlelight flickered and danced on the walls and ceiling as I closed the door after me. I paused, closed my eyes, and made the sign of the cross in my mind before I turned around.

Alec was sprawled under the sheets and propped up on six pillows. His pleasure was evident as his eyes took in every one of my curves. One arm was stretched across the pillows and his other hand was gently tapping the bed at his side. "Come here, Sam," he whispered.

I lowered my head and took measured steps to the side of the bed. When I looked up his eyes drew me the rest of the way. I reached for the top sheet, but Alec brushed it away and turned toward me, his hands—*those massive hands!*—roaming from thigh to breast as he sucked my lips and probed my mouth. His fingers prodded and poked in places that hadn't been touched in a very long time, in ways I'd never experienced. My breasts heaved and my nipples rose in response to his fingertips.

Alec rolled back onto the pillows and pulled me on top of him in one motion. He spread my jacket and cupped my breasts, framing each nipple with thumb and index finger, and pausing for what seemed an eternity before pulling me closer. But Alec wasn't in a hurry as he traced my nipples for several moments and then suckled them with the abandon of a child. Shock waves of pleasure traveled from my nipples to my toes and back, again and again . . . and again.

He wants me . . . and he can have me.

SIX

I slept well and woke up before Alec did. His snoring might have had something to do with that, but my mind was racing as soon as I opened my eyes, and that was the more likely explanation. I slipped out of bed as quietly as possible, then paused for a moment as I stood in the early morning light that streamed through a crack in the drapes.

The deed was done, and done well enough, as was clear in Alec's soft smile. I just hoped that the rest of the family would be discreet enough not to embarrass me by making some kind of joke at our expense.

I rummaged through my suitcase for my old terry-cloth robe and slippers and once more said a short prayer that I wouldn't bump into anyone in the hall. As I stood under the shower, I wondered where Alec and I would go from here. Would this weekend mark the deepening of our relationship? Or was I just another notch in his belt, another conquest for a young warrior? I figured that I'd find out soon enough.

Alec stirred as I reentered his bedroom. I tiptoed to the bench at the foot of the bed and managed to slip on jeans and a bra before he opened his eyes and rolled onto his elbows.

"No repeat performance this morning?" he said with a jumbo-sized grin.

"I'm embarrassed enough as it is," I said, slipping on a white T-shirt.

"Trust me, you don't have a thing to be embarrassed about."

"I'm referring to your parents, Alec."

"They're the ones who should be embarrassed," he said, "if they didn't have as great a time as we did."

I put my hands firmly on my waist. "Get a move on, will you? I'm not facing them alone."

"Yes, ma'am," Alec said, lumbering out of bed.

I averted my eyes as he slipped on a black terry robe that looked as if it weighed more than I did. "Back in two shakes," Alec said, closing the door behind him.

I moved to the window and swung the drapes open. Outside, the water lapped quietly at the shore behind the beach house as sloops with virgin white sails dotted the bay.

Odd as it was, I didn't feel out of place. *I'm Samantha Bonti, no matter where I might find myself.*

I could hear the sounds of others rustling throughout the house and the clanking of pots and pans in the kitchen below. Alec burst through the door, his hair matted and darker than usual from the shower. I was never so glad for how fast he could move.

"Miss me?" he asked as he headed for the closet.

"Counted the seconds."

I averted my eyes once more as he dressed, and returned my attention to the window, where I could now see families strolling on the beach.

"You smell like you, Sam," Alec breathed into my ear as he came up behind me and pulled me close. "We could skip breakfast with the folks, you know," he said playfully.

The very idea of Alec's missing a meal made me laugh. "What's next?" I chuckled, breaking free and turning around. "You gonna switch to social work?"

"Very funny," he said. "A regular comedienne."

"I have my moments."

Alec's eyes drifted toward the window and he whispered, "You can say that again."

Breakfast in the sunroom was filled with spirited conversation, and I was relieved that no one made any wisecracks about my sharing a bed with the rising star in the family. Instead, they seemed to take my presence as a matter of course, which went a long way to reinforcing my comfort level.

Afterward, the women again made fast work of the dishes, after which Filomena announced that it was time for everyone to assemble out front for the bike ride.

I harnessed my hair with a scrunchy and hopped aboard my new yellow bicycle. Alec gave my ponytail a playful tug and everyone fell in line behind Giovanni as he pedaled to the end of the driveway.

The procession negotiated the gentle curves of the lane and entered a narrow bike path along the beach. A gentle onshore breeze added an additional dimension to the view I'd had from Alec's room. It was all I could do to resist pulling over to the side, sticking my bike in the beach grass, and running into the surf with open arms, clothes and all.

As if he had read my mind, Alec slowed down until I was beside him. "I've a mind to do some skinny-dipping tonight," he said, jutting his chin toward the shore.

"We've managed to avoid parental disapproval so far," I replied without any trace of a frown. "Let's not tempt fate."

"Your words say no, but your face says otherwise," he said with a chuckle. Our procession returned to the country lane half a mile farther on and Giovanni led us toward a small marina in the distance. He wheeled into its gravel parking lot and pulled up to a shack that stood between two docks.

"Anyone up for some homemade Italian ice?" he smiled as he lowered his kickstand.

"Thanks, Grandpa!" the girls cheered in unison from the child seats affixed to their parents' bikes.

"Lemon for me, please," I said, feeling like a kid myself. I'd never known my own grandfather, who died when my mother was only fourteen. In fact, I'd never really had any positive male influences in my life. Maybe I could make up for lost time now with Giovanni.

Back at the house, it was time for the next meal, this one consumed by the pool. There were hot dogs, hamburgers, and Italian sausages served with sides of potato salad and coleslaw, and drinks to satisfy any taste. I tried a peach wine cooler before switching to iced tea and watched Alec put away a six-pack of Peroni without noticeable effect. His three helpings of food might have had something to do with that, but, given his size and his history, it probably wouldn't have mattered if he hadn't even had a bite.

We'd barely finished our lunch when Filomena announced the plan for dinner at a popular country inn nearby. "Let's reassemble at eight, shall we?"

"Perfect," Alec said, rising from his chaise. "That gives us plenty of time to watch the four o'clock game." He reached for my hand as the men started for the den. "Care to join us, Sam?"

"If you don't mind, I'll stay here and enjoy the sun a little longer."

"Not at all," he said with a gleam in his eye, his hand slipping from mine. "But you're all mine later."

I wonder if his mother caught that wink.

As usual, dinner was off the charts, as was cuddling in bed with Alec as soon as we returned to the house. Falling asleep that way, without any demand for more, was a perfect cap to a perfect day.

The next morning, as soon as breakfast was over, he announced that he'd be taking me for a ride. Leading me by the hand to the spacious garage, he punched in a code on a keypad and the door started to rise, revealing a pristine dark blue 1980 Mercedes 450SL. Its top was down, revealing a cream-colored leather interior.

"Nothing like cruising in a convertible in these parts," Alec said.

"Is this yours?" I nearly shrieked.

"Just another toy, Sam," he said with a shrug as he opened my door.

"Just another toy," I echoed. "Like that classic Corvette in the next bay, I suppose."

"The folks are very good about letting me keep them here," Alec said as he sank into his bucket seat and turned the ignition key. "Until I get a place of my own on the water, that is." He fired up the CD player and rolled down the driveway and out onto the two-lane road.

"Ever been to the Hamptons, Sam?" he asked unnecessarily. Just a few weeks ago I'd never even been to Tribeca!

After stopping for lunch in Bridgehampton, we headed toward the ocean. The contemporary homes along the beach that I'd seen photos of in glossy magazines were so much more impressive in real life.

"This is the real deal, Sam," he said. "I've been planning to buy here for a year. My cut from the merger deal alone could make it happen."

Truthfully, I hadn't gotten used to the family beach house fantasy yet, and I couldn't find the words to express how living in this place could ever be real for me.

"Speechless, huh?" Alec asked. I nodded. "I'll admit it, Sam, it took me a while to get used to the idea, but it's closer than you know."

He has no idea how far away something like this still seems to me.

He kissed my neck and a tingle coursed through my body. *I should just give in to everything he sends my way. Let go, and let God.* "It's more than I can comprehend, Alec." I sighed.

"My plans only started to make sense to me after I met you," he said.

My introduction to those nearest and dearest to Alec had gone better than I anticipated. They were a genuine family who had made me feel very welcome, and I believed I'd grow even closer to them over time—especially Giovanni. He was most definitely the patriarch of the family, in charge of his domain, and his rise on Wall Street was no accident, but he also had a softer side, and it was this combination—which I also saw in Alec—that attracted me to both of them.

Diana Ross sang on the stereo as Alec headed for home:

If I don't have all the answers
At least I know
I'll take my share of chances

"Why don't you put on the game?" I suggested, feeling magnanimous.

"Thanks, Sam," he said, reaching for the radio. "There are only a couple of things that interest me more, and you're at the top of the list."

I smiled and pointed my chin at the radio. "Are they ahead of your merger?"

Alec laughed. "No . . . but it's close."

Even though the Yankees lost the game, Alec was in a good mood all the way back to the house. When the family gathered on the deck, cocktails in hand, to watch the sunset, the men gravitated toward one end and began a heated conversation about their favorite team.

Gianna sauntered over and plopped on the chaise next to mine. "The only thing that could get between them and their Yankees is God and family," she quipped, "and I'm not so certain about the first one. I wonder what Christmas would be like if it were in baseball season."

"I don't know," I countered. "But it's hard for me to imagine anything being more important to Alec right now than his merger negotiations."

She raised her glass to me. "Except you, of course." I smiled softly. "A merger of a different stripe." She chuckled. *The kind that heats up in a bedroom, right?*

I looked over her shoulder and whispered, "We have gotten closer."

Gianna laughed, and the men glanced our way but never stopped talking. "I'm sure you have," she said.

I was sure my face went beet red because Gianna rested a hand on my arm to reassure me. "I'm just teasing, Sam," she said softly. *I wondered who would be first in Alec's family to call me that. I was betting on Franco.* "I think we've all gotten closer to you, and we're all pleased as hell."

"I appreciate that, Gianna."

"Everyone here appreciates *you*," she continued. "Alec is always ready to jump in and help anybody; he's generous to a fault, so it's nice to meet someone who won't take advantage of him." With that she grabbed my glass and rose to her feet. "Here, let me refill that for you," she said insistently, then moved toward the patio bar.

At that moment, Giovanni stepped away from the other men to make an announcement.

"Anyone object to pizza tonight?" he said to the sounds of boisterous approval all around.

I'd barely digested my lunch, but I always had room for good pizza.

Later on, stuffed again, Alec and I finished the night as we had the one before, cuddling in bed, fondling and smooching, and sharing some pillow talk.

Monday morning I dashed down to the kitchen having already determined to take charge of the eggs and bagels. I was looking forward to treating the family to a slice of my past— those mornings with Grandma that I still cherished. Samantha Bonti put on a show and it was a hit with everyone, Alec most of all. As I put away the last of the strawberries I also put away any further thought of being embarrassed around Alec's family.

Afterward, Alec and I took a walk on the beach, hand in hand, hardly talking. He squeezed my hand every few yards, immersed in feelings that I was sure mirrored my own. After half an hour we retraced our steps, and when we were in sight of the house he stopped, swept me up into his arms, and locked his lips on mine in the way that was uniquely his. The tingle from head to toe was resurrected, and the path to our future together was wide open again.

Franco was alone on the deck, talking on the portable phone, when we walked up onto it.

"Where's Dad?" Alec asked when he hung up.

"In his office. I suppose none of us has had a total break from work."

Alec leaned close to me. "I've got to talk to him about something," he said, heading inside. "I won't be long."

Franco smiled broadly and patted the chaise next to his.

"Let's bond a little, Sam," he said as I sat down and swung my legs onto the lounge. "I don't think I'll be seeing you in my office anytime soon," he teased, blatantly looking me over from head to toe.

"I don't think so," I agreed.

"So Dad tells me you're religious." *Franco doesn't waste any time getting down to it.*

"I'm not as familiar with all the rites and ceremonies as I probably should be," I replied. "But I'm definitely among the faithful."

"Dad's a real believer, too. He's always trying to get us to go to church, or to one of his retreats on Staten Island."

"You're not interested?"

"I get to Mass, mostly for Monica and the kids," he said. "Mount Manresa is something else entirely. Those Jesuits are tough, but I'm not sure they could handle me and Alec." He let out a chuckle. *Whether I can handle you guys isn't a certainty yet, either.* "Besides, we've got our hands full with the NIAF functions that Dad drags us to," he added.

"What's the NIAF?" I asked, wondering if I should have heard of it.

"The National Italian American Foundation. It represents over five million *paesanos.*"

"Doesn't sound like you're interested in that, either."

"There's more of a payoff for business types," he said, eyeing me up and down, and not for the first time since I sat down beside him. "I can find patients anywhere."

I looked over Franco's shoulder toward the people strolling along the shoreline. *Especially in this neck of the woods, I'm sure.* I fidgeted and pondered how to change the subject, but just then Alec reappeared, coming to my rescue.

"Is he behaving himself?" Alec asked, taking my hand.

"She's not in any danger, bro," Franco said.

"Not anymore," Alec answered, pulling me gently to my feet. "We're leaving," he said.

"Before lunch?"

"I wanna beat some of the ungodly traffic back to the city."

Alec and I said good-bye to Franco and made the rounds. Filomena gave me a polite peck on the cheek, but Giovanni hugged me as if I were one of his own children.

Of course, Alec wouldn't venture out on any trip destined to last more than an hour without proper provisions, so he rummaged through the kitchen cabinets and the refrigerator and packed enough food and drink to last at least three days.

"You sure we have enough to eat?" I cracked as we rolled out of the driveway.

"You probably could get by on a small bag of pumpkin seeds," he countered, as he turned on the CD player. "I, on the other hand, am headed into battle on the LIE and an army travels on its stomach."

I gazed pointedly at his midsection, which almost touched the bottom of the steering wheel even though his seat was as far back as it could go. "Yeah, well, in that case you'll certainly survive the whole war."

"Well, I wasn't only thinking about the trip," he explained a bit sheepishly. "I figured there'd be plenty left over for a late night snack."

"Of course." I smiled.

"Listen, Sam," he said softly, "I had a tremendous time with you this weekend."

I touched his arm. "Thanks for having me, Alec," I said, double entendre unintended. "I had a great time, too. I felt right at home."

"That's because my family fell in love with you right away." *Tony Kroon said over and over that his mother loved me.* "I don't know if I'd go that far, Alec. Maybe 'fond of' would be a better way to describe how they feel."

"It's just a hop, skip, and a jump from fondness to love, you know," he said with a smile. *True, if they move even half as fast as you do.* "Anyway, the weekend couldn't have gone better."

That was true enough, if you discounted a previous marriage. I'd just have to accept that he was being honest when he said it didn't mean anything. And, in any case, whatever trepidations I'd had about meeting his family and measuring up had turned out to be completely unfounded. It was obvious to me that they were all in Alec's corner and they never made me feel as if I threatened their bond with him in any way. In fact, they had been amazingly generous and genuine in the welcome they gave me.

SEVEN

I showed up at my cubicle well before nine on Tuesday, much to the surprise of both Priti and my boss.

"I half-expected to not see you at all today," Priti said as she rolled back from her desk, "much less this early."

"First day of the rest of my life." I sighed, eyeing the non-blinking message light on my phone. *Nothing from Alec? Now that is a surprise.*

"What's that supposed to mean?" Priti said, shooting a glance toward our boss, who was buried in his work. "I'm not reading any vibe from you at all, Sam. You gonna fill me in now, or make me wait until lunch?"

"Everything's fine, P," I said as I pulled my chair back. "I fell asleep on the phone with Alec last night."

"Speaking of sleeping . . ." Priti said, stopping in midsentence. Her eyes were wide open and focused on something over my shoulder. Before I could say a word, two massive arms circled my waist from behind, one hand clutching a long-stemmed rose.

"Good morning, Samantha Bonti," Alec whispered, nipping an ear.

Priti's eyes opened wider, if that were possible, as she lowered her head and made a move to roll back into her cubicle.

"Wait, Priti," I said. "I want you to meet Alec."

Alec looked toward her without letting go of my waist and she got to experience his jumbo grin for the first time. "So this is the friend I've heard so much about." Alec reached an arm toward Priti and squeezed her hand. "It's a pleasure to make your acquaintance, Priti."

"Likewise, Alec," Priti said, a blush evident even on her caramel skin. "I'll leave you two alone," she spluttered as she rolled into her cubicle.

I turned around in Alec's arms and caught the boss looking our way. "If you don't get out of here, Alec, I'll be in hot water," I said.

"Any water you're in positively boils," he said, pulling me close with a smile. I was certain my boss could see my face turn red from twenty feet away. "And you make my blood boil, too," he whispered before planting a kiss smack on my lips.

I don't care about the boss right now.

"I'm leaving anyway," he said as he separated from me. "Just didn't want you to forget me today."

As if.

With that, he slipped the rose into my hand and his fingers traced my arm as he stepped back and leaned against the end of the partition. "I hope you don't have any plans for Saturday," he added. *Gee, I'd planned to spend the day looking at my four walls.* "Jack's invited us on his boat . . ." he said, the words trailing off as he disappeared.

Priti's voice wafted over the divider. "Consider me totally filled in."

It was a cool, crisp fall day when Alec and I arrived in the Rover at the Seventy-ninth Street Boat Basin on the Hudson River.

Alec took my hand for the short stroll to the end of a floating dock, raising his hand to Jack and Patricia Bronson in response to their hearty wave from the deck of their thirty-foot sailboat.

He steadied me as I stepped down into the dinghy that would take us to the larger boat, then followed me aboard, rocking the small boat more than I would have liked. The attendant pulled the crank on the outboard motor and shoved off.

"Ahoy there!" Jack yelled from the stern as we came alongside. He took my hand and helped me on board.

Alec refused a hand, lumbered aboard the sloop, and saluted his friend. "All hands on deck, captain," he said with a big grin, then handed a bag to Patricia. "Some champagne to christen the voyage."

"We'll keep ours as backup, then," Patricia said before heading to the galley below. "I'll be right back."

"Why don't you two sit down while I cast off," Jack suggested.

Alec and I took our places in the stern and he wrapped an arm around me as Jack negotiated the slick deck to the front of the boat and untied the bowline. Then he straightened up, put his hands on his hips, and surveyed the river for a moment before scrambling back to the helm.

"Have you sailed before, Samantha?" Jack asked, gunning the engine.

I've been sailing along for weeks. "No, it's my first time."

"First time for a lot of things lately." Alec chuckled.

"I'm sure," Jack said as Patricia reappeared with flutes and champagne. "We'll cruise to the Battery and unfurl the sails when we hit the bay."

"And toast the Statue of Liberty," Patricia said.

"That'll be the second one," Alec said, reaching for two flutes.

"But of course," Patricia said as she filled the flutes and passed one to her husband.

Jack kept one hand on the wheel as Patricia moved to his side and rested an arm on his waist. "To the best first mate anyone could have," he said, raising his glass to his wife.

Alec pulled me close. "I'll drink to that," he said, "and to my mate, too."

"Cheers, everyone," Patricia said as we sipped.

We passed the aircraft carrier museum *Intrepid* anchored opposite Forty-sixth Street and the helicopter pads just below Thirty-fourth Street ten minutes later. The World Trade Center, only a couple of blocks from Alec's apartment, dominated the view off the port bow even though it was still a couple of miles away, and I had a tiny first glimpse of Lady Liberty dead ahead.

The sleek boat cut through the water, seemingly without effort, and the only sounds I heard were the gentle purr of its small engine and the Hudson lapping at the hull. Alec, lost in thought for a minute, ran his finger through my long hair, which was flying behind me in the breeze, and then bent over and gave me one of his soulful kisses. I hadn't quite gotten used to these public displays of affection, but I didn't resist when he went back for a second helping.

"I'd tell you two to get a room"—Jack chortled—"but I need you now, Alec."

He turned the wheel over to Patricia and Alec followed him to the furled sails. The two of them unbuckled the bindings and pulled on the lanyards, and I was impressed not only that Alec seemed to know what to do but also that he did it with aplomb. The men ducked aside and their faces broke out in broad smiles as the sails billowed, the sloop leaped forward, and Patricia steered us to the left of Lady Liberty. Jack retook the helm then, and I craned my neck as we sailed past. "I'll get us something to snack on," Patricia said, relieved of her duties, and once more she disappeared below.

"I'm starved," Alec announced, squeezing next to me again. "How about you?"

"I could use a bite."

Alec leaned over and nipped my ear. "Happy to oblige," he whispered.

Jack set the wheel, heading us toward the Verrazano-Narrows Bridge miles away, and joined the rest of us in the stern.

"What a way to go, eh, pal?" he asked rhetorically, raising his glass to Alec.

Alec returned the gesture. "First class, as usual," he said.

"Wind's at our back," Jack continued, "in more ways than one."

"Smooth sailing, all the way to the top."

Patricia gave me a wink. "You guys aren't going to start talking business now, are you?"

"We can discuss the Yankees if you prefer," Alec cracked.

"We women will have none of that," Patricia scoffed. "You're on our time now."

"Okay, then," Alec said, "let's talk about Sam joining us in Bermuda."

Patricia smiled in my direction. "That's a fabulous idea," she said. "What do you think, Samantha?"

"First time I'm hearing about it."

Alec pulled me close. "I was gonna lay it on you later, Sam," he said. "We're entertaining a major banking client there for a week and I would love to have you with me."

I fidgeted in my seat. "When?"

"Week from Monday."

"I can't get away for a whole week, Alec," I said softly. *And I'm not sure I'm ready for a whole week with you, either.*

"Then I'll fly you down on Wednesday," he said. Problem solved. "I'll just have to do what I can to survive until you show up," he added, laughing.

"I don't know."

"C'mon," Alec purred. "I'll take care of everything. There's even a set of Lugano luggage in it for you."

"Ooh," Patricia gushed toward me. "I'd hold him to that, whether you go or not."

They're all so casual about it, I thought, still torn between jeopardizing my job and just saying *screw it.*

"You need me to talk to your boss?" Alec the problem solver asked.

"I'll see what I can do."

"The big guy won't take no for an answer," Jack said, smiling.

No, I suppose he won't.

My boss probably knew where the chips lay because he didn't put up much of a fuss. The week flew by, and Priti was almost as excited as I was about my going to Bermuda, which the well-heeled knew was absolutely ideal in September and the peons only dreamed about.

Alec did take care of everything, and neither the leather luggage he had promised nor the first-class booking came as a surprise. I felt like royalty from the moment a driver picked me up early in the morning and stowed my bags in the limo.

I could get used to this.

I did find it somewhat odd when the solicitous flight attendant addressed me as "Mrs. DeMarco" but it seemed natural to just go with the flow. It was also natural to order a mimosa when she asked if she could get me anything, and to ponder my immediate and long-term future with the man I'd gotten to know very well, but who was still somewhat of a mystery to me. And then, there it was: a woman getting on the plane carrying a white Vera Wang garment bag. I took it as another sign.

I had little doubt about Alec's strengths—his intimidating size with an ambition to match, and the softness that he showed so spontaneously, at least to his family and to me—but I wondered if his weaknesses—his lack of caution when plowing straight ahead and his seemingly insatiable appetites—would eventually prove problematical, if not destructive. I hoped that the days ahead would provide me with more knowledge about, if not answers to, the mystery of Alec DeMarco.

When we got to Bermuda the jet banked above the island then glided down onto a glistening white runway. As I exited the terminal, I was engulfed by the tropical sun and a warm ocean breeze. The driver who met me apologized for Alec, saying that he was tied up in a meeting, which was okay with me since I'd have some time to take in the scenery on our way to the hotel.

A doorman and a bellhop, outfitted in bright red, British-style uniforms and quaint, bill-less caps, approached the taxi as it rolled to a stop. The doorman helped me out of car while the bellhop grabbed the bags in the trunk.

"Mr. DeMarco is waiting for you in the lobby," the doorman said when we arrived, with a wave toward the entrance. Sure enough, Alec rose from a wicker chair, signature grin in place and a vanilla ice-cream cone in hand.

"Do you mind taking care of this?" Alec asked the bellhop as he handed him the cone. "I've got what I need now."

"Not at all, Mr. DeMarco," the bellhop replied, taking it from him as Alec scooped me up into his arms, squeezed tight, and said hello with a deep kiss.

"I can't tell you how happy I am to see you," he gushed. "Let's go change into swimsuits and grab a bite of lunch. After that I have a few things I need to take care of, so you can do some shopping in town and we'll meet up again later."

The bellhop was just leaving the suite as we approached. Alec slipped a bill into his hand as I paused just inside, mesmerized by the view of the bay beyond the veranda and by the ocean breeze that filled the room. Alec engulfed me with his arms from behind, and I closed my eyes as he nibbled at my ear, his halting breath as warm as the island air.

"You don't know what you do to me, Sam," he moaned as he wrapped his arms around me. "I'm not going to wait anymore." And with that, he swept me up off the floor and headed for the bedroom.

Less than ten minutes later, he sat up on his side of the bed, feet planted on the floor. "I gotta get going, Sam," he said over a shoulder.

"I thought we were going to have lunch together."

"No time to eat with you now," he said as he turned and patted my arm. "Not after the, uh, appetizer. Order something for yourself here or at the pool, anywhere you like. Just sign our room number."

With that, he stood up, letting the sheet slide away as he turned around, his nakedness in full view for the first time. Every inch of his body was bathed in tropical light, and although his midsection had a few extra curves and folds, I couldn't imagine him looking any other way.

"I can't keep Ted Ross waiting," Alec said, snapping me back to attention.

"The senator's brother?"

"Yup," he replied as he disappeared into the bathroom.

Five minutes later he was showered and dressed, moving fast again. "I'll meet you back here at five, okay?" he asked and I nodded. "We'll have an early dinner, just the two of us, before meeting up with the others." He smiled, opened his wallet, and tossed his AmEx card onto the bed. "Just in case you see something in town," he said as the door closed behind him, leaving me alone in the suite. Suddenly I couldn't help wondering why Alec even wanted me here when his real priority was clearly the merger, and not our still only six-week-old relationship.

✧ ✧ ✧

Alec returned shortly after five looking so pleased with himself that I knew his deal was going well and he hadn't given me a moment's thought.

"You didn't go shopping?" he asked, picking up the AmEx card from the bed, right where he'd dropped it.

"I just needed to chill for a while," I said with a shrug. In truth, I hadn't felt comfortable throwing around someone else's money on things I could never justify needing.

"Well, I picked up something for you from the shop downstairs," he said, reaching into his pocket and pulling out a small white box, which he handed to me. I slipped the cover off and saw the sterling silver rosary nestled in white cotton.

Maybe I was on his mind this afternoon after all.

"It's beautiful, Alec." I sighed as I slipped the rosary into my fingers and lifted it up.

He grabbed my hand, kissed my fingers and the rosary, and looked me in the eyes. "Not as beautiful as you are, Sam," he said softly, "and not as beautiful as what we have."

I smiled and wondered if it was the right time to ask him the question I'd been asking myself all day: *Where does our relationship stand?* "Thank you, Alec," I said, squeezing the beads.

"I picked up a rosary for Dad, too," he announced gleefully. "And I think I'll get that purse you said you liked yesterday for Mom."

I stiffened as soon as he said that, as Tony Kroon and his jewelry purchases came to mind. *What is it with these Italian guys? Can't they buy something for their girl without thinking about someone in their family at the same time?*

The Four Lanterns restaurant was in a converted stone and cedar Georgian house. The dining room, with its mahogany beams and linen tablecloths, was perfectly understated, and the food easily lived up to the setting. The baked bananas we had for dessert were almost as sinful as Alec's past, but not as sinful as the check—so sinful, in fact, that American Express had to call the restaurant to confirm that Alec DeMarco was indeed using the card.

"Three thousand dollars?" I exclaimed when Alec told me how much the tab was.

"That bottle of wine alone was worth every bit of twenty-one hundred bucks." Alec shrugged as he took my hand to leave. "C'mon, beautiful," he said then, quickly changing gears. "Jack and Patricia are waiting for us at the tiki bar."

After a couple of drinks with Jack and Patricia, Alec and I walked hand in hand to the terrace and rode the elevator to our suite. A semi-cuddle in bed was all I could manage after our decadent meal, but he seemed content with that and quickly dozed off.

The next morning I was showered and dressed before Alec stirred. Feeling somewhat renewed by a sound night's sleep, I waited for him on the veranda.

Alec shuffled to the doorway in his robe a half hour later. "How about breakfast downstairs on the terrace?" he said with a smile.

"Perfect," I said, figuring that if I was distracted it wouldn't be so noticeable when we weren't alone.

Halfway through our lobster omelets, two young women in high-heeled sandals pranced over to our table. Alec sat back and smiled up at them, calm as could be, while I said a silent thanks for the dark glasses that hid my startled expression. The taller of the two stood there with tight lips and arms crossed as the other reached into her pocketbook and tossed a rolled-up belt onto the table. "You left that in our room the other night," she said with a smirk.

"It isn't mine," Alec said without missing a beat.

"Whatever," she huffed as the two turned on their heels and slunk away.

Alec shook his head, chuckled, and looked at me. My lips had gotten tighter and I was wringing my hands under the table, stunned into silence.

"I could cut the tension with my knife." He smiled thinly as he looked at me.

Or your wrists, for all I care, I thought bitterly. *It seems that six weeks really isn't enough time to get to know someone, inside and out.*

Alec's smile disappeared and his eyes searched for mine. "What's the matter, Sam?"

"Oh, nothing," I scoffed. "Every guy I date has women he slept with show up at the breakfast table."

"I'm serious, Sam," Alec said, grabbing the belt. "It isn't mine, and I didn't sleep with them. They're hookers working the conference here. Gotta keep my clients happy."

"So you're a pimp, then."

"I do what I have to," he said, recovering his Wall Street bravado.

"Whatever," I huffed, sounding a lot like the recently departed hooker and looking right through him. *Why didn't I hang on to that AmEx card? I could be on the next flight out of here. Even better, charter a private jet. That would serve him right.*

Alec leaned forward and slid his hands toward me. I shivered, tropical sun and all, at the thought of him touching me. I was glad my hands were still under the table, because that saved me the trouble of pulling them away.

"Sam," he said, "you can ask me anything."

My head swiveled from one table of happy diners to another.

"I'll tell you whatever you want to know, except the names of the guilty parties."

As I turned to face him, I shot daggers through my

sunglasses. "I find it hard to believe you really didn't do anything with those women. They seemed to know you pretty damn well."

Alec laughed out loud, shaking me to the core. My mind was going off in all directions and I couldn't think of anything to say. But Alec jumped right in to fill the agonizing pause. "Listen, Sam," he said, leaning back. "This isn't easy for me to talk about."

I'm all busted up about your discomfort.

He struggled for words, as if he were in a confessional. "Sometimes you have to do things you aren't necessarily proud of to get to the top, Sam. But I promise you that I didn't sleep with those women." I still felt numb. I didn't know what to think. "There's no one else and nothing else matters since I met you."

I wanted to believe him. I'd come to trust Alec in a way I didn't think was possible after Tony. But I could tell I wasn't getting the whole story—and I wasn't sure I wanted to know it. "I want to believe you, Alec." I sighed, relenting a little.

"Do you have any reason not to?"

"Well, you've got to admit you're a little crazy," I said with a cynical smile.

His big grin returned in all its glory. "Crazy for you, Sam."

He leaned toward me to plant a kiss on my cheek, but I placed a hand on his chest and stopped him.

"Alec." I turned to look him in the eye. It was the same probing look that my mother and grandmother had used on me countless times, as if reading my answer to their question before I'd even given it. "Listen, I didn't come out of dating a gangster without a few battle scars. And trust is a big one. If we're going to have any sort of future together, I have to know I can trust you. I have to know I am not making the same mistake my mother made." I paused and looked down. "You need to tell me everything. I'm a big girl; I can handle it. I just need to know the truth."

"Sam, I've always been honest with you. I just worry that some of the rough stuff in my past is going to change your opinion of me . . . and I'm crazy about you."

"Alec, the past doesn't matter to me. Believe me, when you read my book, you'll learn a few things about me you'd rather not know." He shifted in his seat, clearly uncomfortable thinking about the men in my past. I leaned in conspiratorially. "Don't let my spirituality fool you into thinking I'm some kind of nun; I like that you've been a bad boy." He looked up and I gave him a sly smile.

"Really?" he asked, sounding at once hopeful and relieved.

"Really," I said reassuringly. "I'm not judging you at all, Alec. We all have skeletons in our closets we'd rather forget. I just need you to be honest with me about yours so I won't obsess over imagining you with women far more experienced than me. I want to know everything about you—kinks and all."

Alec looked at me with such tenderness, I felt the full force of his love for me in that instant. He exhaled. "It wasn't until I met you that I knew exactly what I wanted out of life, Sam—the minute I laid eyes on you I vowed to become the kind of man who deserves you." He gazed at me so intensely that I blushed and looked away. "Are you sure you want to hear this stuff? I will tell you every last detail if that's what you want . . ."

Fair warning. I looked at him and smiled. "I want every last dirty detail."

Over coffee, Alec proceeded to tell me everything. And I mean everything. He started with the story of the hookers from the night before I arrived. Apparently, his client, a paunchy middle-aged golf nut with a Junior League wife and two kids in Connecticut, had a taste for bondage. After getting sauced and horny at a strip club, the client asked Alec to get him "a shot and two girls." Alec paused then and looked at me to make sure I was still with him. I nodded, doing my best to reserve judgment despite now having the visual of the two skanks implanted firmly in my head.

He continued: "By 'shot,' he didn't mean alcohol, Sam . . . He meant a cock shot."

"What?" I practically spit out my water and then laughed uncomfortably. "What's a cock shot?"

"A while back we made a connection with a doctor in the porn industry who hooked us up with injections so we could last as long as we wanted."

We . . . he said "we." "And . . . did you do one that night?"

"I'm not going to lie, Sam: I was tempted. Old habits die hard, you know. But all I had to do was think of you being in my arms the next day and the temptation passed. I might have even gone through with the injection if your flight were getting in sooner." I raised an eyebrow. "But I realized that I didn't need a shot to be with you. Those girls from last night tried to get me to join in—that's probably why they were pouting this morning: I rejected them, left a generous wad of cash on the coffee table, went to my room, poured myself a scotch from the minibar, and watched a porn flick."

Well, he certainly doesn't mince words! Alec leaned back as I took it all in. "I'm glad you told me, Alec. This whole world of yours is so foreign to me and I really want to understand it since it is such a big part of your life. I want you to let me in and tell me everything."

"Are you sure?" He raised an eyebrow at me this time, then signaled the waiter for a grappa.

"I'm sure." I reached over and took his hand in mine. "If there's one thing I learned in writing my story down over the years—even if I am the only person who ever reads it—it's that we have to be honest with ourselves and each other if we are ever going to move forward with our lives. Confession absolves us of our sins. I believe that as sure as I believe that the Blessed Mother is always watching over me. So tell me everything, Alec DeMarco."

Well, I asked for it . . . And I got it. *Fair warning,* I reminded myself. I sat there reeling, and hearing without really listening as Alec confessed one debauchery after another in an effort to expunge his past. I went numb after a couple of minutes of his brutal honesty, but was somewhat surprised that I was bored by the time he'd finished the entire litany of his experiences with porn stars and Penthouse Pets.

"Do you need those types of things?" I asked matter-of-factly, crossing my hands on the table.

"No, Sam. That's the point I'm trying to make." He sighed, resting a hand on mine. "I don't know how else to tell you." *His childlike innocence is back in full bloom.* "I love the game. I love making money. I love spending it. But it adds up to a whole lot of nothing without someone meaningful to share it with. You wanted to know about my past—do you see now how meaningless all of the sex and drugs and partying were? I don't need any of it now that I have you in my life."

Alec smiled at me and I knew he meant it.

On Friday morning, as we were having our breakfast on the veranda, Alec informed me that he had chartered a forty-foot sailboat for just the two of us. I was excited when we arrived at the dock and were greeted by a leathery-skinned captain who introduced himself and his mate with a classic Bermudian accent. "Name's Amado, and this here is Mac," he said warmly, welcoming us aboard.

Alec and I relaxed in the sun as Amado sailed around the bay and out into the Atlantic, dropping anchor in a secluded cove where we took a dip, while Mac, in tattered tan shorts and a shirt with the sleeves cut off, went about spearing some fish, which he then cooked for our lunch. "Perfect, isn't it?" Alec asked as we nestled together in the stern, my head resting on his shoulder.

"Couldn't be better, Alec," I agreed dreamily.

"Oh, yeah?" he drawled, reaching into his shorts pocket. "Just wait till you get a load of this." He handed me a long white box.

His pockets are deep indeed. "What is it?" I asked, sounding just like a schoolgirl.

"I scored a little something for you yesterday when you went off looking at some handbags in the gift shop." He grinned.

I lifted the cover and the tab at the Four Lanterns lost its shock value. "Is this a Rolex?" I cried.

"I couldn't believe what I got that rose gold model for," he said. "In fact," he continued, reaching again into his pocket, "the price was so good that I couldn't pass up getting a matching one for myself."

"I can't accept this, Alec," I said softly, rubbing the watch between thumb and index finger. "Really, I don't need such extravagant gifts . . . I really only came here to spend more time with you . . ."

"If you don't put it on right now, I'll give it to Gianna," he admonished me.

"Okay, okay, I give in!" I squealed and kissed him square on the lips.

I slipped the Rolex onto my wrist, thinking, *This thing is worth more than everything I've owned my whole life.* "I don't know what to say, Alec."

"The way you look right now says enough for me." He smiled hugely, then gave me a kiss. "I swear, I never thought I'd meet a girl like you."

✧ ✧ ✧

My fantasy trip to Bermuda had been sprinkled with rocky moments, but when I awoke on Saturday morning the stress I'd endured as a result of Alec's confession was gone. We had made love the night before, a tender and unrushed coupling, and now, as I sat on the veranda waiting for him to arise, I reflected on how close we'd become in spite of everything that might have driven us apart.

After another room-service breakfast on the veranda, Alec took my hand as he had taken my heart and led me to the elevator and down to the front entrance, where the white Bentley he'd reserved was waiting.

"A regular cab is beneath you, I suppose," I said.

"*Au contraire,* buttercup," Alec said. "It's beneath *us.*"

After a couple of hours spent shopping, we stopped for hot dogs at a stand overlooking the marina. I'd never had one that tasted as good. That night, the same white Bentley took us to Horizons for an amazing meal. Alec and I talked for hours, and I found my gaze drawn again and again to the water, stretching as far as the eye could see, as I contemplated an unending future with him.

When we left the restaurant, intending to call it a night, our driver, Donnie, made us an offer neither one of us could refuse. "You must take a walk on Elbow Beach first," he said with a smile as he opened the rear door of the Bentley for us.

Donnie drove a couple of miles to the southern shore of the island, turned onto a narrow winding lane, and dropped us off in a secluded area of the beach. "Enjoy the beautiful views!" he called out as we stepped onto the pink sand.

Alec and I strolled hand in hand over a low dune and down to the shore, alone with the moon and stars and the breaking surf. The salt air and ocean breeze enveloped us as we stood with our arms locked around each other's waist and gazed up at the heavens. Alec pointed to a shooting star that streaked across the sky, and together we exclaimed our amazement and watched until it disappeared. Neither of us said another word for a few minutes, content to be alone and kissing by moonlight.

Finally, Alec squeezed my waist tighter and broke the silence. "I felt like that star spoke to me," he said softly as he twirled me into his arms and looked into my eyes. My heart raced as he kissed me full on the lips. "Call me crazy"—he sighed when he came up for air—"but I love you, Samantha Bonti." With that, he kissed me again before I could respond, then dropped to one knee and reached for my hand. My heart was practically beating out of my chest as he looked into my eyes again.

"I love you," he repeated, slipping the Rolex from my wrist without taking his eyes off mine. His smile was both childlike and powerful as he raised the watch toward my pounding chest.

"Will you marry me, Samantha Bonti?"

My heart stopped racing, and I felt as if I were floating toward the stars as my mother, my grandmother, the Blessed Mother, and my entire past flashed through my mind.

Do I truly love this man? Do I really know what I'm getting into? Although I don't discount his flaws, I know he can give me the kind of security I truly need, but would he be the kind of husband I want and need?

I hated having to ask myself these questions, but the truth was, I was afraid—afraid of getting hurt again, afraid of having yet another man abandon me like my deadbeat father and Tony the sociopath had done. I shook off the fear and bid good riddance to them both. I'd made my decision. I knew Alec really loved me, and I truly believed this could work.

"Yes, I will," I whispered, delighted to see Alec breaking out into perhaps his biggest grin of all time.

EIGHT

All the way back to the hotel my brand-new fiancé alternated between kissing me and hooting it up with our driver, who seemed almost as happy as we were. Although I was well acquainted with how fast Alec could move, I was still stunned by his proposal, coming as it did only two months after we met. As we strolled arm in arm into the lobby I was sure everyone who saw us could tell what had just happened.

After tossing our clothes onto the floor, we fell into bed with the bottle of champagne Alec had ordered while we were still in the limo. We cuddled, kissed, laughed, and chatted about everything and nothing until we both fell asleep with the empty bottle on the covers between us. The last thing I remember was Alec telling me he thought the shooting star we saw from the beach was my mother passing by to give us her blessing.

I woke up the next morning, still dazed, when Alec rolled on top of my thigh.

"I want to make love to my fiancée for the first time," he said, pulling the sheet down. He kissed me on the lips, and after a slow, gentle lovemaking we pulled on our robes and went out to the veranda. Alec ordered breakfast and then placed a call to his mother.

I don't have anyone to call . . . I said a prayer for my family and for Alec's and resolved to just relax and enjoy the moment.

"Are you sitting down, Mom?" Alec asked, unable to keep the excitement out of his voice. "Sam and I are engaged."

I could hear her shout from my seat across the table.

"I know, I know," Alec said. "I surprised myself, even."

He gave me a wink as he listened for a moment.

I still can't believe it. I guess that comes from growing up poor and waiting for the other shoe to drop whenever something good happens.

"No, we haven't made any plans yet," he went on, covering the mouthpiece and whispering, "Dad's picking up the extension." There was a momentary silence and then, "Thanks, Dad. We're thrilled, too."

After a minute of spirited exchange between father and son, Alec reached over to me. "Here," he said, handing me the phone. "They want to talk to you."

"Welcome to the family, Samantha," Giovanni said.

"We couldn't be happier for you," Filomena added.

"For us, too," Giovanni said.

"Of course, dear," Filomena said, and I wasn't sure if she was speaking to her husband or to me.

Perhaps it's both. "Thank you," I said. "It's all kind of a blur right now."

"Don't worry about a thing," Filomena said. "I'll take care of all the arrangements once you set a date."

I thought of Mom and Grandma and almost cried. "Thanks again, Fil," I managed.

"Don't mention it, Samantha," she said. "We'll talk as soon as you get back. Would you put Alec on again?"

Alec listened to his mother go on and made clown faces for my benefit.

He always knows just how to calm me down.

"The sooner the better, as far as I'm concerned," he said after a while. "I'll call you from the airport. Bye, you two."

Alec disconnected and glanced at me as he dialed another number. "One more call and then I'm all yours." He held up a finger and then said into the phone: "Victor? Sam and I just got engaged."

I wonder how long it will be until I get used to hearing that.

"Yeah, thanks, buddy, but listen—I need you do me a favor tomorrow. Call Linda and cancel our date for Wednesday and tell her I don't want her showing up at my apartment anymore. Okay? Her number's in my calendar. Yeah, thanks."

Date?

"I know, I know," Alec went on. "Sudden as a heart attack." He laughed as he hung up, but his expression changed as soon as he looked at me.

"What's with the long face? I told you I was dropping girlfriends left and right, and she's the last," he said, soothing me again. "Last night just came out of left field, Sam. If I'd had any idea I'd propose to you down here I would have dumped her before I left." It was like something came over me.

I felt a surge of anger. *What else is he going to reveal before we leave this island? And why didn't he tell me about Linda last night?* I took a deep breath and reminded myself that as brutal as Alec's honesty could be sometimes, he was a straight shooter. I'd asked for complete honesty and I had to give him credit for coming clean. We had only known each other for two months; my life had taken as much of a 180-degree turn as his had. I decided to let it go—I was the one marrying Alec DeMarco after all, not "Linda"—and I'll admit, the fact that he had his Victor dispatch with the relationship with her made me feel almost instantly better. He had chosen me.

"You have Victor doing your dirty work?"

Alec chuckled. "Teammate and friend, and as far as I'm concerned you can't be one without the other," he said, dead serious. "Now get over here and jump in my lap so I can kiss my fiancée. If we didn't have a flight to catch, I would have thrown you back on the bed for round two." Alec gave me a huge smile as he spread his arms wide, and my face lit up. I couldn't resist this man. I pulled myself out of my chair, ambled over, and wrapped my arms around the neck I'd wanted to strangle a moment earlier. Alec did what he wanted to do. And I loved that about him.

I laughed to myself then, crazy for my crazy guy, and hugged him tight.

"I really wish your mother were alive," Alec said, brushing a strand of hair off my face. "I would have loved her."

"Maybe," I mused, "but I doubt it. She was crazy. It wasn't all bad, but she wasn't good crazy like you are. It was never a good idea for me to have Mom around a boyfriend, and you wouldn't have been an exception."

"Fiancé," Alec corrected. "A whole 'nother ball game."

Like everything that stands in your way. "I must admit it would have been interesting to see you two go at each other," I said, imagining the scene in my mind.

"Trust me, it woulda been a first-round KO."

"I don't know, Alec. She was a pretty good fighter herself."

I looked over his shoulder at the beach below, and for some reason was reminded of a picnic I'd gone on with Tony and my mother and his aunt on Gerritsen Beach in Brooklyn. His aunt had been jealous of the way I looked in the skimpy bikini I'd worn just for Tony and she got him all riled up about how indecent it was. Mind you, this was a woman who had stolen her daughter's boyfriend. She kept ranting and raving to the point where Tony came at me, put his hands on my shoulders, and started shaking me hard back and forth, cursing and muttering and asking me over and over again, "Why the hell are you wearing that bathing suit?" Mom came at him with a kitchen knife, and she would have stuck him if he hadn't taken his hands off me.

Turning back to Alec I had no doubt that he'd come to my rescue on a beach or anywhere else.

"Well," he said, "we'll never know, will we? So let's forget about it. I'm taking you to that fancy jewelry store in town."

"I don't need anything, Alec," I said softly. "Really. Why don't we just take it easy until it's time for our flight?"

"No fiancée of mine is showing up back home without a blinding rock on her ring finger, and that's that," the lion commanded. "You won't be coming back to our room empty-handed this time."

I looked at the beach again.

"Thinking about what you want?" he asked, sliding on his shoes, grinning with pride.

"You always make me feel like a princess, Alec. You make me so happy; I don't need a fancy ring to remind me how much I love you." I sat in his lap and kissed him gently.

"Nah, you need a fancy ring, Mrs. DeMarco." He kissed my nose and popped up, determined to get that ring on my finger before we made it to Customs. *I do have something to declare.*

Alec asked me to choose any stone I wanted. I was overwhelmed by the selection of gems, each more gorgeous than the last. Finally, with Alec's help, I settled on the perfect stone. But the jeweler balked at setting it right away. No problem, Alec just slipped five crisp one-hundred-dollar bills into his hand and told him there'd be five more to match if the ring was ready when we got back from lunch.

Later that afternoon, as Alec and I packed the last of our things before heading to the airport, my new flawless diamond sparkled in the tropical sun filtering in from the terrace, almost as much as my eyes did.

"I'll never forget the way you look right now," Alec said, taking a swig of the complimentary champagne sent up by the concierge.

"And I'll never forget these past few days, Alec." I sighed, unable to take my eyes off the rock on my finger. "Especially last night."

"I'm planning to crowd your memory with visits to every corner of the globe."

The world is his oyster, and I'm his pearl.

"Gianna and Mom both have four-carat diamonds," Alec said between bites. "We should have gotten you a five-carat stone. I should have never listened to them when they told me a five-carat would just be too big for your tiny hands."

Really, Elizabeth Taylor had small hands, too. Betcha Mike Todd never listened to his mother.

"Three is outrageous enough," I said. "I would have been happy with a chip!"

"I wouldn't have been." He growled playfully, as he scooped me into his arms while reaching for a second scone.

I had to pinch myself every couple of minutes on the flight home to make sure I wasn't in a dream. As we landed at JFK Airport, however, my elation turned to anxiety. We were about to be greeted at the gate by Alec's parents and sister. Any lingering fear dissipated, however, as I saw Gianna holding up a bunch of pink balloons and Giovanni waving a bouquet of roses.

There were hugs and kisses and smiles all around as I lost myself in the bosom of my new family.

"Alec's proposal was bit of a shock to us all, Samantha," Filomena said, grabbing my hand, "but a distinct pleasure, nonetheless."

"Mom put together a little reception for you two on Saturday," Gianna gushed, "at our house in Brooklyn."

"If that meets with your approval, of course," Filomena added.

"I'll look forward to it," I said, a tinge of worry reemerging.

There aren't many single-family homes on large plots in Brooklyn. Janice Caputo, my best friend when I was growing up, had lived in one of those free-standing homes, and I'd seen a couple of others that were owned by mobsters like Tino Priganti, but none of them came close to the one Alec had lived in.

The stately brick home was set atop a gentle rise overlooking Fort Hamilton and the Verrazano-Narrows Bridge. A lush green lawn was accented with a few apple and cherry trees, which were dwarfed by the giant oaks that stood guard on each side of the house. The property was surrounded by a low stone wall interrupted by the wrought-iron gate at the entrance to a brick driveway.

Alec steered the Rover up the driveway and I caught a glimpse of a Saint Joseph grotto twenty feet in front of the white portico.

"Home, sweet home," Alec said as he killed the engine.

I smiled, checking myself in the visor mirror.

"Mere bag of shells compared to where we're headed, Sam," he added. "Ready to go in?"

"As ready as I'll ever be," I replied, one eye on the grotto.

Alec's parents greeted us in the marble foyer and escorted us to the solarium in the rear of the house, where an intimate group, including his brother and sister and their spouses, as well as two couples I didn't recognize, rose as one, clapping and offering congratulations.

"This is Angelo and Connie, my godparents," Alec said, introducing me to a traditional-looking Italian couple. "And these two lovely people," he added, pointing to the other couple, "are Sid and Betsy, my parents' best friends."

"I've heard so much about you," Betsy said, taking my hand in hers.

Sid touched my shoulder gently. "Alec is certainly blessed to have you in his life," he said.

"That's for sure," Connie said lightly. "He needs all the religious influence he can get."

"You holy rollers gonna preach to me all day?" Alec erupted in mock indignation.

"God forbid," Franco chimed in.

"There's room for Him here, as always," Giovanni said as he wrapped an arm around his wife, "but Fil wants to talk about the wedding first."

"Have you two discussed a date, Sam?" Filomena asked.

"November second," I replied.

"All Souls' Day," Alec said. "As if you people didn't know that."

"Her influence seems to be working quite well," Connie said, beaming.

"A Saturday this year," Filomena said. "Perfect."

"So let's toast the perfect couple." Giovanni popped a bottle of prosecco as Filomena distributed glasses.

"Let's sit down, shall we?" Filomena said after the toast. "We can talk about the details while we eat."

"Great," Alec said. "I'm starved."

"What else is new?" Gianna countered, and everyone laughed.

"If it's all right with you, Samantha," Giovanni said as everyone settled into their seats, "I'll make arrangements for the ceremony at Our Lady of Victory."

"That would be lovely, Mr. De . . . Giovanni," I said.

Giovanni smiled warmly. "I'd love it if you called me Dad from now on." *I always wanted a real father. I missed out, but this may work out after all.*

"Thanks . . . Dad." I smiled as I tested the unfamiliar word, thrilled that it felt so natural to say it to Giovanni. "I'd like to have a priest I know from Brooklyn do the officiating. Would that be a problem?"

"Not at all," Giovanni said.

"Not if they want the DeMarco contributions to keep coming," Franco cracked.

"Enough of that." Filomena silenced him. "We've got important matters to discuss right now, starting with pre-Cana."

"What's that?" Alec asked, sounding slightly suspicious. He loved that I embraced my Catholicism but I got the sense that he wasn't particularly interested in participating in the rituals of the church. *One step at a time, Sam . . . this is all happening fast enough*, I reminded myself. Besides, I didn't exactly have a perfect attendance record at Mass, either, except my weekly novena thirty-minute Masses with Priti.

"Before you commit to the sacrament of marriage, you have to take pre-Cana classes at the church. You didn't go the last time around and look where it got you," Giovanni chided Alec.

I'd almost completely forgotten about her . . .

"Sam, you've made all your sacraments, haven't you?" Giovanni turned to ask me.

The sacraments . . . I'd forgotten: "You know what? As Catholic as I am in spirit and belief, I've never made any of my sacraments. I wasn't baptized, haven't received Holy Communion, nor was I confirmed. But I am beyond thrilled to receive them all before getting married—it's something I've always wanted to do, but never had a reason until now." *Maybe I'll ask Alec's parents to be my godparents.*

Giovanni, dear that he was, squeezed my shoulder and gave me a warm smile that spoke volumes. "If it's all right with you, Sam, I'll pull some strings and get you into a crash course at Our Lady of Victory. They're . . ." Giovanni's voice trailed off for a moment. ". . . willing to overlook Alec's previous marriage and allow him to remarry in the church."

The thought of not being able to marry in a church because of Alec's divorce hadn't even occurred to me. *It's a good thing I'm signing up for classes. I really do have a lot of catching up to do on my religion.* My mom would have been so disappointed if I couldn't be married in a church even if she wasn't there to see me walk down the aisle. I couldn't have borne it—even after her death. "Thank you . . . Dad," I said again, squeezing his hand in acknowledgment of his thoughtfulness.

He winked at me, then turned to Alec with a warning: "I'm afraid this time there's no talking your way out of pre-Cana, Alec—six classes. Make time."

I expected more grumbling, but Alec scooped me up and said, "For this woman, I would do anything! Anything!" He kissed me full on the mouth and reached for the prosecco.

"So, now that that's out of the way," Filomena said, "I've got some wonderful rooftop places in mind for the reception, Samantha."

Alec paused in the middle of a sip of prosecco. "We're saving the big reception for Bermuda, Mom," he said, to which everyone reacted with stunned silence. "Sam and I are thinking about having a small ceremony on the second at Our Lady of Victory," he continued, turning toward his father, "in deference to you, Dad. A gathering for just the immediate family and close friends will follow." Alec turned toward me then and broke out his trademark grin. "But we're planning an island blowout the next weekend for the reception."

The only planning I'd done was to nod approval as I listened for the first time to Alec's vision for our wedding. I nodded because it didn't seem that I had much say in the planning of the wedding anyway. I couldn't even afford to pay for so much as the invitations. I would never dream of complaining. But there was a part of me that was bothered by my total lack of control in the relationship—he always called the shots. Yet on the other hand, part of me loved how Alec took control of every situation; I loved how masculine he was. But more than that, Alec made me feel safe—I didn't mind letting him lead. I was content to fold myself into his world, the world I'd finally found across the Blessed Bridge. I was ready to leave the old Samantha Bonti behind. Alec loved me for me. And I felt like I'd been waiting for him forever.

I was marrying the man I loved, with my eyes open. I realized that he wasn't perfect—but then neither was I. This fairy-tale life I was about to embark on with Alec far outweighed the alternative—I loved him and there was nothing I could do about it now, except trust in the Blessed Mother, take the leap, and see where I ended up.

I looked up at him, testing the words *Mrs. Alec DeMarco* on my tongue. The grin that spread across his face as they escaped my lips said it all. Our mutual excitement over the engagement quickly overpowered any flicker of resentment I might have felt about Alec taking charge without consulting me. I loved my bully of a fiancé.

Filomena's voice lifted me out of my reverie. She frowned at her son and said, "You expect everyone to just get on a plane and show up there?"

"If they want to party," Alec cracked.

"You may want to rethink that, son," Giovanni said. "Some guests who will be on our list aren't as affluent as we are."

"I'm footing the bill for anyone who wants to be there," Alec said.

"Whoa," Franco exclaimed. "That's gonna be a tidy sum."

Alec gave me a wink. "Mere bag of shells, bro." He chuckled.

Giovanni's frown matched his wife's. "You'll be spending a chunk of your commission for the merger before it's in the bag," he said.

"Oh, it's in the bag all right," Alec said. "We pretty much put that to bed last week."

"'Pretty much' isn't a hundred percent, Alec," Filomena warned.

"I've got it covered, Mom. I'll break into my piggy bank if I have to."

A pregnant pause ensued before Betsy jumped in. "Sid and I were hoping you'd have the reception on a yacht or some other location where our company could do the catering," she said. "It was going to be our wedding gift to you two."

"We'd be honored if you took care of the small reception at the house," Alec said. "Right, Sam?"

I nodded.

"It'll be our pleasure, then," Sid said. "But that won't be enough of a gift. We'll have to add something else."

"Do what you gotta do." Alec laughed.

"And, if your mind is made up, your father and I will do what we have to as well," Filomena said.

She knows there's no way she could talk him out of it.

"What about the wedding party?" Gianna bubbled toward me. "I'd love to be your maid of honor."

"That's very kind of you, Gianna, but I already asked my friend Priti," I said, and Gianna seemed crushed. "But I'd love you to be a bridesmaid."

"Sure," Gianna murmured.

"And you, Monica," Alec said to his sister-in-law. "If you'll do us the honor . . ."

"Of course," she replied.

"Awesome," Alec said. "I'll pair you with Franco."

"Very funny, bro," Franco said. "If I'm not your best man, count me out."

"Okay, then. Franco, you'll walk down the aisle with Priti."

"How many ushers are you going to have?" Gianna said,

already calculating seating arrangements in her mind. "There must be twenty guys you could choose from."

"I've whittled it down to five, sis," Alec said and turned toward Gary. "You'll be with Gianna." Gary nodded, ever the devoted husband. "Victor and Jack are in, and I'm gonna ask Ted Ross."

"The senator's brother?" Angelo whistled.

"He owes me." Alec smiled. "And I want to keep him close."

"I can't wait to meet your other bridesmaids," Gianna said, squeezing my arm for emphasis.

I pursed my lips, searching for something to say. *There's no one I could ask, and I certainly didn't want this huge affair. Aside from Alec's sister and sister-in-law, Priti is the only friend I really have aside from John—and he would look terrible in a bridesmaid dress. I have to think fast!*

Alec came to my rescue before I could give it another thought. "Sam bounced around from job to job the past couple of years and didn't have many opportunities to get close to anyone. It was a miracle she connected with Priti," he began. *I'll say.* I looked at him, grateful to the verge of tears, and he nodded with understanding. Alec knew how hard on me the years I'd spent with Tony were—not to mention all those years spent looking over my shoulder once he went to prison. Alec understood how isolated I'd felt and wanted me to know that I had family now and would never feel alone like that again. "Sofia and Pat will be paired with Victor and Jack," Alec added, turning toward his sister-in-law. "That leaves you with Ted, Monica."

"I'll show him a good time," Monica said, raising a comically arched eyebrow toward Franco. He just laughed and encircled Monica in a playful hug. Perhaps it was the result of having twin girls, but even though Franco and Monica teased each other mercilessly and complained about each other constantly, they were a team. Just like Filomena and Giovanni, Gianna and Gary—and now, me and Alec.

"Now, time for some espresso over vanilla ice cream, please, and limoncello," Franco chimed in, settling the matter with food—the Italian way.

I smiled. The way Alec had come to my defense, knowing how sensitive I was about my past, made me realize that I loved the blustery side of his personality for the same reasons I adored his intimate side. For once, I no longer felt threatened or inadequate. I was beginning to see myself as the confident woman Alec saw in me, and his encouragement gave me a feeling of security I'd never felt before—not at home, not with friends, and certainly not with men.

The wedding was less than six weeks away; sacraments and pre-Cana aside, it could have been the next day, as far as I was concerned. Priti and John were the only people on the invitation list Filomena had asked me to provide, and those two had already assured me they would be there, whenever and wherever I tied the knot. The only thing that could have stood in the way of an immediate ceremony was Father Rinaldi's availability. When I spoke to the good father at Our Lady of Guadalupe after his Mass on Sunday, he echoed my friends' sentiments, saying he would move heaven and earth to be there when I needed him. His constant support over the years meant the world to me. I felt a little less alone just knowing he'd be there for me on the most important day of my life—even though Grandma and Mom hadn't lived long enough to see me happily married to the man of my dreams.

I truly wondered what they would have thought of Alec. Would Mom have mortified me the same way she did at Tony Kroon's house on Christmas? Would Grandma have proudly brought a *babka* without the Italians understanding what a *babka* cake even is? But I believed it would have been different this time. I really thought that even from heaven they were happy with my choice and with the world I had fallen into. *I think I just have to stop asking myself if I belong.*

With all of the important parts of the ceremony covered, the only thing left for me to worry about was my dress. Although time was short, I had always dreamed of wearing a gown designed by Vera Wang, though I never even imagined that it would be a possibility for me. But suddenly, it was more than a possibility—it was about to become a reality. Priti and I took a personal day to go to the Vera Wang shop on Madison Avenue. Ever since I saw that woman on the plane to Bermuda holding that white garment bag a month earlier, I simply knew it was a sign. Who knew it would be a sign of my future? This would be the last bit of money I had left in savings and I was determined to make this purchase on my own.

We took the bus uptown together, reminiscing about the first shopping mission she'd accompanied me on, to Saks just a few months before. If it weren't for seeing Priti at work every day and filling her in on my whirlwind courtship with Alec on a daily basis, I am not sure I would have believed it myself. I still had to pinch myself to prove that this was really happening. To me, Priti was a friend who came into my life at the right time. And no matter if our lives went off on different paths, which so many did, she would always remain special—one of the first people in New York who believed in me.

As if under a spell at Vera Wang, I tried on the first dress I saw on the sample size rack and it was perfect. Angelic white with a sheer, button-down back and a removable bottom flounce for the beach party.

Filomena, on the other hand, was frantic from the start. It was *damn the torpedoes, full speed ahead* for her, and I sometimes felt like a guest in my own life. She had two events in two countries to plan and hundreds of people to consider for an invitation. As a result, I think she was genuinely relieved when I declined her offer to help me pick out a dress.

I could have been caught up in the hubbub leading up to the wedding. I could have been dragged into the battles over tuxes and gowns and menus and seating arrangements. I could have gotten my nose severely out of joint over the groom's name being listed first on the ostentatious invitations Filomena selected without any input from me, a Pamela Kroon move if ever there was one. Something Tony Kroon, like Alec, would have had her back for. However, none of it mattered to me. The DeMarcos were footing the bill and they could do as they pleased as far as I was concerned. What mattered most to me was getting the rest of my life under way—and starting my new life with Alec. Love was what it was all about; so I hoped.

Alec, meanwhile, was like a kid on Christmas throughout the engagement. I was glad we'd decided on a short engagement; frantic as that period of wedding planning was, had we waited any longer Alec would have probably self-combusted. I shook my head and laughed, thinking of him waiting even one more day to marry me. *That's my guy,* I thought. *He's fast, all right.*

My guy. I finally had a *my guy.* I finally found home.

Alec, of course, spared no expense on himself, either. He wouldn't hear of letting either Priti or John pay for their flights or accommodations, but his support as I made the necessary sacraments, and his generosity in taking my feelings into account, meant far more to me than his generosity with money and gifts.

He insisted on a custom-made tux, and I didn't want to know how much of a premium he paid to ensure on-time delivery. He also had a four-day bachelor party in Monte Carlo with Franco, Gary, and ten of his closest friends. I didn't want to know what went on there, either. *Alec's going to do what Alec's going to do.* The words came to mind like déjà vu; they sounded at once threatening and born of resignation when I'd first thought them. Now they just made me love him more. *Alec's going to do what Alec's going to do. But he comes home to me. He chose me.*

I thought about Tony Kroon and how trapped he'd made me feel. I didn't want to be held back and I didn't want to hold Alec back, either—that's not why I was marrying him. I was marrying him because I trusted him to do right by me.

I looked at Alec, *my guy,* reading in bed, and my mind raced with all the terrible things that could go down in Monte Carlo . . . So I did what a girl does best: I tied him up, teased him, and tormented him until he begged for more—so he'd remember just who he was coming home to marry. The harder I rode to get him to climax the more convinced he was that it didn't get any better than sex with me.

The ceremony at Our Lady of Victory, with just Franco and Priti to attend to Alec and me, and the intimate reception at the De-Marco home in Brooklyn were just perfect. Filomena prepared a beautiful champagne brunch with the help of her friend Betsy, who also made my husband's first wedding cake: coconut and pineapple with homemade rum ice cream. There were about twelve of us at this very intimate gathering since the big wedding was to take place the following week. The house looked so festive. As Alec and I toasted to life and love, I truly felt that I was finally home. Thank God we didn't go with Alec's original plan to get hitched and head to the Yankees playoff game. That would've been a great wedding night.

I would have been happy to start our honeymoon immediately instead of waiting a week before the reprise in Bermuda, but, good wife that I now was, I did nothing to dampen Alec's enthusiasm for the decadent celebration he had planned down to the smallest detail and had looked forward to for weeks. It was all he could talk about in the limo on our way to his apartment after the reception, gulping champagne he didn't need, and I was sure he wouldn't stop even when we got up to his—our—bedroom.

But I was wrong.

Alec went silent behind me just inside the door. I braced myself, expecting him to tear my dress off, scoop me into his arms, or toss me across a shoulder and throw me on the bed.

He placed his hands gently on my shoulders, twirled me around just as gently, and kissed me softly on the lips.

"Welcome home, Mrs. DeMarco." He sighed, and I gazed into his dreamy eyes.

Then he reached into a deep pocket and pulled out a small rectangular box. "I've got a small gift for you," he said, kissing me again and placing the box in my trembling hands.

"C'mon, open it," he said with a gentle smile.

I slipped the cover off and my smile, for once, was bigger than his at the sight of the diamond eternity band.

"I had been saving it for the ceremony in Bermuda, but I just couldn't resist giving it to you now. You deserve it, Sam, and so much more."

I couldn't stop staring at the sparkling stones.

He swept me up into his arms and headed for the bed with his eyes locked on mine. "I'm going to make love to my wife for the first time," he breathed.

We awoke on Sunday as Mr. and Mrs. DeMarco, and always-in-charge Alec delivered his first husbandly command as soon as his eyes opened.

"Resign from that job of yours first thing tomorrow morning," he said. "Do it over the phone."

"Yes, master," I said, giving him a playful elbow.

For the first time in my life I wouldn't be responsible for supporting myself, and while in one sense that was a great relief, it was also a bit of a struggle for me to contemplate giving up total control of my future. It meant a lot to leave my job behind and rely entirely on a man for income and security, but I'd always gone with my gut and I knew that, at this point in my life, I wanted to fully embrace the role of "dutiful wife" to my new control-freak husband. That said, however, it was still important for me to retain my own identity and to continue pursuing my writing. I could still be myself without a job, but not without what I considered to be my true and most important work.

Meanwhile, I got out of bed and took control of making breakfast.

We spent a lazy day at home with the Sunday papers in our laps and football games on the television. Alec handled some last-minute problem solving related to the Bermuda festivities, and I took some time to think about how much more time I'd have to write once I wasn't working anymore.

When we arrived in Bermuda the following Saturday, the weather was markedly cooler than it had been on our previous visit, but the sun was still there to greet us. We settled into the bridal suite, which was, of course, larger than the accommodations we had stayed in previously. The bathroom alone was more expansive than the Brooklyn apartment I had finally left behind for good.

The tab for another dinner at the Four Lanterns—Chateaubriand for two and a 1970 Château Lafite Rothschild Bordeaux that went down like grape juice for me—was also bigger than the already astronomical one we'd run up before. *I could buy a decent used car for the same amount he just added to his AmEx card!* After some fretting, however, I decided to leave all financial matters in my husband's capable and powerful hands.

The full-blown ceremony late on Sunday afternoon was straight out of a fairy tale. I arrived at the famous limestone cliffs where the ceremony would take place in a horse and carriage, with my maid of honor and Alec's two cousins, two beautiful white horses in front. The weather couldn't have been better, and I couldn't help thinking that Grandma Ruth was still watching over me. The women in the wedding party wore gowns that matched the sand, and Alec and I repeated our vows under a virgin-white silk canopy overlooking the beach. As the bluish-green waves crashed seemingly after every sentence we uttered, it felt like I was in a dream, one so far away from my past, I could finally exhale. Again, I could have left for the honeymoon immediately, but there was still a blowout party to attend before my husband and I could finally make our getaway.

So instead of heading for the airport we went back to the hotel to change for the beach reception—for me, a simple white dress that was more like a slip or a nightgown, and for Alec, jeans with a button-down shirt. We checked our shoes at the shoe check, which had been my idea—the only one I was allowed—and made our way to the paradise seafront feast. There were restrooms disguised as palm-covered cabanas and bars were set up everywhere. The bay looked like a small corner of Polynesia, transported onto the sands of Bermuda. Colorful flower petals decorated the many overflowing hors d'oeuvre stations, where the guests were helped by attentive servers before settling down at tables warmed by a giant bonfire, to eat and drink while being entertained by mesmerizing fire dancers and a fierce limbo contest before they moved to take their seats for dinner.

Franco rose from his seat and, with the ocean at his back, made a toast about finding love and keeping it that brought a tear to the eye of his brother and everyone in attendance.

Alec drained his glass and wrapped an arm around me. "I love you, Sam," he whispered, warming me more than the champagne I was sipping. He gave me a prolonged kiss and the crowd cheered anew, another public display from which I didn't recover until well into our first dance.

"You do look wonderful tonight," Alec said with a huge smile, echoing the words of the Eric Clapton tune being played by a full orchestra. *I didn't remember ever picking a wedding song. Oh, well.*

"I feel so special, Alec," I whispered. "I don't know what to say."

"That's okay with me," he said, laughing. "I'll do all the talking."

That's for sure.

When our wedding song ended we partnered with his parents for the next dance. Alec played to the crowd, steering Filomena around the floor, and I felt as secure with Giovanni as I had with Alec the night before.

"Thanks, Dad," I said when it was over.

Giovanni gave me a peck on the cheek, and I made my way back to my seat. Alec was in his element, bouncing from table to table and accepting toasts right and left.

Priti leaned over and touched my hand. "Unbelievable," she bubbled.

"Tell me about it, P," I said. "Don't pinch me. I don't want to wake up."

"Trust me," she said, "you're a real princess now."

But I'm also still Samantha, no matter what the last name is. "I just hope I get the hang of being among royalty."

"If it gets to be too much for you, you could always come back to your cubicle," Priti said.

"No, thanks," I said, and we shared a laugh as Giovanni slipped into his son's vacant seat.

"Nice to see you gals enjoying yourselves," he said. "I can see I'm not needed here."

"That couldn't be further from the truth, Dad," I said. "You're one of the few people I know here and I love having you stop by."

Giovanni waved an arm at the crowd. "There are more than a few people here who aren't strangers to you," he said.

That was true enough. John was nearby and I was glad for the handful of others who didn't make me feel like a guest at my own wedding. But I wondered if I'd ever be on a first-name basis with men like the two with whom Alec was lost in conversation, Grigor Malchek, the CEO of the New York Stock Exchange, and Senator Robert Ross.

Giovanni squeezed my hand and kissed my cheek. "I'll give some others a chance to stop by," he said, rising.

"You sure hit the jackpot with him," Priti said.

"I'm blessed, P."

"Tell me about it," she said, and we shared another laugh.

Alec came back to my side as each course was served, and a procession of visitors filled his seat whenever he rejoined the ongoing revelry. I was particularly glad when Betsy and Sid came, because I already had warm feelings toward them.

"Holding it together?" Betsy said, resting a hand on my shoulder.

"Sure, although I will admit it's a bit overwhelming."

"You'll get the hang of things in no time," Betsy said. "We knew the minute we met you that you were as sharp as Alec said you were."

"Talented, too," Sid added. "I was really impressed when I heard you were a writer."

"Thanks," I said, genuinely meaning it.

"We'll have you and Alec over when you get back," Betsy said as she started to leave. "We'll chat a lot more then."

At that point, Victor left the scrum of guys whooping it up at the bar and came back to our table looking for his wife.

"Where's Sofia?" he asked.

"I think she went to the ladies' room," I replied, as I looked away, not particularly interested in striking up a conversation with him. It wasn't that I didn't like Victor, or Sofia for that matter. I just thought they were typical of the type clawing their way up the financial ladder, which admittedly wasn't so different from what Alec appeared to be doing.

Victor, however, didn't take the hint and sat down beside me. "Gotta hand it to Alec," he began. "The guy really knows how to throw a party."

"Thanks," I said drily, looking around for an out to this conversation.

"You two make a great couple," Victor continued.

"Thanks again."

"I'm serious, Sam," he insisted. "Every successful guy needs a good woman to stand behind him, and Sofia and I think you've got what it takes to help Alec go all the way. We're ready to help you any way we can. Alec has an awful lot on his plate and that can be hard for a wife to handle."

"Alec does fine with eating." I laughed.

"A shark if ever there was one," Victor agreed, "but he's gotta be on the lookout for even bigger ones." He drained his glass and leaned toward me. "Such as Grigor Malchek and his crew," he whispered, and I shivered as he stood to leave. *I know what a crew is. I met Tony Kroon's.* "Alec's got to keep feeding them or they'll have him for lunch."

I fidgeted in my seat and looked away again. "Thanks again for the support, Victor," I said quietly.

"Don't mention it, Sam," he said as he walked away.

Alec as shark food? That required some sober consideration.

"I don't mean to ignore my lovely bride," a boyish-faced Alec said when he returned to the table moments later.

"I'm enjoying myself," I said, in half a lie.

"Just had to make the rounds," Alec said. "Starting tomorrow it'll be just you and me for a week in the best hotels Europe has to offer."

"I can't wait," I said with a sigh.

"Speaking of offers . . ." He pointed to the line that was form-ing at the end of the dais.

Two by two, the guests approached and handed over fancy envelopes to Alec and me. It was a scene right out of *Goodfellas*. I just placed them in the satin drawstring bag secreted under the table. But most of the guests, especially those in the Wall Street community, frowned upon the Italian tradition of handing over money at weddings and opted for more traditional gifts, from Tiffany to Steuben, to a large bond for my unconceived child.

"Might be enough in there to carry us for a year." Alec chuck-led as the last envelope was delivered.

Probably enough to last for the rest of my life.

The celebration wound down fairly quickly after that, except for Alec and the boys, who showed no sign of leaving.

"It's a pretty night," Alec said, breaking out his biggest grin. "What say we put a cap on this celebration in fitting style?" The glint in the eye they all shared foretold exactly what they had in mind as they headed toward the water.

Alec gave me a fast kiss on the cheek as he stood up. "I won't be long, buttercup," he promised on his way to joining the exodus.

The boys drained their glasses, tossed them in the sand, and made a mad dash to the ocean, shedding garments along the way. Bare cheeks and cocks were the last thing I saw before I turned to Priti, the disbelief evident on my face.

"Boys will be boys," she said.

True to his code, if not to his promise to me, Alec was the last man standing at the bar, and it was 2 a.m. by the time my bedraggled husband staggered over to the table where I was dutifully waiting and we retired to the bridal suite. I'd changed three times, had three different parties, with wedding costs ballparking to the tune of at least three hundred grand, but that was merely lunch money for a guy who made it on Wall Street.

The semiconscious, semicoherent man I'd married twice in one week stumbled into the bedroom using my slight frame as an unsteady crutch until his massive upper body, followed by his legs, crashed onto the mattress. Removing his damp clothes and helping him crawl under the covers was my final wifely duty at the end of a very long day.

NINE

"My head . . ." Alec moaned from beneath the tangled sheets.

"Serves you right," I said, yanking open the drapes. "Do you know I had to carry you over the threshold last night?"

"Oh, baby, I'm sorry." Alec laughed and rubbed his eyes. "Don't be mad. I overdid it last night, but I promise to make it up to you on our honeymoon." He stood up and wrapped me in his arms. "Finally, I'll have you to myself . . ." Luckily we had an evening flight from Bermuda; Alec sorely needed the whole day to recover.

By the time we arrived in Amsterdam at six-thirty Tuesday morning, after changing planes in New York, I was both tired and cranky. I was not used to such long flights or to the time difference. But it was the beginning of our honeymoon, so my crankiness didn't last, even though I figured I could get away with it a while longer because of Alec's bad behavior at our wedding reception.

Alec had planned this trip down to the smallest detail, as he had everything we did together from the moment we met. Even so, I had to admit that the way things kicked off when we exited the terminal came as a total surprise—not only to me but also apparently to Alec.

Even he hadn't expected to be greeted by an imposing six-foot, four-inch man, who introduced himself as Gustav and informed us that his boss, Hans Voorhees, had instructed him to watch over us during our stay in Amsterdam. We'd already received plenty of outrageous gifts from Alec's family and associates, all of which he had taken in stride. But receiving a personal bodyguard as a present actually left my usually loquacious wheeler-dealer husband speechless.

"I haven't seen Hans for a year or more. He was so happy when I told him the news of our wedding and that we'd be coming to Amsterdam," he said, shaking his head as we entered the limo.

"Who is he, anyway?" I asked.

"A former shareholder in Transglobal Equities," Alec replied.

Gustav and the driver sat up front, and Alec popped the bottle of champagne that had been wrapped in a gold bow, another gift from Hans. I could tell as he poured the bubbly that he was trying to figure out what he had done to merit such service.

"I had no idea I'd made such an impression on him," he said finally, shaking his head again. "I'll have to give him a call when we get to the hotel."

The imposing InterContinental Hotel abutting the Amstel River took my breath away. *I hope I never become so jaded as to take such gems for granted.*

"It's magnificent, Alec," I said, my nose almost touching the window as we pulled up to the entrance.

"This beauty was built in the 1860s and it's the grande dame of Dutch hotels, but it's just the first stop, buttercup," Alec said with a promising grin. "Wait until you see the rest."

All I could think about at that moment was luxuriating in this stately place. It took several minutes after we entered our suite before I felt comfortable enough to sit on any of the

antique furniture, or even to touch any of the blue Delft porcelain vases and knickknacks that occupied every shelf and table.

After we'd both freshened up a bit, with Gustav in tow Alec
took me out on the town. We shopped in quaint boutiques, and
Gustav was there, handing our packages off to our driver. We ate
a late lunch at a trendy café on the river, and Gustav was there,
grabbing a bite at the small bar a few feet away. We got out of the
car to visit a landmark, and Gustav was there, rotating his head
a yard or two behind us. We leaned on a railing along one of the
canals just to chat, and Gustav leaned back against the railing a
stone's throw away.

Alec kissed me and took his time about it, and I felt Gustav's
eyes on our embrace.

I nodded toward our shadow when we leaned over the railing again. "He expecting a spy to show up?" I said with a giggle.
"Or an *assassin*?"

"There's a handful of characters I can think of who would
want to know what Transglobal is up to, and more than a couple
in Zurich who wouldn't shed a tear if I wasn't around. Come
on," Alec said, changing the subject, "let's go back to the hotel
and relax before dinner." He winked at me then and said too
loudly, "Gustav! The car, my good man . . ." I stifled a laugh and
shadowed our shadow on the way to the car.

When we returned to the hotel Alec had the concierge confirm our dinner reservation at La Rive, which was right in our
hotel and one of the finest restaurants in Amsterdam. Then,
after a quick tour of the hotel's grand ballroom, shops, and
restaurants, we wound up at the spa, which boasted a heated
pool, Turkish baths, a solarium, and aestheticians in addition
to the usual complement of exercise equipment, masseuses, and
personal trainers. I was jet-lagged and tourist-tired and totally
ready for some pampering, but I wasn't prepared for the shock I
received when I emerged from the ladies' dressing room. Breasts

were bobbing and swaying, and male genitals dangled all over the place, but by the time I emerged for my rubdown by a male masseur I was as nonchalant about the whole thing as he was.

Back in the suite Alec popped a favorite Billy Joel CD into the top-quality sound system before he jumped into the Jacuzzi, claiming he just couldn't wait to give it a spin. I was watered out and opted to sit at the Italian marble vanity and fuss with my hair to the booming sound of the Long Island crooner:

Darling, I don't know why I go to extremes
Too high or too low, there ain't no in-betweens

I couldn't think of any words that would be more appropriate for the Wall Street titan-whale flopping around in the artificial surf nearby.

The next day, Hans Voorhees, who insisted on being our Amsterdam host, took us on a boat ride through the canals. The cold air was invigorating, and Hans proved to be the perfect historical guide to the ancient houses we passed as well as to the farms and windmills on the outskirts of the city. On our way back, we pulled up to a picturesque house where one of Hans's colleagues and his wife treated us to a midday spread.

Then off we went to a wild soccer game, and while Alec wouldn't have minded being in the middle of the riotous crowd, I was more than happy to take it all in from Hans's private box. For the next two days, always accompanied by Gustav, we made forays around town during the day and indulged in five-star dining at night. Alec would sooner be dead than show up at home empty-handed, so he put his buying skills to good use and selected gifts for everyone in his family. I picked up a porcelain Buddha for Priti and a kissing couple for John, to bring him luck in finding a mate. The pinnacle for shopaholic Alec, however, came on our last day, when he bought us ski gear and shipped it home for future use on trips to Aspen and Tahoe and Switzerland. He never asked me if I even knew how to ski.

Finally our limo whisked us to the railway station, where we bid farewell to Gustav and waited on the platform for an early evening train to Paris, the next stop on our itinerary. Standing there wrapped in fur surrounded by our stacked belongings, I looked like an extra in *Doctor Zhivago*.

I felt like royalty, however, in our private compartment and at dinner in the dining car. My thoughts on the four-hour trip were filled with good memories of the last five days that I knew would last a lifetime.

It was almost bedtime when we arrived at the Hôtel Plaza Athénée, a grand art-nouveau marvel from 1889 and a landmark of discretion and style that was within eyesight of the River Seine, the Arc de Triomphe, and the Eiffel Tower. I didn't expect Alec to be quite so knowledgeable about the city's history and geography, but I couldn't have had a better guide than my husband to the many wonders of Paris.

That night, I fell asleep as soon as my head hit the pillow, in a bed the size of a small swimming pool. I awoke the next morning refreshed, to the tantalizing aroma of buttery croissants and rich black coffee that Alec had ordered from room service.

Henri Bouchard, our driver for the next two days, was a native Parisian who more than fulfilled his promise to take us to places we shouldn't miss, places that even Alec, seasoned traveler that he was, wouldn't know about. But Alec, of course, also found time to shop, and bought me so much beautiful lingerie at La Perla that, despite my growing accustomed to his extravagance, I was left speechless. But I repaid him in spades when we got back to the hotel that night after dinner.

After leading him to an antique love seat and giving him a playful twirl and push that sent him plopping onto its cushions, I leaned over and undid his shirt buttons down to his belt, then grabbed the end of his tie and pulled him toward my lips.

"Don't go anywhere," I breathed. I planted a slow, wet kiss on his lips as he placed his hands on my waist. "It's *Samantha's Secret* for you tonight, dear."

He started to tighten his grip and pull me toward him, but I backed away before he could lock down his prey and pranced toward the bedroom. "I'll be right back," I said over my shoulder, with enough syrup in my voice for a whole stack of pancakes.

Giggling and flushed with my newfound power, I reached for the bag holding my new lingerie and slipped into a stone-colored satin baby-doll top and matching panties. Then, throwing my head forward and back to toss my hair around my shoulders, I glanced in the full-length freestanding antique mirror in the corner and liked what I saw.

He'll be uncontrollable by the time I get to the black lace bra and matching garter belt.

On Sunday afternoon Henri drove us to the airport for the long flight home and insisted on giving us an early-nineteenth-century porcelain bell as a souvenir. I tucked it into my pocketbook and into my heart, where the other cherished memories of my honeymoon had been stored for safekeeping.

It was still late Sunday night in New York when we got home, and when I woke up the next morning the first thing I thought about was how different my life had become in so many ways, and seemingly overnight. I was married, and I was secure beyond my wildest dreams. I had a future straight ahead that was every bit as real as tying the knot had been. I'd been to Europe for the first time and had added reams of worldliness to the sophistication I'd already been exposed to during Alec's courtship. And Hans had given me a taste of how the super-rich, whose ranks Alec aspired to join, actually lived. I had also gotten a healthy serving of life's raw underbelly in Amsterdam, and a taste for the two sides of Paris—an urban center of sophistication by day and a sexy, mysterious City of Light after sundown.

To think I didn't even know the difference between lunch and brunch a few months ago, and look at me now!

When Alec showed the first signs of stirring, I pulled on my robe, tucked my toes into my slippers, and headed to the kitchen to brew the coffee and rustle up some breakfast for him. I'd gotten used to lingering over coffee and the paper with him every morning. But when he dashed into the kitchen ten minutes later, fully dressed in a snappy suit, I realized that he'd already reverted to his quick-moving, hard-driving Wall Street mode.

"That's sweet of you to be cooking eggs," he said, pecking me on the cheek. "Hate to dash off like this, but I'm already late for work."

"You gonna go into battle on an empty stomach?"

"I'll order something as soon as I get to my desk," he said. "We're closing the merger this week and there's no time to lose. As soon as I put it to bed, I'll be promoted to partner and the money will be beyond anything you could even imagine."

I'm standing in a gourmet kitchen with the Manhattan skyline out the window. How much more could we possibly need?

"I couldn't be happier than I am right now," I said.

"Stick around, Mrs. DeMarco," Alec said. "I ordered a second AmEx card in your name last week, and I'm sure you'll have fun using it."

I didn't know what to say. I'd never had any credit cards, much less an American Express card, in my name. He kissed me on the cheek as I stood in the kitchen, stunned.

"Good luck!" I called, switching off the burner as I heard the door close behind him. The apartment was silent. *What do I do now?* If Alec didn't have a housekeeper I would have tidied up the apartment and done the laundry. Instead I decided to call Priti and set up lunch. She sounded almost as excited as I was to get together, and showed zero concern about ducking out for what was sure to be a longer-than-allowed midday break. Practically as soon as we hung up, the phone rang. It was Filomena, calling to check in. The next call was from Sofia.

"How's the new Wall Street wife doing?" she asked.

"I'm settling in, thanks."

"You free for lunch today?"

"Gee, Sofe, no. I just made a date."

"Playing the diva already, going shopping and getting your hair and nails done?"

"Just catching up with Priti, is all."

"What about tomorrow? You free then?"

Oh, I'm free all right . . .

"That'll work," I said.

"Great. Lena and I have a darling place where we can bond. My treat." I knew that Lena was a friend of Sofia's who traveled in Alec's circle. She and her husband, Tom, had been at our wedding but I'd barely had a chance to say hello to them.

"That would be wonderful. I've been looking forward to getting to know Lena better," I said, not really sure whether I meant that or not. And I really didn't know Tom at all.

"Tom's a social misfit." Sofia chuckled. "I'm sure Lena will get around to telling you all about him. We just want to show you the ropes first."

"I'm looking forward to it," I said.

"I'll swing by and pick you up at noon." Sofia bubbled with enthusiasm.

I hung up, thinking, *What kind of ropes are these Wall Street wives going to show me? There is only one thing I know for certain: I'm not in Bensonhurst anymore.*

✧ ✧ ✧

A couple of hours later, I stepped out into a brisk fall day and hopped a cab to a tiny café just around the corner from Priti's office. The stars must have been aligned because she was walking up to the entrance just as I opened the cab door.

"Hey, P!" I called to her.

She pivoted, danced to the cab, and grabbed my hand as I paid the driver.

"Timing is everything," she said, quickly dragging me to a minuscule wrought-iron table by the window, which had become available right when we entered.

"I see what you mean," I said, laughing as we squeezed into our chairs.

The Financial District was teeming with life and Priti was more upbeat than ever.

"Gotta love the energy in this city, P," I mused, taking it all in.

"Gotta love the situation you find yourself in now, too."

"I'm not complaining." I grinned.

"I'd slap you if you did," Priti teased as a waitress came over. "Let's order right away so we can get to the juicy stuff."

"Have whatever you want, P. It's on me."

"*I* won't complain about that," she said, and we shared a laugh that reminded me of many we'd had before.

"It feels good to be with you again."

"I don't think we were alone for a single minute at the wedding." Priti sighed.

"Get in line—I feel like I didn't see anyone for more than a few minutes the whole night."

"Well, we're together now, and I've got some news of my own."

"Oh, wow, P. What is it? I should have known something was up when you seemed even more cheerful than usual."

"It is good news, Sam, at least for me, but I'm sorry to say I won't be around much longer." She was trying to look serious but couldn't keep the smile off her lips.

"About a month ago," she said, "my parents set up a meeting with a guy from a family in India they're close to. I didn't even mention it because you were so wrapped up in everything going on in your own life."

"I always have time for you, P. You know that."

Priti paused a moment and gazed out the window before turning back to me. "The whole truth, Sam, is that I just didn't think it was going to go anywhere."

"Like a couple of other arranged dates you had."

"Exactly. I don't have one foot in India and the other here, which is how my parents live."

"You're as New York as they come, P."

"Not anymore, Sam!" Priti grinned. "We hit it off big-time last week and I just know he's going to propose to me."

"Wow, P," I said softly. "It seems whatever I had is catching."

"I'm sick with joy, Sam."

I wonder how well I'll do without my security blanket.

"I suppose he'll take you back to India?"

"He's a brilliant oncologist in a famous practice, so I don't have a choice if I want a life with a guy who turns me on."

"Don't tell me you did him already!" I teased.

"Oh, no." Priti blushed. "He's much too proper for that."

"You talk a big game, but you aren't exactly a slut."

"Nope," she said, pursing her lips. "I'm a lady when it comes to that . . . Just like you."

"I'm gonna miss having you around, P."

"You never know," she said, pensive again. "The circle of life, right?"

"Our paths will cross again."

"If not in this life, maybe in the next. But I have to tell you, getting to know you and seeing how self-assured you've become these last few months gave me the confidence to just go with the flow."

One day I want The Blessed Bridge *to do that for millions.*

"Don't kid yourself, P. I've still got a roller coaster rumbling around in my stomach and my head."

"As I said, you're a lady." Priti smiled again, as I wondered how many more of those smiles I'd get to see. "And you're on your way to being a grande dame who can handle anything with class."

The budding grande dame stopped into Our Lady of Victory on the way home and said a prayer to the Blessed Mother, the grandest dame of all. As I left the church I knew I would be losing Priti soon, but my soul was at peace because I also knew I'd always have guidance whenever I needed it most in the uncharted waters ahead.

It was late afternoon when I got back to the apartment. When I got in I was startled by muffled sounds I couldn't place.

No way Alec is home already.

I took a hesitant step and the round, red-splotched face of Zosia, Alec's—and now my—elderly Polish maid, poked out from the bedroom doorway.

"Oh, it's you, Mrs. DeMarco," she said in her thick accent.

I still got a thrill out of hearing "DeMarco" at the end of my name. I reminded the precious old lady that she should call me Samantha and asked how she was.

"Veddy well, tenk you. I a little late today."

"That's okay, Zosia," I said. "I'll stay out of your way."

"I almost done. I can stay if you wan' and help prepare the food for Mr. Alec," Zosia said, bringing up a topic we'd discussed when I met her for the first time shortly before the wedding. She had pulled me aside and asked if I was comfortable in the kitchen, and I confided that, when it came to dinner, my skills were somewhat limited.

"That won't be necessary, Zosia," I said now. "But thank you, anyway."

"Anytime you wan', I cook with you."

"Yes, we'll do that," I said. "Soon." And I meant it, particularly since I'd had the pleasure of sampling some of her culinary delights.

"I'll be back on Tursday, Mrs. Samantha," the maid said as she got into her coat.

"Be well, Zosia," I said. *There but for the grace of God* . . .

I bought some time by straightening Alec's desk, which didn't really need straightening, and finally went into the kitchen, wondering what I could come up with to feed my husband. A fast search of the nearly-empty refrigerator, freezer, and cabinets had me second-guessing my decision to let Zosia leave and also made me realize that I needed to do a good amount of food shopping. Thank God for the endless number of places to order in from in New York.

In the end, I needn't have worried because Alec didn't come through the door until almost nine, and when he did he was surly and totally exhausted, on edge after a long day. I ordered a pizza, which I thought would be the surest bet.

Alec barely said a word as we ate, and I didn't bother him with questions about how his day had gone. Afterward he pushed away from the table and shuffled off to bed with his dutiful wife close behind. The good-night kiss he gave me wasn't one that will go down in the record books.

The next day was a repeat of the previous one, except that this time I knew better than to make any breakfast. Alec was up and out the door before I even got out of bed. Lying there and contemplating all the time I had before Sofia would arrive to pick me up for our lunch, I realized that this was a golden opportunity to get back to my writing and revise the manuscript for *The Blessed Bridge* before sending it out to publishers again.

I hadn't touched a word of it since meeting Alec, but I was still determined to get it published.

I'd moved most of my possessions into Alec's apartment before our first wedding, and my manuscript was already sitting on the closet shelf. With a renewed sense of purpose, I headed for Alec's desk and started to reread what I'd written so long ago. Pretty soon I'd lost all sense of time and was startled out of my intense concentration when the house phone rang. *Shit, it's already twelve o'clock. How did that happen?*

"Mrs. Falco is here," the doorman said when I picked up the phone in the kitchen.

"Tell her I'll be down in a couple of minutes," I said.

Ten minutes later, surely a showering and dressing record for me, I breezed into the lobby to find Sofia checking her nails and chatting with the doorman.

"Fashionably late," she teased. "I can see you've got potential."

"Sorry. It wasn't deliberate, Sofe."

"Well, no problem," she said, ushering me out the door and into the cab waiting at the curb. "I had the cab wait for me so we don't have to worry about finding another one. A little trick of mine—Lena and I have so many tips we could write a book!"

I thought of the stack of pages on Alec's desk, suddenly wishing I could be back upstairs working on my own book . . .

Less than twenty minutes later our driver pulled up in front of what even I knew to be one of the trendiest new ladies' lunch places, on Madison Avenue just above Sixtieth Street.

Lena, perfectly groomed, with her stick-straight blond hair impeccably highlighted, was already waiting for us at a prime table near the window, and as soon as we'd ordered, my hostesses got down to the business of beginning my "education."

"Now that the honeymoon is over, you're gonna need all the tricks of the trade you can learn to handle Alec," Sophia said to begin, turning to Lena for confirmation.

"We're a good team," I said.

"Sure you are," Lena agreed. "It's just that things tend to get crazy in his business."

My crazy guy can handle it.

"Not that there aren't benefits," Lena added, and both she and Sofia smiled like two cats who had each swallowed a canary.

"The money is as crazy as the work is," Sophia continued, "which is a good thing because there is so much shopping to do!"

"We'll get you started on that if you want," Lena said. "We know all the right places, and we can help you redecorate your apartment to make it yours, too. Right, Sofia?"

"Absolutely."

"Money isn't everything," I said, starting to get annoyed at their attitude.

Sofia and Lena looked at each other and their smiles were matched as perfectly as their shoes and gloves.

"Sometimes that's all there is," Lena said.

Maybe for you two.

"Of course," Sofia said, "kids are part of the equation. But we're talking about having a life of your own."

"I have that."

"Oh, right," Sofia said. "I remember—you're a writer. How's that going?"

Good timing. "Pretty well, thanks."

"You gonna be published soon?" Lena asked as the waiter brought our food.

"Working on it," I said with a thin smile. "Writing can be crazy, too. I'm not sure where it will end up."

"Well," Sofia said, picking up her fork, "what you *can* count on is Alec getting to the top of the heap. Victor says he rules a room like nobody he's seen, including the infamous Gordon Gekko."

We all chuckled.

"Tom's thrilled his wagon is hitched to your husband's," Lena continued.

"There are a few others, too," Sofia said. "But there are plenty in his firm who aren't in his corner."

I flashed back to Bermuda. "Victor mentioned the sharks that are about," I said.

"Exactly," Sofia said. "Like that Harvard graduate, Ted Ross."

"He seemed nice enough," I said.

"They all come off that way," Sofia scoffed. "But he's the one who came up with the idea of a merger and he's none too happy about sharing the glory with Alec."

"Not to mention the money," Lena said.

"According to Victor," Sofia added, "there probably would have been no deal, and no money, if Alec hadn't taken the bull by the horns."

"He spearheaded the whole thing," Lena said.

That's my guy.

"But at the end of the day," Sofia continued, "senior management doesn't care who brought them the money. And they don't hesitate to throw whoever it is under the bus if he stops being useful."

I looked her in the eye. "Alec's a big boy."

"With big appetites," Sofia said, and Lena laughed knowingly in agreement. "Clothes, cars, gadgets, games . . . whatever."

"Not to mention food and wine," Lena chimed in.

Sofia paused, as if considering whether or not to say what she had in mind. "The scuttlebutt is that Alec's big appetites include risky stock positions, and the honchos are worried about keeping him under control."

Join the club.

Lena rested a hand on my arm. "I think there's more than a little jealousy involved, too," she said. "Alec's so young, and so talented."

And I'm so proud of him!

"The higher-ups are always worried about an upstart tipping the scales," Sofia continued.

"And we all know Alec's a big tipper," I said, bringing another round of laughter to our table.

"Good for you, Samantha," Sofia said. "Gotta keep a sense of humor about all this stuff, or we'd lose our minds."

"And not be able to enjoy dessert," Lena said, signaling the waiter. "The crème brûlée is to die for, Sam."

"I'll have one of those fresh fruit medleys I saw on the cart."

"Sorry, but that's a little too healthy for me," Lena quipped.

"And speaking of healthy, how are you in the cooking department, Sam?" Sofia asked.

"I can do breakfast with my eyes closed, and I'm okay with salads, but I have to admit that dinner is a little daunting," I answered honestly.

"Well, we can give you a few pointers in that department, too," Sofia said, with Lena again nodding her agreement. "And we'll throw in a few for the bedroom." She chuckled. "No extra charge."

I'd had every intention of tidying Alec's desk when I got back home, but my eye caught the last notation I'd made before the house phone interrupted me. So I sat down to finish what I'd started and the next thing I knew, I heard the front door opening. A quick glance at my watch confirmed that I'd once more lost track of time. As I quickly gathered the pages now covering the desk, Alec stuck his head in the door. "What are you doing?" he asked, eyeing the manuscript clutched with my arms.

"Just getting some work done on my manuscript," I said, moving away from his high-backed leather chair.

"Oh, that," he said with a shrug, dropping his briefcase and sitting in the chair I'd just vacated. "Unfortunately, nothing's come of those calls I made." He spread his hands along the edge of the desktop and surveyed his work area.

"That's okay," I said, smiling to mask the lie, and the disappointment I felt.

"When do I get to read it?"

"Whenever you want," I assured him, trying not to show how excited I was by the offer. Reading it, I was sure, would prove to him that I was a serious writer, and it would also give him much greater insight into who I was and where I had come from.

"Just leave it on my night table," Alec said, still inspecting the desktop.

"How was your day?"

"Merger went to escrow," he said.

"That's good, right?"

"No, it's great," Alec said, still not looking at me.

"Sounds like we should celebrate, then," I said.

"We'll do that after I get my money."

"Whatever you say."

"Listen," he said, resting his massive arms on the desk, hands clasped, head down, pausing a moment, "I can't have you messing things up here."

I swallowed hard and pressed the manuscript to my chest. "I didn't disturb anything, Alec, and I have to work someplace."

"Can't you use the kitchen table?"

"I suppose so, but I'm also going to need the PC."

"So pick up a laptop tomorrow. You should have your own computer anyway." Alec reached for his mouse and started clicking away.

"Okay," I said softly. "What would you like for dinner?"

"Why not order up some Chinese," he said, scanning the latest stock quotes. "I'll eat here while I finish what I have to do."

I took a few steps on my way out and paused at the doorway. "You know," I said to my eyes-glued-to-the-monitor husband, "I could have a decorator come in to carve out a little workspace for me, if that's okay."

"Don't bother," he said, peering at the screen. "By the time one of those broads makes up her mind and draws up specs, we'll be long gone from here."

TEN

The first order of business over the next few days was entering the edits and notations I'd made on my novel into the electronic file *on my brand-new laptop*—the first purchase I'd made with my brand-new AmEx card. It sounds silly but I felt like such a grown-up handing over my card. (It was not lost on me, however, that I was more like a spoiled child since I wasn't the one footing the bill.) I had to admit, though, I did feel an unexpected rush as I walked out of the store. I immediately thought of Sofia's and Lena's cavalier attitude toward spending their husbands' money. *Sometimes that's all there is.* They made it sound like revenge. I dismissed the thought as quickly as it came and chalked my exhilaration up to excitement—the laptop was just the first step toward my dream of getting *The Blessed Bridge* published.

When I was done revising the manuscript, I printed a copy on the printer I'd bought to go with my laptop and left it on Alec's night table. I had butterflies in my stomach just thinking about what he'd have to say once he had read it. With that mission accomplished, I set about becoming the best wife any Wall Street titan could have. Although I certainly intended to enjoy every material comfort every step of the way, I was also determined to stay true to myself—that girl from Brooklyn—and not get swallowed up by the shallowness I saw all around me. So with my priorities in check, I jumped with both feet into a life where money would never be an object and I would never again have to stand in line anywhere. I had gone from nothing to instant gratification in a few short months, and now it seemed as if Alec had given me the keys to the city. It felt surreal and real at once, and I was grateful.

Although I did my fair share of running up the AmEx bill, I wasn't in Sofia's and Lena's league, and never would be. So while I indulged in Dolce & Gabbana, Versace, and Armani, I didn't overindulge (at least by Wall Street standards), and I didn't shop out of spite. I mean, the occasional Hermès Birkin was always a huge purchase, but anyone who had any money had one. I didn't think owning four was a big deal, but hey, who was counting.

Over the weeks that followed Alec worked nonstop and was distracted much of the time when we were together. I didn't begrudge him his dream—I knew all about dreaming myself—and vowed to help him in any way I could. But staying upbeat was difficult, especially when the titan-to-be to whom I was married had to dash off to one far-flung city or another to handle a "sensitive negotiation." At the same time, Priti was about to leave for India to get married. Inevitably, I grew closer to Sofia and Lena, who introduced me to other women in the Wall Street wives club, and they were soon inviting me to join some of their charities and causes.

Sometimes self-doubt reared its ugly head and I questioned whether I was worthy of my own good fortune, but I tried to remain grateful for what I'd been given, which included my dear father-in-law, Giovanni, who shared my faith in God and also seemed to have faith in me. Giovanni made me feel like I belonged in the DeMarco clan, even on days when I felt completely out of my league with them.

At our family Thanksgiving dinner at the DeMarcos'

Brooklyn home, I ticked off my many blessings in my mind, but in the midst of all the goodhearted chitchat, I was also aware that no one really cared about the one thing that meant the most to me—my writing. All the women wanted to talk about was an upcoming charity luncheon or shopping expedition or a planned vacation trip, and the men, drunk on football along with an array of wines and vintage ports, weren't of any use as company.

It's funny, but even though the women in my new family ran in a more affluent crowd, they still seemed so Brooklyn to me. They were as consumed with shopping and lunching and spas and salons as my friends from the old neighborhood were. Except with better highlights. Still, as much as they tried to make me feel like I belonged, I wasn't any more like them than I was the gum-snapping disco queen and wannabe moll that Tony had wanted in a girlfriend. I did my best to hold my own with them and appreciated being part of a loving family for the first time in my life. Our lunches and other get-togethers were pleasant enough, and, as I figured, having finally made it across that coveted Bridge, I intended to stay and make the best of it.

I didn't begrudge the women the perks that went along with their marriages—Lord knows I enjoyed those myself—or the men the opportunity to relax and enjoy the fruits of their hard work. But I began to feel that there was more to life than this. I wanted to know how these women defined themselves apart from their husbands' power and the multimillion-dollar bonuses they provided. And I wished that they could be more interested in me, Samantha Bonti, apart from seeing me simply as Alec's wife. But I held my tongue.

Of course, I wanted to help Alec fulfill his dream, but I too had a dream and it seemed to be getting lost along the way. Trying to maintain my sense of self was growing more difficult every day as my husband's huge presence took precedence over everything else in our lives. I could begin to feel Samantha

Bonti getting swallowed up by Mrs. DeMarco—and I missed the old Sam.

I dropped a hint about how lonely I felt to Alec one night as we were getting ready for bed, and he took me in his arms and promised that work would let up soon. He told me that all of these changes would just take some getting used to. And then, ever the problem solver, he suggested we get a dog as a companion for me when he was away. I agreed that I would love to have a little dog, but, of course, in Alec's world of huge appetites a huge dog was the only way to go.

Not one to put off what could be done immediately, Alec arranged for us to pick out our new pet the very next weekend. We drove out to the east end of Long Island and, after winding our way through the country, found our way to a farm, where the owners proudly displayed their litter of eight Bullmastiff puppies. We picked a big, strapping pup, named him Hercules, and took him home that day.

The first few months of my new life as Mrs. DeMarco saw the escalation of Alec's wheeling and dealing. He made no effort to conceal how crazed he was, and he made no apologies for being that way. He saw stocks as a game and, as with any game in which he found himself, he played to win. Period.

He was like a silverback in a pen with other angry gorillas, all competing for the same prize. In this case it was selling the stock at the highest price. Sell-side feared him, buy-side embraced him, and when a two-dollar broker wasn't looking he was there to take a bite. He was the true master.

Each day at Transglobal Equities brought a new contest for Alec's magnetism. He continued to attract colleagues into his orbit who were worthy of being on his team. His main competition at Transglobal Equities was Ted Ross, who was vying for the best players in the company to join his own. Both men were driven, and determined to win over the senior partners at Trans-global. Both also had their eyes on the even bigger prize—being in Grigor Malchek's orbit. After all, Alec said, if you're going to run things you might as well run with the man who ran the entire stock exchange. In fact, he was so determined to get close to Malchek that he sometimes let someone else higher up take credit for his ideas just to increase his popularity and keep his name out there in the ether. It made no sense to me, but Alec assured me that he knew what he was doing when it came to pleasing Malchek. Keeping a low profile—that's what appealed to Malchek.

Ted Ross was short and stocky and showing early signs of going bald. While his brother Robert, the senator, went on to New York Law School after college graduation, Ted had followed their father into the financial world, where his salesman's energy and bravado allowed him to shine. Nowhere near the imposing physical specimen Alec was, he nonetheless didn't shrink from throwing his professional weight around and leaving others in his wake. He didn't care at all that, behind his back, people whispered about his having a Napoleon complex that manifested itself not only in the office but also at home, where he was working on his seventh child. God knows these types needed more offspring.

The end of every day brought a comparison of their trading activity and the awarding of an unofficial, virtual trophy that the winner got to keep only until the market opened again the next morning—unless one of them had got the jump on foreign exchange activity the night before. Alec preened most when he strolled into the office with that day's trophy already in hand. He'd bested Ted on the merger deal, and he never tired of throwing a triumph in the face of the guy who had tried so hard to keep him down.

When he came home now, he was so exhausted that most

evenings he fell into bed with no more than a cursory "How was your day?" tossed my way. But on those rare occasions when he was in the mood for conversation, we didn't talk about much of anything other than business. He just assumed that I was fitting in and enjoying the life he had given me as much as he enjoyed his own, right up to his nightcap in bed of Johnnie Walker Blue, green chartreuse, or a joint—or some combination thereof.

I *was* enjoying myself, but I ate dinner alone, save for Hercules, and far too often for my liking. And I didn't count the formal client dinners Alec dragged me to as quality time with my husband. Our life together was changing rapidly, as his all-consuming climb up the ladder of success seemed to demand more and more of his time. Clearly our courting days were over, but I understood that now more than ever, he needed my support to reach his goal. So I didn't complain, and I listened attentively to anything Alec cared to share, even on those occasions when he came home loaded and shared stories about the seedier side of Wall Street that left me tossing and turning all night. As his dutiful wife, I told myself that, right now, his needs came first.

Over time, it became abundantly clear that the sexual escapades to which he'd confessed before we married were not a thing of the past. Alec had his secretary handle all the arrangements for "business entertainment," but I overheard more than I wanted to about five-hundred-dollar-per-champagne-bottle strip clubs or all-out penthouse romps. Alec's early adulthood knowledge of S&M came in handy, too, as it appeared that a lot of his partners at Transglobal had kinky fantasies involving leather and latex that could go all night with the right amount of blow and pills. He never had less than ten thousand dollars cash on him, and he salivated about the power he wielded in sexual arenas as much as Tony had about a score or kickback opportunity. Memories of my past flooded back and demanded comparison to my present. My eyes always widened as Alec's pillow talk got around to highlights in which he seemed to take pleasure in recounting these stories from "business" trips that included porn stars flown in on private jets at a cost of twenty thousand dollars a day.

Meanwhile, the shortest trip my husband had taken was for three days in Aspen, Colorado, so it wasn't hard to do the math. It didn't matter to Alec whether the powerful titans in his orbit were insecure about the size of their dicks or were willing to pay any amount of money or take it from the big companies they worked for. A CEO could do that and hide it well and, for a woman to give them attention their wives did not, it was sure as hell worth it to them. Alec was a provider, and he would provide for himself and his family by providing something of value to somebody else.

One of Alec's favorite stories was about when Mitch, one of his bosses, who had married a former model and had six kids with her, came to him and said he couldn't take the pedestrian sex anymore and needed to get laid. So Alec secured the services of Heather Frankel, a porn star with more than a hundred movies under her belt. Then he segued from that tale to one about a vice president at the firm who was a small-dicked Irish Catholic who could hardly ever get it up, and when he did it was pitiful. The only way he could fuck his wife was in the shower because he needed water on his back to have an orgasm.

And I needed a chalice of wine after hearing about an even seedier side of my husband's pimping—the enforcement side. When one of the hookers on one of these trips charged a Rolex on his AmEx card, Alec tore it off her wrist and threw her out. I had barely digested that borderline-violent scene, however, when my on-his-way-to-being-a-titan husband trumped it with one that could have ended up with physical harm to *him*.

It seems that an hour into Heather Frankel's "date" with Mitch, she was no longer satisfied with the twenty thousand she'd been paid, and came out of the bedroom demanding more money from Alec, who was waiting in the living room of the suite he had booked for the occasion. Fat chance. These were ruthless bitches who only wanted money and this one had already gotten more than she was worth.

I knew what Alec would say before he told me there was no way he would let her set him up like that. When he refused, Heather dug her cell phone out of her purse and stormed back to the bedroom. Ten minutes later a three-hundred-pound black man with a shaved head showed up at the door to the suite with a gun and demanded twenty-five thousand in cash. Alec, of course, told the "gentleman" that wasn't possible, whereupon the man threatened to expose what he knew about Mitch and his colleagues to their wives and the media.

Alec-the-peacemaker smoked a joint and downed a Quaalude with the guy, and then gave him two grand to go away. To preserve my sanity, I got extremely good at tuning out while listening in. I didn't want to have to imagine what two of his bosses did with the three women they paid for or who did what to whom. The only thing that kept my antenna up was the possibility that Alec had been an active participant in any of the lechery he orchestrated. I knew that the women he paid for were only interested in his money, and so far he hadn't exhibited any of the telltale signs that he was getting sex elsewhere, but he was, after all, a man, and a powerful one at that.

When I raised this possibility with him one night, Alec swore up and down that he would never be unfaithful to me. But most important, he wouldn't ever want to lose the upper hand by showing any interest in sampling their wares. He insisted that picking up the checks and pleasing others were simply the means to get where he wanted to go. Knowing Alec, that made sense to me. He got off on knowing the girls wanted him, but giving in would be giving them too much power. He always wanted to be in control, even at the cost of denying his own pleasure. Then he explained to me that he had fallen in love with me because I was the first woman he'd actually wanted to have intercourse with in a long time. But that made no sense to me at all, because we'd been married for almost a year and you could practically count on the fingers of both hands the number of times my maniacally focused husband and I made love since returning from our honeymoon.

Alec's efforts on the merger paid off shortly before Thanksgiving, to the tune of several million dollars. Unreal as that amount of money seemed to me, I wondered if it was worth the constant lack of quality time for Alec and me, or the painful hemorrhoid attacks his fast living had brought on. I was starting to worry about his getting sick.

Much as I'd tried to warn him about his prodigious eating habits, my words fell on deaf ears and he just kept on as usual. Nor did he listen to my gentle suggestions that he spend more quality time with Hercules. My exhausted dragon-slayer husband didn't really want to be bothered with the family dog, even on weekends, and he made it clear that he would prefer Hercules to be in his cage when he got home. I felt bad for the dog, but tried my best to comply. It wasn't always easy, though, because I was never sure when he would walk through the door, and I wanted to give Hercules as much love and freedom as I could before consigning him to his cage for the night.

Week after week, Alec went on taking big stock positions and satisfying big appetites, and I soldiered on lunching and shopping and hitting the beauty salons. He was particularly proud that one of the bonuses of the score he'd made was being able to grab three hungry junior associates for his team. Alec let them run the smaller deals, which not only kept him stocked with plenty of cash but also gave him time that could be put to better use. He had Grigor Malchek on his fishing line and fully intended to land him.

The reeling in was to take place in San Francisco, and I was especially excited because Giovanni and I were both going to join him. Giovanni's firm had a minor interest in the deal, and the plan was that Alec would go out ahead (in a private jet, of course) to do some hunting and fishing. It seemed that all the Wall Street big shots enjoyed killing animals just as the guys in the mafia enjoyed killing people. Giovanni and I would join him a couple of days later.

Since the merger had gone through, the next step was to see where all the players found their seats once the music stopped. Some pretty powerful men were angling to run things, and Alec had lines into all of them. He fully intended to help Malchek get what he wanted, which was to have his handpicked guy become CEO of the newly merged firm. But that wasn't all. Alec also fully intended to climb over everyone else and become Malchek's right-hand man in the near future.

I was looking forward to the trip because it would give me some time along with Giovanni. We shared a limo to JFK, and when we were settled into our wide leather first-class seats for the long flight to San Francisco, he warmed my heart by saying just what I'd been thinking.

"Alec and I have a lot of business going on where we're headed," he said as we buckled up, "but what really excites me is that I get to travel with you, Sam."

"You took the words right out of my mouth . . . Dad," I said.

We each accepted a glass of champagne from the flight attendant, and I could see where Alec's joie de vivre originated when Giovanni continued.

"I can't wait until I take you to the Napa vineyard we took a large position in," he said. "Putting a new management team together at the merged firm is big, especially for my son. But being around grapes is my soul."

I know all about feeding the soul. "Connects you to your heritage, I suppose."

"Exactly," Giovanni said.

"You were born in Italy, right?"

"Came here as a young boy," he said, and then pursed his lips. "With my brother."

"You two didn't get along?"

"We were family, but my brother and I always had that Italian macho competition thing going."

"Hmmm," I said. "Sort of like Alec and Franco, I guess."

"Right again, my smart new daughter."

"What about your mom?"

"Passed away from smallpox when I was just a baby."

I rested a hand on his. "That must have been pretty rough."

"We all have our crosses to bear, child," Giovanni said softly. *I know all about that, too.*

"What did your dad do to feed his family?" I asked.

Giovanni brightened. "He boxed. Got pretty good at it, too. My brother and I called a truce to our private punching matches on the nights we got to go watch him."

"I can see where the DeMarco sports heritage began," I said, laughing.

"I love that my boys are so into the Yankees," Giovanni said, "but I could do with less of the competition they've got going with professions and status."

"Who gets where and who owns what."

Giovanni smiled. "Right you are yet again. My sons are always jockeying for position in their respective roles of older brother and young upstart. Filomena and I are proud of them both no matter how high they climb, and all we really care about is for them being happy."

Spoken like a true parent. "That's how I want my child to be," I said, surprising myself.

Giovanni beamed and I saw a hint of Alec's wide grin. "You trying to tell me something, Sammy?" he asked. *Only Mom and Grandma ever called me that.* "Making an announcement?"

"N-o-o, not at all." I blushed.

Giovanni looked crestfallen but recovered quickly. "All in good time . . ."

Alec, fresh from a duck and goose hunting expedition in Montana, was waiting for us in the lobby bar at the San Francisco Luxe Regent Hotel. Still wearing his canvas Beretta pants and vest, and his calf-high boots, he had a blast for ten minutes impressing us with his skill at bringing down winged creatures.

Alec-the-tour-guide then went off on how plush the Luxe Regent hotels were, and added that he would love to own one of their apartments. I didn't ask what the tab for that would be. Since most of the sums Alec threw around were basically incomprehensible to me, I just decided to go with the flow, counting my blessings along the way. But that didn't stop me from worrying about money and wishing that we were saving some of it. Having grown up with nothing, I'd never stop fearing the loss of what I had gained.

At the end of three days of mixed business and pleasure, Malchek's man was confirmed as the new CEO of the merged specialty trading company, just as Alec had predicted. Ten of the major brokers and power players celebrated that night with a sumptuous dinner in a private room at the Drake Hotel. Only a couple of the men had brought their wives on the trip, but I would have felt just as alone if every one of them had, because Giovanni, who wasn't in the inner circle, hadn't been included, and Alec was far too preoccupied keeping things smooth as silk to keep close company with me. I smiled and kept silent as usual, and set my heart on the three-day side trip to Napa Valley that was to begin the next morning.

Alec rented a black Mercedes convertible, and the three DeMarcos were all in high spirits as we headed north for the four-hour ride. Alec insisted on driving with the top down even though the early December air was chilly. Giovanni and I bundled ourselves against the wind.

We stayed at Auberge du Soleil, a spa resort, mostly made up of cedar and glass. Our private chalet was decorated in a style that merged quaint and cozy with New Age. The place was famous for fostering renewal in mind and body as well as in relationships, and the bright yellow and hot pink throw pillows that were scattered all around were full of positive energy. Alec must have caught some of it, because he was ebullient on the couple of private wine tastings we went to, and he couldn't have been more solicitous of me—both in and out of bed.

Napa Valley renewed my hope for a better future with Alec now that he seemed closer to his goal, the top of the Wall Street ladder. Sadly, however, what hope I had was pretty much dashed when he reverted to Wall Street mode almost as soon as our plane touched down at JFK. Somewhat deflated, I nevertheless did what I could to get into the holiday spirit. One of the best days I had was when Zosia showed up at the apartment with an armful of groceries. She would have dragged me by an ear into the kitchen if I hadn't agreed to assist her in baking honey cakes and rum *babka* and whipping up a hearty veal stew. It felt good to relax and laugh as we cooked, and I couldn't wait to present my husband with my first home-cooked meal.

As Zosia was leaving, I dragged her into Alec's study and grabbed a bottle of red wine from the hundred or so in racks along one wall. "I want you and your husband to enjoy this, Zosia," I said, forcing her to accept it over strenuous objections.

Alec's mood was pretty flat when he arrived home, but he

perked up considerably at the prospect of some home cooking. He immediately went over to the pot and pulled out a healthy chunk of veal with his fingers. "Wow, this is good," he remarked with more enthusiasm than I'd heard from him in a long time. Then, after taking off his jacket and loosening his tie, he headed into the study to pick out a wine to go with our dinner. Two minutes later, however, he was back in the dining room with a huge frown furrowing his brow.

"The '62 Rothschild isn't where I left it," he said. "Can you shed some light on the subject?"

Uh-oh. "I think I gave it to Zosia by mistake, Alec," I said. "I wanted to thank her for cooking with me. I didn't realize it was special. All those bottles look alike to me."

"Of all the fucking wines there, you really picked a doozy, Sam," Alec said, seething. "That was a five-thousand-dollar bottle of some of the best grapes ever grown on this planet."

I thought steam was going to come out of his ears and I had no one to stick up for me. *I'm alone in this, too.* "I'm sorry, Alec," I said. "I didn't know. I thought it was just a bottle of wine. Do you want me to try to get it back?" I asked, and knew instantly that there was no way Alec would allow me to do that.

"You must be out of your mind," he said, turning away.

I guess it wouldn't be a good idea to mention that he throws around five-thousand-dollar wads like most people do singles.

"Listen, Sam," Alec continued. "Just do me a favor and ask me the next time you want to give away anything of mine—especially when it's something you don't know anything about."

Although I wasn't in the mood to go anywhere the next day, I had to get ready for a luncheon. Our fight last night had me rattled, as did my realization that I'd now missed my period two months in a row. At least it was a benefit sponsored by Too Many at Risk, a charity. If anyone could relate to disadvantaged children it was Samantha Bonti. But I couldn't get Alec's outburst out of my mind, even as I listened to the speeches, ate my poached salmon, and wrote out a check for a thousand dollars, and it didn't help that he came home that night, just after eight, in a totally foul mood.

After giving me a perfunctory kiss, he tore off his jacket and tie and stomped into his study, spraying the air with homophobic slurs about his various rivals. For the next half hour I could hear bangs and muffled grunts through the closed door. Finally, from my position curled up in the corner of the sofa, I heard him curse one last time and slam down the phone several times.

Unbelievably, when he emerged, his scowl had been replaced by a boyish grin.

"I was asked to join the board of the Too Many at Risk foundation," I ventured, taking advantage of this miraculous transformation.

"That's great," Alec deadpanned. "It'll give you something to do. So what's for dinner?"

I was nowhere near ready to fly solo at the stove. "I picked up sushi on the way home."

"You should take some cooking lessons from my mother," Alec said. "Or at least call her and ask for some of her recipes."

I served what I had on hand and we ate mechanically. Alec was civil but still distracted during dinner, so I let my mind wander. I understood that it wasn't easy to become a self-made millionaire, let alone a billionaire, and I was all for striving and achievement, but not at the price of disturbing the peace—the peace of one's soul or the peace of a relationship with a soul mate. I worried that Alec's job was getting to him, and I prayed that his volatility was a normal part of what he was going through and that it would dissipate when he had achieved what he wanted.

We shuffled off to bed after dinner and watched some TV until Alec said he had just thought of something and picked up the phone on his bedside table to call Victor. That call ended better than the last one in the study had, since Alec slammed the phone down only twice, creating enough breeze to ruffle the top page of my manuscript, which, luckily, was held together with a sturdy rubber band.

"I can put that away until you have more time, Alec," I said softly.

"No, don't do that," he said, slumping into his pillows. "I'm sorry, Sam. I've just been too exhausted after what I've been going through at work."

"There might be something else coming along for you to devote some energy to," I said, opening the drawer of my night table and taking out the narrow plastic stick I'd placed there a few hours before.

"What the hell is that?" Alec asked, looking confused.

"It's a home pregnancy test," I said, getting his immediate attention. "I'm pregnant, Alec," I went on, searching his eyes with all the hope I could muster.

ELEVEN

"Oh my God, Sam, that's great!" he exclaimed with genuine pleasure, and I was never so happy to see that jumbo grin. "I have you, I have the best job in the world, and now I have a baby!" It seemed that he couldn't get the words out fast enough, which was all right with me since I was totally speechless. "I don't want anything to change when you have this baby. We'll still travel and enjoy life. Our child will become part of our world, not the other way around."

"I'm happy that you're happy, Alec."

"You better believe it. I can't wait to start a family in that new apartment I've been eyeing."

Words didn't fail me then. "You want us to move? Is that really necessary?" I asked, knowing the answer before the words had left my lips.

"This place won't do," Alec said, his boyish face filled with wonder. "Not for where I'm going. Moving up in address goes hand in hand with moving up the financial ladder, Sam."

In the weeks that followed Alec seemed beyond happy, vowing that we'd have the best ob-gyn in the city and the best help money could buy. Christmas at Alec's parents' house was a joyous occasion, with many blessings and extravagant baby gifts from Giovanni and Filomena, and the following week, as we ushered in the New Year at the Rainbow Room, high above Manhattan, it seemed to me that the entire world was at my feet.

Alec greeted the New Year by immersing himself in his work, and I immersed myself in my pregnancy. I was constantly aware of being responsible for everything that would happen to my child in the foreseeable future. I became more vigilant than ever about healthy eating and did everything in my power to make sure that peace reigned in the DeMarco household. I listened politely to the advice of friends and family but secretly knew that my parenting plan meant doing everything exactly opposite to the way my mother had handled it.

Meanwhile, I vowed to continue doing whatever I could to help my husband achieve his goals. If I wanted my home to be happy and harmonious when this baby arrived, there would be no complaints from me about anything related to my pregnancy or to his preoccupation with his work. Most of all, there would be no complaints about the unread manuscript on his night-stand. In fact, after seeing it lying there for another couple of months, I quietly put it back on the closet shelf. Playing dutiful wife to Alec had left me with no time to write or revise, anyway.

Alec was still micromanaging our life together, but I told myself that he was doing it to protect me, not to put me down, as my mother had. Although he could certainly be heavy-handed, even dictatorial at times, I didn't resent his control. I liked my life, I believed his intentions were good, and I knew he had a concrete and laudable goal. So what if he preferred going out to cuddling on the couch; so what if he always had something to say about the styles and colors of my clothing? After all, he did have impeccable taste, and he had the right to showcase his wife the way he wanted.

I kept telling myself that I was one lucky girl who was blessed beyond measure, and those blessings seemed to grow month by month. When I hit my second trimester, the flirting that had come my way courtesy of some of Alec's associates totally stopped. It was a pleasure not to have to deal with their veiled sexual innuendos, but Alec might well have missed the attention his competitors gave me as additional proof of the winner he was.

Winning for Alec also meant the ability to pick up and leave for some exotic location pretty much whenever he wanted, and when he suggested a winter getaway just for the two of us at the Ocean Club on Paradise Island in the Bahamas, I agreed without a moment's hesitation. Although we were both excited about our impending parenthood, our life was still extremely stressful, given Alec's ever-escalating financial battles and my ever-expanding body. It was a blessing to be able to leave New York in early February for a few days in the tropical sun and sand.

Our private villa was set among luxurious gardens inspired by the grandeur of Versailles. Alone on our lanai after checking in, Alec and I soaked up the ocean breezes perfumed with hibiscus and bougainvillea, getting a full dose of stress-relieving tranquility to kick things off.

Of course, Alec also kicked things off with the local drink, called a Bahama Mama, made up of coffee liqueur and two kinds of rum, while I just had coconut and pineapple juice with a hint of grenadine.

Over drinks and our first serving of conch fritters, we talked about family, and I felt blessed that Alec didn't bring up business even once. The evening gave me hope that once the baby was born, Alec would slow down, not be so career-driven, and devote more of his time to his family. I knew that he was looking forward to being a father; I just couldn't be certain how he would interpret the role.

By the time our last full day in the islands dawned, we were both in a Zen state. I could have pitched a thatched hut somewhere close to the beach and stayed forever. I even thought for a brief moment that I could convince my husband to stay with me, but, serene as he was in our surroundings, he was already being drawn back into the world we would be returning to the next day. On the lanai at sunset that night, he lit one of the joints he'd gotten from a solicitous bellhop and waxed expansive about his work.

"I'm responsible for the supply-and-demand formula for pricing stocks," Alec said. "What I'm doing now, Sam, will lock up becoming a partner."

He had my full attention, although I had no idea what he was talking about, which did not go unnoticed by my joint-smoking husband.

"I won't burden you with the details, Sam," he said, pausing to take another drag, "but Malchek has some very rich friends, guys like Miles Blackmon, who want to manipulate buys of their company stocks." I didn't know a lot, but I knew Blackmon owned one of the largest media companies in the world. "That's our specialty. What I'm doing may fall into a gray area, but everyone everywhere does it, and no one raises a stink."

It's pimping of a different stripe. "Are you in any danger of being carted off in handcuffs, Alec?" I asked.

"You can't say no to Miles Blackmon, Sam, and you can't say no to Malchek. Besides, if they lock *me* up, he'll be going before me."

Just like the hookers would be ahead of him on the chain gang.

Alec took another drag from the joint, held his breath for a moment, and watched the exhaled smoke waft into the island air. "I'll admit it gets pretty hairy at times, especially when we have to deal with a kingpin who threatens to take his company to NASDAQ, Malchek's competitor, like Peter Vici did."

I gasped softly. *Maybe I know more than I want to know.* "He's

that cell phone company guy who got pinched for insider trading, right?"

"Yup."

"And that can't happen to you?"

"Vici got caught because his greed crossed the line."

That didn't make me feel any better, as Alec's prodigious
appetites flashed through my mind.

"I'm not really worried, Sam," he continued. "Transglobal is
too smart for that, and nobody is going to go to Yale."

"Yale?"

"Code for jail," Alec said with a chuckle.

A shiver ran up my spine. *The Brooklyn Boys always said they
were so cool they could get by in Yale or in jail.*

"You don't have to worry, either, Sam," Alec continued. "We
follow SEC rules to the letter and buy stock at the going rate,
fair and square. That props up its value for guys like Blackmon,
but who cares? It's strictly legit, even if it costs us a bundle
sometimes."

"I didn't think you were in business to lose money."

"We're not. We treat it as an investment."

"In what?"

"Going public."

"Selling your own stock?"

"Right again, buttercup. That's the real game being played,"
Alec, titan husband, said with a self-satisfied grin.

"And you play to win."

"My team won't come in second, especially to Ted's boys.
He's helping Blackmon, which has nothing to do with me, but
we're both on the floor of the exchange, so we're both working
for Malchek in the end. I won't be coming out with the short
end of the stick going up against that Italian."

"I always forget they changed their name from Rossi way
back," I said.

"I never do," Alec said. "And I always bust Ted's balls about it."

We spent the next day soaking up the sun, until it was time to get ready for our evening flight. Relaxed and content as I was, I still wasn't ready to get back to reality, back to the Wall Street world that was still so foreign to me.

As the weeks passed, I now had a definite bump. Even though I wasn't bloated or carrying any extra pounds, none of it seemed to matter to Alec, who was growing less and less interested in having sex with me. According to Sofia and Lena, that wasn't unusual, so I followed his lead and settled for a contented cuddle, telling myself that as an Italian Catholic expectant father he believed in keeping hands off when it came to the holy goings-on in my body.

I nurtured myself by mastering the culinary tips my girlfriends sent my way: I'd feed Alec food I'd ordered in and reheated to perfection in the microwave on only the finest china. And I fed my soul by joining the board of the foundation for at-risk children and using my newfound clout to do some good in the world.

Hercules, however, wasn't adapting as well as I was. He started urinating a lot in his crate, probably in defiance of his captivity, and when I allowed him to roam the apartment when Alec wasn't home I was terrified that he would pee on the rug. Alec rescued me by hiring a dog walker to take him out for four hours a day, which also went a long way toward assuaging my guilt about leaving Hercules alone so much.

By the time I was in my sixth month it was harder for me to keep up with Alec's hectic entertainment schedule, but I put on a cheery face when he mentioned that a big-shot client had invited us to a Knicks game at Madison Square Garden in mid-April.

"Emmanuel and his brothers, Spiro and Sal, ran an oil

tanker business along with their father and uncles. The Greeks are very tight that way. They like family businesses and don't let outsiders in much," Alec said. "I'm helping him on some futures contracts, and Stavros Shipping is going to take a nice position in Transglobal."

"Sounds like more teamwork." I smiled.

"Game on," my husband-competitor said.

Of course, whether it was Wall Street money or oil money, we wouldn't be taking in the game with the peons in the nose-bleed section. For us it was the private box owned by Stavros Shipping. I wasn't surprised by the royal treatment, although I was somewhat taken aback by the youngest brother, Spiro, who appeared to be about my age. Instead of the expensively trimmed hair and conservative business suit I'd grown accustomed to seeing on all Alec's clients, Spiro was wearing jeans and a black silk jacket over an open-necked white silk shirt. He was also sporting a full beard and wore his gleaming chestnut hair in a ponytail.

"So pleased to finally meet the woman who made Alec here legit." Emmanuel smiled with one arm draped across Alec's shoulders as we were introduced. "Why don't the two of you take a seat," he went on, nodding toward my bump and waving toward one of the suite's leather couches. "Just let me know what you want and I'll have it brought over to you."

"Thank you for the hospitality," I said.

"Don't mention it—Alec is a tremendous asset to our firm," he replied, echoing Hans Voorhees. "Nothing is too good for him and his family."

Hors d'oeuvres were served and everyone in the small crowd save yours truly had champagne and cocktails as we watched the shoot-around on the hardwood floor below. I thought the view we had was spectacular, but Alec pointed out that the only way to see a basketball game was from the folding chairs at courtside—which is exactly where he and Emmanuel headed as the game was about to tip off.

By the time June rolled around, all I was looking forward to was having my baby. I couldn't wait to get rid of those extra twenty-plus pounds and to get started on my ever-growing mental list of what I would do with and for my child. I wasn't in the mood to go anywhere, and I begged off both daytime outings with Sofia and Lena and every evening event that I could. And it took all the self-discipline I had to make it through the family gatherings with a pleasant expression on my face.

What wasn't hard to take was Alec's suggestion of another extended weekend getaway, this time to the Ram's Head Inn on Shelter Island, off the eastern end of Long Island. He said it would be an ideal place to start the summer, and a great way to rest up before the blessed event scheduled to take place in a few more weeks. Enraptured with helicopters, he added that taking the 120-mile trip in one would be the perfect way to go.

I didn't put up any resistance to that suggestion, either.

The sun and salt air worked their magic as soon as we touched down, and the three dozen red roses awaiting me in our suite, along with the scores of red rose petals on our bedspread, had me falling in love with my husband all over again.

I just know the big lug is a pussycat at heart.

I was touched by Alec's romantic gesture, and didn't even mind that I wasn't going to have him all to myself on this trip. Truthfully, I wasn't looking or feeling very sexy and was happy to have both Sofia and Victor and Lena and Tom, as well as a few other couples, at the so-called Transglobal mini-conference to fill some time and take up the slack when I dragged myself back to our suite while the rest of them continued to party.

The only downside to their nonstop celebration was the toll I feared so much overindulgence, combined with so much stress, was taking on my husband's body. Even a guy as big and strong as Alec couldn't stand up to the booze and the drugs, the pressure and the pace, forever. He was already starting to gain weight, and the hemorrhoids he'd confessed to have been battling for years were getting worse and flaring up more frequently. That problem would definitely have to be addressed, but for the moment I pushed it to the back of my mind, telling myself that he'd been handling it all for years and knew what he was doing.

In the last days before giving birth, I came to understand why it's said that life would come to an end if men had to have the babies. My guy was no exception, and while there was no way he could avoid noticing my almost-hourly visits to the bathroom or my tossing and turning all night, he refused to acknowledge any problem he didn't know how to solve. Instead, he stuck with what he *did* know how to deal with—such as hiring a young woman who worked for him on and off as a concierge to be at my service from the moment our baby was born. And preoccupied as I was, I didn't waste any time wondering why on earth I'd need a concierge while I was in the hospital.

My water broke when I was alone at home and I called Alec immediately. He chuckled and told me I didn't know what I was saying, there is no way my water had broken this early. But in fact it had. I went into labor a month early to be exact. So I hung up and called a man of reason, my father-in-law, who rushed right over. He took Hercules out for a quick walk and left him downstairs with the doorman. Then he phoned his son and told him to get his ass home immediately because he was going to have a baby and the NYSE could do business for a day without him running the show.

We waited an hour for Alec to swing by in the limo, and I was never so glad to take a ride in it than I was that day. I was also thrilled to find that I was already three centimeters dilated by the time we were settled in a private labor room at New York Presbyterian/Weill Cornell Medical Center with a view of the East River. We still didn't know the sex of our baby, but having a girl had been in my heart since the moment I found out I was pregnant.

Alec spent more time on his cell phone than he did at my side, but I didn't blame him, as the stark reality was that, for the moment anyway, there wasn't really much he could do for me. After I was wheeled into the delivery room, however, Alec bent over me, kissed me on the forehead, and went into action. He held up one leg while the nurse held up the other and I pushed and screamed and cried. That was the Alec I knew. All game.

To his credit, he was also at my side as soon as I got back to my room, cooing and giggling with joy over our Isabella Rose while I basked in the reflection of his joy. For all the expensive gifts he had given me since we met, I had finally been able to give him the most priceless gift of all. I was still amazed that I was actually a mother. I was on an island every bit as peaceful as any tropical paradise, and I said a few silent prayers of thanks for the newest blessing I'd been able to give and receive. I didn't yet know who this little person I'd brought into the world and held in my arms was going to turn out to be, but I understood that she would change my own life forever.

The peace was short-lived, however, as the DeMarco family showed up in force within an hour of the glorious event. I vowed to be alone with *my* family as soon as possible, but managed to get into the spirit of celebration my in-laws were so good at creating.

Warm and loving as their visit was, however, I sensed that Franco and Monica were somehow distant from each other, and I thought that Giovanni was trying to hide some kind of stress. But I was exhausted and preoccupied with my baby girl and dismissed such thoughts as creations of my own imagination.

Almost as soon as they left I fell into the first sound sleep I'd had in many days if not weeks.

Early the next morning an energetic young woman with short blond hair burst through the doorway bearing four over-flowing shopping bags from Barneys. I'd been having a private conversation with baby Isabella but the interruption didn't seem to disturb her one bit.

"Hi, I'm Caryn from Gotham Concierge," the bouncy young bottle-blonde said in introducing herself, dropping the bags on the floor next to my bed and squeezing my hand. "Pleased to meet you and your precious baby, Mrs. DeMarco."

"Samantha," I said. "Likewise."

Caryn pulled a couple of boxes out of the bags and handed them to me. "Wait until you get a look at this lingerie, Saman-tha," she gushed. "Alec's got some trip in mind for just the two of you. He insisted I pick out some sexy things for you—you're gonna die!"

I almost did when I got a look at the black satin robe and almost-sheer nightgown, and I nearly lost it again when Caryn insisted on putting the black satin slippers with two-inch heels on my still-swollen feet.

What did he have mind? Making up for lost time?

"Of course," Caryn continued, "Alec also had to do some-thing special for the three nurses who took care of you." She reached into a bag and pulled out three familiar red boxes. "So, Cartier watches all around," she announced

"Of course," I said, kissing my daughter's dark hair.

"Do you need anything else?" Caryn asked, squeezing my hand again.

"No, I'm all set," I said.

"Okay, then," she said as she started to leave. "Just remember, I'm only a phone call away."

I was fortunate to have the connections and the money that

got me a three-day stay in the hospital instead of being kicked out the day after I gave birth. So I took advantage of the rest and spent time bonding with my daughter. On my last day in the hospital, Alec showed up to take me home with a Filipina nanny in tow. I was already feeling overwhelmed by the prospect of taking care of this baby on my own, without the helpful hospital staff surrounding me day and night, so I was immeasurably grateful for the help.

From the very start, Alma was much more than a nanny. Though she was only in her early twenties, she had a strong maternal instinct, along with a generous spirit, and I felt as if she had been sent by God just for me. For the next several days we talked openly about life and love as she shared her tips about caring for a baby, which I had no idea at all how to do in the first weeks of Isabella's life. Just knowing she was there made me feel more secure, and she always made sure Alec was comfortable and well fed, even changing the sheets stained with blood from his worsening hemorrhoids on Zosia's day off.

Of course, Alec had been ignoring my pleas to have his condition taken care of. He avoided doctors like the plague. He had too many other pressing matters to take care of, such as finalizing the lease on the new apartment, which had two very large terraces with fabulous views of the water and Lady Liberty. He was also busy making arrangements for taking Transglobal public. But bloody sheet incidents became more frequent, and when he hemorrhaged so much one night that I thought he was going to bleed to death, I was all ready to call an ambulance. Of course, Alec wouldn't hear of it, but he did finally promise to see a doctor. For a moment I flashed back to the way I had lost my mother as a result of her drinking and drug habit. Was this happening to me all over again? I couldn't bear to think that the husband I loved so dearly might have the same self-destructive gene as my mother.

got me a three-day stay in the hospital instead of being kicked out the day after I gave birth. So I took advantage of the rest and spent time bonding with my daughter. On my last day in the hospital, Alec showed up to take me home with a Filipina nanny in tow. I was already feeling overwhelmed by the prospect of taking care of this baby on my own, without the helpful hospital staff surrounding me day and night, so I was immeasurably grateful for the help.

From the very start, Alma was much more than a nanny. Though she was only in her early twenties, she had a strong maternal instinct, along with a generous spirit, and I felt as if she had been sent by God just for me. For the next several days we talked openly about life and love as she shared her tips about caring for a baby, which I had no idea at all how to do in the first weeks of Isabella's life. Just knowing she was there made me feel more secure, and she always made sure Alec was comfortable and well fed, even changing the sheets stained with blood from his worsening hemorrhoids on Zosia's day off.

Of course, Alec had been ignoring my pleas to have his condition taken care of. He avoided doctors like the plague. He had too many other pressing matters to take care of, such as finalizing the lease on the new apartment, which had two very large terraces with fabulous views of the water and Lady Liberty. He was also busy making arrangements for taking Transglobal public. But bloody sheet incidents became more frequent, and when he hemorrhaged so much one night that I thought he was going to bleed to death, I was all ready to call an ambulance. Of course, Alec wouldn't hear of it, but he did finally promise to see a doctor. For a moment I flashed back to the way I had lost my mother as a result of her drinking and drug habit. Was this happening to me all over again? I couldn't bear to think that the husband I loved so dearly might have the same self-destructive gene as my mother.

strong as Alec couldn't stand up to the booze and the drugs, the pressure and the pace, forever. He was already starting to gain weight, and the hemorrhoids he'd confessed to have been battling for years were getting worse and flaring up more frequently. That problem would definitely have to be addressed, but for the moment I pushed it to the back of my mind, telling myself that he'd been handling it all for years and knew what he was doing.

In the last days before giving birth, I came to understand why it's said that life would come to an end if men had to have the babies. My guy was no exception, and while there was no way he could avoid noticing my almost-hourly visits to the bathroom or my tossing and turning all night, he refused to acknowledge any problem he didn't know how to solve. Instead, he stuck with what he *did* know how to deal with—such as hiring a young woman who worked for him on and off as a concierge to be at my service from the moment our baby was born. And preoccupied as I was, I didn't waste any time wondering why on earth I'd need a concierge while I was in the hospital.

My water broke when I was alone at home and I called Alec immediately. He chuckled and told me I didn't know what I was saying, there is no way my water had broken this early. But in fact it had. I went into labor a month early to be exact. So I hung up and called a man of reason, my father-in-law, who rushed right over. He took Hercules out for a quick walk and left him downstairs with the doorman. Then he phoned his son and told him to get his ass home immediately because he was going to have a baby and the NYSE could do business for a day without him running the show.

We waited an hour for Alec to swing by in the limo, and I was never so glad to take a ride in it than I was that day. I was also thrilled to find that I was already three centimeters dilated by the time we were settled in a private labor room at New York Presbyterian/Weill Cornell Medical Center with a view of the East River. We still didn't know the sex of our baby, but having a girl had been in my heart since the moment I found out I was pregnant.

Alec spent more time on his cell phone than he did at my side, but I didn't blame him, as the stark reality was that, for the moment anyway, there wasn't really much he could do for me. After I was wheeled into the delivery room, however, Alec bent over me, kissed me on the forehead, and went into action. He held up one leg while the nurse held up the other and I pushed and screamed and cried. That was the Alec I knew. All game.

To his credit, he was also at my side as soon as I got back to my room, cooing and giggling with joy over our Isabella Rose while I basked in the reflection of his joy. For all the expensive gifts he had given me since we met, I had finally been able to give him the most priceless gift of all. I was still amazed that I was actually a mother. I was on an island every bit as peaceful as any tropical paradise, and I said a few silent prayers of thanks for the newest blessing I'd been able to give and receive. I didn't yet know who this little person I'd brought into the world and held in my arms was going to turn out to be, but I understood that she would change my own life forever.

The peace was short-lived, however, as the DeMarco family showed up in force within an hour of the glorious event. I vowed to be alone with *my* family as soon as possible, but managed to get into the spirit of celebration my in-laws were so good at creating.

Warm and loving as their visit was, however, I sensed that Franco and Monica were somehow distant from each other, and I thought that Giovanni was trying to hide some kind of stress. But I was exhausted and preoccupied with my baby girl and dismissed such thoughts as creations of my own imagination.

Almost as soon as they left I fell into the first sound sleep I had in many days if not weeks.

Early the next morning an energetic young woman wit short blond hair burst through the doorway bearing four ove flowing shopping bags from Barneys. I'd been having a priva conversation with baby Isabella but the interruption didn seem to disturb her one bit.

"Hi, I'm Caryn from Gotham Concierge," the bouncy your bottle-blonde said in introducing herself, dropping the bags o the floor next to my bed and squeezing my hand. "Pleased t meet you and your precious baby, Mrs. DeMarco."

"Samantha," I said. "Likewise."

Caryn pulled a couple of boxes out of the bags and hande them to me. "Wait until you get a look at this lingerie, Samar tha," she gushed. "Alec's got some trip in mind for just the tw of you. He insisted I pick out some sexy things for you—you'r gonna die!"

I almost did when I got a look at the black satin robe an almost-sheer nightgown, and I nearly lost it again when Cary insisted on putting the black satin slippers with two-inch heel on my still-swollen feet.

What did he have mind? Making up for lost time?

"Of course," Caryn continued, "Alec also had to do some thing special for the three nurses who took care of you." Sh reached into a bag and pulled out three familiar red boxes. "So Cartier watches all around," she announced

"Of course," I said, kissing my daughter's dark hair.

"Do you need anything else?" Caryn asked, squeezing m hand again.

"No, I'm all set," I said.

"Okay, then," she said as she started to leave. "Just remember I'm only a phone call away."

I was fortunate to have the connections and the money tha

After emergency surgery to repair twenty internal hemor-rhoids, Alec remained hospitalized and in a morphine haze for a week, insisting during his more lucid moments that he could recuperate just as well in his own bed. That didn't make me feel much better, since recent events were just the latest reminder of how precariously he lived his life and the likelihood that I would be without him long before we'd grown to a ripe old age.

As soon as he was released from the hospital, Alec an-nounced that he needed to spend some more time recuperat-ing alone, so he flew off to Aruba. Truthfully, I didn't mind much because I was much more interested in bonding with my daughter than traveling with a husband who seemed completely uninterested in having sex with me. I still hadn't had the oppor-tunity to show off any of the lingerie he'd bought for me, and the promise of a renewed romance that the kinky gift implied had long since faded away.

Alec called home at least once a day, always bemoaning the fact that he missed kissing his daughter at the start and end of each day. He insisted on hearing Isabella's cooing, so she and I would share the phone as Alec's voice boomed through the receiver.

"Oh, Sam, I miss the two of you so much," he said when he'd been away five days. "But I really needed this trip and I'm feeling much better."

"That makes me happy, Alec," I said.

"You'll be even happier when you get a look at the dream house I found on the Internet while I was killing some time down here."

What house? I'm still getting used to the idea of moving to a different apartment.

"It's on the North Fork of Long Island," Alec continued. "I already put in a bid."

"I thought you had your heart set on the Hamptons," I said.

"You can't get the kind of property there that's available on the North Fork."

"How much property do you need?"

"Enough for a compound, which I plan to start developing right after the company goes public."

Now he's Alec-the-Godfather. Or is it Alec-the-Kennedy?

"You don't think your mom and dad will actually want to move, do you?" I asked.

"Sooner or later that house will be too much for them and they'll want to be close by."

"Have you mentioned this to Franco and Gianna yet?"

"No, but they'll be on board as soon as I do."

I've got my hands full with you, and now you want your family to move in, too?

Alec returned from Aruba with renewed vigor and threw himself into his work and into his plans for Isabella's christening, which would be taking place at Our Lady of Victory with Franco and Gianna as godparents. An Alec DeMarco blowout with two hundred guests at the Hudson River Club in Battery Park City overlooking the Statue of Liberty would follow immediately. He insisted that the old players on his team as well as guys like Grigor Malchek and Ted Ross be included on the list of invitations I was to send out—with Alma's assistance, of course.

Too bad she couldn't help me improve the conjugal situation with my husband. Lately it seemed that nothing I did, from modeling my most seductive lingerie to lighting scented candles, was enough to get his attention away from his business or distract him from his self-medication with alcohol and pot at the end of most days. And still I deluded myself by clinging to the hope that his self-destructive behavior as well as his lack of interest in me as a sex partner were temporary and would resolve themselves with just a little more time, and a little more support from me.

I clung to my daughter as I clung to my hope, although I was still insecure in my skills and instincts as a mother. I certainly had no role model. My own mother was a model only for how *not* to raise a child, so I was more or less on my own. Sometimes the job seemed so overwhelming that I just had to hand the baby—and the responsibility—off to Alma and be by myself. Mostly, however, I wanted to be with Isabella, and most nights I read to her, which my mother had never done for me, and sang her to sleep with the most soothing words I knew.

Amazing Grace, how sweet the sound, that saved a wretch like me.
I once was lost but now am found, was blind, but now I see.

TWELVE

The first six months of Isabella's life flew by as Alec continued to climb the ranks and spend more and more money. On the first of December we moved into our new three-bedroom, three-bathroom duplex apartment overlooking the Hudson River, which he deemed appropriate for his new status. The terrace was barren in midwinter but beautiful nevertheless under a blanket of snow. One thing I was really looking forward to was planting a few small trees in the spring.

I probably shouldn't have been shocked when, just a month after we moved in, Alec mentioned the next move he had in mind, to an apartment in the Luxe Regent, which was just being built. I wondered where we'd finally put down roots—aside, that is, from the summer house compound on the North Fork property that Alec had in fact bought using his shares in Transglobal (which would certainly skyrocket as soon as the company went public) as collateral. It hadn't taken him long to start putting in motion his plans for a helipad and the toy that went with it.

Alec went on slaying dragons and I went on making a life for me and my daughter, who was the center of attention at all DeMarco family gatherings. I was thankful Isabella had a genuinely loving family and thankful, too, that I had these people as an anchor in my fast-paced and sometimes lonely life. The only thing I didn't have was someone with whom I could discuss my deep-seated and long-held belief in the subjective value of personal striving and self-worth as opposed to the objective value that was calibrated in terms of financial worth.

The women in Alec's circle, including those I worked with on the charity board, were pleasant and well-meaning but had no interest in delving beneath the surface pleasantries we exchanged. And whenever I tried to bring up these feelings with my in-laws, they would find some way to distract me or change the subject. So gradually I stopped trying to share what I felt and simply accepted them all for what they were and what they were able to provide for me and my baby.

One day, I hoped, when *The Blessed Bridge* was published, I'd be able to share my thoughts with the world. For now, I confided only in Isabella and in Hercules, both of whom I talked to when we were alone. They may not have been able to respond, but at least they didn't try to shut me up.

Alec and I ushered in the New Year following Isabella's birth high atop the north tower of the World Trade Center, home to some of the most powerful Wall Street firms and to Windows on the World, where we attended a black-tie ball, given by Barklay & Sons, a New York–based hedge fund. Alec, who easily held his own with Grigor Malchek and Senator Ross, spent the entire night with a self-satisfied smile plastered on his face. With our current and future homes in the immediate neighborhood, 107 stories below, our world was literally and figuratively at his feet. The celebration was lavish beyond description and symbolic of a world that was still so foreign to me, but I still clung to the hope that Alec was ever closer to making his dream come true and being happy with our family.

The future was also the topic of discussion when Monica,

Franco's loyal wife, asked me to lunch at Café Boulud the following week. She was already there when I arrived and could hardly wait for me to take my seat before she started to unburden herself. "Franco's away more than ever," she began. "From our home . . . and from me when he is at home."

"I can relate," I said. *That's the most honest thing I've heard or said to anyone in months.* "It isn't easy supporting such ambitious, driven men."

"I knew you'd understand." She sighed. "It's really getting to me, Sam. Franco is never satisfied, always trying to keep up with Alec," she said, and then she looked me in the eyes. "I'm not blameless, either. I've nagged him more than once to get me the kind of diamonds Alec gets for you."

"It's not bad to want things, Monica."

"Yeah, well, some people want the wrong things," she said, her eyes filling with fire. "I found a black thong that wasn't mine in Franco's pants pocket last week." I shivered, as the memory of finding someone else's lipstick in the back of Tony Kroon's car came rushing back. "Of course, he swore it was just the result of some boys' night out at a strip club," she continued. "With Alec and his clients."

Of course.

The pricey fashions and jewelry on and all around us, and the fancy china and food on the table in front of us, didn't seem to matter all that much to either of us in that moment. I tried to be as supportive and encouraging as I could.

"I'd love to hear more about your book, Sam," she said as we started on dessert.

"Thank you, Monica," I said, surprised. "I'm genuinely touched."

"I've wanted to bring it up a couple of times when everyone got together, but it never seemed to be the right moment," she said. *Join the club.*

"It's pretty simple, really. I write about being who I am and chasing my dream."

Gazing over my shoulder, Monica seemed to be lost in thought. After a minute, she began to speak. "That's just it," she said, turning to me. "I don't know who I am, so I don't have any dreams. Sure, I've got a dream husband and dream house, but so does everyone else I know. There's nothing special about me."

"I think talking about it is how a dream starts, and how it stays alive," I said. "Every one of us is special, Monica. There are disfigured children in Asia who've been saved because of the foundation you belong to, and you've got two precious daughters to be proud of."

"I don't think those things make me all that special, Sam," she said, shaking her head.

"Well, you're special to me, and you've got a great life while you go about finding out who you are."

Monica gazed away again. "I don't think I want to go on being just a mother in the Italian version of a family that minimizes the husband-and-wife part," she said. "If you get my drift."

"I hear you." I frowned.

"I'm actually glad I haven't gotten pregnant again." Monica sighed.

God works in strange ways.

It was a beautiful early summer day when Transglobal was to become the first specialty trading firm to go public. Needless to say, my husband was salivating at the thought of collecting his just reward for hand-to-hand combat, which had also included plenty of the kissing-up that he always cursed under his breath. Alec appeared to be a superior trader, more so than any of his counterparts on the Street. But he needed to be validated like the rest of us, and he should have taken credit for all the ideas he gave away. For everyone on Wall Street it was all about money, all about who had the biggest cock and the biggest bank account. That was the real reason Alec was driven to take the risks others wouldn't and make the trades that would satisfy the toughest customer, the biggest scumbag client. This was a minefield, stocked with greedy men who were secretly running the world. Every political campaign in the country was somehow funded by Wall Street money. And my husband was part of that world. I'd always thought that the mafia ran things, but they were small potatoes compared to this kind of power.

Alec assured me that I would never want for anything ever again, that no harm would ever come to me and we would always be rich. But silently I wondered if the loss of our time together was worth whatever monstrous increase in wealth was coming our way, particularly since, in my opinion, we already had enough to last us through at least a dozen lifetimes. After all, I was a girl who had spent long stretches surviving on toast for dinner *without the butter*.

The Wall Street buzz on that day was all about Transglobal, and about the new partner, Alec DeMarco, who had been asked to ring the opening bell. The entire family was present and I was at his side with Isabella in my arms when the moment arrived. Alec did the deed, champagne was poured, and he preened as I had never seen him do before. Even Grigor Malchek seemed to be under his spell. When Alec was asked where the guys were that he used to hang out with, he simply replied, "I'm just too busy celebrating my greatness, that's all."

I secretly flinched in the midst of all the joy I felt for Alec because he showed no sense of humility whatsoever. Don't get me wrong, he had worked hard and deserved his reward, but he'd caught a couple of breaks along the way, too, and there were a lot of other people who had a hand in his success. It would have been nice to see him acknowledge someone or something other than himself that morning. Commitment before ego, he'd always say.

I had to admit, however, that all the fawning his parents and sister did over Alec made it easy for him to lose himself in the celebration on the floor of the exchange, and afterward at the Hudson River Club. As off-the-charts as that celebratory blowout was, Alec no doubt thought it an inadequate acknowledgment of the score he had just made. For him, a castle high in the Alps would have been a more fitting venue than a mere restaurant.

As for me, I had no idea if any venue could deliver appropriate recognition of his partnership and the two million shares in his personal trading account that opened at fifty-five dollars per share. I'll admit, too, that I was intoxicated by the hundred-plus millions he had, on paper. But what meant even more to me than that crazy sum was that a different kind of Brooklyn boy had made a different kind of mark on the world, and that I was a different kind of Brooklyn girl who intended to put my mark on my daughter and make her proud of her mother.

Alec spent more money over the next month than he'd earned the previous year, and by the time Isabella's third birthday party came around, Franco had completely given up trying to compete with a brother who now owned an executive-model Sikorsky helicopter—the "Rolls-Royce of the sky," Alec called it—to go along with his North Fork compound and who now had his eye on a huge villa in Italy for the entire family. Not even the Barnum & Bailey clowns or strolling minstrels who provided the entertainment for the birthday party Caryn had arranged for Isabella at the Boathouse in Central Park could erase the scowl from Franco's face. He seemed resigned to just go along for the ride Alec was on. For my part, I was thankful that Alec had managed to inject some magic into at least one of his primary relationships.

In terms of his business relationships, there were new deals in the works with his friend, the Greek Emmanuel Stavros. These brothers were also huge venture capitalists, never mind everything else they owned. I was surprised to learn that at least one of those holdings might have something to do with me, but I couldn't pry any specifics from my husband, who was playing his cards close to his custom-tailored vest. I allowed myself to think it somehow involved *The Blessed Bridge* and felt a rush of hope.

Of course Emmanuel and his family were at Isabella's party, and I was surprised to see how his down-to-earth wife mothered their toddler son, who laughed with joy as he clung to her skirt, and the way she spoke with quiet confidence to everyone regardless of rank. To me she seemed the picture of self-assurance and contentment, and I wondered if she and Emmanuel had managed to find for themselves what was missing from my relationship with my husband.

Alec's increased obsession with luxury showed no signs of slowing down, especially during his two-month-early fortieth-birthday blowout. He flew his immediate family to Los Cabos, Mexico, on a private jet and chartered a Boeing 757 for fifty of his closest friends. It was to be four days of sun and fun, and Alec made sure the festivities started off right by finding a way to take chocolates out of wrappers and replace them with medical marijuana lozenges for all on the plane to enjoy. He also filled up empty protein shake packages with more marijuana and hash to be consumed during our stay.

The four-day event included yachting, drinking the finest tequilas, and indulging in the best foods and fish Baja had to offer. The culmination was a beach party with fire pits that burned into the wee hours of the morning. It truly was the ultimate dream birthday for the ultimate King of Wall Street, who oversaw every detail, including his-and-hers custom-monogrammed bathrobes in every room, and of course footed the entire bill. I was nervous about the cost but went with the flow.

The King also received the dream gift of a lifetime from a dear friend who played for the Yankees: a 1998 World Series ring set with diamonds and designed by the great DiMaggio himself. I mean, what could get better than that? Of course, I later found out that we'd almost lost the Yankee when he fell head first into the hot tub after way too many mushrooms and weed. Luckily, Alec's brother, the good doctor, rescued him—and us—from what could have been a tragedy, not to mention some serious trouble.

All in all, Mexico made Isabella's party look like an afternoon tea.

The festivities were interrupted, however, when the birthday boy had to fly back on the eve of his actual birthday dinner to be on the floor of the exchange for the opening of a huge IPO he'd won over all his competitors, including Ted Ross. Of course he made a big deal of it, so when his friends offered him a jet so long as he paid for the fuel—which in and of itself was a hefty chunk of change—Alec went for it. It cost eighty-five grand to fly Alec back on a G5 that reportedly belonged to Paul McCartney so that he could open the new listing at the nine-thirty opening bell the next morning.

When he returned to Mexico that same evening, we partied hard and were lucky to be flying private when we left the next morning. Unfortunately our flight was stopped at Customs in Texas because of a tip that there were drugs on board. I sat frozen in fear as the agents came on board to search, but their professional expertise wasn't up to my husband's unlimited ingenuity. As soon as they departed empty-handed and we were once more airborne, Alec gave me one of his biggest, most self-satisfied grins and said, "I knew they'd never think to look for the stuff I Crazy-Glued onto the inside of my jeans!"

The whole birthday extravaganza was the talk of Wall Street for a month.

✧ ✧ ✧

Alec's investment in a partnership that owned a preserve on the North Fork was but one of the more sizable ones he made in the early fall, and he always seemed to have something on the drawing board, such as a limousine that was being customized with more than two hundred thousand dollars' worth of appointments. He was always adding members to his team, in and out of the office, and he planned to hire a full-time chauffeur to go along with his Vietnam War veteran helicopter pilot, who was on permanent standby.

Only the best of everything would do, Alec reminded me often. Why own a helicopter with only one engine when you could have one with two? Such excesses were becoming overwhelming and I started to wonder where I belonged in all of it, especially after Alec ignored the advice of his lawyer and named Franco executor of his estate instead of me. I felt that was wrong, and for once I spoke up. After all, I was the one with the child, and his child had to be protected in case of his death. Luckily a kind female lawyer agreed with me. Hence the twenty-four-hour turnaround.

I'll get by.

Of course, "getting by" wasn't anything like it had been before I met Alec. We ate sushi at Nobu or had their takeout at least once a week; we attended every Broadway opening and film premiere, took tables at political and charity functions, and there was always a major trip or two on the horizon.

Alec flaunted his successes and everyone in his orbit attached themselves to him for the ride, including those from his past who came crawling out of the woodwork. One of them was his ex-wife, Katie, whom I'd almost forgotten about, as had Alec, until she phoned one night to tell him that she still thought they were soul mates. He told her she was out of her mind and threw some money at her, after which she disappeared, never to be heard from again.

My generous husband never turned down any request for money, nor did he ever ask my opinion before writing the check. Although I had unlimited money to spend, I didn't have any real say when it came to family finances.

In early October a Brink's truck delivered his new, titanium black AmEx card, which he put to good use as soon as we arrived at the St. Regis Hotel in Washington, D.C., for the NIAF ball later that month. Jim and Jeff, two divine creations of the concierge god, had taken care of our airline tickets and had even arranged for shipping our luggage ahead via FedEx. When we strolled up to their desk upon arrival they informed us that they'd made all the sightseeing arrangements as per Alec's instructions and that our evening wear had been pressed and was waiting for us in our suites.

Alec, his parents, and I toured the capital in a stretch limo. I was so grateful for the extra time I was able to spend with Giovanni during the whirlwind trip. He connected me to shared roots and to my husband, and his faith in God and in me always restored my faith in the future.

Giovanni was beside himself with pride at the cocktail party Friday night when he introduced his son, who would be officially inducted as a member of the NIAF the next day. His buttons positively burst when some senior members speculated that Alec might be designated as Man of the Year someday.

The ball that followed the next night was as festive a black-tie affair as could be. Giovanni was handsome and elegant in his dinner jacket, and when he took me out on the dance floor, I was thrilled that he complimented the understated Dolce & Gabbana black silk cocktail dress I'd chosen for the occasion. I knew we could easily have been mistaken for father and daughter, and, in truth, Giovanni was more of a father to me during that one evening than my own father had been my whole life.

Upon our return to New York, Alec and I resumed our

crazy-millionaire existence with helicopter hops to the North
Fork or Atlantic City on the weekends and over to Teterboro Airport in New Jersey for regular getaways by private jet to Arizona,
the Florida Keys, and the Cayman Islands, where much of the
lucre from Wall Street deals is stashed away. As much as I loved
traveling, I was relieved to get home to New York. I was happier
when we stayed at home, especially during the year-end holidays,
so that I could enjoy quiet family time with just my husband
and Isabella.

Alec was more than restless by the time we rang in the New
Year, and he came home after lunch one day in early January an-
nouncing his plans for a one-week getaway to Puerto Rico just
for the two of us. Isabella would stay with his parents, as she
often did when we traveled, and we'd put Hercules in a kennel,
which always made me sad, but I was looking forward to the
warm weather I found myself missing and to having some quality one-on-one time with my husband. He was unusually excited
about the trip and more animated as he ticked off items on his
latest itinerary, but what really surprised me was his suggestion
that we take a walk around our neighborhood. Normally, my
larger-than-life husband was the sort who would take a Segway
to get around our apartment if that were practical.

He was also the sort who had ulterior motives most of the
time, so it shouldn't have surprised me when he happened to
steer us toward the site where ground had been broken for the
Luxe Regent.

"Would you prefer to live in the suburbs?" he asked as he
reached for the door to the sales office.

*Hardly! Not after I've spent my whole life getting to this side of the
bridge.*

"You know, we could just buy the condo we're renting now
for half a million," I said.

"I don't want the hassle of having to unload it eighteen

months from now," he replied as he waved me inside. "Besides," he added, "I can get in on the ground floor here and negotiate a great deal on spec."

A tall, elegant South African woman named Mirabelle ushered us to plush chairs and spread out blueprints on a teak cocktail table. Alec dove right into the possibilities, and I could see the wheels turning in his head. It didn't take him long to settle on combining three units into one six-bedroom, five-bath penthouse with an unobstructed view of Lady Liberty, my favorite statue besides any of the Blessed Mother.

Recognizing a live one when she saw him, Mirabelle smiled broadly. "Maybe you should consider taking the entire floor," she said to Alec.

"Don't tempt me," Alec said, laughing. "I'll let you know if I can pull that off down the road."

I wouldn't bet against him.

"Are dogs allowed?" I asked.

"Absolutely," Mirabelle replied. "We'll take any animal you have."

I guess you would, at these prices.

"I'll have my people get in touch with you, then," Alec said to Mirabelle.

"We'll look forward to having you with us," she replied, rising to shake our hands.

I'm sure you will. "Would you mind if my husband and I talked privately for a moment?" I asked.

"Not at all," Mirabelle said, scooping up her purse and heading for the ladies' room.

"Is all this really necessary, honey?" I asked when we were alone. "We have all the space we need right now."

"It's not where I want to be, Sam. Besides, I plan on our family growing."

I skipped mentioning the critical activity necessary to

make that a reality. "I don't think I want more than two kids," I said.

"We can stop as soon as I have a son," Alec said.

Who am I to disagree with his plans? Do I even have any negotiating power anyway?

When we arrived in San Juan at noon a couple of weeks later, we went directly to the private pool adjoining our private villa. As usual, my husband cleaned out the minibar and smoked a joint, courtesy of another solicitous bellhop. He never seemed to have any problem identifying just the right one to suit his needs.

Later, after a quiet dinner, we hit the casino where I watched Alec play poker and declined his repeated invitations to sit in. He pocketed a cool twenty thousand that night, and upon our return to the villa insisted we celebrate by skinny-dipping in the pool, a bottle of champagne in a bucket on its ledge. I couldn't remember the last time Alec had been so attentive to me, and I was thrilled by his pampering.

As we sat by the pool the next day, Alec started once again to talk about the big plans he had for the millions he was making. I wasn't surprised to learn that he was planning to open his own brokerage firm, but what did surprise me was that he saw this as happening in less than two years.

"We just started a family, and we've made a huge commitment to a new multimillion-dollar home," I protested. "Do you really think you should be leaving the security you have at Transglobal so soon?"

"I'm only as good as my last score, Sam," he replied, using the word that never failed to remind me of Tony, as did Alec's tendency to make snap decisions and the pleasure he took in "scoring" at somebody else's expense.

"The senior partners hold all the cards when it comes to the deals I get to make. I'd rather control the game than keep looking back over my shoulder for the axe they would never hesitate to use. That's why I'm naming my company DeMarco Futures.

"Besides," Alec added, "the Luxe Regent pad isn't going to cost as much out of pocket as you think."

"What do you mean?"

"They include a generous construction allowance. We only have to cover whatever we spend on top of that, and most of it will just be added to the mortgage."

"You mean you're not buying it outright?"

"No way, Sam. Can't tie up that kind of dough. The whole key to success is using other people's money."

"I see," I said, but I didn't, really. I'd always thought owning a place outright was the way to go assuming you had the money to do it.

"Just leave this kind of stuff to me, Sam," Alec said, patting my hand as if I were his child. "You just take care of Isabella and pray for a boy every chance you get."

Do I have a choice? "Okay," I said softly, privately deciding that, should I become pregnant, praying for a healthy and happy baby was really all that mattered to me.

"You should think about what you want to do with your life, too," Alec continued.

I already have, and we talked about it, remember?

"Emmanuel and his brothers invest in different things all the time, show business being one of them. You know those Greeks, their hands are in everything, and I think that investing in a play would be a great idea. Aside from the opportunity to make some money, it's a great way to entertain clients."

"So? What's that got to do with me?"

"We know plenty of guys who would put up ten or twenty Gs for a show, and you could produce it."

"I'm not a producer, Alec. I wouldn't even know where to start."

"It isn't rocket science, Sam. You just flash your tits and your happy smile, and then tell other people what to do."

I notice he left out my smarts and my moxie.

"The Stavros brothers are gonna hook you up. They know a few people in show business and Emmanuel said he'll point you in the right direction. I really think you're cut out for this, Sam," he concluded, and for a moment I was touched because it sounded like he really meant it.

I don't know. Maybe this is up my alley. "I'm not sure I'm comfortable being responsible for the kind of money a stage production would require, especially if it's someone else's."

"Yeah, well"—Alec smiled—"the kicker is the investors don't have to make any money. It would be great if they did, but even if they don't, they can use the write-off. It's a win either way."

"If you say so." I shrugged

"I do. And no matter how it turns out, you'll get some great experience, so it's a win-win for both of us."

If you say so.

The next four months flew by for Alec, but not so fast for me, since I was the one who had to remain steadfastly supportive, no matter what mood he was in. Whenever I tried to help boost his spirits when he was down, it didn't seem to have much positive effect, and no matter how hard I tried to help him pause and revel in his success after a victory, his mind was always focused like a laser on his next target. And although he adored our three-year-old daughter, his fixation on having her say hello and good-bye, good morning and good night, to him with a kiss every single time without fail could make it difficult for her (and for me) to feel that love. And though Alec was always playful around Isabella, it saddened me that the time we spent as a family was so limited. For me it was family that put everything else in perspective, but Alec couldn't seem to find that balance.

It was always up or down with my husband, so I rode the roller coaster with Isabella and said prayers of thanks that the highs were more frequent than the lows.

I kept myself busy writing and volunteering at the women's domestic violence shelter and spending time with Isabella. I really wanted to be there for my daughter the best way I knew how, but I was still a bit fearful of who I was and my past and how I would eventually impact my child for the rest of her life. I had to learn to hold back my fears and live more in faith when it came to Isabella. I tried not to bring my relationship with my mother into play. I wanted to do this differently and guide Isabella into the right direction of life. I'd learned a lot from Alma, and my guiding principle was never to be like my own mother, but I often felt like I was flying by the seat of my pants, and that was scary, even though Isabella appeared to be thriving. She was a bright, happy kid who brought me continuous pleasure, and the one thing I continued to love most, and felt truly confident doing, was reading to her at bedtime whenever possible. Seeing her face light up as she crawled into my lap and I opened a book never ceased to thrill and amaze me. Her long dark hair reminded me of mine as a child, before my mother got high one day and cut it all off. I knew Isabella was nothing like her maternal grandmother, although she did inherit my mother's big green eyes and full lips. She was a sweet child who often seemed serious beyond her years. Maybe I didn't have the true mother gene because of my past. But I was sure as hell working on it.

I was thrilled when Alec surprised me with a family trip to Italy in the spring, because it was only when he was miles from work that he truly seemed at peace.

Alec-the-tour-guide couldn't resist pointing out that the name Roma (Rome in Italian) was almost like *amore* spelled backward, and the glint in his eye as he conveyed that information gave me hope that seeing the sights and eating fabulous meals wouldn't be all we did. And the fact that Giovanni and Filomena would be with us on the trip gave me hope that he would do less drinking and forgo his usual recreational drugs. While I was sad to leave my daughter behind, Isabella would be staying with her aunt Gianna, so I knew that she'd be well taken care of.

On the plane, I sat next to Giovanni, who kept me entranced with his stories about the rich history of the places we'd be visiting. "Growing up in Sicily," he told me, "was a lot different from the way my own kids, and you, grew up in Brooklyn." *And my Brooklyn was a lot different from yours.* I urged him to tell me more about his own childhood, which, I realized, was probably a lot like that of my own father, who had also been born in Sicily.

"Well," he said, "for one thing, we didn't go to any market to buy our fish. We ate what we caught, preferably sardines, which we fried in oil over an outdoor fire. My mamma made the pasta and salad and my sisters baked the bread. Our family's life revolved around cooking and eating, and we all contributed what we could." I loved hearing him talk, and I also loved gaining some insight into the source of Alec's infinite love of food.

In Giovanni's company the trip literally flew by, and almost before I knew it we were landing. We were met at the airport by Andrea, who would be our limo driver throughout the trip. Although he spoke mainly in Italian, which both Giovanni and Filomena spoke fluently, I sensed just from the tone of his voice that he was a happy and passionate man. He couldn't stop talking about his *bella ragazza,* his beautiful girlfriend, and I couldn't help feeling, as most Italians do, that we're all part of one great big family.

We had lunch at a charming restaurant, seated on a patio surrounded by olive trees, and took the proprietor at his word when he begged us to pick as many olives as we wanted to eat. After a delightful, sun-kissed meal accompanied by homemade limoncello served ice-cold in Venetian shot glasses, we checked into our hotel and took a long afternoon nap before descending again for another unforgettable meal.

For the weeks that followed, we toured the Eternal City and ate one meal after another, each of them more fabulous than the last. Our travels took us to Florence, and then to Venice, a city of breathtaking beauty that felt like a dream. Every one of us was enjoying the vacation of a lifetime but none of us more so than Giovanni, who was in his element as he paused at nearly every church to pray and sing with the local priests and monks. I was just thrilled to once again be making up for lost time with my husband.

Thankfully, there was no sign that his hemorrhoids were recurring, despite the richness of our meals, and Alec remained upbeat, willing to embellish the historical lessons Giovanni provided, and always gentle with me. When we got back to our room in the evening and he took me in his arms, he was once more the gentle giant I'd fallen in love with and who I knew was hidden beneath the tough Wall Street titan exterior he showed the world. Since we were never far from a religious painting, a cathedral, a convent, or a monastery, I had plenty of opportunities to say prayers of thanks for these blessings. What I was most grateful for in the end was simply having made love with my husband more in those three weeks in Italy than I had in the preceding three months.

I never wanted our fantasy trip to Italy to end. As I expected, within just a few days of returning to Manhattan, my husband got his game face back on. Gone were all signs of the gentler Alec I'd known in Europe. For my part, I resumed the role of supportive wife and doting mother to Isabella, attended the occasional charity function, the usual luncheons, and visits with my in-laws.

And I shopped.

There was no getting away from spending money, as almost every interaction outside my home involved large quantities of it, whether for a new outfit, a gift, or a charitable contribution. I knew, because Alec had told me, that any check I wrote or any swipe of my titanium AmEx card would be covered without question, and that he knew I wouldn't take advantage of that fact.

On the few occasions over the next year that he asked me if I needed anything, I thought better of mentioning that the only thing I lacked was enough time with him.

Instead I marched on side-by-side with Alec and cherished my attachments to my daughter and to Giovanni, which made everything worthwhile. Spending time with the people I loved was what mattered to me the most. So when Giovanni called me in early July, inviting me and Isabella to lunch in his Wall Street office so that we could discuss his idea for Isabella's fourth birthday party, I counted the hours until the day arrived. I had decided I could talk to my adopted father as I would to a priest and had just been waiting for the right opportunity to broach the subject of my concerns about his son, my husband.

"How's my little princess?" He beamed when we arrived, sweeping Isabella into his arms, cooing, "Who's the prettiest little girl?" while she giggled with pleasure. Isabella loved her grandpa, and also loved dressing up. On this occasion she really did look like a princess in a delicate green silk dress that matched her eyes and the two big bows in her hair.

Tucking her into the crook of his arm, Giovanni settled at one end of the overstuffed leather couch opposite his desk, while I sat in a matching armchair close by.

"I'm thinking the Bronx Zoo," Giovanni began.

"That's a wonderful idea!" I beamed.

"We're all going before they open on her birthday," he continued. "The monsignor up at Fordham owes me a favor, and the zoo butts up against his campus. Apparently, someone connected with it owes the good priest, so what goes around comes around."

I shook my head in amazement. "I swear, sometimes it seems as if my life is make-believe."

"Well, believe it, Samantha. I'd do anything for my family."

"I know that," I said. *The time is now.* "And there's something I think you could do for me, Dad."

"Anything, Sam. Just say the word."

"I'm worried about Alec," I began tentatively.

Giovanni reached his free hand across to mine and squeezed. "The crazy pace he's on, right?"

I gazed into his sympathetic eyes and nodded slowly. "I'm not sure it's good for his health or for . . . our relationship."

"Don't think my wife and I haven't had our share of bumps in the road, especially early on, Samantha. And don't think his mother and I haven't talked about his excesses. But he's a grown man who has to do what he has to do." *Spoken like a true Italian.* "All we can do is keep praying that God watches over him, and keep telling him how much we love him and that he doesn't have to prove anything more to us."

"I just wonder sometimes how much more he has to prove to himself." I sighed.

"Join the club." Giovanni smiled.

"I didn't mean to spring this on you," I said in apology.

"Don't be silly," he said. "That's what parents are for, and you are both my children now."

"Thanks, Dad."

"So," he said, "why don't you sneak over for dinner tonight so we can talk more about it. I'm making some sausage and broccoli di rape with orecchiette."

"That's my favorite!"

"I know, I know, already." Giovanni feigned insult. "If I learned nothing else about you in Italy, it was that."

On the way back to the apartment I picked up some fresh flowers and chocolate-dipped strawberries so I wouldn't walk in empty-handed that evening, and I let Alma give Isabella an early bath so that she would be ready for bed and I could read her a story before I left.

My cell phone rang before I'd gotten to the third page.

"Jesus fucking Christ, Sam!" Alec screamed as soon as I flipped the phone open. I didn't have to bring it to my ear to hear the rest. "Dad just had a heart attack! I'm on my way to the exchange garage where they're working on him. They said they'll be taking him to St. Vincent's. Sonofabitch!" he raged.

I didn't know what to say. I could barely breathe, let alone think. "I'll be praying for him, Alec," was all I could manage.

I wasn't at my mother's side when she died, because I was aware the end was near and had been off making her funeral arrangements. No cell phone for Samantha then. I was determined to make amends for that now with the only other parent I'd known.

Remaining as calm as I could so as not to scare her, I explained to Isabella that Grandpa was sick and that I was going to see him. Then I grabbed my bag and ran out the door, pausing only long enough to tell Alma what was going on and that I might be very late returning. She made the sign of the cross as I bolted out the door.

Alec was nowhere to be seen when I arrived at the hospital, and a nurse informed me that no one in the family had shown up yet. He must have missed them at the garage and still be on his way. I told the nurse I wanted to see my father, and she asked me to wait where I was while she checked Giovanni's status.

When she returned a few minutes later, she was accompanied by a young doctor who had a long face that made him look older than his years.

"I'm so sorry," he said, taking my hand. "Your dad didn't make it."

Oh my God, I can't believe this is really happening.

"Can I see him?" I asked.

"You'll have to identify the body," the doctor said softly. "Can you handle that?"

"Yes," I whispered. *I hope so.*

He escorted me to a dimly lit refrigerated room that adjoined the ER, and I stood stock still inside the doorway as he went over to a steel table with a long white zippered bag on it. I steeled myself as he opened the zipper. I closed my eyes for a moment when he motioned me over, and said a fast, silent prayer.

Thy kingdom come, Thy will be done.

I nodded my head in recognition of the face, which was as peaceful as I'd ever seen it. He was still tan from our trip, and with his eyes closed he appeared to be taking a nap. There was even a hint of a smile on his lips. *I was just with you and now, just like that, you're gone?*

"Are his personal things here?" I asked, collecting myself.

"On the shelf below," the doctor replied.

I lifted the sheet and reached for Giovanni's suit jacket. My hand went immediately to the right pocket, where I knew he always kept his grandmother's black-beaded rosary, and I kissed its white gold cross before tucking the rosary into my palm.

"I'm so sorry," the doctor said once more.

"So am I," I whispered.

I bent down then and kissed Giovanni's forehead, startled by how cold it already was. The only father I ever knew.

I love you, Dad.

Standing straight and looking down at him once more, I squeezed the rosary beads, closed my eyes for a long moment, and said a silent prayer before turning for the door.

Nothing's going to be the same ever again.

THIRTEEN

"He's gone, Alec," I whispered when my husband stormed up to me in the emergency room waiting area, a mixture of rage and resignation on his face. "I was just with him at lunchtime . . . and just like that, he's gone."

Alec heard me without hearing me, and said nothing as he pivoted toward the nurse's desk. I saw him without seeing him as he gesticulated, and then went motionless. I have no idea how much time elapsed before he lumbered back to me on his way to the exit.

"Everyone's waiting at Dad's house," he said.

I'm not sure if he would have noticed had I not followed him out the door.

I was the last person in the family besides Isabella to see Giovanni alive, and the first to see a fatherless Alec DeMarco. He didn't say much on the drive to Brooklyn and what he did say consisted mainly of cursing under his breath. He did, however, let me know that he'd almost been arrested for bowling over a cop who was on crowd control at the exchange garage when he made a futile attempt to catch up with the ambulance speeding away with his father.

Filomena was seated in a large stuffed chair in the living

room as Alec and I joined the others, who had gathered around and were talking with bowed heads and lowered voices. Swallowed up by the chair as she was by her circumstance, she appeared oblivious to what was going on around her. I said a fast prayer for her, as well as for me and my daughter.

It was painfully obvious to me that I wasn't the only one in the room who was going to miss Giovanni's help. He had been the linchpin holding the family together. Everyone, from his shattered widow to his elder son, who was as disconnected from his wife as he now was from his father, to his daughter, who wouldn't have the joy of being given away by a beloved dad, to Alec, the raging bull, was going to be set adrift without his presence to anchor them.

No one said much to me, and I didn't mind; in fact I wasn't sure that I'd be able to stop myself from spilling all my worries to anyone who approached. I stood to the side as everyone gathered around Alec, who was explaining that Giovanni had headed to the garage earlier than usual to cook dinner. He had put the bag of fruit he had bought from a sidewalk vendor on the seat beside him, started his car, and had a massive heart attack before he had a chance to put it in gear.

There was no doubt that Alec would be in charge of all the funeral arrangements. I also overheard a word or two about what should be done about the summer home. I had neither the inclination nor the time to care about any of it. All I could think about was how much I had grown to love the man I was proud to call "Dad," and to wonder how on earth I would keep my soaring husband grounded without his help.

Lord, help us all.

Giovanni's wake in Bensonhurst, where he had grown up, and his burial in the family plot on Staten Island were both typical Alec DeMarco productions. He really did it right for his dad. The entire funeral home was given over to the overflow crowd that showed up over the course of three days, and the Verrazano-Narrows Bridge was closed down by a police brigade escorting the hundred-car procession. Several cars carrying nothing but flowers followed the hearse, reminding me of the showy tributes accorded to important members of the mafia. In this case, however, Giovanni deserved it. He was truly a great man.

Isabella's birthday celebration a week later was subdued, and I don't think she really minded. I could tell by how unusually quiet she was that she sensed the loss of her grandfather, even though she didn't say anything about it. And her mother certainly didn't miss the extravaganzas Alec had orchestrated in the past. Instead, the three of us spent the day together at home looking at old photos and our wedding video before joining the family for dinner and a birthday cake in Brooklyn.

Filomena's grief turned to bitterness over the next several weeks, and she seemed to lose all connection to the family. Monica was about to lose Franco and my mother-in-law couldn't keep it together, so Alec took over running the family. He wanted me to call his mother every day and see her as often as possible. And he gave the same instruction to Gianna, who had set her wedding date for May 7, the same day her parents got married.

While Alec stepped into the role of family patriarch, he kept the others at arm's length emotionally. As I tried to figure out what he was going through, it seemed to me that he felt he couldn't let down his guard either on the job or at home, because displaying any sign of weakness would cause him to lose control. I almost wore out Giovanni's rosary beads praying for strength, understanding, tolerance . . . and the ability to forgive.

I considered that my husband must have been dealing with guilt from the past and his relationship with his father, that he was worried about his mother and his older brother, while at the same time pursuing his continuing quest to prove that an Italian kid from Brooklyn without a college degree could rise above everyone else on the Street.

I would have loved getting closer to his family, but I often felt as if they were putting up barriers. I sometimes wondered if I was the one to blame, if I was unintentionally giving off the wrong vibe, but when I was being honest, I understood that they really weren't interested in being any closer or in finding out who I really was and what was important to me. They were much too concerned with sticking to *omertà,* the Italian code of silence, when it came to discussing serious family issues.

The DeMarco family had always fancied themselves cut from the same privileged cloth as the Kennedys, and the women were constantly trying to get me to dress more like them—in tailored suits and long sundresses that simply weren't my style.

I knew that I'd never succeed in getting them to accept me for who I really was—a lesson I'd learned the hard way from Tony's mother, Pamela Kroon. And, as a result, at least for a while, I lost a piece of myself in exchange for fitting in.

As for Isabella, my precious little daughter was animated and inquisitive but much too young to be a confidante or companion to me, and a lot of her daily care was handled by Alma, whom I trusted implicitly—in fact a lot more than I trusted myself. I was always afraid I'd screw up in some way and often thought of the many times I'd wished my mother would just leave the mothering to Grandma. I had total faith in Alma, and in the teachers at the nursery school near Our Lady of Victory that Isabella attended.

My instincts told me the best thing I could do for my daughter was to become the person I wanted to be, so that she would know she too could be anything she wanted.

✧ ✧ ✧

Now more than ever, with Giovanni gone, I sensed I didn't really belong in Alec's family, or among his elite Wall Street crowd. I often felt, as I had at various points in my life, as if I were living on an island, separated from others and unable to control my own destiny. When those feelings threatened to overwhelm me, I did what I'd always done in the past: I reached deep down inside me and rediscovered the Samantha who had always believed in her ability to get through whatever life threw her way.

Rather than giving into feelings of loneliness and inadequacy, I committed myself anew to *The Blessed Bridge*. I knew that the novel would still be the source of my salvation and I renewed my determination to get it published. I had no idea when or how that would happen, but I believed in my heart of hearts that it would. I still had faith that God had a plan for me and that the Blessed Mother would watch over me.

As hard as it was to live with the loneliness that resulted from Alec's work schedule, the nights when he came home after a bad day in the office were a much heavier cross to bear. I remember the first time he snapped. "You are a terrible mother. Did you even stay with Isabella today? How many times do I need to tell you that you should be taking her to visit with my mother? What do you do all day, anyway?" he bellowed at me.

I was completely shocked. Memories of Tony came flooding back, and all I could do was take Isabella to her room and stay with her behind the closed door until my crazed husband ran out of steam. As these episodes became more frequent they ceased to take me by surprise, but that didn't make them any easier to live with. If it wasn't my mothering he was screaming about, it was my cooking, or failing at my duties as a daughter-in-law. And God forbid Hercules was out of his crate or even making a sound when Alec came home. That always sparked a barrage of loud curses followed by a smashed telephone or a shoved dog.

✧ ✧ ✧

There are only so many candles one can light and journal entries one can pen, only so many charity board functions to go to, so when Doris Bernstein, a Broadway producer so well-known that she actually had a theater named after her, called me out of the blue in late August I was not only surprised but also thrilled at the opportunity she presented.

"Samantha," she said, without preamble, when I picked up the phone, "I got your number from the Stavros brothers. You come highly recommended, and they suggest that we get together, before the Labor Day weekend if possible, to discuss the possibility of you producing a play for me. It's not Broadway, but it's going to be in a well-established off-Broadway theater in the West Village, and I think you might find it interesting."

Interesting? Was she kidding? This was the most exciting opportunity I'd been offered in my entire life! "Thank you so much, Doris," I replied, trying to sound like a professional rather than a kid who'd just been offered an entire box of chocolates. I wanted to jump up and down and shout "Yes!"

"I'd love to meet with you. Just tell me when and where," I said.

I sensed that if I could pull this off, it would be life-changing for me—a chance to give me a purpose and to be involved in something far more fulfilling than my increasingly lonely duties as Alec's stay-at-home wife.

We met a few days later in Doris's office, which was filled with a vast collection of trophies and plaques as well as some striking antiques. But Doris herself was even more impressive than her surroundings. In her late fifties but looking much younger, she was elegant, trim, and full of self-confidence. What impressed me most, however, was the genuine warmth she exuded from the moment she rose to greet me.

"As I told you on the phone, you come highly recommended," Doris said as we sat down.

"I want to be honest, Mrs. Bernstein," I said, looking her in the eye.

"Please call me Doris," she interjected.

"And I'm Samantha." I smiled. "I just want you to know I don't really have any experience as a producer."

She laughed. "I didn't have any, either, until my husband dropped a show into my lap."

"Well, I'm honored that you're considering me for the job."

"It's yours if you want it, Samantha. The money is there and the Stavros brothers, who are putting it up, are behind you."

I looked away for a moment. "I just don't want to screw anything up, Doris."

She laughed again, louder this time. "*Everyone* screws up, darling. The trick is always to land on your feet."

Getting by, as I say. Maybe I can do this.

"It isn't rocket science," Doris continued. "The key to having a success, Samantha, is to know from the start that it's not about show business. It's about organization and discipline and details . . . and staying on schedule."

"Well, that sounds like something I can do. I may not know a lot about producing plays but I do think I'm disciplined and organized, and I never miss a deadline."

"That's exactly what I thought, and now that I've met you, I believe you'll do just fine."

"Thank you."

Doris laughed yet again, and I loved being around her. "You may not be thanking me after you've spent a few days and nights pulling out that lovely hair of yours," she said.

"You're scaring me now," I said.

"No guts, no glory." She chuckled. *I'm familiar with that lesson.* "If you pull this off, there's no telling where it could lead."

All roads lead to The Blessed Bridge *getting published.* I smiled.

"Take it from me, Samantha: I meet people all day long. Over the years I've gotten pretty good at figuring out who can do what, and there's something about you that tells me you can pull this off. You aren't all bluster and show, you don't put on airs, and your whole demeanor tells me you're a quick study."

"Thanks again, Doris. I look forward to learning a lot from you."

"I've put together a marvelous group of people for you to work with," she said, leaning back in her chair. "Mary Davies, my assistant, will be your go-to person and I'll introduce her to you on your way out. Everyone loves Mary and you will, too. She's the mother we all wish we had."

Mother Mary. I smiled inside at that as Doris paused for a moment.

"As for the rest, they're all talented people who are fun to be around. You'll meet them soon, starting with Marvin and Gregory, who wrote *A Gay Day.*"

"I can't wait to get started," I said, and my mind went into overdrive, wondering about the first steps I would take.

"Read the play as soon as you can, Samantha. Make any notations you want and jot down any questions you have. Call me as soon as you're finished because we'd like to stage it this holiday season."

"I'll do it over the weekend," I promised. I was used to using the power of the written word to convey ideas and emotions, but staging a play meant getting that power from the page to the stage and the way the actors delivered their lines. This was different from anything I'd ever done before, and my mind was buzzing with new possibilities. It would be quite the challenge, but I was game; I had to be.

"Welcome to my world, Samantha," she said.

✧ ✧ ✧

On the Friday before Labor Day weekend, the whole family, with Hercules and his crate included, packed up and made the usual farm stand stops on the way to Alec's mother's house on Long Island, but the atmosphere when we arrived was nothing like it had been in the past. Filomena was zoned out in her chair, Franco was slumped into one corner of the long couch, and Gianna and Gary were in the other corner, blank stares on their faces. It felt as if Giovanni's wake still hadn't ended.

"Gotta kick Boston's ass this weekend, bro," Alec said, trying to raise his brother's spirits.

"I'm down with that." Franco smiled thinly.

"Where's Monica and the kids?" Alec asked.

"She decided at the last minute to visit her folks at the Jersey Shore and take the girls with her."

No one raised an eyebrow, and I wondered if I was the only one who wanted to ask a question or two.

Or three.

After a moment of awkward silence, Alec continued as master of ceremonies. "Let me just get our luggage out of the Rover. Then I'll order some pizza and everyone can eat where they want."

Sounds real homey.

"What—you didn't come in a helicopter?" Franco prodded his brother.

"Had to bring the mutt along," Alec said complainingly. "The damn walker is away, and Sam didn't want to leave him in the kennel over a long weekend."

Hercules could use a vacation like everyone else, out of his crate, and Isabella loves being around him.

Alec, Franco, and Gary camped out in the den well before game time, and the rest of us gathered at the kitchen table. Although Filomena remained largely silent, she did emerge from her solitude long enough to engage with Isabella for a few moments at a time.

The Yankees ended up beating Boston on the road, but even my husband's celebratory mood couldn't prompt him to touch me when we made our way to the bedroom that night.

The atmosphere at breakfast the next morning wasn't much improved, but at least everyone was gathered around the table together. Alec had planned a deep-sea fishing trip, and so he bolted for the marina, Franco in tow, right after a second helping of pancakes, eggs, bacon, and sausage. Soon after that, Gianna and Gary excused themselves to go for a bike ride. Filomena took Isabella's hand, and I followed them out onto the deck, where Hercules, anchored to a long rope, stood up on his hind legs to greet us.

The moderate breezes coming off the bay already held a hint of fall. Although it wasn't exactly tanning weather, it was still warm enough to enjoy the sun. Filomena sat on a chaise as I slid onto another, raised my knees, and pulled out the manuscript Doris had given me from my beach bag.

I read through the morning, and after lunch, Filomena got Isabella to take a nap in her room. That left the two of us alone, and, to my surprise, my mother-in-law began to open up a bit about what she was feeling. She reminisced a bit about the good times she'd had with Giovanni and confided that she was feeling lost without him. I simply listened and commiserated as best I could.

Just as she was slipping into a reflective silence, Alec and Franco came home with the catch of the day and news of another Yankee victory. That was enough to keep Alec in a magnanimous and entertaining mood throughout our grilled-fish dinner and dessert on the deck. By the time we retired to our room, he was exhausted from his Old-Man-and-the-Sea day and an evening of nonstop drinking, so any further entertaining was out of the question. I reached for the manuscript on my night table as he rolled over, and enjoyed the last few pages of a simple but wonderful story about a day in the life of two people in love before drifting into a peaceful sleep.

Alec holed up in his father's office right after breakfast on Sunday, saying he'd be working until around 8 p.m. when he could once more be found in the den for the Yankee game, and I was grateful for the opportunity to join Filomena at Mass with Isabella in tow.

When we got back, we once more settled on the deck, and I had just about finished making my notes on the play when Alec emerged from the office.

"What's that?" he asked, pointing his chin at the manuscript in my lap.

"The play you and your friends are backing."

"Oh, that," Alec said. "How's it going?"

"Just getting my feet wet. It's hard to know yet."

"You remember what I told you about how to get by in this deal?"

Do I ever—tits and ass. I don't think I'll be following that advice. "Yes," I said through thin lips. "I think it's going to work out just fine."

"Great," Alec said. "What's for dinner, Ma?"

"I thought we'd order Chinese," Filomena said.

"Good by me," Alec said agreeably, which might or might not have meant that he'd been having a good day so far. "Just send my Kung Pao chicken into the den with some chopsticks," he added, before disappearing again.

Alec surprised me after breakfast on Labor Day when he suggested that he and I take a walk on the beach, and I was baffled when he added that I could bring Hercules along.

The stroll felt like old times, and I said a couple of silent prayers that the calmness we were experiencing would be the rule rather than the exception going forward. I also fretted a little about how to make that happen, and, lost as I was in my own thoughts, I didn't see the dog that Hercules spied on a far-off bluff. I was stunned when Hercules ripped the leash from my hand and dashed off before I even knew what was happening. Alec's loud curse as he broke into a sprint after our family dog put an end to whatever calm there had been.

I jogged as best I could trying to catch up, and had to stifle a laugh or two at the sight of my massive husband zigzagging in pursuit of our spry and no doubt horny dog. I couldn't blame Hercules for exploiting his newfound freedom, and I couldn't really blame Alec for being a bit hot under the collar when I caught up to him, kneeling and gasping for air with the end of the leash in hand. I couldn't blame him, either, for the stream of curses that flowed from his lips as he reeled Hercules in.

What I *could* blame him for was the fist he delivered to the dog's jaw as soon as he got within striking distance. I was stunned. This was the first time Alec's mounting hostility and verbal abuse had actually exploded into physical violence, and although I was fighting back tears I said nothing as he dragged our still-whimpering pet back to the house and threw him into his crate. I was so appalled by my husband's behavior that I couldn't even bear the sight of him. A part of me feared that the next time Alec lost control like that, the object of his fury would be me. But even in my own mind that didn't excuse my silence. *Why didn't I do anything to defend poor Hercules?*

We barely spoke for the rest of the day or on the ride back to the city, and I pretended to be sleeping when he got out of bed early Tuesday morning for a one-week business trip to Washington, D.C. Truth be told, I hadn't slept much sharing a bed with a man who'd acted like a beast, and I was in no mood to say an obligatory good-bye to someone who suddenly seemed like a stranger to me.

The only thing that really kept me sane was going full steam ahead with the off-Broadway production, so I called Doris to set up a meeting with Mary Davies and the rest of the staff.

"There's my girl," Mary said brightly, rising and taking my hand in both of hers when I arrived at the West Village theater.

"Samantha, this is Marvin," she said with a wave of her hand toward a clean-cut young man with short, wavy blond hair wearing preppie tan slacks and a crisp blue and white checked shirt. "And this is his partner, Gregory," she continued, wrapping her arm around a dapper guy dressed in designer jeans and a tight-fitting black nylon T-shirt. His dark hair was parted in the middle and hung almost to his shoulders.

"Pleasure to meet you, Samantha." Marvin smiled broadly.

"Likewise," Gregory added with a smile to match.

"The pleasure is all mine," I said in return.

"I'm going to do everything I can to make sure there's more pleasure than pain in delivering this play to the public," Mary assured us.

"Sort of like childbirth, I suppose," Marvin said.

"He's the writer in the group," Mary said to me as we sat down. *Not the only one.* "Probably belongs on the *Saturday Night Live* staff, but he's stuck teaching English lit and composition in a high school up in Rhode Island."

"It has its rewards, you know," Marvin said.

"Of course it does, darling," Mary said. "But Gregory has designs on a huge PR career, and if he handles the promotion for this play as well as I think he can, there's going to be a lot more of a payoff right here in the big city."

"I'm looking forward to that," Marvin said, resting a hand on his partner's. "We've been together fifteen years and this is the most exciting thing we've done together."

"Careful there"—Gregory laughed with a raised eyebrow—"or you'll ruin my reputation."

It was obvious they were excited about what they were doing, and obvious, too, that they were in love, which I already knew from reading the play.

"You're my kind of people," I said.

"Now it's your turn to be careful, Samantha," Mary said. "No telling what these two will do to you if you fall under their spell."

"Just between us girls," I said to all three, "I can handle myself."

The group laugh was just what this girl needed to forget her problems, at least for a while. When I opened my eyes early Sunday morning I felt refreshed for the first time in a week, even though I had stayed at the theater until nearly midnight. It was a joy to be with creative people who accepted me at face value and wanted to work with me, and to feel, for the first time since my whirlwind wedding to Alec, that I was beginning to reclaim control over my own life, my own destiny.

Alec wasn't due back until late Monday night, so I had two whole days to work on budgets and schedules, make the calls that needed to be made, and, best of all, think about the door that was opening up for me. Sadly, there was no one with whom I could share my excitement, especially not with my husband. I wasn't in the mood yet to talk to him about anything, but even if I were, he wouldn't understand what could be so exciting about an artsy project involving a couple of gay men and not much monetary reward.

I was under the covers and barely awake when he lumbered into the room and got undressed on his way to the bed.

"Trip go okay?" I mumbled.

"Coulda been better," he said as his head hit the pillow. "See you in the morning."

"G'night," I mumbled, squeezing the rosary beads under my pillow and saying a prayer for a better tomorrow.

Alec's alarm clock woke both of us up, as usual, on Tuesday morning. He groaned, poured out of bed like molasses in winter, and plodded into the bathroom. Hearing Alma already in the kitchen, I jumped out of bed, quickly got dressed, and went to get Isabella so that she could say good morning and good-bye to her father as soon as he got out of the shower.

I sat down on my daughter's bed and, as she wiped the sleep from her eyes, had some fun pointing to the blue sky and puffy clouds visible through her window and telling her we would be out there soon on this glorious late summer day. After a quick bowl of her favorite cereal in the breakfast nook, I got her dressed in her favorite outfit—jeans (the umpteenth reminder that I hadn't been allowed to wear jeans, favorite or otherwise, until I was ten years old) and a frilly pink T-shirt—and escorted her to her father, who stopped fussing with his tie to fuss over her.

When I got back from walking her to nursery school Alec had already left, so I camped out in the breakfast nook with my laptop and started to make some notes for the show. I was soon lost in my work and a half hour or more had flown by when I heard a muffled explosion somewhere in the neighborhood.

What the hell was that?

Before I could get to the window, the phone rang.

"A plane just hit the World Trade Center, Sam," Alec said, his voice as cold as ice. "No one knows what the fuck happened. Could be some moron flying a commuter plane back from the Hamptons for all I know. But it's only a couple of blocks away and I'm not taking any chances. I'm going for Isabella."

He hung up without waiting for a reply.

This has got to be bullshit.

I switched on the TV. There was no mention of a commuter plane, but there was plenty of information about a full-sized commercial jet crashing into the north tower. *What on earth is going on?*

I couldn't pry my eyes away from the television as I, along with the rest of the world, watched a second jet hit the south tower only minutes later.

The phone rang again seconds after that, and Alec huffed on his cell phone. "We're getting the hell out of here, Sam. Meet us at the garage."

Still in a state of shock, I grabbed my purse and Hercules's leash, and Alma, the dog, and I all bolted out the door, down to the lobby, and out onto the street, headed for Isabella's nursery school. *I'm not taking any chances, either.*

I craned my neck toward the top of the towers as we hustled along. The smoke, the flames . . . the *holes* . . . seemed surreal. But the blaring sirens and frantic activity everywhere—thousands and thousands of people running in all directions—were all too real.

Please, God, keep my Isabella safe.

I broke into a run and arrived at the school almost at the same time as Alec. Despite the chaos all around, I suddenly remembered the first time I'd run into him in that very same neighborhood. The children were gathered in the bomb shelter belowground, so Alec and I raced down the steps as he ordered the first woman he saw to *"get me my child . . . NOW."*

Alec swept Isabella up into his arms and we all hurried back up to the street. Alec-the-former-football-player barreled and cut his way through the crowds with me on his tail, and more than one person ricocheted off his midsection, spinning around and almost falling in his wake as I had that day just over five years before. By the time we got to the garage and joined the line at the attendant's booth, we were gasping for air as if there would be no tomorrow, and in all the chaos it seemed as if there might not be.

We were just about at the head of the line when a collective scream rose on the block as people started to jump from the burning towers. We shielded our daughter from that horror, but before we could even process what was happening, the south tower started to crumble onto itself. The roar when it crashed was from the bowels of hell itself.

"Oh my God!" a chorus of people nearby screeched as the possibility that all of us would soon perish became all too real.

I was afraid I'd lose my mind first.

"The train went *boom,* Mommy," Isabella said.

We reached the attendant's window just as a wall of smoke and debris blew down the street and a mounted policeman showed up in the driveway.

"No one's driving into or out of this area," he barked. "Everyone below Canal Street has to evacuate on foot—*now*."

"Where the hell are we supposed to go?" Alec and a host of others shouted.

"There's a ferry being set up at the Battery Park marina."

"Let's go!" Alec shouted, and I was never more grateful for his ability to move fast as he led our escape.

We arrived at the ferry point completely out of breath again, and we stood in line for a spot on one of the boats making round trips to the New Jersey side of the Hudson River. It was less than a mile away from where we were and I prayed to the Blessed Mother that we would be among those who made it out alive.

I was still praying when we finally made it onto a deck that was enveloped in gray smoke and more crowded than the worst subway at rush hour. The ferry shoved off as everyone on board looked back at Lady Liberty being swallowed up in smoke and at the fire that still raged near the top of the north tower.

When that tower started its collapse, we gasped as one. More than a few clutched their hearts, and scores cried.

I have no idea how many were crying inside, as I was. I reached for my daughter, pulled her head to my lips, and closed my eyes.

I'm a refugee again.

FOURTEEN

My heart was in my throat as everyone shuffled off the ferry in eerie silence, and I had no idea how we arrived at the Newark Armory. I could, however, explain the car that was waiting for us there, as Alec maximized comfort in whatever situation he found himself; he must have made a call from the ferry while I was losing my mind. Thank God his cell phone was working, because many were not.

Getting into a limo restored a measure of sanity to the DeMarco family, even though we were surrounded by camouflaged military trucks and National Guard soldiers. The driver snaked his way to the George Washington Bridge, and we made it across just as the Guard was sealing it off to civilian traffic. By that time I'd regained a semblance of sanity, but it still seemed as if we were in some kind of post-apocalyptic war movie.

We made our way out to Long Island, a trip that took six hours instead of the usual two. Franco and Monica were already there, physically if not mentally, and he informed us that there had been no way to talk Filomena into leaving the Brooklyn home she had shared for decades with Giovanni. If we were all going to die, she said, she wanted to do it there. Gary, who had managed to get a call to her while he was walking across the Brooklyn Bridge, said that Gianna was meeting him there and they would stay with her in Brooklyn. Alec said we'd stay on the island until things calmed down and then join them when we could.

My laser-focused husband scrambled to work long-distance while I scrambled to keep my sanity over the next two days. He holed up in his father's office, and I camped out on a couch in the solarium or a chair in Isabella's room while she played or slept.

I'd been having enough trouble trying to make sense of the life I was living; now I found myself trying to make sense of life itself.

Who would do such a thing?

I hadn't made much progress by the time we pulled ourselves together for the trip to Brooklyn. I went to the TV to switch off the nonstop coverage of the destruction mere blocks from my home and froze in my tracks when I caught the image of the most recent discovery amid the ruins.

As I stared at the perfectly formed steel cross sticking out from a pile of rubble under a clear blue sky, a spark of hope for the future ignited in my soul.

Over the course of the next month, it was a mixed bag of hope and despair at the DeMarco residence in Brooklyn. Alec made a couple of trips by limo into Manhattan to take Hercules to stay with our dog walker, to get us some clothes, and to enroll Isabella in a West Village nursery school, so a semblance of order was restored. He took me with him on one excursion to our apartment so I could scrounge up any personal items I wanted, but other than the first book I'd read to Isabella and my rosary collection, the only thing I cared about was my manuscript. The apartment was covered in soot and dust that got in through a window I had left slightly ajar at the time the buildings collapsed and the place would have to be professionally cleaned before it was even safe for us to live there.

I reconnected with Mary, Marvin, and Gregory as soon as possible, and we got back to working on the play.

Compared to so many others, I was safe in a world that had just been turned upside down. Every night after my head hit my pillow I said prayers of thanks for my family's safety and for Alma's reassuring presence. I also prayed for Filomena, who was still so devastated by the loss of her husband that the terrorist attack barely registered, and for Franco and Monica, whose marriage was disintegrating before my eyes. Still, the irony wasn't lost on me that, because of Alec, I was once more back in Brooklyn, whether I liked it or not.

The last thing I prayed for every night was for enough strength and wisdom to narrow the distance between us, created not only by his short temper and inexcusable treatment of Hercules but also by the fact that he was working late in Manhattan almost every night and entertaining without me most of the time. These days, even when we did go out together socially or to a business function, he barely acknowledged me, and when he did it was usually pointing out how hot I was to one of his cronies. He was barely more than cordial whenever he was at home, and usually medicated in some fashion, legal or otherwise. He issued orders about everything from having dinner ready to getting Isabella to and from school on time, and there were few opportunities to connect with him, let him open up, let him know how I really felt about things. No matter how hard I tried to talk to him, he blew me off every chance he had, saying that he had no time for my selfishness. *My selfishness . . . really?* And I could count on the fingers of one hand the times I remembered that we were husband and wife in bed. It was as if he had put me and Isabella in a nice little box that he kept on a shelf to be opened up when he was in the mood to do so.

By this time it was hard to even recognize him as the same man who had courted me so extravagantly, who had constantly told me how beautiful I was, and who had showered me with gifts and attention. I suppose the warning signs had been there in his relentless drive to reach the top, the confessions he'd made about the "favors" he did for clients, and in his giant appetites. But those had been overridden by his generosity and kindness toward me, and I could never have imagined that he would turn into the man with whom I now found myself sharing my life.

The question I kept asking myself over and over—with no satisfactory answer—was whether the price of staying in my marriage would be greater than the cost of breaking free. And, either way, how much was I willing to pay?

I did the best I could to accept being alone most of the time. I went about my work and took care of my charitable responsibilities. I chauffeured my daughter around, cobbled together dinners from local restaurants, which I served on fine china, and presented a tidy Isabella to her father every morning and evening to say hello and good-bye.

The irony was, with all the practice I'd had at being on my own and alone for most of my life, I wasn't getting any better at living like that. I was never resigned to being a refugee, which I'd been more often than not from birth, and I wasn't about to start.

As it turned out, the environmental effect of the dust and debris downtown after 9/11 was more severe than anyone had thought it would be. *A Gay Day* had to be postponed, which wasn't necessarily a bad thing because I'd have more time to keep working on my notes. We'd debut during the Easter holiday, and that time of resurrection seemed perfect in more than one way.

The same could not, however, be said of my living arrangements, as one month in exile in Brooklyn turned into four. I did my duty and got by, and I cherished the positive reinforcement I received most days from my daughter and from my work. Marvin and Gregory were delightful, while Mary patted me on the back at every turn and never seemed condescending even when she was advising or correcting me.

Sadly, Alec didn't want anything to do with my new friends, didn't even want to hear about them. He said they were crazy, and I didn't get into what did or didn't define crazy for him. I was sorry I'd caught him on a good day when I invited him to an informal play reading, because, once he got there, he made no effort to hide his disdain for the gay lifestyle in general or for Marvin and Gregory in particular. I didn't know whether to chalk that up to Alec-the-macho-homophobe, Alec-the-garden-variety-Republican, or Alec-the-disinterested-in-anything-Samantha.

One of the very few times Alec-the-romantic miraculously resurfaced was when he insisted on a special celebration for Valentine's Day, thus feeding the small flame of hope in me that was about to blow out. He laid on a big splash at the Plaza hotel that was to start for me with several hours at the spa. Of course, concierge Caryn handled all of the arrangements and met me there in midafternoon. After making certain that everything for my pampering was in order, she told me to enjoy myself while she went about seeing to the other details of our stay.

Never had I needed a top-of-the-line spa treatment and the quiet time to ponder more than I did on that day. During my massages and mudpacks, I replayed in my mind the five years since I'd met Alec and took stock of my life.

The years of poverty between leaving Tony Kroon behind and meeting Alec DeMarco had flown by before I knew it, and the years since the latter seemed like a month. My handsome bear of a Prince Charming had come along to rescue me from the humdrum, dead-end life I'd been living and introduced me to a vast array of material pleasures as well as an equally vast array of luminaries who wore their power like a fashion label. Without him I wouldn't have my beautiful daughter who gave me the chance to set some things right. I couldn't deny that I had the best of everything at my fingertips, and I had no doubt that the riches would continue to flow as Alec kept raking in—and spending—enormous sums of money. The way he talked about some very powerful people, including Grigor Malchek, who made many, many millions of dollars as the head of the stock exchange, and Senator Ross, who, with the help of his brother's millions, was now being mentioned for governor of New York, and the hints he dropped about the skeletons they had in their closets meant that he was at the top of his game and the "trophies" would keep on coming.

As my makeup was being applied following my facial, it struck me that cosmetics covered blemishes in much the same way that wealth and power covered the gaping holes in people's lives—surface interactions instead of real connections, hollow striving for the next best thing and the best invitations, gray-area business deals done behind closed doors by ravenous sharks who didn't care who got eaten up along the way—or the strippers and hookers who were always around to help everyone feel good.

I could only hope that the man I thought I'd met, the one who spoke from the heart about family and love, was still there somewhere and that I'd somehow find him again.

Ever-efficient Caryn showed up just as I was finished and took me by the hand to the elevator bank.

"Top-floor suite," she said, pressing the button. "You know Alec—nothing but the best."

She opened one of the double doors to the suite and escorted me onto the raised marble foyer. "Make yourself at home, Samantha. Alec said he'd be over as soon as he could clear his desk, but you know how Thursdays are. If you need anything, I'm on my cell around the clock."

Nothing but the best.

I stood for a moment when the door closed behind her and surveyed the latest palace that had been set before me. There wasn't a thing out of place in the sunken living room, and the kitchenette, which I glimpsed beyond a large dining table to the left, looked as spotless as I assumed Martha Stewart's would be.

I made my way to the master bedroom on the right. It was no surprise to find my clothes hanging in the closet, which had been left open for proper inspection, but I have to admit that the red petals strewn about on the king-sized bed and the trail of red petals that led to the master bath left me catching my breath. I followed the trail, one slow step at a time, and pushed the door that was open halfway.

The light from a hundred red candles danced off the polished mirrors and gleaming tile, making each red petal that led to the whirlpool seem like a ruby. I took a few more steps to the end of the trail—a small white linen envelope and a bed of petals floating on clouds of bubbles that offered promise to a girl who so longed to rest a weary heart. I held the envelope for a long moment before sliding the note out and reading it.

Mi Amore,
   Hope to make it there in time to share some "bubbly" with you before dinner.

A.

"Sorry I'm so late, Sam," Alec said in a rush when he burst through the door at eight-thirty. "It was unavoidable." He bent down to give me a hurried kiss and then looked me in the eyes. "You're beautiful," he said, and walked away.

I watched from the couch as he slipped his jacket off and loosened his tie.

"At least the chef arrived on time," he said with a nod toward the kitchen, where the personal chef arranged for by Caryn was hard at work. "C'mon, let's start eating." He waved toward the table. "I'm starved."

So am I.

Alec rambled on about the headaches of handling his father's estate and about the ins and outs of keeping Grigor Malchek happy, and got around to the forelock-tugging he'd had to do for him.

"You don't have to kiss anyone's ass, Alec," I said.

"I do if I want to get where I want to go."

"But where do you want to go? Don't we have enough?" I asked.

"No way," Alec scoffed. "Not until I'm out on my own and call all the shots."

"Speaking of shots," I blurted, "do you think all the alcohol and other stuff you consume is really necessary?"

Some pauses are delicious; the one that hung over the table as I toyed with the black truffle linguine on my Waterford china plate was not.

"I can drink anyone under the table, Sam," Alec said at last, his voice low but firm. "And out-party anyone."

"You're preaching to the choir," I said. "I'm just worried that the toll it's taking on your body isn't worth it."

"I am fine," Alec said, his voice rising, "and it won't. When I'm at work I'm all business."

And all business when it comes to play. "But for you entertaining is also work. Do you really need to entertain *so* much, Alec?" I asked.

"I get more done after the closing bell than I do during the day," he said. "That's just the way it is, Sam."

"If you say so."

"I do. I'm locking things up nice and tight. With Malchek's blessing I'll be able to get my bond trading company off the ground by the end of the year."

"You never mentioned bonds before."

"There's a killing waiting to be made now in real estate funds and investment mortgages, and I intend to get in on the ground floor."

From a penthouse high atop the Luxe Regent. "But do you really know enough about the real estate game to make your stand there?" I asked. *Other than collecting properties like I collect rosaries, that is.*

"Bonds, stocks, real estate, it's all the same to me," Alec said. "The structure of the deal, what's in it for me, is all that counts."

Being responsible for several hundred thousand dollars, as I was producing a play, was more than enough for me. I couldn't even imagine what handling a billion dollars of other people's money must be like. "Don't your investors think the same way?" I asked.

"Sure they do," Alec replied. "Everyone plays the game to win, and I wouldn't expect anything else. But if I structure things right everyone gets what they want."

Really? "I sure hope so." I sighed.

"Listen, Sam—leave this stuff to me. You just concentrate on Isabella."

"And the play, of course." I smiled thinly. *Not to mention my book.*

"Whatever you do is fine by me, as long as it doesn't take time away from the family," Alec said. "And as long as you keep those fag friends of yours far away from me."

I toyed with my food while Alec polished off a few more forkfuls of pasta in rapid succession.

"How's your wine?" he asked when he came up for air.

"Perfect, as usual."

Alec smiled ear to ear, and I couldn't remember the last time I'd seen that jumbo grin. "Nothing but the best, Sam," he drawled. "Nothing but the best."

Alec's Valentine splash faded into history in a matter of days as he put me back into my box and went on to the next splash, the custom-designed limousine and full-time chauffeur Caryn had arranged. The limo had every conceivable appointment, including an espresso machine, a DVD player, a hidden stash box for drugs, and a mini toilet that I could never imagine using. God only knows what went on in that traveling office-cum-bachelor-pad when I wasn't there, which was most of the time, as Alec-the-toast-of-the-town squired clients to restaurants and shows and clubs.

With the able assistance of his new secretary, who, in addition to her routine duties booked the special services of high-priced "escorts," and of Caryn, his trusty concierge, who juggled time and place, secured impossible reservations at the trendiest restaurants, and delivered last-minute gifts ranging from engraved Cartier pens to floor tickets for a Knicks home game, he maintained his steady rise on Wall Street. I didn't really mind, because I wasn't comfortable riding around in an extravagance that cost as much as a nice little vacation condo would have, and I didn't want to be privy to my husband's escort service, which I feared was as much in the gray area as the ones advertised in the Manhattan Yellow Pages. I had as little interest in porn and pot and pills on the road as I did at home.

In the meantime, *A Gay Day* had a spirited debut in front of a packed audience that included Alec and the Stavros brothers. He fidgeted in his seat, more interested in the after-party than in the play, as I said every line to myself along with the actors.

Our limited run was a modest success as show business goes. To me, however, it was a smash because it glorified love between two human beings, and I couldn't think of being involved with anything more important than that. I patted myself on my back for the work I had done bringing it to the stage—I was filled with a sense of purpose, a sense of true accomplishment, and for the first time in a long time, I felt happy.

Gianna and Gary tied the knot later that spring as scheduled, but that splash faded quickly, too, in the shadow of Franco's continuing slide into divorce. Monica and the children were no longer present at family gatherings in either Brooklyn or Long Island, and Franco swung back and forth between wallowing in depression and extolling the virtues of his impending bachelorhood. He was most animated, however, telling tales of the entertaining adventures with Alec in which he was now included.

Alec's fixation on material possessions and power was only growing more urgent. I didn't even raise an eyebrow when he mentioned the private jet he had his eye on. These trappings were just part of my life, as was the nagging feeling that I'd never really belong in my husband's world and the nagging fear that I'd never reconnect with the man I'd married. He added a second summer home in Quogue because he just had to be closer to the social scene in the Hamptons, and he continued entertaining not only clients but also his new friends, the ballplayers and their wives or girlfriends whom he'd met thanks to his legendary seats behind home plate at Yankee Stadium, and who appreciated his intimate knowledge of restaurants and clubs, including the ones where tits were exposed. To return these favors a couple of the players introduced him to Kevin O'Brien, a former EMT who was a fabulous personal trainer and advisor on the very latest approaches to exercise and peak performance.

Unfortunately, the positive side of my husband's new

interest in working out was far outweighed by something else—the inclusion of human growth hormone (HGH), testosterone, and steroids in Kevin's training regimen. Although these drugs were strictly forbidden by Major League Baseball, the players swore by their merits, and Alec-the-experimenter as well as Alec-the-experienced-needle-man jumped right in. That Kevin insisted on a doctor's supervision and monitoring of doses did little to alleviate my fears. Nor did running Alec's program by Dr. V, a world-famous internist with his own morning TV show, who told me there was a risk of potentially serious side effects.

Kevin was a likable guy who knew a lot about alternative and natural medicine, which had been an interest of mine all my life. But that didn't change the fact that Alec's headfirst dive into designer drugs—a marvelous new service he discovered his money could buy—was causing him to have the worst mood swings I'd ever experienced. His eyeballs would suddenly seem to be bulging out of his head and he would fly into a rage and snap at me or, worse, at Isabella, for absolutely no reason. The drugs may have been legally prescribed by the top anti-aging doctor in Manhattan, and according to my husband they made him feel great, younger and more alive. But no matter how good he felt after a back adjustment and an injection from Kevin, I was walking on eggshells whenever he was around, as I waited for the next explosion. It was becoming more than I could handle, and for the first time in my marriage I suddenly began longing for a way out.

Luckily for Hercules, he had stayed with the dog walker after the WTC bombing and was now living with her on a permanent basis. I hated the fact that Alec hadn't made any plans for his inclusion at the Luxe Regent palace he was building and I still blamed myself for not having defended him, because both Isabella and I loved Hercules very much, but at least I could be sure that he was now safe from Alec's fury.

My only escape from Alec's increasingly erratic and volatile behavior was my work—as a producer, I felt like I could truly be myself. Doris Bernstein and I became good friends as we worked together on another play, and I also struck up a friendship with Debbie Warren, who was married to the Yankees pitcher Presley Warren. I accepted her invitation to join her animal rights charity board and felt blessed that I could add these nurturing relationships to the ones I had with Marvin and Gregory. Being with these people kept me connected to Sam Bonti, rather than the increasingly submissive Mrs. DeMarco, who had taken to tiptoeing around her husband and shrinking into the background of his life.

Alec took care of the special needs of anyone who could help him on his rise to the top, and it broke my heart that he didn't believe me to be of any use at all. All that mattered to him was an adoring child and a dutiful wife he could show off to colleagues and clients at social functions. In truth I got ten admiring looks from those colleagues and clients for every one my husband gave me in the bedroom or anywhere else. It broke my heart, too, that the home life I always wanted—a child safe asleep and a husband at my side on the couch as we watched TV and ate popcorn—remained only a dream.

Alec fell into a routine of hitting the liquor cabinet as soon as he walked through the door, smoking pot constantly, and popping the occasional pain pill, particularly Percocet, which he obtained courtesy of his doctor connections. You'd think that all this self-medication would have at least relaxed him enough to communicate, but he kept all of his feelings bottled up despite my many hints that I would be more than receptive to his opening up. I racked my brain thinking about what I could do to hold on to my husband, and I had more time to do that than I would have liked.

Alec didn't call home often, and when he did it was usually

because he had some function that involved me. When he was home, if he wasn't watching a Yankee game in the den or playing with Isabella for the couple of minutes he allotted to that activity, I wouldn't even have known he was there. The rest of the time he was holed up in his study, assumedly working on his deals, or in the place he'd rented on Wall Street, initially because he needed a private place to shit. He hated shitting at the NYSE bathrooms; he needed room to spread out. This had become his part-time residence, which he and his buddies called the "lair." They used it as a recreational pad where they banged their girls on the side, stored the weed that was dropped off weekly at great expense, and made their chocolate-covered mushrooms. He also kept all his Yankee memorabilia there, along with suits for work. He had developed another life outside the home, our home.

He did, however, manage, with Caryn doing all the work, to plan a fifth birthday party for Isabella at Disney World, complete with fire-eaters on stilts, for family and close friends. At the same time he was working toward opening a company of his own that would be a major player on Wall Street. As usual, getting by was all I could do. I went to meetings with my team, attended charity events and board meetings, spent time with my delightful and insightful little girl, who was well on her way to becoming her own person, and did everything I could to keep my dream alive.

Before I knew it, another year was just around the corner.

More than seven years already since I met Alec.

I wasn't ready for Broadway, but my second and third plays had done better than the first and I was earning at least entry-level respect from the show business crowd. That was the topic of discussion when Marvin and Gregory invited me to their Rhode Island home early the following April.

"At least you're making a name for yourself," Marvin said,

as we sat bundled up on the deck with a salty ocean breeze wafting over us. "You don't need Alec to do that."

He was the steady, sensible half of the couple and I appreciated his encouragement, but his words didn't change the fact that my marriage was crumbling under my feet. Of equal concern was the fact that the "name" I was acquiring wasn't the one I really wanted—author of *The Blessed Bridge*.

"You just keep doing what you're doing," Marvin said, "and let the chips fall where they may."

"I'm on board with that," Gregory said. "Plenty of people would kill to have what you have," he continued, and then a devilish smile appeared on his face as he pointed to the seven-carat yellow diamond on my ring finger. "Especially Precious there."

"You're just talking about material things," I said.

Gregory laughed. "I will admit plenty of people would trade it all for a good screw at least once a week."

"Don't mind him, Sam," Marvin said. "You've got an awful lot going for you."

"And we sure as hell don't mind going along with you," Gregory said.

"I'm just not sure producing plays is the right path for me," I said softly.

"What—you've got a better one available?" Marvin asked.

"Maybe," I mused, and the shrill cries of seagulls flying low were the only sounds to be heard for a long moment.

Gregory leaned forward. "Give it up, Sam. It's just us girls here."

The three of us laughed freely. I was amazed at how different I felt around them—how at ease—as opposed to the tension I felt at home.

"I really want to be a writer." There, I'd said it.

"I should have known," Marvin said, "what with all the little touches you've contributed to our scripts."

"How long have you had that dream?" Gregory asked.

"Ever since my grandma gave me a portable Smith-Corona for my fourteenth birthday."

"Whoa." Marvin whistled. "That's quite a long time."

"Don't remind me." I frowned.

"Good for you for sticking with it," Marvin said.

"Doesn't surprise me," Gregory said. "If we've learned anything from working with you, it's that dogged determination is your strong suit."

"And what, pray tell, have you been secretly creating lo these many years?" Marvin asked.

"A novel about a girl growing up in Brooklyn."

Gregory frowned. "I can't believe you didn't mention it before now."

"You two already know everything that's in it," I said. "Growing up poor and being abused in and out of my home, and wanting to make my mark in the world."

"But you conveniently forgot to tell us how you intended to do that," Marvin said.

My eyes traveled from one to the other. "Forgive me?"

"Of course we will," Gregory smiled. "As long as we get to read your manuscript."

I delivered my novel to my friends with renewed hope for its publication. By the spring of 2005, the time for Alec to open his own business was approaching, as was the completion of our Luxe Regent apartment. I still didn't control our checking account, although I had opened one of my own for the small sums I was earning as a producer, and I didn't get to make any major decorating decisions, but I did get to choose among the options Alec's decorator laid out.

Marvin and Gregory helped me with those decisions, and they commiserated with me about the marble columns, the tile, and the massive, dark-wood antiques that would fill my new home no matter what small decorative details I decided on. The way I saw it, my new home was going to be as cold and sexless as my marriage.

By the time Alec, Isabella, and I moved into our palatial aerie that June, my husband had amassed a private helicopter, a private jet, and two summer homes, and he had access to the highest levels of society. He used his new toys to whisk himself to Washington, D.C., to Albany, where Senator Ross was now angling to be governor, and to any other city where a critical business meeting or a huge event, such as the Super Bowl, was taking place.

The wealth that surrounded me had long ago ceased to shock or even impress me, but our new, six-million-dollar home on the thirty-eighth floor of the Luxe Regent Hotel took my breath away. The columns, the marble, and the furnishings may have been gaudy and not to my taste, and the script *D* engraved in the foyer tile may have been over the top, but looking through the floor-to-ceiling windows for the first time in the finished space was still spectacular. The Manhattan skyline was on one side of the sunken living room, New York Harbor and the Statue of Liberty on the other.

For the first time in years, I felt myself filling up with a renewed sense that the world was at my fingertips. I couldn't help thinking that my mother and grandmother would have been as blown away as I was, but also that, ultimately, they would have been as critical of the flash as they had been of the flashy gifts Tony Kroon was always giving me. Still, in the midst of it all, I had the nagging feeling that I was standing in quicksand.

One wall of the foyer was covered in a mosaic mural that a sweet Jewish lady had created on-site, sweating under a wig she refused to take off. Flowing water spewed from the mouth of a ceramic fish into a marble fountain just beyond the *D*. I was surrounded by Italian antiques and custom pieces; I had Versace rugs and china and Biedermeier tables to beat the band; there were gold fixtures in all five of the bathrooms. I had eleven rooms—a "mini-mansion," Mirabelle, our saleswoman called it—that were filled with only the best, and my daughter had her own wing, which was at least ten times larger than the room I grew up in. And still I had an empty feeling in the pit of my stomach. I couldn't be farther from the Brooklyn I had so wanted to put far behind me, I had everything a girl could ever want, but I was no closer to the dream I had been certain would be mine in Manhattan—my dream of being a bestselling author, making my own way by sharing my story with the world, and having a loving and supportive family to come home to.

Over the next few months I discovered that the services and staff at the Luxe Regent lived up to their reputation for delivering luxury. I was truly living "the suite life." Whatever I needed would show up at my door; whatever I wanted done they would do. Since we were connected to the hotel any service they provided we received as well. Room service at 3 a.m., massages and manicures at midnight. Groceries and dry cleaning were promptly delivered and stowed in my refrigerator and cabinets and closets, whether or not I was at home. If Alma was off or out on an errand and I needed a babysitter, one magically appeared in a manner of minutes. If I needed nonscheduled maid service, all I had to do was pick up the phone.

Alec was in his element with an army of servants scrambling for the outrageous tips he gave them like pigeons going after breadcrumbs tossed from a park bench. Everyone was happy to assist Mr. DeMarco, which made him happy, too. He was particularly fond of Eddie, one of the doormen, who delivered his weekly supply of pot and extra painkillers whenever he requested them.

Kevin O'Brien continued to show up regularly for training sessions in the spa and HGH injections in our bedroom. Even the staid, generally unflappable crowd who populated the Luxe Regent went gaga whenever Presley Warren and other baseball cronies joined Alec's workout sessions. He extended Caryn's concierge services to anyone in the building who needed that impossible reservation or ticket, and it didn't take long for Alec to be "the Man" around the Luxe Regent, just as he was around Wall Street. He basked in all the attention.

One night later that fall, our house phone startled us awake with its blaring ring just as we were starting to fall asleep at around midnight.

"What's up, Rob?" Alec mumbled, and I could hear the raised, frantic voice on the other end, although I couldn't make out the words.

"I'll be right down," Alec said, as he hung up and bolted from the bed at the same time.

Moving fast yet again. "What's the matter?" I asked as he pulled on his pants and a shirt.

"Nothing," he said. "Go back to sleep."

Sure. No problem. Right.

I spent a fretful half hour sitting up in bed, all manner of scenarios playing out in my mind, until Alec returned and, without saying a word, crawled into bed, rolled over, and turned off his night table lamp, throwing the room into darkness.

"You gonna fill me in?" I asked.

"I told you it was nothing."

"Had to be something."

"Just the usual business. No concern of yours."

I switched on my night table lamp. "The usual business doesn't usually disturb my home, Alec."

"It was just some crazy broad," he said, without rolling over.

Oh. And here I was thinking it was something to worry about. "*What* broad?" I screeched.

Alec rolled over, narrowing his eyes and pursing his lips. "I don't want to go into it," he muttered. "I've got a big day tomorrow and I gotta get to sleep."

"Well, before you do, I gotta know what the hell is going on."

"Suit yourself, then." He sighed, raising his massive form on one elbow. "Ted Ross scored fifty mil when the company he put together went public. Seems he promised to take care of this dame."

"For what?"

"Services rendered, Sam."

I'm sure she wasn't providing stellar financial advice. "What's that got to do with you?"

"She did a few favors for some of my clients, and she came to collect."

I shuddered, as a scene from our past burst into our present. "Like Heather Frankel's pimp?"

"Something like that." Alec grunted. *Business as usual.* "I got rid of her."

"What'd it cost you?"

"Nothing." Alec grinned. "But ol' Ted is gonna be a mil lighter."

"Oh, is that all?"

"Can't have a crazy broad shooting her mouth off about Ted when brother Robert is about to become governor, not to mention the senator's married aide, who had a heart attack while he was doing her in her bed."

And white-collar workers supposedly don't get their hands dirty? "Still delivering the coffee and lunches, I see."

Alec slumped into his pillow. "Not for long, Sam," he said, closing his eyes. "Not for long."

I switched the light off and sank into my pillow knowing that my eyes would remain wide open for much of the night.

Franco and Monica ended up in divorce court just a few months after we moved. She wound up with everything after discovering that for years Franco had been secretly involved with a black woman from the South. But that was just a side-bar to Alec's relentless march toward starting his own mort-gage and bond trading company. Nothing would stand in his way: not the hemorrhoid condition that had reappeared, or the strange bumps and shingles on his back that came and went—which he claimed were the expected result of the growth hormone injections he was taking—and certainly not a wife who often felt like just another decorative object in his man-sion.

It pained me to feel that way on the sunny morning when he was finally able to leave the stock exchange; when I stood with him at the official ceremony on the floor as he and I rang the closing bell with Filomena and a wide-eyed Isabella at our side; when cakes in the shape of his and his dad's badge numbers, 3333 and 788, were rolled in, and when I presented him with his and his father's badges, which I'd had dipped in gold; and at the bash to beat all bashes, held at the Downtown Athletic Club afterward. Alec beamed with pride. Marvin and Gregory weren't among the two hundred invited guests, since Alec wouldn't hear of their attending, so once again I felt utterly alone. In the midst of that joyous crowd, I was as much a trophy as the Heisman award, which the Club had displayed for years. If I hadn't had a chance encounter with Olivia, a beautiful raven-haired woman who was about my age, the best day in my husband's life would have been a total loss for me.

We greeted each other politely as people do when they're circulating among strangers at these events, and as soon as she said hello I could tell that she was as indifferent to all the wealth and power in the room as I was.

"Is this decadent, or what?" she remarked.

"Par for the course in this game." I smiled in return.

"I often wonder if my career is even worth it."

"So you work on Wall Street? How long have you been at it?"

"Ten years already," Olivia said wistfully. "Where did the time go?"

Tell me about it.

"If I weren't sleeping with the boss," Olivia continued, "I think I'd be off on an island somewhere, or back in Madrid where I came from."

As she seemed to ponder that, I stole a glance at her ring finger, which was bare.

"So what's your story?" Olivia continued after a moment.

"I sleep with the boss, too," I said wryly. *That's about all I do in bed with him.*

"Oh yeah, Alec," she said. "Brendan and he are thick as thieves."

"Will you two get married?"

"I gave that up a while back," Olivia said softly, shaking her head. "His Irish Catholic mob family would crucify him if he got divorced."

"You're still young," I offered.

"I suppose," she replied. "But . . . the devil you know and all that."

Do I ever know.

It didn't take more than that brief conversation for me to be convinced that this was a person I wanted to know better, one of the few people in the Wall Street world I could relate to, and I was equally certain that she felt the same way. So, before we went our separate ways, we promised each other that we would stay in touch.

❖ ❖ ❖

At long last Alec had what he wanted. He was calling all the shots and spending his backers' money—along with fifteen million of his own that he'd put up—left and right to get DeMarco Futures off the ground and flying high. Victor Falco and the rest of Alec's team had followed him to his new offices and were rewarded with hefty raises. A support staff of twenty also joined them, enticed by generous salary and benefits packages.

Deep-pocketed investors couldn't get in line fast enough to cash in on the funds Alec put together, and ungodly sums of money kept flowing into his hands. I truly hoped that his friends as well as his colleagues really appreciated all that he was doing for them—all the money he made them and everyone on the Street, and all the sacrifices being made by his family.

Billionaire-in-the-making Alec knew just what to do with the mega-millions that came his way in his first year of business. He leveraged the money to build an ever-growing bond empire, and he greased the coffers of Robert Ross and other politicians to ensure that any door he wanted to go through would be open to him.

Meanwhile, I spent my time keeping the only door I had open—producing another play for Doris Bernstein with Mary and my gay partners—and preserving my sanity by spending as much time as I could with the regular people in my life. If I didn't have them to lean on when things got crazier than usual, I would have ended up in a rubber room somewhere.

And I also did my best to keep others out of rubber rooms whenever I was called upon to do so. I let Alec rant and rave about problems at work without saying a word about his cursing, the smashed phones, or his continuous lack of attention to me. I let Franco cry on my shoulder now and then about his broken family, without pointing out that he was in large part responsible for his plight. I turned a sympathetic ear when an eight-months-pregnant Sofia showed up at my door dying to tell someone about finding a coke-addled Victor in a bar at two o'clock in the morning with some floozy right out of college. And I even managed not to throw up when she added that he had told her he was saving his marriage by letting off some steam. I counted my blessings after that tale of woe, as I was again reminded that things could be even worse than they were.

Then one day, they got worse. Alec was leaving on one of his endless business trips and Isabella and I were standing in front of the building to wave him off when Becca, Isabella's best friend in the world, came bounding out the door with her nanny and shouted to Isabella to come play in the park. With a glance in my direction and a quick good-bye to her father, she bolted after her friend.

"No good-bye kiss." Alec seethed.

That fixation could be endearing, but sometimes it struck me as insane. "She's just a normal kid, Alec," I said.

"I've told you time and time again how important it is to me," Alec spit through gritted teeth, almost foaming at the mouth.

"I'm sorry, Alec."

"That's not good enough."

"What was I supposed to do? Chase her down and drag her back here?"

"Keep her at your side, you stupid cunt," Alec roared, "like a real mother would."

My cheeks turned beet red and I was glad I had my thousand-dollar Valentino sunglasses on as my eyes filled with tears. "Screw you, Alec," I hissed through gritted teeth, years of unexpressed anger and frustration finally released in an instant.

I didn't see the massive palm coming. The slap to my face, which cracked my sunglasses and sent them flying to the sidewalk, left me as paralyzed as Lot's wife when she turned around to look back at Sodom burning in the fires of hell.

I covered my throbbing face with my hands as I stared at Alec in shock. The handful of people who had watched the scene unfold, including two young doormen and an officer in the private security car parked near the entrance, remained motionless as Alec got into the limo that had been waiting at the curb and slammed the door. No one dared interfere with "the Man."

Only when the limo was rolling away did one of the doormen come forward to help me.

"You okay, Mrs. DeMarco?" he asked, placing a hand on my elbow.

For the first time, I hated hearing that name associated with me. "Yes, I'm fine," I managed to say briskly.

"Here, let me help you up the steps," the doorman urged, squeezing my elbow gently.

"No, I'm fine," I lied. "Please, just get me a cab."

"Yes, Mrs. DeMarco," he replied, and I grabbed his arm as he started to turn around. "Is there something else?" he asked.

"Please have a babysitter pick up Isabella in the park and stay with her until I get back."

"Yes, ma'am," he said.

I dialed Marvin and Gregory's Greenwich Village apartment number on my cell and, thank God, Gregory picked up on the second ring.

"Okay if I come over?" I asked, tears in my voice.

"Sure, Sam—what's the matter?"

Gregory cursed under his breath as I gave him a fast recap. "Beast," he growled just before I hung up.

I hopped in the cab and rubbed my cheek as my mind raced and the bustling world of Manhattan rolled by outside the window. It was as if that blow to my face suddenly snapped me out of the trance I'd been in since my wedding day. All the abuse I'd suffered, from the time I was a child, throughout my adolescence, during my years with Tony Kroon, and, I had to finally admit, during the time I'd been with Alec suddenly came rushing back and overwhelmed me. Luckily I arrived at my safe haven just in time to save me from sinking into total despair.

"Despicable." Marvin steamed as the three of us sat down in their small living area. I was still shell-shocked. "Who the hell does he think he is?"

"Gordon Gekko, probably," Gregory said.

"Alec's worse," Marvin said. "Gekko wore his greed and lust for power on his sleeve. This guy hides behind words like *team* and *family*." He shook his head slowly from side to side. "I know Alec is in his own world most of the time, which is abuse enough," he went on, "but did you have any inkling he would do something like this?"

"I've been burying my head in the sand . . . turning a blind eye to everything," I admitted aloud to myself.

"Don't beat yourself up, Sam," Marvin said. "Alec just over-powered you in every way."

"So what are you going to do now?" Gregory asked.

"I have no idea," I said. "I don't really have any money of my own . . ."

"You and Isabella can stay here for as long as you need to," Gregory said. "We're in Rhode Island most of the time, anyway, and we can stay with friends when we're in the city."

"Thanks, guys. Really." I paused, my mind still reeling. "But I don't think it's come to that . . . not yet." But my voice wavered as I considered my next move. I wasn't ready to abandon Alec and destroy the family we'd created together, but any feelings of love I still had for him were dashed out of my heart the moment his palm made contact with my face.

Gregory leaned over and squeezed my hand as his partner had done. "Whatever you need, Sam, just ask," he said.

"I will."

Marvin sat back and crossed his arms. "You have to make a life for yourself and Isabella, Sam."

"Easier said than done," I said.

He rose to his feet and headed for the desk in front of a picture window that looked out onto West Fourth Street. "You've already made a start with your producing," he said as he opened a drawer. He turned around and my eyes were drawn to the bound pages in his hands. "And this novel of yours isn't a bad way to go from there."

The pain from Alec's slap started to heal as soon as I heard those words.

"We loved it, Sam." Gregory smiled, and the healing continued in earnest.

"It might need a good editor," Marvin said as he sat back down and slid my manuscript onto the cocktail table. "But I've seen coming-of-age stories get published that aren't half as good as this one is right now."

"He's right, Sam," Gregory said. "Why don't you get a copy to Doris? She knows a lot of people who could help you."

If they keep this up much longer the slap will seem like just a bad dream.

In the taxi on my way back to the apartment I considered the future that Marvin and Gregory had allowed me to believe might be within my reach.

FIFTEEN

When the cab pulled up to the curb I kept my head down and moved as quickly as I could to the elevator. There was no doubt in my mind that the DeMarcos would be the lead item on the Luxe Regent's extremely active gossip grapevine, and I had no desire to make eye contact with anyone at that point.

Isabella, who was blissfully ignorant of the spectacle her parents had created on the street, lobbied me for a playdate with another friend from the building, and I was only too happy for the time alone to gather my thoughts.

There was no getting away from the sad fact that, however luxurious it might be, any home I shared with Alec would now be nothing more than a prison to me. Nor was there any way to avoid the conclusion that I bore some of the responsibility for making it so. I realized that somewhere in the back of my mind I had known this for a long time, but it had taken my husband's public burst of fury and my own public humiliation for me to admit it even to myself.

Alec had the same rescue gene as Tony Kroon, and the refugee I was had been only too willing to grab on with hands and heart to the lifeline he tossed my way. If anything was going to change I needed to keep reminding myself that I deserved more from life than acting as someone's grateful and silent decorative appendage, and I needed to acknowledge that throughout the course of my marriage, I had gradually allowed myself to disappear. I went over and over in my mind the two options I had going forward: move out with Isabella or stay where we were, at least for now.

The first course would free me from daily suffocation, but there would be constant battles with Alec over the money I'd need to live, no matter how modestly, and over our daughter, who would have her world turned upside down. The second course would avoid those direct confrontations and buy me more time to consider the best plan for my future, but I'd be at constant risk of becoming the target of another one of Alec's explosions.

After an hour of going back and forth I still couldn't make up my mind, and I decided to call a truce on the internal battle, since Alec would be away for a week. The one thing I did know with certainty was that I would have to be my own savior.

I still had faith in Samantha Bonti, and I recommitted to using my writing to acknowledge both my virtues and my weaknesses, my despair and my hope. And at the same time, I recommitted to my faith in God and the Blessed Mother, who had always helped me through the darkest times. Getting up from the corner of the couch where I'd been huddled since I got home, I went into the bedroom and reached for the rosary under my pillow. Clutching it tightly, I sat down on the bed and prayed to be forgiven for all the months that had passed since I'd last visited a church, and then prayed with all my heart that Alec would be the last cross I'd have to bear before I could truly be happy again.

When I got up the next day, I at least knew what course I would take in the near term. I'd change the things I could change, praying for the courage to do so; I'd endure that which

I couldn't change, praying for the strength to do so; and I'd pray always for the wisdom to know which was which.

I wouldn't move out, at least for now, because I couldn't risk the full brunt of Alec's fury or the emotional harm the break might cause for Isabella. And I still felt there was a chance, however slight, that Alec would come to his senses. I left that in God's hands and turned to the things I could control.

First on the list was my writing career.

With the help of Mr. Wainwright, my high school English teacher and mentor, I'd applied to and been accepted at New York University, but despite a partial scholarship and government grants I just didn't have the means to attend without asking Alec for help. I had been in total survival mode when I first crossed the Brooklyn Bridge in search of my destiny in Manhattan, and I cursed myself for not enrolling in college when I had the chance after meeting Alec. After chastising myself once again for letting my husband take total control of my life and for succumbing to the temptations of ungodly wealth, which got me far off course, I investigated my options for higher education and settled on a creative writing seminar at NYU. I also decided that I'd take my time telling Alec about it.

Next, I summoned up my courage and got a copy of *The Blessed Bridge* into Doris Bernstein's hands, as Marvin, bless his soul, had suggested. If I'd learned anything from Alec it was the importance of "who you know," and it couldn't hurt to have the most successful creative person I knew involved in some way. At the very least, I knew Doris would offer moral support and an honest opinion.

The final course of action I laid out for myself before Alec came back was to increase the time I spent with "normal" people. It had been months since Olivia and I had promised to stay in touch, but I took a chance and phoned her office to set up a lunch date for the next day. I also made a date with Debbie

Warren, and I accepted a standing invitation from Marvin and Gregory to visit them in Rhode Island over the weekend before Alec returned.

As I had hoped, lunch with Olivia proved to be just the confidence booster I needed. Even though we hardly knew each other, I felt comfortable enough to talk about my upbringing, complete with welfare and blocks of American cheese for dinner, as well as my abusive first boyfriend. And, as a Wall Street insider herself, she was uniquely able to understand and empathize with my current concerns and frustrations. Best of all, she was genuinely interested and supportive when I told her about my writing aspirations.

"When I saw you at Alec's sendoff my first thought was that you were just another rich bitch who lived at the Luxe Regent," she said, "but I knew you were something else entirely as soon as we started to talk."

"I'm not much for pomp and circumstance."

"Sort of an earth chick, it turned out." She laughed. "But who knew there was an earnest writer inside?"

"What about you?" I asked. "What's your 'inside' story?"

Olivia looked into space. "Nothing as earth-shattering as yours," she said softly. "I just want to have someone to cuddle with." She sighed.

"All things come to those who wait."

"And pray," Olivia added, and I thought for sure someone was going to have to pick me up off the floor.

"Is that something you do often?" I asked.

"All the time," Olivia said. "I spend a lot of lunch hours at Our Lady of Victory."

Who knew? "I go there a lot . . . at least I used to," I confessed. "Ironic, isn't it, that we might have met in church rather than at Alec's ostentatious extravaganza?"

"God sure works in strange ways, doesn't He?"

The Blessed Mother Mary had Martha, and now He's given me a sister.

"Amen to that, Olivia."

I was just as comfortable with Debbie Warren the following day. She handled her role as the wife of a baseball icon with a carefree spirit, and she showed as much interest in me as Olivia had. She was also as forthcoming about the trials and tribulations of her life, and just as nonjudgmental about my own, past and present.

"After hearing what you've had to overcome I'm embarrassed to complain about anything," Debbie said.

"Well, from what you've told me about the groupies who throw themselves at ballplayers, I'd say you have every right," I said.

"Presley's got plenty of teammates who manage to resist," she said. "There's no excuse for abusing a wife."

You're preaching to the choir.

"We met when we were both on spring break in Cancún, and we've been together ever since. I thought his lustful escapades would have ended long ago," she said with a sigh, the emotional pain clearly evident on her face. "And I never thought I would have to read about his indiscretions on the back page of the tabloids. I could just scream every time someone mentions the night when he was on the road and exposed himself in a disco to some college chicks."

"Men." I sighed, truly at a loss for words.

"*Some* men, Samantha."

"The crazy ones."

Debbie shook her head slowly. "Like my husband," she said softly. "Who gives away a World Series championship ring?"

"Alec treats it as if he were on that 1998 team," I said. "Lord knows what he did to earn it."

"Amen, sister."

"Have you thought about leaving Presley?"

"Every day," Debbie said, looking straight into my eyes. "But it's so hard."

Tell me about it.

"It'd be hell for our three kids, who adore their father, not to mention for me."

"Pulling up stakes and all that," I said.

"That's the least of it. My Italian Catholic family would be devastated by a divorce and I'd never hear the end of it."

"You're *Italian*?" I asked, wide-eyed.

"Hundred percent."

"I guess the blond hair threw me off."

Debbie laughed. "Only my hairdresser knows for sure."

We continued the girl talk for a while, neither of us mentioning the crazy men we were married to, and then Debbie shared her hope that she would eventually be able to use the degree in child psychology that had been gathering dust from the day she graduated from college. Like me, she mourned having allowed her own identity to be subsumed by that of her powerful husband. "Women." She smiled. "Hear us roar."

As we parted ways on the sidewalk outside the café we promised to get together again soon. I hailed a cab and thought about what it would be like to have two sisters in my life.

And I was thrilled to have something positive to talk about when I showed up in Rhode Island on Friday afternoon. By the time I left Marvin and Gregory at the end of the weekend, I felt that I was as ready as I could be to deal with Alec and the gilded prison in which I lived.

From the moment he walked in the door late Monday evening, Alec acted as if nothing out of the ordinary had happened, and there was no way I was going to bring it up. He didn't so much as ask me what was new as he grabbed a bite from the kitchen and "medicated" himself, and only mumbled "good night" when he turned off the light.

It was the same old, same old for Alec in the months that followed. Wheeling and dealing continued apace, and he piled up the millions in contemplation of ever greater wealth, as he made money for Grigor Malchek and other well-heeled investors. It became clearer and clearer to me that Alec was an easy touch for just about anyone who bowed to him in the process. He was constantly talking on the phone or at an event with someone who bent his ear about a worthwhile project, and he was as loose with his checkbook as he was morally with his business entertaining. When Gary wanted a Porsche, there was Alec to purchase it for him, and when Gianna and Gary had their eye on a condo in Brooklyn Heights with a to-die-for view of the Brooklyn Bridge and the Manhattan skyline, he loaned them most of the down payment. Alec-the-new-patriarch just couldn't say no to the sister who worshipped the ground he walked on, and the three of them knew the loan wouldn't be repaid for a long time, if it was paid back at all. But this was his family, so who was I to judge? If I had a family I'm sure I would have done the same.

Filomena still seemed oblivious to most of what was going on around her, including the string of loose young women on the arm of her elder, newly divorced son, but did she ever raise an eyebrow when he strolled into a family gathering with his black Southern belle on his arm. If she did have any opinions about Franco's new taste in women, she kept them to herself, with pursed lips. And whatever opinions I had on the matter, well . . . I kind of enjoyed the added color in the family.

Nor did I—or anyone else in the family—say a word about the extra pounds Alec was piling on. And although Isabella, who was growing into an ever more precocious child every day, didn't mention her father's weight gain, she did tell me about watching him eat an entire box of dry Cheerios in bed, and she was forever running to me or Alma with a wide-eyed tale of discovering a stash of Oreos and Nutter Butter cookies, Kit Kats, Twizzlers, or Skor bars hidden under the bed.

Alec continued his workouts and human growth hormone injections with Kevin O'Brien, and he was beyond thrilled when his trainer introduced him to Calvin Ransom, the most famous pitcher on the Yankee staff. Alec acted like a child for days afterward, but it tortured me when our young daughter came to me one day because she'd seen "Daddy getting a needle" and wanted to know if he was sick.

"Oh, honey," I said, wanting to reassure her, "Daddy isn't sick. He just gets those vitamin shots to give him more energy because he works so hard every day."

She seemed to accept that explanation, but I hated the fact that she was being exposed to things no child her age should have to see.

I shouldn't have been surprised that even after achieving what he claimed to be his ultimate goal of striking out on his own, nothing had truly changed in Alec's world—not the money, or the self-medicating and partying, or the constant striving for more and more . . . and more.

Bloody bed sheets were still a part of our life as well, as I discovered one morning when he bolted out the door for work as usual, failing to say a word about the mess he was leaving behind. Alma, saint that she was, helped me dump the blood-soaked sheets into the bathtub, and cleaned up the drain clog they caused, without a word of complaint.

Isabella was not quite eight yet, but she was inquisitive and precocious, as her teacher was all too willing to tell me when I attended a conference with her. And she had certainly been witness to more than a child of her age should have seen or heard.

Clearly I needed to start talking to her about what was going on. Sometimes I would try to normalize things by chatting with her about what Daddy did at work and explaining that what was going on wasn't really so unusual, even though she was still too young to understand it all. It was difficult at first—for both of us—but it was far better than letting her imagine things that could have been even worse than the reality.

"You know," I said, "Daddy is working really hard and he's under a lot of pressure because he's set a really big goal for himself. But no matter what, the most important thing for him is to give his family the best of everything.

"It's important to have goals for yourself and to follow your dream no matter what. But the most important thing of all is to figure out how to reach your goals and stay focused. That's something you're going to have to do for yourself when you grow up."

"But how do *you* do that, Mom?" Isabella asked, looking very serious.

"Well," I said, "you say your prayers every night, because God always answers. I haven't always prayed as often as I should have, but I hope you will."

From that moment onward, I made it a point to share as much of my life as I could with my daughter and try to be the best role model I could. She loved hearing about whatever play I was working on, and she was always begging to go with me to meetings and rehearsals. It hurt me to tell her she'd have to wait a bit longer for that, but that pain was nothing compared to the hurt I felt because of Alec's lack of interest in our sweet daughter. Despite the fact that he was such a family man. The pressure of being rich finally caught up with him.

That holiday season I was overjoyed to be offered the opportunity to produce a play that would open between Thanksgiving and Christmas in a theater on West Forty-second Street.

It wasn't Broadway, but it was the closest I'd come so far. The production budget was also twice as large as any of the others I'd been responsible for and it would have been nice to have my financial-wiz husband to help me with it, but I'd long given up that hope. The status meetings Doris Bernstein held from time to time were generally opportunities for me to shine, but I was beyond nervous when she called around noon one day in early November to say that the next meeting had to be moved up and asked if I could be in her office in an hour. I was unshowered, un-made-up, still in sweatpants, with an unfinished report on my desk, and I knew that the Stavros brothers would be there checking on their investment.

I told her not to worry and then sprang into a panic as soon as I hung up the phone. I threw on my best pair of jeans, a great cashmere sweater, and a kick-ass pair of boots, grabbed my three-thousand-dollar Dolce & Gabbana jacket and a wide-brimmed Lanvin hat, and was out the door in minutes.

Talk about "getting by." I laughed silently as I pressed the elevator button.

Heart racing, I breezed into the meeting and through the production details that I'd rehearsed in the cab on the way over. The few questions anyone had were by and large about the dollar figures associated with each budget item.

When Doris finally asked, "Are there any other questions for Samantha?" her two partners, Spiro and Emmanuel Stavros, shook their heads. I hadn't seen them for quite some time and this guy Spiro seemed to be giving me a hot flash. *A girl like me should not be having these thoughts.*

"What's that perfume you're wearing?" Spiro asked warmly. *I don't think that's the kind of question Doris had in mind.* "It's as lovely as you are."

"Eau d'Hadrien, and thank you very much." I blushed, taken aback for a brief moment.

"And thank you, Samantha, for coming in on such short notice," Doris said, rising.

"Yes, thank you," Spiro chimed in, "and please, let me walk you out."

"You don't have to do that," I said as I pushed away from the table.

"It's no trouble," Spiro said with a smile. "I'm on my way to '21' for a stuffy business lunch anyway."

"You did a great job in there, Samantha," he said as we waited for the elevator.

Yeah, right. A snow job. "It's kind of you to say that."

"The people I do business with aren't much concerned with kindness," he said. "It's all dollars and cents to them, and they liked your bottom line."

"You're not shy about making money, are you?" I asked as the doors opened.

"I'm not shy about anything," he said with a grin as he ushered me into the elevator.

Spiro escorted me to the lobby and out into the cold, gray, blustery early afternoon, and then he insisted on hailing a cab for me even after I told him two or three times that that wasn't necessary. As I watched and hoped for luck at the curb, Spiro stood five feet out into the street with his right arm raised, his chestnut ponytail gleaming against the collar of his camelhair topcoat.

After three excruciating minutes, Spiro turned to me. "Perhaps I should have let you fend for yourself."

Wouldn't be the first time.

"Do you want to wait inside?"

"I'm okay," I said, lying, and shivering from head to toe.

As Spiro started to turn back to the street, a gust of wind caught the brim of my hat and carried it to the sidewalk ten feet away. Before I could say a word, he was already in motion, and I was thankful to be in the presence of another man who moved fast.

Winds being what they are—relentless—and New Yorkers being what they are—blasé—my hat resumed its sailing as Spiro cut through the crowd and leaped onto a concrete planter like a running back evading would-be tacklers, raised his right arm again, and snatched my hat from its perch atop a naked hedge.

Hopping off the planter and strolling back to me hat in hand, he was grinning broadly as he dusted it off, fit it snugly on my head, and paused for a long moment to survey his handi-work. His eyes were silvery gray, and they danced with life as his hands slipped to my shoulders, seemingly in slow motion.

"Can't have a hot producer losing her fancy chapeau, now, can we?"

I was loving that hot producer comment, but it also kind of took me aback.

Then, spying an available taxi, he sprang into action again. He held the door open, ushered me inside with those eyes, and leaned in, one arm on the door and the other on the roof. "Until next time, Samantha," he said softly, giving me a peck on the cheek and closing the door before I had even a chance to thank him for rescuing my hat . . . and me from what had started out as a rather stressful day.

I felt like I'd been to a coming-out ball when I got back to the apartment. I kicked off my Manolo boots, slipped out of my sweater and jeans, and wrapped myself in a robe before settling into the rose-colored ottoman, which matched the plush pile carpeting in my apartment-size dressing room, to contemplate what I'd just experienced.

Although I appreciated the positive reinforcement I'd re-ceived for my work, I appreciated even more the positive rein-forcement I'd received as a woman, which is something I'd been lacking for a very long time. Dying to share it with someone, I reached for my cell and dialed Olivia in her office, hoping she'd pick up her extension.

"It's been too long, Samantha," she said, answering the phone and my prayer. "How are you doing?"

"Well, funny you should ask. The strangest thing just happened. There was this man . . . I mean out of nowhere." It all came out in a rush as I filled her in quickly before pausing to catch my breath.

"They're never out of nowhere, trust me. You sound like a girl who just came back from a first date."

"I know. Crazy, isn't it?"

"Slow down, sister," Olivia said. "Maybe he was just being a nice guy."

Starved as I was for affection, she had a point. "Maybe."

"Or maybe he's like all the rest of them, just looking for the next conquest."

"Perhaps . . ."

"Take a cold shower and call me in the morning," Olivia said.

"Maybe you're right, but I just can't help feeling that when he said I was hot, he wasn't talking about my career as a producer."

"All the more reason for taking that cold shower," Olivia said, and I laughed with her then.

"What do you think I should do?"

"What *can* you do?" Olivia exhaled. "Wait, like we all do."

"Thanks for being there, Olivia."

"No worries," she replied, and we said our good-byes.

My friend's wise words aside, I still had more than enough worries that wouldn't be fading away for quite some time. The positive reinforcement I had received did nothing to alleviate the stress of the prison I was in, my deep concern for Isabella's well-being, or the doubts I had about my own murky future. And now a huge "maybe" had been added to that list.

Am I reading too much into what could well be a meaningless encounter?

I wasn't going to come up with an answer on that ottoman, so I headed for my desk to fire up my laptop, because I couldn't think of anything else to do. On my way out of my dressing room, I glanced at the painting of the Blessed Mother hanging in a recess among the white lacquer shelves and said a fast prayer before turning out the light.

I didn't expect to find the answer to that "maybe" anytime soon, but it was right there on the screen as soon as I opened my email:

You're amazing, Samantha. This will be a great production.

Spiro

My heart was racing again, and an ocean of cold water wouldn't have been enough to counteract the heat coursing through my body.

SIXTEEN

After taking a few calming breaths, I dashed off a short but carefully considered response.

> Thank you for your kind words. Till we meet again, as they say in the theater.
>
> Samantha

I was still stunned after hitting "Send" and just sat there staring at the screen. I pictured Spiro at '21' discussing whatever deal he was working on, and wondered when I'd hear back from him.

I didn't have to wait more than a couple of minutes for the telltale chime on my laptop:

> There is something wrong in a world where your openness, unselfishness, and regard for others don't amaze at least one person every day. As if that weren't enough, your combination of confidence and innocence is indeed rare, and totally irresistible. I'd be less than honest if I didn't add that I've never before come across your intoxicating combination of wide-eyed girl and mature woman in the same person.

Shame on anyone who doesn't notice what is as clear as
day, or doesn't say a word about how amazing you truly are.

                                                        Spiro

I didn't know how he could be participating in a lunch
meeting while meeting with me online, but I didn't care. I didn't
care about anything but those words at that moment—not the
trials and heartaches of my past, not the prison and heartaches
of my present, and not the uncertainty about my future. All that
mattered to me was that an honest man seemed somehow to
have recognized the Samantha who had to deal with it all.

Of course, I knew that Spiro could have been just another
powerful man who enjoyed tossing a lifeline to a vulnerable girl.
But I also knew that if I reached for it with both hands this time
it would be on my terms. Instead of a desperate grab for any life
preserver in a stormy life, I'd be reaching for a strong hold on
the peaceful life I always wanted.

I told Spiro again how surprised and touched I was, and
we exchanged a few more emails acknowledging our circumstances—his arranged marriage to a wonderful but incom-
patible Greek woman, and my marriage-in-name-only to a
self-destructive man—which made any kind of meaningful and
regular relationship between us difficult if not impossible. We
bemoaned our fate and agreed to let go and let God.

Spiro began emailing me every other day. Over the next
several months I found myself dreaming up reasons to attend
social functions that would be excuses for me to see him. Alec
didn't seem to care that I was out and about by myself in the
evenings. He was only too happy to have me occupied while he
drifted into his office and away in a haze of marijuana smoke.

When May 2007 rolled around and the warm weather set
in again, Alec arranged the first weekend blowout of the season
at the Long Island compound. In the helicopter on the way out

I looked down at the line of cars on the expressway and found myself wondering if Spiro was driving one of those indistinguishable vehicles on the road below. Then I immediately felt guilty.

How could something so wrong feel so right?

The DeMarco family was its usual dysfunctional self, which mattered less than ever to me. While Alec's sister and mother wallowed in the misery that was mostly of their own creation, and assorted guests joined them in milking the trappings of wealth, I thought about when I'd be able to steal away and spend time with the normal person with whom I had an anything but normal relationship.

So on Sunday I decided to fly back to New York by myself and do the unthinkable—have a coffee with Spiro. I doubt that Alec even noticed my absence.

"I want to leave my own mark," Spiro confessed solemnly as we sat in an almost-deserted coffee shop on Madison Avenue.

"I had no idea that you wanted to separate yourself from your brothers. Why didn't you mention it before?" I asked.

Spiro sighed. "It's been hard enough just to be together . . . We haven't really been alone."

"And what is it you want to do? What do you want to be remembered for?"

"My dream is to build a chain of state-of-the-art retirement communities that have on-site recreation and activities, companion services, and senior care. Each facility would have everything right on site, including a full-service hospital. I guess you could say that I want to be in the business of helping others."

I know all about dreams. "So what's stopping you?" I asked.

"I don't control the money, Samantha. I have two brothers."

I know about that, too. "You *will* someday control your own fortune, Spiro."

"But that's only part of it," he continued, and then he paused and gazed into my eyes. "I want to be with someone who shares my dream, Sam."

That was the first time he'd called me by that name, and it never meant more to me than it did then. "My dream is to be with someone who just wants to curl up on a couch with me and eat popcorn." I sighed.

"I'd do that right now if I could," Spiro said solemnly.

Propriety be damned. I wish he'd take my hand right now.

"I want to leave my mark, too," I said softly after a few quiet moments.

Spiro smiled. "You're well on your way, from what I can tell."

"That's just it, Spiro," I said. "I do enjoy producing, and it brought us together, but it's not how I plan to make a name for myself."

"And what do you really want to be doing?"

"Writing. Getting my novel published. That's how *I* dream of making my mark."

"So you're an author," he said, without a hint of condescension or doubt in his voice. His eyes found mine again. "You still amaze me, Sam."

Spiro held my eyes for another moment.

"I'd love to read your novel."

I smiled and touched his hand.

As the days went by Spiro and I continued to exchange emails about separate lives and the platonic relationship we had. There was always a hint of the spark we'd felt on that day when he rescued my hat, and there was no denying the desire building up inside me.

Over the summer, Alec continued to revel in his millions and his minions, but from time to time there was a hint in his facial expressions and halting speech that something was bothering him. He still spouted his maxims about "team" and "commitment before ego," but they didn't seem to have the same ring of conviction. The one thing I knew was that whatever was bothering him this time had nothing to do with me. I'd certainly been the source of his bad moods before, but this was different.

What wasn't different was that he continued to pack on the pounds as he ramped up his use of recreational and prescription drugs, which Franco would supply when "fill-in" prescriptions were needed.

In mid-June, when he was called to testify before Congress about the use of performance-enhancing drugs in Major League Baseball, I thought that might be the source of his bad mood, but he went down to Washington as if he were on just another business trip. He was a legitimate, upstanding citizen, and a good Republican to boot, and he told the truth about what he knew, which had nothing to do with PED use by Presley Warren or Calvin Ransom or any of the rest of the Yankees. Alec just told the committee that he was under a physician's care for his health and training needs, and that was that.

All I knew was that Alec was committed to everything but me. But for the first time in a long time, that was okay, because *I* was committed to me.

I kept on seeing Spiro but always in the company of other people. It was only when reading his emails—like the one he wrote about *The Blessed Bridge*—that I truly felt alone with him.

Forgive me for not getting back to you sooner, but I wanted to read it twice. It was as if the angels themselves were whispering in my ears, and there is no doubt in my mind that young girls and grown women would learn from your story and be inspired by your words.

You've had to fend for yourself for most of your years, Samantha. If only one person changes the direction of her life because of the story you tell, its value would be immeasurable. Stop all you are doing and publish this book. It will be your ticket to freedom.

As I read those words, my commitment to my novel reached a new high. His praise made me realize that I hadn't written much of anything for too many years. I'd put my manuscript in a box for safekeeping, just as I'd put aside my visits to Our Lady of Victory, and went on trying to be what someone else wanted me to be, even though I doubted that I'd ever live up to Alec's expectations of what a perfect wife or a perfect mother should be. It was finally time for that to stop. I had to do more than sign up for a single writing seminar. I also had to let the Blessed Mother out of the box I'd kept her in.

I dashed off a fast thank-you to Spiro for both his compliment and his inspiration, and he replied almost as soon as I'd hit "Send."

Taking this journey with you is an inspiration to me.

And his words continued to come as we led our separate lives.

You're tough, you're strong, you're resilient. Stay focused—don't let anyone take you off your path.

Easier said than done, but I get it.

Go to church. Light a candle. Sit down and relax.

Thanks for the reminder.

You have your health, a wonderful daughter, your writing, and . . .

Me . . . whenever you need me.

Since life with Alec was as frightful as ever, I had never needed anything more.

Stop everything you're doing. Stop producing other people's plays, stop writing any other stuff, and just focus on *The Blessed Bridge*. That's your ticket, that's who you are. Take it out and get it published.

Alec remained in his own world and I stayed in mine. The more I saw of his, the more I wanted to go in the direction my heart was taking me. I had no idea how my relationship with Spiro would go in the long term, but I knew that I wanted to be with someone who wanted me to be me, even if we were just flirting friends.

When Doris's invitation to a swank reception showed up in the mail late in August, and I knew that Alec would be out of town, I jumped at the opportunity to shed my identity as Mrs. DeMarco and just be Samantha.

In a drawing room high above Central Park, I circulated among the black-tie guests for a polite fifteen minutes and then made my way out to the terrace to soak up the energy of the majestic city.

"I was simply dying until you showed up," Spiro said, his silvery gray eyes smiling.

I've come alive a bit myself recently. "I'm all about life," I said softly.

After hesitating for a moment in the stillness of a humid summer evening, he raised one eyebrow toward the double glass doors behind us and pulled me into his arms.

"I'm all about life, too," he said, and kissed me as every girl should be kissed.

Finally, he tilted his head back and drank me in with his eyes. As his mouth took mine again, I heard Rhett Butler's words to Scarlett in her well-appointed dressing room: *You should be kissed, and often.*

As summer turned to fall, I fretted constantly over all the reasons I shouldn't be involved in a relationship that was no longer platonic. Even though my marriage was falling apart, I'd still taken an oath before God that I should keep unless it ended in His eyes. Also, there was Isabella to think about. The consequences for both Spiro and me would be dire if our friendship became public, and I'd have the frightful prospect of dealing with Alec, who had a black book filled with high-priced lawyers at his disposal. It just wasn't worth it . . . but I needed love now more than ever.

Still, what it always came back to was how good—how *right*— it felt. Spiro was in my life, and for all I knew, Grandma, or even the Blessed Mother, had sent him to me. I wasn't trying to complicate my life, but I also wasn't going to stop being me. If someone couldn't stand not being around me, Lord knew I deserved something better. God works in strange ways—and who could blame me for injecting some normalcy into my life? Truth be told, I wasn't being given any glaring stop signs to halt the progress I was making in my life. Quite the contrary, all I saw was repeated encouragement to keep going.

As Spiro had told me, *No person can keep you from your God-given destiny.*

My destiny was *The Blessed Bridge* and I intended to get it out there.

Alec's self-abuse was growing harder to watch. When his weight got to the point where even he was concerned about his health, he decided to go on a crash weight-loss program. After a course of laxatives and enemas failed to do the trick, he came up with the idea of gaining twenty more pounds so he'd qualify for lap band surgery, another luxury available for only forty thousand cash.

One day Isabella found a half-smoked joint that Alec had left on his desk. When she asked me about the "funny-looking cigarette," I had to do some quick thinking and creative lying, but that was nothing compared to the morning when he had a shot of twenty-year-old scotch with his Cheerios—his "breakfast of champions"—before leaving for work. We were all sitting at the table in the kitchen when his mood turned suddenly darker for no apparent reason. He rose with palpable menace, lunged over our daughter and toward where I was sitting, and swiped at my laptop, nearly knocking it to the white Italian tile, all the while letting out a stream of invective about what a "shitty" mother I was.

Try explaining to a nine-year-old that parenting is more than securing a fifty-thousand-dollar trip to Disney World to meet Cinderella herself and that her mother was trying to be her own Cinderella in the face of all that. When Alec returned home from work that night, he tested my sanity once again when he shocked me with an attempt at lovemaking. For a change, I had fallen asleep first, so I kept my eyelids shut, which seemed only natural since every other part of my body was suddenly paralyzed. I thought of the Blessed Mother hanging in my dressing room, and I was thankful she wasn't above my bed, as she had been when Tony Kroon took my virginity in his parents' bed.

God, please . . . I don't want to do this.

I stirred when feigned sleep would have been far too obvious to the three-hundred-plus-pound behemoth who kept jostling me.

Alec didn't say a word about how long it had been.

Probably more than a year.

And he said nothing about my mechanical submission

to his sudden appetite, as he did what he wanted to do, and I vowed that it would be the last time.

Alec barely acknowledged our anniversary that fall, which was fine by me. And then Doris Bernstein came through with an agent who wanted to talk to me about *The Blessed Bridge*. Shortly after I gave her the manuscript she'd told me how much she liked the book, which meant the world to me coming from her. And she'd promised to "talk to a few people" about it. But then months had gone by and I was beginning to think I'd hit another dead end. So hearing that someone was actually interested enough to meet with me was the greatest anniversary gift I could have received.

Alec waltzed through the year-end holidays, as ebullient as ever about the festivities he both attended and arranged, but the fact that something was bothering him was still evident beneath the surface. In fact, it was bothering him so much that he barely uttered a word when I said that I thought it would be better if I moved into the same room with Isabella. I knew I could have claimed one of the many empty rooms, but, truthfully, I wanted to be near my daughter.

I told him my plan right after I cleaned up his bloody sheets one morning. Self-preservation always being at the top of my list, I left unsaid that I had hated waking up next to him every day for too long. I did say, however, that it would be the last time I'd be picking up his soiled sheets. I moved to the couch in Isabella's room, telling her that Daddy snored a lot, which he did, and that it would be easier if he had the bed to himself.

My daughter's eyes revealed that she knew the truth—that Mommy would sleep better this way—as well as the relief she felt knowing that she wouldn't be alone when Daddy's next temper tantrum erupted, which I sadly realized was not unlike the way I'd felt when I was with Grandma in our room while Mom was having one of her intoxicated explosions. Though I said a prayer that she and I would support each other as Grandma and I had, it was with a heavy heart that it dawned on me I hadn't been able to spare my daughter from the heartache I'd been suffering for years.

More and more frequently, Alec's explosive tantrums risked turning into trips to the ER. One night, I heard him screaming my name at 2 a.m. and found him sweat-soaked and on his knees at the double sink in the master bathroom, his breathing labored. He tried to get up but almost passed out. I grabbed a couple of towels and wrapped them around him, biting my lip the whole time, as images of my mother crashed out on her chipped-tile bathroom floor flashed through my mind. Less than a minute later, however, he calmed down and his breathing stabilized. Remembering Mom's two ambulance trips, I asked him if he should go to the hospital.

He shook his head slowly. "No way," he muttered. "Just give me a minute and I'll be fine."

I pivoted on my bare feet and headed out.

"I'm just getting old," Alec called after me.

I didn't care to know if he was trying to smile when he said that.

From then on Alec and I communicated mostly via Black-Berry, even from room to room in the house. For him, it was the easiest way yet to keep communication going from the box he kept me in. For me, it was the easiest way to keep his tantrums at arm's length. But that didn't mean I wasn't worried about him.

Abiding faith in the Blessed Mother had always given me strength when I needed it most, and I always prayed hard for Alec. I had always gravitated toward others who shared my faith, and Spiro had used the word *God* more often in the short time I'd known him than Alec had in more than ten years of marriage.

I took this as further evidence that it was right for us to be together. And when the other mother Mary, Doris's assistant, sent me a rosary from Ireland while she was on an extended visit with her family, I realized that no amount of money could buy the love that came with her gift. It was these touching expressions of caring that got me through being untouched most of the time—yet another item on the list of things I vowed to change in my life. *Money doesn't define you. You should be the one who defines what it can do for you.*

After checking in on Alec one evening when he was in the bedroom, only to find him watching porn on his laptop with his hands under the sheet and my thousand-dollar jar of La Mer skin cream opened at his side, I stopped going in there at all, and generally cringed when I heard him come out. His only comment was "I can't believe how soft my cock is. This cream is really something else." Of course, his BlackBerry communication after that little encounter was noteworthy. I mean, this was an extraordinary man that I loved so much.

What had happened to the amazing man I married? Did Wall Street do this to him? Was this his chosen path now?

If only there were more humorous moments, like the time Alec's hundred-thousand-dollar Italian antique bed crashed to the floor with him in it, my prison sentence would have been easier to take. Lucky for Alec, Olivia had stopped working full-time for her boss and was dating a construction worker, of all people, who worked at a new hotel site close to the Luxe Regent. He came right up with two Mexican buddies, and I laughed right along with them as they did the necessary repairs.

In the new year, the literary agent whom Doris had recommended finally gave me a call to say that she wanted to set up a lunch, and I jumped at the lifeline that was being offered—tenuous though it might be.

This is going to be the most important meal of my entire life.

Moira Jewison made a reservation at Nello on Madison Avenue, but I would gladly have met her at a hot dog stand. She was already waiting at the table when I arrived. She appeared to be in her mid-forties, wore heavy designer eyeglass frames, and struck me as the high-end frumpy type, which was just how I'd pictured a literary agent would be.

"Samantha, I'm so pleased to meet you. I read your book and I just love it," Moira said as soon as I was seated. "I couldn't put it down."

I love you, Moira.

"I want to do something for you, but right now I'm going through a divorce," she continued. "On top of that, I'm not fully recovered from a shattered elbow, and don't ask how that happened!"

"Oh, I'm so sorry," I said softly.

"Don't be," Moira huffed. "I was in the last two weeks of full bed rest and climbing the walls to get back into the game when your manuscript landed in my lap."

And I've just landed at the foot of another bridge.

"Don't get me wrong," she continued. "It has to be cleaned up before I can send it out. I'll give you the marked-up copy I have that will point you in the right direction, but you'll have to do the work."

I was already visualizing *The Blessed Bridge* in the window of Barnes & Noble.

SEVENTEEN

After that lunch I attended my writing seminar with a totally different attitude. I wasn't showing up just to become a better writer; I was showing up to be the best storyteller I could be. I was no longer thinking *The Blessed Bridge* would get published "hopefully, one day"; I was thinking "probably, soon."

Soon is a relative term, as I soon found out. Over the next few weeks I churned out revised pages and added new copy according to Moira's suggestions. But the turnaround from her was much less than ideal. She told me her divorce and her recovery from elbow surgery were still more time-consuming than she would have liked, but I couldn't help thinking she had many other writers in her stable who were higher in the pecking order than I was.

That's okay. I'll be at the top someday.

Progress toward publication might be slower than ideal, I decided, but it would be progress nonetheless, and every step would bring me closer to the validation of my dream. But it was Spiro who validated me as a woman. I felt truly blessed, and I made sure to acknowledge those responsible every day, in bed at night with my rosary, or on my knees in Our Lady of Victory.

By early summer I finally learned what had been bothering

my husband. For more than a year he had been distracted and edgy beneath the self-assured front he continued to put up. I'd had a sense of foreboding that disturbed me, but the signs of unrest he'd been showing were nothing compared to the behavior that ensued when DeMarco Futures was hit with a large margin call. Apparently, the real estate bonds that everyone had scrambled to scarf up had underwritten a whole lot of mortgages that were shaky at best, and the funds Alec managed— along with those of many others who were heavily invested in the mortgage market—weren't worth the rating they'd been given at the start.

Having overheard enough of his conversations on the phone to know there was a problem, I asked Alec if everything was okay, but he dismissed the concern evident in my voice with a curt "No big deal. I just have to cover a few shortages with some of my stock."

Oh.

I hadn't been plugged into the Wall Street grapevine for at least two years, but I still caught wind of major developments during one conversation or another with people who were. I still saw Gary at family gatherings and Sofia at company functions, and I connected with Olivia regularly and with Spiro all the time. All of them mentioned the margin call, and all of them more than suspected that it was a bigger deal than Alec let on.

Of course, the biggest news was always splashed in huge headlines on the front page of the *Wall Street Journal,* which arrived at my doorstep every day, so no one had to tell me that Grigor Malchek was under fire from Spencer Edelman, the New York State attorney general, who had seized an opportunity to drag him through the mud. Malchek, however, didn't get where he'd gotten by being a shrinking violet, and he sued Edelman for defamation and false prosecution.

From what I heard after that bomb hit, Alec didn't think it

was that big a deal, either. He said the investigation would likely drag on for years, but he swore to more than one party that "Edelman was jerking off" and "no one was going to 'Yale,'" at least no one who mattered. However, the recent chink in Alec's armor made me think there might be more to the story, so I asked Spiro, whose opinion I knew I could trust.

According to him, Ted Ross was in it up to his eyeballs because his team had handled the bulk of the transactions being looked into, but many suspected that the investigation was more political than anything else. Democrat Edelman would love nothing more than taking Ted's scalp and also implicating Republican senator Robert Ross, who was leading in the polls for governor of New York, along the way. Spiro said that sliming the candidate would be reward enough for Edelman, but if he found something that actually incriminated Ross, he himself would be in the running for governor in the next election cycle. He said that the only thing men like Edelman and Malchek, and soon-to-be-governor Ross, really wanted was power. These men ruled the country in secret, and no one—no one—could be elected president without the support of Wall Street, where the game was really played.

Alec seemed to be as blasé about Edelman's investigation as he had been about the investigation into baseball's connection with performance-enhancing drugs, and it wouldn't have shocked me in the least if he had had some skeletons involving the major players tucked away somewhere.

The more I thought about my life with him, the more it seemed like just a more polished version of the mob I had known in Brooklyn. It involved the same thirst for power, the same mix of sex, drugs, and gambling. What the Wall Street Boys did might have been legal, but that was just bookkeeping. They wrote the laws they manipulated every day. Their violence—the hostile takeovers and insider trading—might not have been literal murder, but they took the life of everything in their path, and the souls of many. Grigor Malchek was as much of a mobster in my book as mob boss Tino Priganti; Ted Ross was interchangeable with Rocco Caputo, my friend Janice's father who owned the Cue Ball, where mob business was conducted; and I had my very own Tony Kroon in Alec DeMarco. I'd thought I'd landed in the legitimate world when I met Alec, but all I'd done was switch deck chairs on the *Titanic,* and what a view I had.

Despite what Alec said about Edelman's investigation, he was still visibly affected. He warned me that things could get really ugly if there was a run on his company's holdings as a result of an initial call, and he mumbled more and more about "those bastards" while lapsing into deeper and more frequent self-induced stupors. By this time his excesses were too much even for his coterie of sycophants—Franco, Gianna, Gary, and Victor—who urged him to get some therapy.

Psychologist Donna Purke was sixty years old and carried her slim, elegant body well. Her self-confidence was evident in every gesture and every word, and it didn't take her long to size up what she was dealing with. Alec moved very quickly through analysis, getting tossed out on the first visit for having smoked marijuana just prior to the session.

After Donna suggested that a few one-on-one sessions with me might help, I figured that I'd do my duty and go for at least a couple of them. I was shocked when, after less than five minutes of conversation, she casually mentioned the divorce she herself was in the midst of and added that there was little likelihood either of us would be able to avoid the split that was on the horizon. After that, we talked more about stores and shoes and salons than about my marriage, and after a month she came to the conclusion that I wasn't the one who needed head-shrinking.

"Writing is my therapy," I said at the session we both knew
was going to be the last.

"I figured it was a special man."

"I may have one of those, too," I said.

"Good for you," she said. "I met a great guy who was married
with three kids, but he was self-aware enough to know he had
to get out and courageous enough to do it. We plan to marry as
soon as we can."

So there is hope.

"Listen to me, Samantha," Donna continued. "If you reveal
yourself in your writing and with others who care about you,
you don't need a professional listener. It's no wonder to me that
the ones who repress everything get sick most often, and really
sick a lot sooner than those who don't."

"I only wish my mother could have unburdened herself." I
sighed. *Sometimes good things fall apart so better things can fall into
place.*

"I suppose she was abusive to you as well as to herself."

"How did you know?"

Donna smiled. "It's what I do. But here's the thing, Samantha. Even if your mom had been the perfect mother, I'd still give
you the same advice I give to every patient—God bless the child
that's got his own."

Wish I'd written that. "Is that something original?"

"I wish," Donna said. "It's from a Billie Holiday song, but it
makes as much sense as anything I was taught over ten years of
formal education."

Stately and elegant though Donna was, until that moment
pretty much all I'd gotten from her was where to get a great pair
of wedges or a new hairstyle. I thought I'd rather spend two
hundred bucks on something else. But those eight words of
advice she passed along to me on the day we parted were worth

more than all of our sessions had cost, and much more than she could know.

Alec's financial scrambling trickled down to Gary and then Gianna, and suddenly *their* lifeline was a little tenuous. There was a lot less extra cash for them, particularly devastating as the Christmas bills came due, and they even started having trouble keeping up with the mortgage payments on their dream house. It wasn't long before the first hints of the DeMarco relationship curse reared its ugly head, and it wasn't long after that when the thought struck me that they'd end up in a therapist's office soon to hash over their marital strain.

In the meantime, Sofia's marriage to Victor was also falling apart. They had tried therapy, too, but his prying into her emails and phone messages hadn't abated, his philandering hadn't stopped, he still smacked her around without warning, and, from what she told me, his self-medication was on a par with Alec's. Sofia was all ears when I shared my problems, but for her it was more than the usual "misery loves company." She seemed to love wallowing in misery, and she never once took my hint that her time would be better spent planning a way to rise above it. When I discussed her attitude with Olivia one day, her wise words rang true.

"Sofia can't help herself," Olivia said. "She has no vision for a way out, so she'd prefer to see you wallow with her. When you succeed she'll be forced to come face-to-face with her own failure."

Victor's money problems also paralleled Alec's. He no longer had the wealth to support his lifestyle and smooth things over with his wife, and he started sponging off her family.

Suddenly it seemed like that "no big deal" was an awfully big deal for some people. But I couldn't do anything about other people's problems, and precious little about my own. I was doing what I could outside the Luxe Regent and inside my laptop, and I was still strapped financially. Isabella was too wise a child not to sense a lot of what was going on, but she mostly didn't talk about it.

The play I was working on at the time went off without a hitch, which is more than I could say about working with Moira. She still hadn't sent the novel out to publishers and was asking for still more revisions. I made the changes she requested while I prayed for patience and for gratitude, and was especially thankful for a reminder of God's love that came my way when I needed it most.

In March Olivia sent me a beautiful rosary of blue and crystal beads from Spain, and I gave those beads quite a workout. By that time Alec was deep into his slide both at the office and at home. He sold off his helicopter, started jettisoning other possessions, and passed it all off as "retrenching." To me, however, these seemed more like acts of desperation. But along with his increasingly foul mood, I also noticed a humbling in Alec—not so much as first, but enough for me to be aware of it. Finally, he confessed that he'd borrowed two million dollars from Ted Ross. I assumed that he'd had no intention of ever paying it back, but my woman's intuition told me that this wasn't going to end well.

In the midst of all this, Spiro had a way of pouring himself out in a handful of words that captured exactly how I felt about our relationship:

> As I drove around today with my family, I was thinking and re-flecting, and trying to decipher both the joy and the pain that has come our way. I felt bound in the confines of our SUV, and never so free at one and the same time. I saw God in the sunset . . . as I see Him in you.

I didn't see God in my husband's world, although my faith told me He was there somewhere. Shortly after Grigor Malchek was ordered to pay millions in restitution to the New York Stock

Exchange the pace of Alec's slide increased, and I wondered if that was just coincidence. Truthfully, it didn't really matter, and all either Alec or I cared about was trying to prevent ourselves from sliding down the slippery slope we were on.

Isabella's one-million-dollar college fund soon became a casualty of her father's financial machinations, and it wasn't long after that when nasty letters from people to whom Alec owed money started showing up in the mail. "I can't believe you are not sending me my final payment and you live in a penthouse," his tax attorney wrote, and that was just one of the milder expressions of what his creditors thought of him.

Still, I continued to stand by him. I had to. He was my daughter's father. No matter what we had gone through, I felt I had to be there for him, if for no other reason than that he was the one who had taken me out of the world I'd been living in and so badly wanted to escape. That didn't mean I loved him, or even liked him, and I didn't want to feel indebted to him, but no matter what happened, I knew I would always be there to help pick up the pieces. There was a part of me that had to give him at least that.

The IRS didn't think much of Alec, either, which they made quite clear when they showed up at our apartment unannounced asking to see his private books. It seemed that he had loaned a cousin money to open a deli that ended up being a front for illegal arms dealing.

Alec made a show of being unconcerned about that particular visit, and he slid through yet another investigation, but I felt the slope growing ever more slippery, especially when a tax arrears statement for more than three million dollars showed up in the mail.

Things got so bad, so quickly, that Marvin and Gregory no longer asked me about my financial situation. But just the fact that they were there, and didn't see a single thing wrong in my continuing involvement with Spiro, was enough for me. They didn't care about money; they didn't care what day it was; all they cared about was love.

Spiro was adamant that I should start my own production company, which, he said, made sense on a number of levels that he didn't need to list. "And get a credit card in your own name," he added. To think that Alec had me sign a prenup before we got married. *How absurd. What is that worth now? It will be worth something when I'm the one making the money.*

So, I saw the sense in what he was saying. I had to start generating some income for myself, no matter how modest, and I simply had to get in the game sooner or later. So I didn't refuse the money he offered to get me started, and, combined with the few bucks I still had in an old savings account, it was enough for the lawyers and accountants who—Alec's "faux pas" notwithstanding—would have to get paid for helping me to incorporate, enough for cards and letterhead and such. I said a prayer of thanks that I had a few bucks still left over to spend on the few lunches I was going to have to spring for. The one thing I had no trouble deciding was what I would name my company.

Spiro played cheerleader every step of the way:

I love the name *Bridge Span Productions*.
I love the logo and the colors.
The letterhead is beautiful.
The envelope is great.
It's you.

I got a Platinum Visa card with a five-thousand-dollar line of credit, which I managed to score on my own. I also managed to secure my very own American Express card. It was green and it was all mine. I found myself selling almost everything I had. Little by little to pay bills. I took control and saved our life. From

Silver to Steuben to Birkins to Biedermeiers—it all had to go. What was it really worth anyway? I asked myself time and time again.

To celebrate my strides toward independence, I took myself out to a trendy downtown bar where the oh-so-young, oh-so-gorgeous, oh-so-gay bartender delivered a menu with a winning smile. It took but a second for me to order the special drink that was listed in boldface: the Brooklyn Bridge. I looked around the crowded room and took my time with the only drink I intended to have. And when the bartender dropped my bill on the bar, there was no doubt who'd be picking up the tab. The name on the card was Samantha Bonti.

Alec celebrated the occasion in his own way, of course. That was the night he had a heart attack, and I almost had one when I heard his screams at 4 a.m. and rushed into his bedroom.

Alec dismissed the event as a "mini" one. And, accurate or not, I was happy to hear there was anything small in his life. He did, however, listen to his doctor's advice about ratcheting down his self-medication, and he swore he'd finally get some serious weight off, since the lap-band surgery he'd had years ago didn't seem to have done the trick. But within a few days he was back to his former habits.

First on the list of Bridge Span Productions were stage adaptations of a children's book, *Stalk to the Sky,* about constructing your own ladder, and a documentary, *Hear Them Chirp,* about how everyone has a right to speak, no matter how small or how frail. Good old Mary Davies, my second mother Mary, helped me get those projects off the ground, and good old Spiro and a few other angels kept them afloat. But my main goal was still getting *The Blessed Bridge* published.

So what if all they elicited from Alec were a couple of har-rumphs.

They were all mine.

And for the first time since we were married, I also filed a separate tax return. I needed to separate myself from Alec at least financially as he continued to unload everything he'd amassed in the past few years, and the late notices on the mortgage for our apartment started piling up in the mail, which indeed no longer brought any good news at all.

Although his dramatic reversal of fortune was painfully obvious to me and everyone else in the family, Alec shrugged it off by saying the bigger sharks were doing what they always did—eating smaller fish. When he let go of Victor and officially shut the doors of DeMarco Futures in July, it was anticlimactic. The inadvertent blessing for doctor-brother Franco was that he was finally doing better financially than his little brother.

Eventually, everything went—the homes, the cars, the toys, the club memberships, even the rose gold Rolex he had given me on a sloop off the coast of Bermuda. All of it. In the end, the hookers Alec had hired for others had more than I did.

The seven-carat yellow diamond ring he gave me was the last to go.

"I'll replace it with a better one someday," Alec said. "Soon. You'll see."

Why is it that the fallen king cannot see even though he sits among the ashes and ruins of his once-great empire?

Only one thing remained of Alec's former empire: the World Series ring he'd received from Presley Warren.

I'd always thought all I wanted was to get over the bridge and have money and success, but if the past decade had taught me nothing else, I'd come to realize that all I really wanted was love. Without that, what do we really have? A whole lot of things that can be sold and a whole lot of nothing in our hearts. So when Spiro called and requested a late meeting in his office one August afternoon, I jumped at the chance to see the one man who'd made me feel loved lately. The pleasure that Spiro gave me in ten minutes made every cell in my body become more alive.

He poured some wine, and then made a show of interest in the latest production figures. I could barely pretend to be interested myself, because there were two buttons open on Spiro's white linen shirt, and I was drinking in his rugged good looks. His office was too dimly lit to see the silvery gray in his eyes, but there was enough to see that they were glued to me.

Gentleman that he was, Spiro wrapped up the business part of the meeting after ten minutes, and suggested we just be in the moment.

Fine by me.

Our glasses were nearly empty, so I went to the sideboard, two glasses in hand, and refilled them. As I turned around, Spiro's eyes froze me in my tracks. There was a different look in them, a look that started the butterflies going in my stomach. I was still frozen ten seconds later when he pulled himself up in slow motion and moved toward me.

"Let me take those," he whispered, as he took the goblets from my hands and caressed my eyes with his. He set the glasses on the sideboard, and his hands went to my waist, pulling me closer.

"You don't know what you do to me," he said softly, then paused for a wickedly delicious moment before his lips locked on mine. He kissed me and kept kissing me, and then he pulled my sweater over my head and caressed my neck with his lips as his fingers undid the two hooks on my black lace bra and slid the straps from my shoulders. His eyes widened and caressed my breasts as the bra fell to the floor. Then I stopped him. "I can't. I just can't do this. Not now."

Our eyes locked for another moment.

"You are a good woman, Sam," he said resignedly. "One I will wait for and want forever."

EIGHTEEN

As Alec struggled to stem the tide that was drowning him, he hit up every person he could think of to whom he'd lent money. Perhaps he hadn't been nice enough to them on his way up, or maybe they were enjoying his downward slide, but for whatever reason they were nowhere to be found in his time of need. Of course he was able to scrounge up five grand here and there, this week or next, but that didn't come close to supporting the life he thought he still had. He fought a losing battle, and the coup de grace was the lawsuit Ted Ross filed right after Labor Day to recover his two million dollars after six straight months of no payments from Alec.

"I need whatever money you have in that account of yours . . . badly," Alec whimpered to me one evening in the den, where we were sitting on couches that needed cleaning. "There's nothing there," I said without emotion, and that wasn't a lie. The piddling sum I had was already spoken for, and it was far too humble to make any difference in his life anyway.

"I wish I could help you, Alec," I added, and that was true, too. Although I despised what he had done to us, he still had rescued the refugee I was and had paid my way ever since. One doesn't forget that—or at least I couldn't. I would have coughed up big dough if I had it.

Hell, if I had big dough, I would have already been gone, but I still would have helped Alec.

And he wouldn't have been in this dire situation if I had managed the finances from the start. He'd have owned at least one home outright, and he wouldn't be facing eviction from the Luxe Regent. When he could no longer ignore the notices, Alec shuffled out of his mini-mansion with Isabella and me in tow.

I had no problem facing moving day; in fact, it felt as if I were being released from Luxe Prison, Biedermeiers and all. Of course, the two-bedroom apartment we were moving into back in our old neighborhood was much smaller, but I saw that as real progress toward a simpler life. To celebrate, I made sure I gave the moving guys a big tip to dispose of that hideous fountain in the foyer on their way out. That would not be coming with me.

I hadn't been looking for unimaginable riches when I met Alec; I'd just been looking for love and an escape from long, lonely years of hardship. It had been easy to take, and now it was easy to see that I should have been more forceful with my opinions, or at least spoken up more often and tried to inject some sanity into our financial situation. But the person who had gone along for the ride wasn't me anymore. Of that I was certain.

Moving down the ladder we were still several rungs above where I had been when I started moving up. Scrounging for welfare checks in my youth, enduring the snickers of my peers when I used food stamps to settle up at the register, and receiving all sorts of hand-me-downs had in some way been a blessing. I often wondered what a thirty-five-dollar salad and a block of welfare cheese had in common. It had made me strong, and I had no trouble doing without the trappings of wealth that Alec bemoaned losing and swore he'd get back. I didn't give a shit about caviar and helicopters. What I yearned for did not come wrapped up in a Cartier box; it was love and that was free.

Marvin and Gregory didn't give a shit, either, about my not showing up with a tin of caviar on my next visit to Rhode Island. All they cared about was being with me.

I received another email from Spiro.

> You'll be fine, Sam. The move and disruptions in your personal life are part of the cleansing process. Focus on the lesson now. Once it is revealed, understood, digested, and put away, the reward comes.
>
> Enjoy your new place, enjoy the fact that you're not living some Luxe Regent fantasy anymore, and understand that where you live doesn't define you. You were proud and strong when you lived on five dollars a day and you're proud and strong now.

Spiro always knew what to write and the perfect time to send it. However, that was as far as it would go for now. I knew I had made the right decision

Even though he was still a mess at home, Alec managed to show his pride and strength to the outside world, and he kept repeating his oath that he'd "be back." His resolve took a beating, however, when he had a hard time getting his phone calls returned, and he beat up his body more and more when he was at home, which was most of the time. I was suddenly forced to face my very real fear of his dying.

It was impossible to enjoy our new place. In fact, it was pure misery for Isabella and me. I think she still appreciated sharing her room with me more than she wanted her privacy, although I could tell that wasn't going to last. Neither she nor I deserved the hand Alec had dealt us. What I *did* deserve was having Spiro around to support me with words at every turn:

I'm in pain also for a multitude of reasons, but that's the way life works. We must consolidate and regroup sometimes before we grow. That can be a painful process, but it's necessary. If we focus on the end goal at the expense of the process, all we'll get is more testing and more pain.

There are great forces at work. Be bold, be strong, pray, and place your heart and emotions in the hands of God. He's always there for us. When you let go and let God, He'll reward you beyond your wildest dreams.

It had never been about money for me, so it was easy to accept my present circumstances, and I was always honest about that. But it had always been about finding a mate for that couch and a failed marriage was a lot harder to swallow. Alec was still, however, the father of my daughter.

I'd always been myself; that hadn't changed with my address. I prayed for the strength and courage to prevail. I was not built to break. Then I prayed some more as Alec sank into a greater depression when everyone continued ignoring his calls. As a last resort, he went to Filomena for the rent money so we wouldn't be thrown out of another place. Alec had failed as a man as he'd failed as a husband, and he was well on his way to failing as a father. I was beginning to think it was society that had failed by causing him to believe that it was wealth that defined him. But ultimately it was the prospect of our crumbling family that was proving infinitely harder for me to accept than the crumbling of our empire.

Isabella spent most of her time at one or another after-school club or activity, and she hung out at her "normal" friends' homes as much as possible. I was happy that she had these good examples in her life, and I was determined to be a good example for her, too.

Alec shopped therapists and copped an assortment of

prescriptions for various pills that he continued to mix and match. If he couldn't live the reality he imagined, he'd live in a drug-induced one, which frightened both me and my daughter.

Gradually, however, for both of us fear morphed into pity. Isabella saw her father as tragically flawed and managed to be at peace most of the time when she was home. And the more he lost his bravado, the more I saw him as someone whose soul had been too hardened by the pursuit of money, too enslaved by the sports mentality and the killer instinct, and too destroyed to love. He had played on a street that was every bit as dangerous as the mafia streets of my youth, and he had lost.

It was a blessing that the power of money had brought him down rather than the power of a gun. And it was also a blessing that somehow, the lower he fell, the more powerless he became, the more I was able to forgive him. It was hard to stay afraid of or angry with someone who had become such a pathetic shadow of the person he wanted to be. To me, that was never more obvious than when he had a panic attack as we were driving home from one of the now-rare visits to his mother in Brooklyn, which usually occurred shortly before the first of the month. He jerked the used Toyota SUV he was driving to the side of the road so hard that the right front wheel jumped the curb. Then he slammed the transmission into park, flung the door open, and raced into the alleyway between two buildings to vomit.

But Alec being Alec, he was also still engaging in self-destructive behaviors that were too serious to ignore, let alone forgive.

One of the more regular acts requiring forgiveness was his nearly daily consumption of a liter of cheap vodka, cut with Crystal Light, and the subsequent spewing out of invectives. Alec liked to call it his pink juice, like the juice dogs are fed before they are euthanized.

In the end, I even forgave him for the free blow jobs from

escorts he finally admitted he'd gotten on a regular basis, as a "commission" for his services rendered. I forgave him for being a disciple of Bill Clinton and thinking that blow jobs weren't "sex." I forgave him for debasing women that way because he could, and I forgave him for all the years he had ignored me when we were in bed. I had been through a lot since the world of Tony Kroon and now Alec DeMarco. Different worlds yet somehow the same. Mafia and Wall Street lead by money and self-loathing. Power, sex, and drugs. That feeling of being so important, when in reality you're not. It all made me wonder how Moses felt when the Israelites turned on him in the desert. It's the same in these worlds. People turn, sometimes so far they never can make it back.

I went from Brooklyn to Manhattan but never once, even with all the money, lost sight of who I was along the way. I played the game and did things I wasn't proud of to fit in. I was now done. It was now my turn. My turn to make things right.

Whether God will forgive him isn't up to me, but I think most people deserve a second chance to achieve a better outcome. And that would include me, too. I had to forgive myself for being far too docile while living the high life under a husband's thumb, for turning Isabella's early care entirely over to a nanny, for seeking comfort from another man in my darkest hours, and for failing to take care of myself for far too long.

What was past was past, and I chose to be thankful that I still had my health, my sanity, and hope for my future. I also remained thankful for the few humorous diversions Alec still provided now and then, like the time he burned his hair with a straightening concoction he simply had to try. I also had to forgive myself and my daughter for laughing so hard when he saw his singed hair.

"Can I ask you something, Mom?" Isabella asked after we'd milked the last drop of enjoyment from that more-comical-than-tragic experiment.

"Sure, honey, anything. You know that."

"Why does Daddy stay in bed so much?"

"I don't really know, Isabella," I said, shaking my head. "It could be that deep inside he's not really sure of himself. It could be he's unhappy with himself, or it could just be he didn't get to where he thought he could be."

My deeper thoughts were that Alec didn't even realize just how depressed he truly was. I thought long and hard about all the Wall Street men who must have been. It seemed sad to have so much and be depressed; however, my empathy turned. They should start a committee or something, they were all good at that.

"I worry about Daddy." Isabella sighed.

"Me too, honey," I said softly.

But, despite my intermingling feelings of worry, pity, and forgiveness, I still didn't want to be around him. Like my daughter, I was out as much as possible. There was always a meeting to go to, a friend to visit, a writing class to attend . . . or a friendly interlude with Spiro. And through it all, I always had the publication of my novel—my personal achievement—at the back of my mind.

When Moira Jewison finally called in November to say that *The Blessed Bridge* was ready to go out to publishers, achievement moved front and center, and stayed there even after she added that it was just the start, that I was a first-time author, that it was a tough sell. I didn't care how long it took for her to sell it, because she'd said the words I'd longed to hear for more than half my life, and I planned on enjoying the ride.

What I hadn't planned on was getting tepid early readings and a couple of fast rejections. Moira, however, dismissed the dismissals and said to keep my chin up.

Then, right after New Year's, she called with more bad news about her personal life and not having been in touch with publishers. It appeared that my salvation would be delayed.

"Keep your chin up," she said once more. "I still see good things ahead for your novel, and I'm sorry my own problems are still slowing things down."

"That's okay, Moira," I said through gritted teeth. "Your health comes first."

"Thanks, Samantha. That's very kind of you."

What else can I say? It's not as if I have a line of literary agents waiting at my door.

"Even if I get totally shot down," she added, "it wouldn't be the first time a first novel got published second or even third in line after something else by the author."

If it weren't for Spiro's words of advice I might have lost it right then and there.

Focus on the process, Samantha.

"I don't *have* a second novel, Moira," I said.

"Surely you have a journal."

"Of course."

"Well, start pulling your notes together, Samantha. A writer writes."

And an agent agents.

I clung to my hope and visions of Tim Robbins on the beach in *The Shawshank Redemption*. He climbed through fifty yards of foul-smelling shit and got clean on the other side.

In the meantime, none of Alec's therapists could get through to him, and he descended to a level of despair and despondency that made pitiful look good. Out of common decency, if for no other reason, I placed a few calls to those so-called medical professionals to inquire about the prescription cocktail he was taking. Each claimed ignorance of others who might have been treating the same case and said there was no way of knowing how many mixologists were involved. I replied by saying that even if this was true, surely the therapist had noticed that Alec was not entirely cogent when he was sitting in a session, and that whatever therapy was being applied wasn't having any measurable positive effect. I told them all that they were lucky they could take Alec in measured doses. *I,* on the other hand, had to live with him.

Forwarding Alec's BlackBerry communications to them as evidence of just how crazy he was put an exclamation point on my circumstances, and how hard it was for me to hang on to my own sanity:

I am going home, rolling a doob. Smoking it on our couch. Heating up the horrible trough of food. So if you come home with her, explain that her father is an UNHEALTHY, FAT, STONED, ANIMAL POTHEAD!!!!

In one of his rare lucid moments, Alec told me what he should have been sharing with his therapists: "I feel as though I live my life in a glorified jail."

Gianna must also have felt like she was in prison with Gary, because she ended up having an affair with a high school teacher. A year of therapy hadn't done a thing to save her marriage, and I wasn't surprised about that, either. Gary had always seemed like a nice enough kind of guy, but he also struck me as weak, and I'd never once thought he'd be good in a foxhole. Without Alec to lean on for his livelihood, Gary was a fish out of water and well on his way to failing as a man, too.

Victor and Sofia had also been on life support for a couple of years already, and she finally decided to pull the plug that year. They, too, had lost everything they had, and the finger pointing between Alec and Victor wasn't pleasant to witness.

Quite frankly, with all of the relationship carnage surrounding me I wondered whether therapy wasn't a complete waste of time. The light of hope had always shone on me, however, and I'd always thanked God for that, so I tried to stay positive about the potential of both psychological counseling and romance. I thanked God for Spiro when it came to *affaires d'amour*, and for Olivia, who was living proof that what I reached for wasn't beyond my grasp.

My "sister" had kept up a torrid relationship with her construction worker boyfriend, who turned out to be an avid sailor and a man of means who had grown up in Northport, Long Island, the son of a well-to-do investment banker. He had a trust fund that could easily support a family for life and had only worked construction to keep himself grounded as he did his own searching. Now that he had grasped Olivia, he too was ready to be "off on an island somewhere," as she had mused the first time I met her. Plans for a sailboat charter service on the island of Formentera, off Spain's Mediterranean coast near Ibiza, were well along and they'd be relocating there soon.

God bless the child that's got his own, indeed.

Alec also saw hope in Olivia's good fortune, but it was the warped kind, as pretty much everything to do with Alec was. As soon as he got wind of the frequent trips she was making to Europe, he wondered if I'd mind asking her to smuggle some hash back.

I dove into my journal to take my mind off the dim prospects for *The Blessed Bridge*, and also to give me something all my own to hold on to in the midst of Alec's insanity, clinical or not. And I held on to the promise of having love one day with Spiro.

As yet another unexpected blessing, Alec grew to accept Marvin and Gregory. He got to know that they accepted him for the burnout he was without once mocking him or even condescending to him. He got to know just what good friends they could be in March, after they patted him on his back for being cleared in Spencer Edelman's investigation and having all claims against his former boss dismissed by the New York State Court of Appeals.

Yes, unbeknownst to me *and* Alec, his name had cropped up on several documents and in a handful of recorded wiretaps. The ones in our mini-mansion weren't very hard to arrange, given Alec's proclivity for deconstructing telephones that then had to be repaired.

Of course, if he'd known he was being dragged into yet another investigation, Alec would have let it roll off his back. It was all just business as usual for him. The way I saw it, I'd gone from Tony Kroon's criminal prosecutions in Brooklyn to Alec's fraud prosecutions in Manhattan. One mob to another.

At least this time the guy I was with came through clean as a whistle. Alec, despite everything he'd done, had never done anything illegal—at least when it came to trading. And that was something he could actually be proud of.

It was no surprise that Ted Ross and his brother, Robert, also came through with flying colors. Their Harvard pedigrees and deep pockets kept their names almost entirely out of the court dockets and scandal sheets.

Spencer Edelman, he of his own gubernatorial aspirations, had to have a scalp, however, and he managed to implicate a senior trader. When I saw a headline mentioning Carmine Sacco, the mobster's name splashed above the fold on the front page of the *Wall Street Journal*, it was a delicious irony to me. Alec, however, took it all in stride. "He didn't have a chair when the music stopped," he said.

Sorta like what happened to you, I suppose.

Although he had shown a glimmer of spunk when that news hit the papers, it didn't last very long and he soon resumed his wallowing. Paying the rent or utility bills was always a balancing act, and I had to squirrel food away for my daughter and me most of the time, stocking up whenever a few extra dollars came my way.

Alec, however, never seemed to lack for food—not that I was around him when he ate. As far as I could tell, he hadn't lost a pound, and I was sure he had plenty of snacks stashed away, as well as just enough money to satisfy all of his appetites including booze. He always had a bottle close at hand, even if the label was pedestrian. He always had some loose cash for a magnum of wine or a two-liter bottle of vodka that was on sale.

Whatever income I had from producing plays was still modest and sporadic, and now I had to scrounge for daily living expenses as Alec did to keep a roof over our heads. Scrounging wasn't anything new for me, and I knew I'd get by. I was thinking of getting a steady job, but Alec wouldn't hear of it.

I didn't want to live with Alec another minute, but I could look months into the future without seeing me anywhere else. All I saw was his impending bankruptcy and me being tied up with him still. Isabella, meanwhile, had a way of keeping me focused on my support system. When she spied me in a down mood my daughter-angel would ask, "Did you ask the Blessed Mother to help you feel better?" Tears welled up in my throat whenever she said those words.

"Did you talk to her? Did you tell her what you want?" she would always add. "Whatever it is, she'll give it to you, Mom."

I always took her advice . . . and I always asked for salvation. Salvation for me, yes, but also for the pitiful man I was with, and for my daughter, who had her own cross to bear.

Months of prayerful requests were answered in part just as summer began, when Alec finally roused himself enough to announce that he would lower himself enough to look for a "lowly" Wall Street job that would "only be worth three hundred grand a year."

I could still squeak out ten years with that amount.

He didn't offer any reasons for this unprecedented action, and I didn't care if it was because he was getting his game face on for the long climb out the depths or if he just wanted to have some flash cash for getaway weekends. *Anything* normal coming from him was heaven-sent for me, and I prayed that his lesson in humility would be the start of his salvation.

Even with all of the self-abuse Alec had administered for years, on the day he ventured back into the maw of capitalism he still managed to look more than decent in a business suit. I chalked that up to another one of God's mysteries and kept my fingers crossed.

Even though he was a mere shell of himself inside, he managed to talk his way into a job on his third interview. A regular salary was also God-sent, as was the medical coverage that included psychiatric care. I had no idea if Alec would avail himself of that, however, or whether the therapy would be successful, so I left those things in His hands, as He'd gotten us this far.

The gifts from God continued as Alec's boss turned out to be another angel. He was the perfect combination of shrewd Jewish businessman and rabbi, and he saw Alec as someone who could be saved while he contributed to the bottom line.

Alec, for his part, ratcheted down his excesses and displayed enough flashes as a lowly stockbroker to keep his boss's faith until the fall, but the job just wasn't big enough to keep his attention. "I can't do this anymore," he announced to me in mid-October.

I've been feeling that way for a while.

A long while.

"I'm gonna tell my boss that," he added, and he did—the very next day.

Several times, as a matter of fact, as his boss would have none of Alec's quitting. Alec told me he had shouted, "I'm depressed and just can't take it anymore!" but all that accomplished was his boss's picking up the phone and arranging an interview with the company psychiatrist. But it didn't buy any better results. What it did buy was Alec's tailspin, as he experimented with a new course of prescription drugs. More sordid displays of his appetites were the only thing therapy had resurrected, and I called his psychiatrist when I'd had enough displays of psycho-pharmaceutical experimentation. I got her voice mail, but, as I was as ready as I'd ever be to say what I wanted to say, I left a message:

> *Listen to me. You've got my husband on five different medications—what, was I born yesterday? He staggered into a kitchen chair last night and fell face-first onto the table, busting up his head in three places. I'm documenting all this because if he dies in his sleep, I'm suing you and everyone else who put him on drugs.*

She didn't return my call, but that was okay—my self-assurance and self-support system were all I needed. But what became painfully obvious to us both was that Alec needed some kind of new treatment. His angel of a boss stepped up to the plate again and arranged a stay at a bucolic rehab facility in Connecticut. At thirty grand for the week, still top of the line, even though it seemed to be the end of the line.

He's gone from husband to roommate to patient.

Alec managed to settle in, and the first report from those in charge after his second day there was that he was happy. They did advise, however, that he should be visited only after he'd had a meal, as that was when he was most stable. I had no doubt they'd heard his incoherent ramblings about everything from the food to the facilities, and I was certain they had their hands full with his daily threats of a daring escape, which was among the nonsense he copied me on via BlackBerry.

But I hoped with all my being that his caregivers also saw

the hopeful side I saw on those few occasions when his communications were from the heart, such as when he said he missed Marvin and Gregory almost as much as he missed Isabella, and when, out of the blue, he gave a thought to me:

> I'm sorry hon. I should have treated you way better. I promise
> I'm getting out of this funk.

He followed that shocker up with an even bigger one citing 2 Timothy 4:7: "I have fought a good fight, I have finished my course, I have kept the faith."

However, Alec still being Alec in some ways, he also managed to wrench his knee playing basketball with other well-heeled "inmates," and then he signed himself out declaring he was again in control of his life. I crossed my fingers once more, and made signs of the cross with them often in the days that followed.

Once again my prayers were answered in part, as there were no excessive displays from Alec, but he still showed the listlessness of severe depression.

"It's not as bad as it looks, Sam," he said softly from his bed late one morning when I had to roust him for a follow-up doctor visit. "I have a plan. It's a good one and I feel good about it. A ninety-million-dollar deal with a local cable sports network. I'm just waiting for two things to happen."

I've been waiting for two things, too: a book deal and freedom. Freedom to explore on my own and freedom to choose the person I want to be in love with. Forever.

"It'll be all business next week," Alec continued. "Suit, tie, the works. Just you wait and see."

To his credit, he kept himself together well enough to muddle through at his boss's small stock-trading company. I was hopeful that he was on his way to making peace with himself and that the deal he was working on, which he swore would set things right, would come to pass.

As for our marriage, only time would tell, but I wasn't yet ready to end it. In spite of all that I'd put up with over the more than twelve years we'd been together—his verbal abuse and self-destructive behaviors, his need for control, his neglect, and the financial crisis he'd created for our family—I knew deep inside me that, for a long time, I'd been silently complicit in all of it, and I believed that deep inside himself Alec needed me more than I needed him. I knew that most people would think I should have said, "Sayonara, you brought this on yourself and you're not taking me down with the ship." But I just couldn't do that. I'd stood by him this long, and if I didn't leave when he was on top of the world, I couldn't do it to him—or anyone—when he'd hit rock bottom. And, beyond that, I simply couldn't bring myself to destroy whatever family we'd managed to build together.

But regardless of what happened with us, I truly wanted him to make a comeback. I knew he was still brilliant and sharp; even with all that pot smoking that brain of his still worked like a magician's. He still had some great ideas and business opportunities on the horizon, and if he only conquered those as he did Wall Street in the past, the outcome would be inevitable. I was rooting for him, but in the meantime I had business of my own to attend to . . . and I still had faith in the outcome.

That faith was sorely tested when Alec's bankruptcy forced me to file my own, even though I had no connection whatsoever with the family finances. The cost of fighting to get my name off every docket Alec was on would have seemed enormous when we were living the high life and it was now astronomical. But, as with almost every other money issue in my life, I had no choice.

I also had to swallow the ten grand it was going to cost to

come out on the other side of bankruptcy. There was no way I'd even mention this to him, because I knew what he would say: "Don't pay it."

I knew I couldn't go to Marvin and Gregory. They were comfortable, but wouldn't have a liquid ten Gs to lend me. Moira Jewison was out of the question. Doris Bernstein could work, but I couldn't bring myself to ask her. And I just couldn't ask Spiro—not at this juncture in my life or in our relationship. I decided I'd have to ask Olivia.

What are sisters for, anyway?

My other sister, Debbie Warren, called the day before the lunch date I'd set up with Olivia, wanting to catch up on everything Samantha. I rattled off the latest on Alec and the one or two tidbits about my newest play that were noteworthy, and then I brought her right up to date on my scrounging for the dough to get past my immediate bankruptcy crisis.

"How much do you need?" she asked before I finished my rambling.

"Ten thousand dollars," I said softly, certain she'd seen my blush over the wires.

"Give me your account information and it will be there tomorrow," Debbie said with the self-assurance any woman would be proud to have.

"I swear, Debbie, I've never borrowed anything in my life," I said. "Just give me six months to a year to pay you back."

"Don't say another word about it," Debbie said. "And there's no time limit on paying it back."

"I'm flabbergasted," I managed to mumble.

"Don't be, Sam. You'd do the same for me."

Sisters, indeed.

The dust from our financial Armageddon hadn't totally settled by the time my next birthday rolled around, but there was a semblance of order to the family budget as bankruptcy proceedings went on. The auxiliary blessings of that were numerous, and the lack of threatening notices in the daily mail wasn't the least of them.

To celebrate my day and go out in style I decided we should go ahead and take the nine-day African safari I had booked and paid for almost two years before. What was I to do? It was paid for. I looked at it as a gift. A gift from above for all that I've been through.

Alec adopted a make-hay-from-hash attitude, which he combined with his tour guide persona, while the practical side of me felt guilty as hell for not having tried to cancel and get our money back. But I put my worries about punishment for sin into its appropriate box and set free my feelings about deserving a break. Alec sure needed one, too.

Debbie didn't raise an eyebrow when I told her about the jaunt we were taking in the midst of our dire financial circumstances. Truthfully, I'd already started paying her back, courtesy of medical insurance reimbursements for Alec's care once he agreed that I could handle those "meager" sums. But I know she wouldn't have said a word even if that weren't the case. In the end, I paid her in full within six months of coming back from Africa, and I wasn't even tempted to boast about my financial prowess to Alec. I could handle myself all by myself, and he was going to find that out sooner or later.

"Sooner" had the inside track when Moira Jewison called to say that a publisher was "very interested" in *The Blessed Bridge* and "there was even some talk of a movie."

"They have a new imprint dedicated to women's interests, and your novel is right up their alley," Moira continued. "They want to meet you."

I'd had one of those meetings before, so I wasn't necessarily as excited as I might have been. "What does that mean, Moira?"

"It means they want to make a deal."

All of the blessings I'd had until that moment—and there were many of those—paled in the light of this opportunity to finally make my mark as I'd always believed I could. I kept telling myself that the crazy energy of that year so far just indicated big changes were happening. Those changes couldn't happen without big disruptions and uprooting, which was also why some of the people around me got so bothered, yet others blessed me.

One of those blessings had been my relationship with Spiro, but based on my decision to stay with Alec, I knew it was time to break it off—at least for now. We hadn't been together since that meeting in his office, but I decided we needed to see each other one more time. I couldn't chance being with him in private, because I wasn't sure my resolve would hold up, so I asked him to meet me for lunch in a small neighborhood restaurant where I knew it would be quiet and I was sure we wouldn't bump into anyone either of us knew.

From the expression on his face when he walked in the door I could tell that he had a pretty good idea what I was going to say. But that didn't make it any easier. Telling Spiro that we needed to cut off our communication even by email was the toughest thing I've ever done in my life. I know he was as devastated as I was, but, gentleman that he always was, he made it as easy for me as he could. Looking straight into my eyes, but without reaching for my hand, which would have been more than I could bear, he assured me that he would honor my decision but also that he would always be there for me if and when I needed him. And I knew he would honor that commitment. I didn't want him to see me cry and try to comfort me, so I held myself together until we'd parted ways, and I'm pretty sure he was doing the same. But we both knew that it was for the best.

He would always remain in my heart, and who knew what the future might bring. God had already given me so much; perhaps there might be more. I could only hope that the words of

SUZANNE CORSO

the song were true: *Somewhere there's a time for us, someday there'll be a time for us. Time together with time to spare . . .*

Meanwhile, I had at least one more bridge to cross, and that was realizing the dream of getting my novel published. Once I got to the other side, which I believed would be very soon, I could begin to think about the person with whom I wanted to be sharing popcorn on a couch. Until we both finally resolved our present situations we needed to let go and let God.

EPILOGUE

I'll never get tired of signing my name . . .

I'd seen many gorgeous book jackets before, but never one with the story of my life between the covers. The Brooklyn Bridge was pictured in all its sinew and stone, and there was I, about to cross to the other side and embark on my future.

I took a book from the carton of advance copies that had just arrived at my door and reached for a pen. I looked at my daughter, who was sitting on the couch next to me, her eyes alight with anticipation, and felt the slight resistance and stiffness of the binding as I opened it for the first time. I breathed in the smell of paper and fresh ink as I smoothed the already smooth front endpaper.

I hadn't thought about what I'd write to my daughter, but the words came without effort:

Dearest Isabella,
    Love yourself as I love you, and as God loves us all.
                                      Mom

I handed her the book and waited while she read the inscription. I don't know which of us shed the first tear as we hugged each other tight. She was still much too young to read *The Blessed Bridge,* but one day she would read it and know who her mother truly was.

Three days later, on a bright fall day, I took a late-morning stroll to our local bookstore. The red and golden hues of the autumn leaves on the tree-lined streets reflected the warmth I felt in my heart as I saw, front and center in the shop's plate-glass window, a three-tiered display of my novel, the window into my soul. None of the handful of passersby knew who I was, but that was fine by me. *I* knew who I was.

I stood there for several moments before turning and hailing the taxi that was miraculously empty and coming right toward me. Suddenly, I needed to be in a place where I felt truly known.

"Our Lady of Victory Church, please, Pine and Wall streets," I directed through the open partition.

If seeing my book for the first time in a store window was amazing, it was overwhelming to find myself a week later seated at a table in Barnes & Noble with piles of *The Blessed Bridge* on either side of me, a long line of people in front of me, and representatives from my publisher standing by to hand me books as, one by one, well-wishers came up to tell me their names and ask me to sign a copy for them. One after another they kept coming, until my hand was cramping, but my smile was almost as broad as any one of Alec's jumbo grins had ever been, and I would have been willing to go on signing forever. To think I signed my book deal while Alec was in the psychiatric ward. Now, that would be something to write about. Maybe in my next book.

My publicist had done a great job getting copies out for blurbs and early reviews, and the feedback was unanimously positive. Most gratifying of all for me was the fact that readers really seemed to understand who I was, what I had gone through, and how I had stuck to my dream and triumphed in the end, despite the odds stacked against me. If anyone found my story inspiring enough to help get them through their own personal problems, the purpose of my writing would be fulfilled.

But I knew that books—and certainly first novels by unknown writers—usually reached no more than a few thousand people at best, so when Moira called to tell me that the early buzz had generated even more serious movie interest, I was over the moon with excitement.

I already had a couple of signings scheduled on the West Coast, and she said that she'd be setting up movie meetings for me while I was there.

I was still convinced that Alec would make a comeback. Men like him just don't disappear into the dust. His lion still lay awake. And I also knew that I had finally found a way to fit into his world *my* way and on *my* terms—as a respected writer, not as just another decoration in his mansion, or any mansion for that matter.

Waiting for takeoff on the plane to Los Angeles I had no doubt that this trip would change my life once again and I was willing to take that chance. I reached into my purse for the rosary I'd found on the day of Mom's funeral. As I did so, I heard Grandma whispering in my ear the words that would protect me on my journey, *"Kinehora, Samelah. Kinehora."*

ACKNOWLEDGMENTS

In spite of your fear, do what you have to do.

—Chin-Ning Chu

What I know with certainty: lose all your money and your friends go with it. Well, not your real friends. That's why I always looked at this loss as a blessing. It quickly eliminated all the shit from my life and all the people who I thought were true friends but disappeared in a flash. It allowed me to see what really mattered most. Somehow the simplest of things started to look better, like the leaves on the trees I never noticed before . . . but do now.

This is why God is so good. As long as I've got Him and His mother I am *the* good. I have taken my rightful place in the world, and once you have your God-given power to do so, the world becomes yours, and nothing—and I mean nothing—is impossible. It is so important not to let the money define you. Remember this statement and you know who you are out there. Own it!

I want to thank the people who believe in me and in my stories and who respect my faith. My honest, humble, and supersmart agent, Susan Ginsburg: thanks for coming into my life in the nick of time. I share great gratitude and much laughter with my editor, Trish Boczkowski: thanks for understanding who I am and allowing my words never to fall short. And, wise for her years, Alexandra Lewis, for never doubting a word and making it all flow gracefully. My loyal and fabulous publishers, Louise Burke and Jen Bergstrom, still the hottest blondes in the book business. Once again, the lovely Felice Javitz, who makes legal pleasurable. Of course, the cast and crew of Simon & Schuster, and the team at Gallery Books, the best always. Thank you for a second time around. I think you're stuck with me; I need an office, window view, please. A special thanks to Judy Kern, for making sense of everything, and to my huge supporter and friend Betsy Berg. By far you are one of the best in this business and you have a great sofa.

I have always loved unexpected gifts. When they come in the form of people who help make your life better it is truly a beautiful thing. For my best friends who still vibrate alongside of me, and you know who you all are, I don't know what I would do without any of you. For Anthony, a real Wall Street guy; thanks, my love, for being a sport when it came to this book. You are still one of the best traders on the street and one of the best men I know. *Don't let them bother!* Samantha, my only bloodline: I love you beyond words. You are the best daughter a mother could have. A gift I keep thanking God for. Here is another book for you to see how life works. And of course my three besties, Mary, Jesus, and Moses. How would I have ever survived without all of you? You three are still my original Jews; candles to you forever.

The great city of Brooklyn: may you continue to shine and let your bridge always be the crossover to greatness for millions. I was one of them and I thank you so.

Grateful as ever, *tddup*.

THE SUITE LIFE

Suzanne Corso

INTRODUCTION

When Samantha Bonti meets the man of her dreams in Alec DeMarco, a successful Wall Street broker, she believes she has finally left the insecurities of her hardscrabble past behind. But now she faces a different kind of challenge: carving a place for herself in the lavish, high-stakes world of Manhattan's elite without losing her own identity.

TOPICS AND QUESTIONS FOR DISCUSSION

1. While dating Alec, does Samantha turn a blind eye to warning signs about his true nature, or was she unaware of his dark side until after they married? Does Alec genuinely care for Samantha, or is she simply another acquisition to him?

2. At numerous points in the story Samantha is shocked at Alec's behavior, especially when he punches Hercules and later when he slaps her glasses off her face. Why does she continue to stay with him? Why is she so bothered by her failure to defend Hercules? What larger implications are there in her silence?

3. In what ways does Alec remind Samantha of Tony Kroon, her former boyfriend? Are the two men more alike than they are different? Why does she compare Wall Street to the mob?

4. What role does religion play in Samantha's life? When Alec asks her how she survived her relationship with Tony, she

responds, "My faith sustains me" (page 31). Cite examples of how she draws on her faith during her marriage to Alec.

5. Samantha's grandmother provided her with encouragement and a loving foundation, while her mother was a drug addict and an alcoholic. How do her past relationships with each woman continue to affect her and influence her life, in both positive and negative ways? In particular, how do Samantha's fears about her mother affect her own parenting of Isabella?

6. Of all Alec's family members, why is it Giovanni to whom Samantha feels the closest? Why does she sense she no longer belongs in Alec's family—or his Wall Street crowd—once Giovanni is gone?

7. At one point Samantha wonders, *Do I even have any negotiating power anyway?* (page 203). Why does she feel so powerless in her marriage to Alec? How much of it has to do with her ceding all financial control to him? Does money equal power in a relationship?

8. Compare Samantha's two different worlds—the wealthy Wall Street circle and the theater industry. Why does she credit the latter, including her friendships with Doris, Marvin, and Gregory, with preserving her sanity?

9. How does Samantha stay grounded in Alec's over-the-top world? As he inducts her into his lavish lifestyle, she vows, "No matter what happened, I fully intended to remain true to myself" (page 48). Does she manage to do this?

10. When Alec's career begins to unravel, why is Samantha better able to handle the reversal of fortune than he is? Do you agree with her theory that society was at least partly responsible for Alec's failures—as a husband, father, and businessman—by "causing him to believe that it was wealth that defined him" (page 302)?

11. Why is Samantha so determined to see that *The Blessed Bridge*

be published? What does the book represent to her? How is it a touchstone in her life, especially in darker times?

12. What draws Samantha to Spiro Stavros? What does he offer her that Alec does not? Would Spiro be a good match for her? Why or why not?

13. Samantha finally admits that she no longer loves or even likes Alec. Why, then, does she choose to stay with him? What do you suppose the future holds for her, romantically and otherwise?

14. The recent "Occupy Wall Street" movement brought the country's top one percent into the media spotlight. After reading *The Suite Life,* what is your opinion of the world of high finance? Did the book dispel or confirm any preconceived ideas you had about the Wall Street elite? How so?

ENHANCE YOUR BOOK CLUB

1. Along with *The Suite Life,* read and discuss *Brooklyn Story,* the first book featuring Samantha Bonti.

2. Samantha finds fulfillment in writing a novel and producing plays. Do you have a long-held creative dream you'd like to accomplish? Share it with the group, and see what advice they have to offer. In addition, combine your discussion of *The Suite Life* with a visit either to the theater or to a bookstore to attend an author event.

3. Indulge your sweet tooth like Samantha did during her first visit with Alec's family. Enjoy strawberries dipped in prosecco and then rolled in powdered or brown sugar.

Visit www.suzannecorso.com to learn more about
the author and her books.